Also by Jennie Marsland

Coming Soon:

McShannon's Heart

Published by Bluewood Publishing Ltd

For more information, please visit:
www.bluewoodpublishing.com

McShannon's Chance

by

Jennie Marsland

DEDICATION

To Kathy, for her never-failing friendship and encouragement, and to Everett, who puts the music in my life.

CHAPTER 1

April 1870, Colorado Territory

The rhythm of the stagecoach wheels changed as the horses slowed to a jog, waking her from an uneasy doze.

We can't be here already.

Beth Underhill uncurled herself from the seat corner and peered out the window. A huddle of buildings showed up ahead, blending with the muted browns and greens of the open scrubland. How long had she been asleep? She'd drifted off after they'd changed horses at noon, and now cottonwoods and pines cast long, late shadows on the sunlit landscape. As Beth rummaged in her pocket for her watch the coach stopped, the door creaked open and the driver stuck his sunburned, grit-covered face inside.

"Wallace Flats, Ma'am, here you are."

So this is it. Beth clambered out, holding her aching back. There'd been no glowing descriptions in the letter she'd received, but hope had painted a rosier picture than what she saw around her.

"What a forsaken place."

The driver pulled Beth's suitcases from the top of the coach and dropped them beside her, raising a small cloud of dust to add to the coating on her skirt. "I've seen worse." He wiped his nose with a grimy handkerchief and shifted from one foot to the other, his thoughts as plain as the frown on his face. *You don't belong here.* "Are you sure someone's going to meet you?"

Beth straightened her shoulders and dredged up a smile. "Yes, Mr. Chalmers. I'll be fine. Don't worry about me."

"Well, then, I got to be going. Been a pleasure, Ma'am."

Pleasure hardly described Beth's rough, solitary journey from Denver. She'd never felt hungrier or dirtier in her life, but Mr. Chalmers had gotten her here in one piece, and he was her last link with home. She turned to him with genuine regret.

"Goodbye and thank you."

He tipped his hat, climbed back to his seat and let out a low, keening whistle to start the horses. Beth watched the stage roll out of town, leaving her stranded in this bit of nowhere.

In spite of the sun, the spring breeze nipped at her. Shivering, Beth pulled her shawl tighter and surveyed the town square. The general store, Baker's Mercantile, needed new window trim. The school needed a fresh coat of white paint. The saloon, with a pair of sagging benches out front and 'Neil Garrett, Prop.' painted in bold, black letters over the swinging doors, looked like the most prosperous building in the place.

Iron rang on iron at the blacksmith's forge, and a saw droned at the sawmill. Behind the false-fronted businesses, houses straggled into the distance, most unpainted and bleaching in the sun. The town well stood under a pine in the middle of the square, the earth around it dampened by drinking horses and riders.

Nothing looked solid or permanent compared to the stone construction Beth was used to seeing in Denver. Nothing held the eye in town, but a far-off view of rolling foothills in the late afternoon light caught her attention. If all went as she expected, she'd be headed out there.

Cadmium yellow and orange, some French ultramarine. A touch of Hooker's green. The light's beautiful. I'll have to tell Graham to put some paper in my trunk. She'd brought her watercolor kit along, but she didn't expect to have a lot of time for painting as a homesteader's wife. Not that Beth had a very clear idea of just what that would involve. She pulled the rumpled letter from her purse and read it one more time.

Dear Miss Underhill,

Thank you for explaining your position to me so honestly. I will be honest with you in return.

For the last four years, I have been living outside of Wallace Flats, a day's stage ride south of Denver. It's very typical of the small towns out here, offering the basics of life and little else. It is beginning to grow, but at present, we have no doctor, no bank and no official law. There are good people in it, but it's a rough place in comparison with Denver, I must admit.

My homestead is ten miles from town. Since coming here I have put all my time and energy into getting the place started. I built the house to meet my own requirements, which are simple. I have no idea if you are the kind of woman who could be content with one room, but if you are, you might find it comfortable enough. At least it doesn't leak.

My nearest neighbors are two miles away, and I go to town no more than twice a week. If you are very fond of social life you'll find little to appeal to you here, but if you enjoy solitude, there is no lack of it. I find the country beautiful, but that is my taste; some find it bleak and of little interest.

What I can offer you is this. If you need a home, as you say, and if you think you could be satisfied with my situation here, I will pay your way to Wallace Flats. If a year from now we feel the arrangement has been a mistake you can go your way, no questions asked, and I will pay you a hundred dollars for your time. If this is agreeable to you please let me know through the agency.

> *Sincerely,*
> *Trey McShannon*

A simple business proposal. Wasn't that preferable to promises from men who talked about love, but cared more for the money they thought Beth stood to inherit? This man's offer held just as much real feeling, and a lot more honesty.

Be grateful for that, Beth. It's a rare commodity. One the Matheson matrimonial agency prided itself on delivering. They didn't concern themselves with emotions. Over the last few months, Beth had come to believe she'd be wise to do the same.

"People marry because they want something from each other," she'd told her cousin Graham when she announced her plans at the last possible moment, after

4

receiving Mr. McShannon's confirming wire. "Well, this man needs a wife and I need a home."

As Beth expected, Graham exploded in a fine Underhill temper. "Elizabeth, have you lost your mind? What exactly do you intend to do when this sodbuster wants to touch you?" His fist came down on the dining room table hard enough to dent the wood. "Not only are you making a complete fool of yourself, you have no idea what sort of an animal he is or what kind of a shack he lives in. God, there are still Indians out there. You could have married Jason Pembroke—"

"Who didn't care for me any more than Trey McShannon does."

No, Jason hadn't cared for her, not even enough to speak to her first before testing the waters with Graham. Mr. Pembroke wanted a wife with breeding and the social graces, and he'd decided Beth would look good enough on his arm to outweigh her disappointing lack of money. She had to admit she couldn't say as much for other, more ardent suitors. As for Mr. McShannon, he wrote like a civilized, educated man. What more could she ask of a stranger?

As she scanned the street, Beth caught one of the loafers on the saloon steps staring at her. When she blushed, he smirked and turned away. She could never have imagined a human being like him. With his long, lank, red hair, brilliant green eyes, crooked mouth and pockmarked face, the man looked like a weathered demon with an evil sense of humor.

Thank God, that's not him.

5

She didn't see anyone who fit Mr. McShannon's description, so she picked up her bags and walked over to the store. The woman behind the counter shook her head at Beth's inquiry, setting her long earbobs dangling.

"His place is about ten miles north of here. Haven't seen him in town today."

Beth heard a faint whisper of panic. "But he's expecting me. I sent him a wire last week that I'd be on today's stage. He wired back that he would meet me."

The clerk rested her hands on the counter and looked Beth over while she stood there, feeling like a curiosity. She knew she had a way of holding her head, and her dress wasn't something you'd see every day in a town like this. Even in her most serviceable traveling clothes, she had *good family* written all over her.

"Don't know what to tell you, miss. Are you a relative of his? I heard him say one time that he had a sister, though you sure don't look anything like him."

"No, we're not related. Is there anywhere I can get a room for tonight?" The whisper of panic grew louder. Beth had enough money with her for a return stage ticket to Denver, and not much more. If Mr. McShannon didn't show up, she'd have no choice but to slink back to Graham with her tail between her legs. A less than appealing thought, the more so since he'd put her on the next train back to Philadelphia. After two years in Denver, Beth couldn't imagine living in that smother of convention again.

"Yes, there's Mrs. Grant's place down the street. The yellow house, fourth place from here on this side . . ." The clerk's earbobs swung again as she pointed. "Wait, that's him there."

Beth turned to the store window and watched the man she'd agreed to marry walk toward her.

Six feet tall, dark hair and eyes. She'd described herself to him in similar meaningless terms. She supposed he'd find them as inadequate as she did.

His rangy frame could have carried more weight, but he had the muscle of a man who did physical work. His long stride suggested latent energy. The way he wore his faded denim work pants, collarless homespun shirt and battered cloth cap made her think he rarely dressed any other way. If he hadn't told her he was twenty-seven, she would have guessed him to be over thirty. There wasn't much of youth about him.

That impression didn't change when he stepped into the store. Long, thick dark lashes shadowed his molasses-colored eyes, set deep under heavy brows. His straight, wayward, near-black hair needed a trim. The stubble on his angular jaw didn't make him any less intimidating.

"Excuse me, Miss, are you Beth Underhill?"

He spoke coolly, almost to the point of curtness, with a bare hint of a drawl. Beth saw a stubborn will and a quick temper in his eyes and the set of his mouth. He likely wouldn't be an easy man to live with.

She swallowed and caught hold of the edge of a shelf to keep from stepping back. *Idiot, say something.* When she found her voice, it sounded odd and distant to her ears.

"Yes. You must be Trey McShannon."

It helped that he looked as uncomfortable as she felt. Beth held out her hand. Warm, callused fingers closed around hers and released.

"I am. How was the trip out? The road can be bad in the spring."

"It wasn't too bad."

Meanwhile the clerk stood looking from one to the other, avidly curious. The corners of Trey's mouth tugged upward with subtle amusement as he handed her a list.

"Could you put this together for me, June? We'll pick it up in twenty minutes or so." Without saying anything more, he picked up Beth's bags and walked out.

With a glimmer of mischief, Beth turned to the counter. June was bound to talk, so why not give her something to talk about?

"We'll need one more thing, please. A couple of pairs of waist overalls, my size."

June nodded. Beth turned and followed Trey, leaving the woman staring after her.

Trey crossed the street to a wagon drawn by a team of fine black Percherons and put the bags in the back. When he turned around, Beth spoke first. She usually reacted to fear by charging ahead, and something about this man rattled her. After five years in the marriage market, she hadn't thought that was possible.

"I thought we might as well see the minister while we're in town, unless you'd rather wait a few days." *If he gives me a chance to back out, I will.*

His appraising glance made her feel like squirming. He didn't seem the least bit impressed with what he saw.

Men didn't often react to Beth that way. Graham would have said it was good for her.

As if he'd been looking at nothing more interesting than the goods in the store window, Trey turned away. "The church is this way."

Beth arched an eyebrow at his back. Mr. McShannon seemed to have quite a high opinion of himself.

"Of course. I'm not blind. I can see the steeple as well as you can."

* * * *

Trey had a quick and to-the-point conversation with himself on the way down the street. He wouldn't look at her, but that didn't dull his awareness of the woman walking beside him, with her big blue-gray eyes under dark lashes, pale, creamy, freckle-dusted skin, and heavy knot of burnished auburn hair. Her softly curving mouth matched the slight but sweet figure in her navy blue dress. She reminded him of Cathy Sinclair at home, a lifetime ago in another world. Trey had spent plenty of time wondering what Beth would look like, but he'd never come close to the reality.

You've made a big mistake, Mister. This girl belongs serving tea back in Denver. Too pretty and way too soft to be out here. Get out while you still can.

But you made a deal.

Unmake it. She had no business answering your letter.

Ever since he'd written her to come out, Trey had been swinging back and forth between anticipation and dread. Four years of war and nearly five of battling to win a living from a homestead hardly fitted a man to live with any woman, let alone one like Beth. No woman who looked like she did had any business writing to a mail-order bride agency. Her letters hadn't given him any reason to think she would be anything but, well, ordinary.

. . . I want to be perfectly honest with you, Mr. McShannon. After the recent death of my aunt, I find myself in need of a home. I have no other family except my cousin, who has a growing family of his own. My aunt's home now passes to him and he wishes to sell it. He has offered me a home with his family, but we have never been close and I would prefer to find some other arrangement. I must do this soon, as he wishes to proceed with the sale as quickly as possible . . .

What had he been expecting, then? She'd told him she hadn't done much housekeeping, but he'd pictured someone whose mother—aunt, he corrected himself—had done most of the work while she looked on. He doubted if Beth could boil water, and he'd bet his farm that she'd never set foot in a one-room cabin with a dirt floor before. Trey didn't want a drudge, but he'd sent for a wife because the cattle and horses alone made more than enough work for him. He needed someone who could look after the house at least. Miss Underhill wouldn't have a clue.

By the time they reached the church, he'd primed himself to tell her he was sorry and he'd pay her fare home, but he didn't get the chance. Reverend Baxter happened to be on the roof replacing some damaged shingles. He dropped his hammer and climbed down to meet them.

"Hello, Trey, good to see you. Who's the young lady?" Blond and balding, the minister pulled a pair of round-rimmed glasses from his shirt pocket, put them on and held out his hand to Beth.

Amid a swirl of conflicting emotions, Trey managed a civil answer. "This is Beth Underhill from Denver, Reverend. Beth, this is Reverend Baxter."

"Pleased to meet you, Miss Underhill."

Trey looked down in embarrassment, wishing he'd shown her as much appreciation. Beth glanced at him, then dropped her gaze as she shook Reverend Baxter's hand.

"Likewise." Trey's heart lurched when he saw her take a deep breath. She wasn't going to leave him a way out. "Reverend, I—we have a favor to ask you."

Reverend Baxter gave Beth his most charming smile. "Oh? What's that? It'll be a pleasure I'm sure."

"Well . . . we'd like you to marry us."

"*Marry* you? Today?" His smile disappeared. Trey's face heated. The man's first thought would be that Beth was in trouble. "Why didn't you give me some notice?"

No backing out now unless I want to look like a prize ass. It's a year . . . if she holds on that long . . . and there isn't a snowball's chance in hell of that. Trey kept his explanation brief. "Miss Underhill and I met by correspondence. She'll be staying with me while we decide if we want to make this permanent. You understand, Reverend."

There wasn't much Reverend Baxter could say. He ushered Beth toward the church and gave Trey a perplexed glance behind her back. "Yes . . . yes, I understand. Come inside."

They stopped a passer-by to act as a witness, entered the church and walked up the dimly lit aisle between the rows of rough, low-backed pine pews. Trey felt like an actor in a play when Reverend Baxter took his Bible from the pulpit and turned to face them. The minister looked as if he felt the same way as he glanced from Trey to the bride.

"Do you have a ring?"

Trey reached into his shirt pocket. "Yes, I do."

"Very well. Join hands."

Trey reached for Beth's left hand. Soft and well tended, it trembled in his. Trey's palms dampened and his manhood stirred at the thought of her fingertips gliding over his skin. *Jesus.* She might well be used to the way she affected a man, but he sure as hell wasn't.

Beth looked as pale as milk in the late afternoon light slanting through the plain window behind her. Was she afraid of him? Disappointed? If so, Trey couldn't blame her. This certainly wasn't the wedding she'd have dreamed of. Why on earth had she written him? She must have gotten offers from men who could give her a lot more. Shame pricked him again. He could have groomed himself up a bit.

At least she's seeing you the way you look every day. Spite, naiveté, a misguided yearning for adventure – whatever her reasons, no one had forced her to do this. As for dreams, Trey preferred to do without them.

They didn't make eye contact during the brief ceremony. Trey slipped the ring on Beth's finger and

Reverend Baxter pronounced them man and wife. They thanked him, shook hands with the witness, and walked out.

* * * *

Back in the sunlight again, Beth looked down at the thin, delicately engraved gold circle glowing on her hand. Trey's eyes followed hers.

"It belonged to my mother, and to her mother before that, I think."

Embarrassed, she ran a finger over the engraving. "It's lovely, but you didn't have to give it to me."

He shrugged and gave her a quick, ironic sideways glance. "I don't have a lot of rings lying around to choose from."

He certainly knew how to make her feel foolish. Without answering, Beth quickened her pace to put some distance between them on their way back down the street. *Maybe I don't suit him, but that's no excuse for plain bad manners.* Trey made no effort to catch up.

As she passed the saloon, Beth caught the eye of a dark-haired girl standing in the doorway, wearing a very low-cut, none-too-clean dress. They both looked away. Beth heard a quiet chuckle from Trey, stopped and waited for him. Grinning, he stepped up beside her.

"Her name's Lorie Carter. She comes from a little town in Montana. She was seventeen when I came here."

Beth glared at him. She supposed most of the single men in town consorted with Lorie, but she hadn't married *them*. "How do you know all that? She's a—"

"I asked her." Trey's amusement did nothing to soothe her. "I stopped by the saloon on my second night in town. It wasn't busy and Lorie came to the bar for a drink. We talked for quite a while. She told me her parents had kicked her out the year before because they didn't like the boy she was seeing. She was just a kid with nowhere to go."

Seventeen. Aunt Abigail had raised Beth to pretend prostitutes didn't exist, but she couldn't after looking one in the eye. She resisted an urge to look back.

"You just talked?"

"That's all. When she asked if I wanted to go back to her room I considered it, but I said no. She said I wasn't her type anyway. I don't know what she meant by that exactly."

Beth didn't know either. She couldn't guess how a woman like Lorie might think, nor did she want to.

She waited in the wagon while Trey picked up his order of supplies. When he climbed up beside her and started the horses, she had to suppress an urge to jump down and run, but in a moment they were moving too fast for escape. Beth focused on the scenery around her.

The flat land grew greener and more rolling as they went. Her nerves didn't keep her from appreciating what she saw. The road cut through patches of woods and crossed the same meandering stream several times. They passed two or three homesteads along the way, but it was for the most part open country. As they drove by one small farm, Beth noticed a red-tailed hawk circling lazily above them. She glanced at Trey out of the corner of her eye and saw that he was watching it too.

The quiet felt like a blessing after the rattling stage, but she wished he would talk to her, even if he had nothing pleasant to say. Trey drove with his eyes on the road, silent and looking as if he'd enjoy the chance to bite someone's head off. Beth fought down panic again. That scene back in the little church, was it real? Did she fall so far short of this man's expectations that he couldn't keep it from showing on his face?

After they'd driven a mile, Beth decided it was going to be up to her to break the silence. "Wallace Flats is a bit smaller than I expected."

Trey kept his eyes forward. He wouldn't even pay her the courtesy of looking at her when he spoke. "Well, it hasn't had long to grow. It's only been here ten years. Some of the settlers made their stake in the silver country and then came here to farm. Some of the others made their money mining the miners, selling supplies and liquor. There's more than a few who're just living on hope. The whole place is a gamble, really. If the railroad doesn't come, it'll probably disappear."

Beth realized what he meant by living on hope as they passed a shaky-looking cabin with a couple of fat hogs and six very lean children milling around it.

"Well, Denver's a gamble too. Graham told me city blocks were won and lost playing dice when it was being built."

Trey's accent roused her curiosity. It came and went, only softening an occasional word, making it difficult to place. "When you wrote you didn't say where you were from."

"I'm from North Georgia. Morgan County. How long have you lived in Denver?"

"For the last two years. I grew up in Philadelphia. What brought you here?"

"Well, after the war I had to start over, so I came West. I looked around a bit and this place caught my eye, so I stayed here."

"Do you have family back home?"

"No. My mother died just before the war started and Father took my sister, Rochelle, back to England with him. He's from Yorkshire."

"Oh? Where was your mother from?" That subtle inflection of his didn't sound British to Beth's ears.

"She was Cajun, from Louisiana." That explained it. The French influence showed in Trey's eyes as well as in the timbre and cadence of his voice; a voice Beth found very pleasant to hear.

"Is your sister older or younger?"

"Younger, by five minutes." He smiled, and it made five years fall away from him. "She's married now, with a couple of kids."

Beth breathed a little easier. He wasn't made of stone. She smiled in response.

"As a small child I used to play with a pair of twin sisters. They fought constantly, but I've always thought being a twin must be interesting."

"Yeah." His dry tone made her think Trey and his sister had likely given their parents more than two children's worth of grief. Beth felt a familiar twinge of envy.

"You're lucky. My parents died when I was very young. Uncle Robert and Aunt Abigail brought me up."

"*What*?" Trey almost dropped the reins as he turned to her, staring. "You're Robert Underhill's niece?"

"Yes, did you know him?" It seemed that everywhere Beth went she met people who knew Uncle Robert. He'd made friends easily, but it certainly wasn't pleasure she saw on Trey's face.

With no warning at all, he pulled the team to a stop and turned them around so abruptly Beth had to grab the seat to keep her balance. She righted herself and glared at him.

"What are you doing?"

The look he gave her felt like a physical push. Those dark eyes turned distant and unyielding again. Beth felt as if the air had solidified between them.

"I'm taking you back to town. I'll put you up at Mrs. Grant's. It's a decent place. You can catch the next stage back to Denver, and I'll give you the fare. I met your uncle at a horse auction a couple of years ago, and I'd heard of him before that. I know he was a banker in Philadelphia, and on the side he raised some of the finest racehorses in the country. His niece doesn't belong out here. You'll be a whole lot better off at your cousin's."

Beth sat up straight, prepared for battle. She'd deliberately avoided mentioning her privileged background in her letters for fear he'd react like this. She'd come out here because she didn't want to be pre-judged, least of all by him.

"Mr. McShannon, you're being completely unfair. We had an agreement. If you don't honor it, I'll be within my rights to sue you."

A smug grin. "Go ahead. You wouldn't get enough to pay your lawyer."

Meeting his gaze and holding it felt like lifting a heavy weight, but Beth did.

"Maybe not, but breach of promise is a rather nasty affair. And you do have your livestock."

That wiped the smile from Trey's face. He stopped the team again. Beth didn't lower her eyes. After a long moment, he turned the horses around.

"All right, have it your way, Philadelphia. And you might as well call me Trey. We did just get married." Another smug grin, followed by a measuring look. "What are you doing here, anyway? Were you bored in town?"

Beth crisply gave him the plain, unvarnished facts. "Uncle Robert moved us West because of his health. When he died, Aunt Abigail and I found out he'd lost a lot of money in mining stock. He'd never told us. The war ruined a lot of his older investments too, but he hadn't told us that either. *Ladies* weren't to worry about such things." *They have to deal with them, though.* "By the time the bills were paid there was enough left to keep the house going, nothing more. When Aunt Abigail passed away this winter, the house went to my cousin. I was left with a small trust fund, which I'll inherit in a little over a year when I turn twenty-five. It's enough to live on, very modestly, for four or five months at the most. I had to do something."

While she spoke, Trey's angry look softened to something that might be curiosity. "Why didn't you go to your cousin's?"

Beth decided to be honest. "I didn't want to sit in Graham's house and wait for him to find an acceptable man to take me off his hands—acceptable to *him*." She looked Trey in the eye again. "When I wrote, I told you I didn't know much about housekeeping. What did you think you were getting?"

"That's not the point. I can't expect you to be content out here."

Now he sounded embarrassed. Beth shrugged. "Mr. McShannon, I'm a big girl. I thought from your letter that you'd give me credit for being able to make up my own mind."

Trey's heavy brows lifted as he gave her another measuring glance. "Oh, I'll bet you're an expert at that." Then he turned his attention back to the road and urged the team into a faster trot.

CHAPTER 2

An hour's drive brought them to the homestead. A copse of pines hid the buildings until they rounded a bend in the long lane. Somewhere in the trees, a pair of crows set up a racket as Trey pulled the horses to a stop.

"Well, here we are."

Beth took one quick look at her surroundings before the tall blood bay stallion in the corral captured her attention. He trotted to the gate and stood, poised and alert, watching them with his head high.

"Trey, Uncle Robert would have sold his soul for a horse like him. Where did you get him?"

The horse whistled at the sound of Beth's unfamiliar voice. He stood at least sixteen hands high, with the bone to match the height. His coat glowed a rich red, a shade or two darker than Beth's hair, accentuated by black points. Every line of him showed his racing blood. He was no youngster, but he moved as if he could put most three-year-olds in training to shame.

Why, back East he'd bring enough to live on for a year. But what's he doing out here?

Beth watched Trey read and respond to her appreciation. He didn't do a very good job of concealing his pride.

"His name's Flying Cloud. We raised him at home. Dad scrimped and saved for years to buy a quality mare in foal by a good stallion. When Cloud was born, Dad gave him to me."

Beth still couldn't believe her eyes. "Since Uncle Robert's farm was sold I never expected to be near an animal like this again. You raised Thoroughbreds at home?"

"In a small way. Dad grew up around racing stables in England. We were working on making it a business, but really we were just farmers. We sold our horses when Dad went overseas. I've got four young mares now."

Beth dragged her eyes from Cloud and looked around the homestead again.

"Well, it certainly looks like you've done a good job here."

Trey had built on a rare piece of flat land. The cabin and barn stood at right angles, with a narrow belt of woods behind for a windbreak. The buildings looked solid and well maintained, their wood faded to a pleasing gray. The corral fit neatly into the angle between them. In all directions rolling, spring-green grasslands stretched into the distance. Everything was dwarfed by the sky.

"Thanks." Trey jumped down from the wagon seat, and Beth followed before he could reach up to help her. They each gathered an armload of supplies and carried it inside.

Beth dropped her load on the rough counter beside the door. A bunk built against one wall, a square pine table with four slat-backed chairs and a roomy dresser next to the stove furnished the cabin. Everything looked handmade, not by a master craftsman but by someone who had, nonetheless, put time and effort and patience into the job. A neat stack of firewood stood ready by the stove. A small round mirror hung beside the dresser, and a shelf on the wall by the table held a row of books.

An Indian rug, colorful with geometric patterns in red and white, covered the earthen floor between the table and the stove. Beside the bunk, a ladder led to a small loft. Hams and slabs of bacon hung from hooks in the rafters. A few dirty dishes lay piled on the dresser, the last ones Trey had used; otherwise, the place looked as spare and efficient inside as it did out. There really wasn't much to get out of order.

Beth's gaze lingered for a moment on the bunk, long enough for Trey to notice. He nodded toward the ladder.

"I fixed up the loft for you. If you want to climb up, I'll hand you your bags."

When she did, she found another bunk ready for her. He'd strung blankets across the front and sides of the loft for privacy and put in a row of nails to hang clothes on. A plain washstand filled one corner, a small dresser occupied another and a weathered rocking chair sat at the foot of the bed. That gesture brought quick tears to Beth's eyes. Taken by surprise, she wiped them away with her sleeve before reaching down for her things.

Had Trey thought about the implications of a rocker when he put it there, or was he simply being kind? Either way, the gesture touched her.

Beth, you're getting way ahead of yourself. She laid the suitcases on the bed, made sure her face was dry and hurried back down the ladder.

When they'd finished unloading the wagon, Beth watched Trey unhitch the team. He looked over his shoulder as he led the horses to the barn.

"You might as well come in and see what I've been working toward."

She followed him and stood at the barn door while he put the team away and hung up their harness. Eight roomy stalls ran along each side of the aisle. Their low sides gave Beth a good view of Trey's mares. Even in the scant light filtering through the dusty windows, their breeding showed – the same breeding visible in Flying Cloud. Two, a sleek black and a dark liver chestnut, looked close to foaling. The rich smells of horses and clover hay and the soft sounds of the horses moving filled a moment of silence before Trey nodded toward the black.

"I call her Eve because I bought her first. She'll foal in a month or so. The chestnut's name is Shiloh. She's due a little sooner."

The stall next to Eve's held a lighter chestnut mare, trim and long-legged. When she came to the half-door to meet him, Trey reached under her mane to rub her neck. "This is Chance. She and Cheyenne, the little sorrel—" he glanced toward the next stall "—will be bred this summer. You'll probably want to ride Cheyenne. She's pretty quiet. Chance can be a handful."

Beth didn't comment. If he expected her to insist she could handle Chance, he was going to be disappointed. He'd find out soon enough.

Loosened by the drive, a lock of hair fell from her bun to tickle Beth's ear. As she tucked it back into place, she found herself imagining Trey's fingers in her hair, his hard hand cupping the back of her neck, his thumb stroking the sensitive skin there. Of their own volition, her lips parted. She closed them and blinked.

Beth, you can't be thinking like this. Just a result of the uncomfortable situation, she supposed. Her eyes met Trey's and saw the answering glow there before he turned away. So he'd felt something too.

Trey had just finished introducing the other horses when the sound of hooves drew him and Beth from the barn. They stood at the door while a wagon pulled into the yard, carrying a stocky, graying, weathered-looking man and a trim, dark-haired woman who looked to be a young fifty. The man nodded and gave Beth a friendly appraisal with sharp hazel eyes. The woman climbed down and extended a hand to her with a frank smile.

"Hello. I'm Maddy Kinsley and this is my husband, Logan. Trey told us you'd be coming in today. It's Beth, isn't it?"

No explanations needed. Thank you. Beth took the hand, hoping her shyness didn't show.

"Yes. Pleased to meet you. Do you live close by?"

"A couple of miles due east of here."

"Logan and I run our cattle together. Maddy sells me bread and milk and feeds me when I'm tired of my own cooking." Trey had a warm smile for them both. Beth took notice. He did know how to be pleasant, at least with others. These must be the neighbors he'd mentioned in his letter.

"Speaking of which, I thought this would come in handy." Maddy pulled a basket out of the back of the wagon.

A savory aroma of chicken and herbs drifted from it. "Here's a pot of soup, Beth, along with the bread and milk. Save you some time while you're getting settled."

Thanking heaven for small mercies, Beth took the basket. She'd been wondering what she'd do if Trey expected her to cook supper on her first night. "Thank you. I feel like less of a stranger already. I'll put it inside."

Maddy followed her into the cabin. Something in the older woman's steady dark blue eyes got behind Beth's usual reserve with strangers. She was going to need a friend, and Maddy looked like the dependable kind. Beth put the basket on the dresser and turned around.

"Maddy, I'm going to start right in by asking you a favor. Will you teach me a few things, like how to make bread? I'm afraid I haven't done much cooking."

Maddy looked Beth up and down, much like June Baker had, then she smiled. "No, I don't suppose you have, but we all have to learn sometime. I'll be baking day after tomorrow. Come on over after dinner." She put a hand on Beth's shoulder. "I remember how I felt when I was newly married. You find yourself alone a lot out here. You just come visit any time it gets to you."

Beth's shyness eased a bit more. Just knowing she could go to someone made a huge difference. "I will, I promise. And you do the same."

With a quick squeeze of Beth's hand, Maddy said goodbye. After the Kinsleys had driven off, Beth clumsily kindled a fire in the stove while Trey did the evening barn chores. Once she had it going, she put the soup on to heat and gave the cabin a closer look.

He liked things simple, which would be all the easier for her. She wondered if he'd made the furniture himself. Something to do on winter nights. Whoever had made it hadn't done a bad job. Nothing fancy, but it served the purpose.

Beth walked over to the bookshelf and scanned the titles. Each book looked well worn. Dickens and Thackeray, Longfellow's *Evangeline*, Walt Whitman. A sea story, *Two Years Before the Mast.* She hadn't read that one. It surprised her to see the Whitman and Longfellow. Trey didn't seem the type.

A velvet-covered folding picture frame lay closed beside the books. Beth picked it up, ran a finger over the faded blue fabric and opened it. The middle section held a family picture. Trey looked to be about sixteen.

Seated, he leaned toward the camera, his long frame still lanky and boyish, with a cocky grin on his lips, dark eyes gleaming with careless arrogance. He had his hair dampened down to a semblance of order. Beth saw barely a trace of the stern-faced man she'd met today.

Why, you'd hardly know him.

The blonde, fine-featured girl seated next to him looked no more like his sister than Beth did, but she bore a strong resemblance to the small, light-haired man standing behind her, as Trey did to his mother. Mrs. McShannon had been a beautiful woman. The dark hair that was straight and unruly in her son looked smooth and wavy, caught up in a soft roll on top of her head. Trey had her eyes as well as her coloring.

One side of the frame contained a later picture of his sister with her husband and children. The remaining section held a picture of Trey in uniform.

A Union uniform.

A traitor. Looking at Trey's young face, strained and tired under his forage cap, Beth dismissed the ugly word. How much had he given up when he made that brutal choice?

Across the bottom of the picture, he'd written '60th Cavalry, 3rd Pennsylvania Volunteers'. Beth knew the name. She recalled seeing the regiment on parade in Philadelphia before they were disbanded. They'd seen the worst of the fighting at Antietam, Gettysburg, the Wilderness. Still absorbed with the picture, she didn't hear Trey step up behind her.

"Surprised?"

Feeling as guilty as if she'd been caught stealing, Beth whirled around. "How old were you when this was taken?"

"Eighteen." Tight-lipped, Trey took the frame from her, folded it with a smart *click* and put it back on the shelf. Beth couldn't fathom why he was so annoyed. If he didn't want the pictures seen, he should have put them away.

"I'm sorry. I suppose I was being curious, but the frame was right there. That must have been a difficult decision to make."

With an impatient shrug, Trey moved to the counter. He turned his back to Beth, dipped hot water from the boiler on the back of the stove and washed his hands. "I didn't take things seriously at eighteen. Later in the war, a boy in my company told me he'd joined up because he'd gotten his report from school and he was more afraid of his father than he was of the Rebs. I guess I wasn't that different."

Beth wanted to ask him if he really expected her to believe that, but he clearly didn't want to discuss it. She groped for a change of subject.

"Your sister's very pretty. You'd never know you were twins."

Good Lord, Beth, what a stupid thing to say.

Trey grinned at her embarrassment. "Thanks. I'm sure she'd take that as a compliment."

Beth couldn't help smiling back. "Good. What are the children's names?"

"The oldest girl is Greer. She's Chelle's husband's child by his first wife. The other two are Trey and Sidonie. That was Mother's name. Sidonie Amelie."

The name rolled off his tongue freighted with a love Beth couldn't miss. It touched a carefully guarded empty place deep inside her.

"What a lovely name. I was named after my mother, Elizabeth Marie. I've never seen a picture of her, but Aunt Abigail always said I looked like her. Your nephew looks a bit like you."

"Chelle says he acts like me, too. Serves her right."

That smile. Could he have any idea how it changed his face? Feeling her cheeks warm, Beth peeked into the soup pot.

"This smells delicious. I liked Maddy and Logan."

Trey took an appreciative sniff as he stepped up beside her. "It's hard not to. They're both salt of the earth, but I'd like Maddy for her cooking alone. That does smell good."

"Well, I think it's ready." Beth rummaged for spoons and knives, put Maddy's bread and butter on the table and filled two bowls with steaming soup. Trey lit the lamp and set it at the end of the table.

The twilight faded as they ate. Their own reflections looked back at them from the window, a pair of strangers having a silent meal. After her long day, Beth felt too drained to make conversation. Trey made no effort to. When he offered to do the dishes, she lit a candle and retreated to the loft to unpack.

She'd brought four cotton dresses with her, the plainest and most serviceable she had, but as Beth hung them up she realized none of them was sturdy enough to be of much use to her here. She unwrapped the parcel containing her new denim trousers and pulled a pair on under her skirt. They fit, and they'd certainly be practical.

I wonder how shocked he'll be.

She hadn't brought much else except a few blouses, her riding clothes, her paint kit and easel and a new sketchbook. She opened the book and rifled through the blank pages. One way or another, she'd get some work done out here. This wasn't going to be a wasted year. If she went on her way next spring, she planned to have something to show for her time. She had friends in New York who knew art. Maybe that should have been her choice. Of course, it still could be. She'd always loved the city.

And now . . . here she was.

She sat down in the old rocker and found it surprisingly comfortable. They really should have it downstairs.

Beth, what have you done? It all seemed simple when you were sitting in Denver writing to him, didn't it? Only now he's not a faceless stranger anymore. He's your husband. Are you going to be a coward?

No, but I strongly suspect you've been a fool.

Perhaps, but it would be hard to make a bigger fool of herself than she had over Daniel Hunter. Hurt and anger surfaced at the thought of him, just as they always did. *But you never loved him, not really, any more than he really loved you. Remember that.* Beth's romantic daydream had been shattered cleanly enough when Daniel came to see her soon after Uncle Robert's funeral.

"Beth, you know I love you."

"Yes, I do, but I never get tired of hearing you say it."

He'd been courting her for almost a year. He was the first man who'd really kissed her, really made her feel. Daniel came from a good Eastern family as well, one with expectations of an only son. Beth had made sure he knew the truth of her financial situation, and he'd said it didn't matter. Her mistake was assuming he'd told his parents and they felt the same way.

"You know I'm enrolled in law school for the fall semester. Now Father says he won't educate me if we marry."

"Daniel, I'll wait while you work your way through school. Uncle Robert had a lot of friends. I can help you find a job. And your parents will come around, I know they will."

"But what if they don't? You'd end up hating me, Beth, and I wouldn't blame you."

Beth didn't hate him. She just couldn't believe she'd mistaken Daniel's self-seeking flattery for love. After he left her that day, she'd never said a word in response to Aunt Abigail's questions. Once the worst of Beth's self-disgust had passed, she simply made up her mind to stop looking for something that didn't exist.

Don't fool yourself, Beth. It doesn't exist here either.

She wondered if Trey knew how his tone and expression had changed while they were in the barn. The man had gentleness in him, however well he kept it hidden. If he thawed out a little, she might even find him attractive.

You do find him attractive.

Beth pushed the thought away and got out of the rocker. She was responsible for herself now, and she wasn't going be led astray by her emotions again.

Trey had blown out the lamp and gone to bed. In the deep quiet she could hear his slow, even breathing. Beth got into her nightgown and under the covers. The chaff mattress wasn't uncomfortable and there were plenty of quilts, but lying there in the candlelight she found herself thinking of her room at home. Not the house in Denver but the one in Philadelphia, with the muted sounds of the street coming up to her window and the diamond-patterned wallpaper she could still picture so clearly. Beth thought that wallpaper was partly responsible for her early habit of doodling. She shut off the memory before it could bring on a rush of homesick, lonely tears.

Perhaps time would prove Graham right, but this was the first major decision Beth had made entirely on her own, with no one advising or suggesting. That was worth something. Instead of crying, it made a lot more sense to go to sleep and let tomorrow look after itself. So she did.

* * * *

September sunlight, as thick and golden as molten honey, filtered through the willows and danced along the ripples of the creek. Up to his armpits in the water, a small boy shouted.

"Hey, Trey, you comin' in or not?"

"Yeah, I'm coming, Justin, keep your pants on."

Justin slipped underwater, stroked to the bank and came up splashing, sending jeweled droplets flying. "You're the one with pants on."

Trey jumped back to avoid being soaked, skinned out of his shirt and overalls and tossed them next to Justin's clothes. With a running leap, he cannon balled into the creek. The cold water forced the air from his seven-year-old lungs. He bobbed to the surface, gasping.

Justin was nowhere to be seen. Trey steadied himself, expecting an underwater attack, but nothing happened. A magpie called from a nearby branch, the only sound except for the murmur of the water.

"Justin Sinclair's an old wet hen!" H*e-n* echoed off the bank, but only the magpie answered. The sun slid behind a cloud, stealing some of the day's warmth. Shivering, Trey hugged himself and scanned the creek up and down. Justin must be planning something, trying to scare him.

Slippery rocks rolling under his feet, Trey took a step toward the shore. Something boomed in the distance, loud enough to send the magpie flying. It sounded too short and sharp for thunder, but what else could it be? Trey glanced at the sky, looking for storm clouds that weren't there. Best get out of the water, just in case. He yelled again.

"Hell, Justin, this isn't funny."

That clap should have brought Justin running, but it didn't. Stumbling, fighting the current and his growing panic, Trey headed for shore. The thunder cracked again and again in rapid succession – much too rapid.

Cannon.

"Justin!"

The sunlight dissolved into darkness. The clammy chill on Trey's skin came from cold sweat, not creek water. He sat up in bed, trembling.

He heard nothing from the loft. He hadn't wakened Beth. Trey rested his head on his knees, waiting for his heart to stop pounding in his ears like the cannon in his dream. Over a year. *Congratulations.* He'd hoped his nightmares had stopped for good, but he'd learned long ago to focus on the positive.

When he'd settled down, Trey pulled on his pants and lit the lamp. Reading for a while might calm him enough to go back to sleep. As he lifted *Two Years Before the Mast* from the bookshelf, his hand brushed the picture frame he'd taken from Beth before supper. He'd meant to put it away before she arrived, but in the hurry of getting the place ready for her, he'd forgotten.

If only other things could be forgotten as easily.

* * * *

Beth didn't know what woke her. She didn't think she'd slept for more than a couple of hours when she opened her eyes to dim lamplight and sat up, her body tense as if she'd had an unpleasant dream. Had someone called out?

Confused and disoriented, she rested her head on her knees for a moment. *You're married. That's no dream.* Trey had been in bed when she fell asleep, she remembered that.

Beth crept across the loft and peeked around the edge of the blanket screening her from the main floor. Trey sat at the table with his back to her. Looking over his shoulder, she saw a book in front of him, but his head was turned toward the stove, watching the fire.

He'd pulled on his pants, but hadn't bothered with a shirt. The dim light didn't hide the contours of his strong shoulders and long, tapered back. Every female instinct she had responded to the sight.

Beth, if he sees you! Cheeks flaming, she dropped the blanket as if it were on fire and scrambled back to bed.

What was he doing up in the middle of the night? She considered asking him if he was all right, but didn't have the nerve.

Maybe you're a coward and a fool both. Beth gave herself a stern shake and turned her back on the blanket

34

curtain. The lamp was still burning when she went back to sleep.

CHAPTER 3

Harriet Grant looked up from her dusting and out her parlor window as the stage left town. Hands on her hips, she watched a man crossing the square, headed toward her place. Customers had been sparse this spring, but she didn't know about this one.

He bore a passing resemblance to Neil Garrett at the saloon, minus the scarred face and half his left arm. His nose had been broken, he walked with a slight limp and his clothes had seen better days a long time ago.

Had a rough war, and a rough time since.

He took off a battered hat as he came in, revealing dark blond hair and cool gray eyes. He would have been good-looking as a boy. In spite of his nose, his face showed a hint of refinement. Harriet took in the stranger's solid, compact build. Not one to cross, she decided. He might have only one good arm, but he looked like he could handle himself.

"Good afternoon, Missus Grant—you are she, aren't you?" His quiet, pleasant voice showed a hint of refinement as well. "I was told you rent rooms."

"Yes, I do, Mister . . .?"

"Nathan Munroe." He dropped his dusty duffle bag on the newly swept hall floor, then muttered to himself and slung it over his shoulder again. "I'm looking for a room for a few weeks, 'til I find something permanent. Looking for work if you hear of anything. I'll pay by the week, in advance. Hope the food's good."

Harriet didn't intend to take him any other way. He handed over a ten-dollar bill, and she gave him his key and change with a miffed expression.

"No one's ever complained about my table."

Mr. Munroe mollified her with a smile that started with his eyes. "I'm sure they haven't, Ma'am. Guess I'll drop my things and go take a look at where I've landed."

"Fine." Harriet gave him a crisp nod. *A smooth one.* "Breakfast's at seven-thirty, lunch is at one and supper's at six. You'll find it pretty quiet here. It's a small town."

He turned to the window and studied the street for a moment. "Not too quiet, I hope. I understand people have been moving in around here. Usually livens a place up a bit."

Harriet watched him climb the stairs. A Southerner by the sound of him and, unless she missed her guess, born a gentleman. Not an uncommon type out here. This one made her curious, but she'd learned a long time ago that it was bad business to ask too many questions of her boarders. One way or another, they'd be answered in time.

* * * *

Nathan Munroe dumped his bag and spared the room a quick glance. The iron bedstead boasted a red and white quilt, the chest of drawers in the corner would be more than ample for his meager belongings, and a comfortable-looking overstuffed chair sat by the window.

Luxury, my friend. How long has it been since you slept in a real bed and ate a woman's cooking?

He stepped out, locked the door behind him and headed for Neil's place. It was almost empty at that time of day, and the few customers who were there didn't seem to be the town's leading lights. One man, barely visible in the shadows at a corner table, looked like he hadn't moved since the previous night. He lifted his head for a moment, then slouched in his chair again as Nathan settled himself on a barstool.

"Coffee, please, black. Are you Mister Garrett?"

"Yeah." The scarred redhead filled a cup and slid it across the bar. "Here you are, Mister."

Nathan took a sip then swallowed more. It tasted good, hot and strong. "Nice little town you've got here."

Neil's eyes flashed amusement. "Don't know if nice is the word I'd use, but I've seen worse. You passing through?"

"I'm not planning on it. I'm looking for a place to settle. Looks like decent country. All it needs is some good people and maybe a little more water."

Neil snorted as he topped up Nathan's cup. "Mister, a few good people and a little more water would turn hell into heaven. You can raise cattle around here, though, if you hold your mouth right."

Nathan sipped his coffee and thought about something stronger, then thought better of it. "I'm sure you can. How many people in town?"

"Three hundred, maybe three-twenty-five."

He felt someone's eyes on him and turned around. A young woman stood in the doorway of a back room. A cloud of tousled chestnut hair tumbled around her shoulders, which the stained blue dress she wore left bare. When she caught Nathan's eye her lips curved in a slow, inviting smile. He hadn't seen anything that looked as good as she did for quite some time.

"You keep women here?"

Neil's crooked mouth twisted in what passed for a grin. "Not me. Don't you know that's illegal? I just rent rooms to them. What they do in them's their own business, as long as it increases mine and they pay their rent. Lorie never has a problem doing that. She's real popular."

Nathan turned and mouthed 'see you' at the girl. "Bet she is."

Lorie gave her hair a subtle toss and disappeared into her room, leaving him reflecting on his slim purse. He needed this town to be a lucky one for him.

Three hundred and twenty-five people. There'd been a hundred at Cedarhill all told when he left home. A small town really, in its own right. The largest plantation in Morgan County, next to the Sinclairs'.

It had surprised Nathan once to realize he wouldn't go back if he could. He'd enjoyed spending money when he had it, but it didn't bother him to be without it anymore. The war had given him a different view of what he needed. At home he'd always been restless to the point where it became anger, and now he had freedom. He'd always enjoyed a good scrap and he'd survived a real dandy, only a little the worse for wear. He'd fought long and hard enough to learn to appreciate peace.

That's what a growing town like this needs. Someone who appreciates peace.

CHAPTER 4

The morning sun slanted through the side windows of the cabin and up into the loft, waking Beth early. She smelled ham and coffee and heard the hiss of a fire in the stove, but no other sounds. Trey must be already up and out. She put on her brown gingham, braided her hair and climbed down the ladder, wishing she felt brave and determined.

One day at a time.

When she saw the thick slice of ham sizzling gently in the skillet at the edge of the stove, she decided it needed an egg. Beth had learned to fry eggs on camping trips as a child. She'd seen a chicken coop beside the barn so she grabbed a bowl and went out, but as soon as she stepped inside the coop an angry, squawking bundle of feathers flew at her face. She just managed to put the door between herself and the rooster.

Beth was never in her best mood early in the morning. She muttered something uncomplimentary, marched to the barn and grabbed the first bridle she came to, with Trey watching from Cheyenne's stall.

He put down his currycomb, leaned on the half-door and looked her over. There was nothing bold about it, but it warmed her.

"Morning. Problem?"

"D'you think that rooster's too tough to eat?" Beth grumbled.

A teasing light gleamed in Trey's eyes. "I've wondered that a few times myself. I heard him out there. Need some help?"

She doubled up the reins in her hand and lifted her chin. "No thank you. He's going to learn some manners or he's going to find himself in a stew pot." In spite of his restless night, Trey's face showed no sign of lost sleep. It seemed he liked early mornings. "Did you have trouble sleeping last night?"

He turned back to Cheyenne, reached for the soft brush on the window ledge and ran it along the mare's side. "A little. How about you?"

"Same here. Strange bed, I guess."

Trey kept his back to Beth while the silence lengthened. The warmth she'd just sensed from him dissipated, leaving her feeling annoyed and more than a little puzzled.

"Well, I want an egg for breakfast. Wish me luck."

"Give 'em hell."

Trey left Cheyenne's stall and crossed the aisle to Cloud's, brushing by Beth without a glance. Dismissed, she marched back to the chicken coop and stepped inside. When the rooster flew at her again, he got a sound slap with the reins. That was one effective way to deal with a prickly male. Beth got her eggs.

She'd finished her breakfast and gone up to the loft to make her bed when Trey called to her from the doorway. "You said in your letter you could ride. I've got time to show you around the place this morning if you'd like."

41

Beth had been looking forward to this. Uncle Robert had taught her young how to sit a horse, and she'd taken to it as naturally as she had to drawing. It would feel good to show Trey she had one useful skill at least.

"Sure. I'll change. It'll only take me a minute."

She reached for her denims, then lost her nerve and put on the riding outfit she'd brought with her. She didn't feel ready to parade around in front of Trey in men's clothes. She knew the tan divided skirt and plain white blouse suited her well.

When she stepped into the yard, Trey had the horses ready. She smiled when she saw he'd saddled Chance for her instead of Cheyenne.

Fine, Mister McShannon, you're on.

Beth swung lightly into the saddle. Appreciation showed in Trey's eyes as she reined Chance in with competent hands. Full of pent-up energy, the mare danced and sidestepped as Trey rode beside her. Once the horses were warm, he threw Beth a challenging glance.

"Want to run, Philadelphia?"

Beth returned his challenge with a toss of her braid. "No, I want to see if that old plug of yours has any legs left. Let's race!"

She shifted her weight and urged Chance to a gallop, with Cloud only one jump behind her. He was older and a lot heavier, as well as carrying a lot more weight, but he had the advantage in power. Beth had to ask Chance for everything she had to keep ahead of him. The mare responded, instinctively lengthening her stride and putting her all into the race. Trey and Cloud couldn't run her down.

They let the horses run together for a mile, neck and neck. When they pulled back to a walk, Trey saluted Beth with a tip of his cap.

"You can ride, and that little lady can run. I've never had a chance to try her like this with another horse."

Beth had to catch her breath before she could answer. She hadn't ridden that fast since the day when, aged thirteen, she'd blackmailed one of the exercise boys at Uncle Robert's farm into letting her ride one of their colts in training.

"She certainly can. Has she ever raced?"

"No. I couldn't afford to buy proven winners. I had to go by bloodlines alone and buy yearlings. Her foals might, though, and if breeding means anything they'll do well. Anyway, racing or not, there are people out here who are interested in good horses." Trey tugged at a handful of black mane. "Cloud's thirteen now, but there's still plenty of time."

Beth understood Trey's pride. Cloud certainly did have some legs left, and he clearly still enjoyed using them. He stepped along looking very pleased with himself. "You've raced him, haven't you?"

"Yes, for a couple of years at county fairs, and a few times at larger meets. He lost his first race and he didn't like it. He never lost another. I swear he still misses it." By his tone, so did Trey. Beth conjured a vivid picture of the lanky colt and equally lanky boy as he went on. "We stopped when I turned eighteen. I'd gotten too heavy; it was going to break him down. I should've got Dad to ride him. He's not much heavier than you, but pound for pound he's one of the toughest men I've ever known. At fifteen I was already a head taller than him, but he was boss all right."

Beth felt a surge of admiration for the man. She didn't imagine Trey had been easy to bring up.

"You said he grew up around racing stables. Was he a jockey?"

"Yes. He rode in his first race when he was fourteen. He spent seven years riding other people's horses. I remember what he said to me before Cloud's first start. 'I never raced a horse of my own, but when I went out on the track, it never mattered to me who the horse belonged to. If the understanding's there, it's you he'll kill himself running for.'"

Beth liked the affection behind the words. In spite of what he'd done, Trey's bond with his family hadn't been shattered by the war, nor had it grown weak with time and distance. "How did he end up coming over here?"

"Well, he liked betting on the horses as well as he liked riding. He won a few times in a row, and then he decided to quit while he was ahead. He wanted to own horses like that one day, and he couldn't do it at home. He came over here, met my mother and bought some land. I guess he passed on a bit of his gambling urge to me. On my way west, Cloud helped me earn my grubstake."

Wanting to keep Trey talking, Beth nudged Chance to bring her alongside Cloud. "How?"

A spark of pure deviltry flashed in Trey's eyes. "Well, before I left I bought the wagon and broke him to harness." He shook his head at the memory. "Broke is a good word for it. At first I wondered what was going to get broken first – the wagon, his legs or my neck, but we worked it out after a while. Then whenever we came to a town I made sure he was all covered in dust, hitched to the wagon. I'd find a place to have a drink or two and start going on about my fast horse. When enough people had put their money and their horses up against me, we'd leave them in the dust."

Beth let out a peal of laughter, picturing the faces on race day. "Didn't anyone catch on?"

"Not often. Now and then someone would look closer than the others and bet on me, but Cloud still looked a bit rough from the war and most people didn't give him more than a glance. Some of them didn't take losing to us all that well. A few times we left town in a hurry."

They rode in silence for a while over the rolling landscape. It reminded Beth of the ocean, with the breeze rippling the grass and the immenseness of the distance around them, punctuated only by occasional clumps of pines and cottonwoods. It intimidated and inspired awe at the same time. Beth saw shades of green and gold she knew she'd never be able to mix on a palette, and they changed with every cloud that passed by.

They came to the crest of a hill and looked down into a shallow river valley where cattle grazed. Trey pulled Cloud to a stop beside Chance.

"Mine and Logan's." He pointed to the far end of the valley, where the ground dipped a little lower. "I grow oats and cut hay down at that end, and there are a couple of meadows up in the hills that grow good grass as well. Logan and I drive what's ready for market to Denver twice a year. Money's always tight, but the two foals this spring will make a difference. Then next year there should be four and I'll be able to buy at least one more mare if things go well."

Watching Trey ride, seeing the effortless partnership he had with Cloud, Beth had to ask herself why he wasn't working at a racing stable back East. It would have made more sense than trying to raise horses bred to run in a place like this. What people needed out here was a good cow pony.

"I'm wondering how much sense it makes to try to raise Thoroughbreds out here. You can't get what they're worth, unless you ship them east. And aren't you worried about thieves?" She wouldn't have questioned him at home, but out here he seemed so at ease, so much in his element that she took the chance. Trey kicked his feet from the stirrups, stretched his legs and gave her a rueful smile.

"I know. I've been told I'm crazy so often I'm ready to believe it. Half the kids in town still call me 'Englishman' because I rode in one day with a racing saddle on Cloud. I doubt if anyone in town had seen one before. As for thieves, no one's likely to steal a horse that's going to stand out a mile if they try to sell it. I probably will ship horses back East some day, when the train comes, and some day there'll be a market on the West Coast, too. Everyone likes a good horse race. Meanwhile, I'll get by. I'm not in it to get rich. Anyway, I could never have afforded land back East. This is home now."

Beth saw the determination on his face, heard it in his voice.

"This place is very important to you, isn't it?"

Too important to share?

"Yes, it is. The land here can't be farmed like the land at home. Overwork it and it dries up and blows away, but respect it and it'll feed you. What I have here I built myself, and that feels good. Maddy and Logan's place is just over here."

They splashed through the shallow river, cantered up the opposite slope and stopped, looking down at the Kinsleys' farm. The house was a larger version of Trey's, made of the same weathered, hand-split logs. A rosebush grew under the kitchen window, but everything else was plain and functional.

As they sat there letting the horses graze, Beth recalled the house she'd grown up in. Chippendale and Wedgwood, hardly a blank space anywhere. It had always seemed cluttered to her. Life there had often seemed cluttered as well. Comparing that house to the Kinsleys' really wasn't possible. You couldn't compare two completely different ways of living.

Trey's eyes met hers, as unsettling as they had been the other day in the store. "This is what I hope to have in five years, Beth. Maybe it's all I'll ever have. Do you think you could live in a house like this for the rest of your life?"

Well, Beth, could you? She turned away and looked down at the Kinsleys' place again.

"I don't know, Trey. It's a different world. I need you to tell me what you expect from me."

The words hung in the air between them for a long moment before he answered.

"Well, I'm going from sunup to sundown just doing what has to be done. Cooking meals, looking after the house, the vegetable garden, odd jobs, it all adds up. I need you to take on some of those things and give me some breathing room. The mares don't get enough exercise. I haven't had time to train them to work cattle, so I use Cloud for that."

Beth couldn't keep the surprise from her voice. "You do?"

"Sure. It didn't come as natural to him as it would to a horse that was bred for it, but he learned. Having you ride the mares will be a real help."

"Of course. That'll be a pleasure, and there's no reason why I can't help with the barn work, too."

With his mouth set in a stern line, Trey pulled Cloud's head from the grass and turned him toward her. "No. That's no place for you, not yet anyway."

Beth kept her anger hidden for the moment. She hadn't been here a full day yet, but she could already see that Trey needed help outside the house as well as in. She appreciated him not pushing her, but since she'd offered . . .

"Why not? You've got plenty of other work; work I can't do. Let me guess, no place for a lady, right?"

"Yes, for starters."

Beth let go of her temper with a most unladylike snort. "You're no different than Graham and Uncle Robert. Trey, to be the kind of lady you're thinking of—decorative and useless—takes a lady's income, and I don't have that anymore."

His eyes flashed in response. "Useless! Beth, what's the matter with you? I just told you there's plenty for you to do."

This was exactly how she'd always been treated at home.

'Oh, Elizabeth, I've been looking for you. I've invited guests for dinner and your aunt wants you to see to the dining table. Go and find her, Graham and I have business to discuss.'

'Beth, dear, your work is lovely but a public showing would look far too forward. That is for professionals.'

She wasn't going to be dismissed like that by Trey or anyone else. Not anymore.

"That's not the point and you know it. The barn chores take as much time as everything else you mentioned put together. I suppose Maddy works in their barn? Milks the cows, probably, and helps with the chores?"

He looked at her as if she were a spoiled child. "Yes, but that's different. She's been a rancher's wife for thirty years. I don't have time to teach you."

"Teach me what? How to swing a pitchfork? How difficult can it be?"

Trey's patience annoyed Beth more than anger would have. "Beth, that's not what I'm talking about. You're a good rider, but you've never worked with horses on the ground and my horses don't know you. You could get hurt. Have you ever been kicked? I have, and it's not entertainment. Until I say differently, I'll look after the barn."

A familiar feeling of futility swept over her. New York looked better by the minute.

"Fine. I think your pride's getting in the way of your common sense, but I'll stay out. I'm not a five-year-old, you know."

"I know," Trey muttered, "so stop acting like one. Let's go home."

By the time they got back to the homestead, Beth had decided he wasn't worth the bother of staying angry with, but she couldn't help it. His place, his rules, his limits. She might as well have stayed at Graham's.

She dismounted in the yard with a sweet smile, left Chance standing there for Trey, just as she would have done in Denver, and went inside. She stayed as bright and frosty as a sunny January day over the rest of Maddy's soup, then after doing the lunch dishes she took her sketchbook, easel and a chair outside. *He can go to the devil. I've got my own work to do.*

It wasn't the best time of day for landscapes, so Beth took a charcoal stick and began a sketch of Cloud standing in the corral. She got so absorbed in trying to capture the sheen of his coat, the suggestion of motion he gave even when he was still, that she didn't hear Trey come up behind her. She had no idea how long he'd been standing there when he spoke.

"If this is your way of sulking, I'd say it's pretty productive. This is good."

Beth laid her charcoal on the easel ledge and looked up. "Thanks."

He put on one of his smug looks. "Still mad as a hornet, aren't you? I don't know much about art, but I can tell you've had some training. That's not just a horse, that's him."

"No, I don't suppose you would know much about art," Beth agreed serenely, "but you're right. I took lessons off and on from the time I was fourteen up until Uncle Robert died. It's been a hobby of mine for a long time."

Trey dropped the annoying grin. "A hobby? Beth, you've got talent as well as training. Your teachers must have told you so. Have you ever done anything with it? Ever sold anything?"

The question took her by surprise. No one else had ever asked her that. "Yes, to a couple of family friends before we moved to Denver. They insisted on paying me. Just before I came here, I sent two paintings off to a friend of mine in New York to see if she could sell them for me, but Uncle Robert and Aunt Abigail thought it more appropriate for me to donate my work to charity. After all, a *lady* had no need to paint for money."

Trey stepped closer, looking at the drawing over her shoulder. "Is that what this morning was all about? You're good at holding a grudge. Look, maybe you weren't all wrong, but I can't picture you shoveling out stalls, or figure out why you would want to."

His breath tickled Beth's ear as he leaned over her. Seconds passed before she could trust herself to look at him.

"I want to because it's part of what has to be done here."

Trey picked up her charcoal and twirled it in his fingers. "Seems to me you'd be better off spending your time at this."

Beth took a relieved breath as he stepped back. His warm, outdoor scent made it difficult for her to think. "I intend to, but not all of it. I could have done that at Graham's house or back East. I chose to come here. You didn't send for an artist."

He handed the charcoal back to her, his fingers grazing hers. "Fair enough. I just want you to take your time getting to know the horses and let me show you a few things before you start handling them alone."

Beth thawed a trifle. Trey seemed to have gotten her point. "I can live with that. I just want you to treat me like I have a real stake in this place, as long as I'm here. If you ever get sick or hurt I'll need to know how to look after things, including the barn. Which reminds me, I'd like you to go over finances with me sometime soon. I don't mean to sound rude, but I've had my fill of surprises."

He shrugged. "Well, that sure won't take long. We can do it right now. The place will be mine free and clear later this summer when my five years are up. There aren't any debts. I've got a hundred dollars in the bank in Denver. My will is there, too. The way it stands now, if I die the place and the stock will be sold and the money will be put in trust for my niece and nephew. Of course if you stay, that will change. Anything else you want to know?"

"No." He'd given her what she wanted, some basic respect.

Beth signed her drawing 'E. M. Underhill', pulled it from the sketchbook and held it out to him. He'd appreciate it more than anyone else would. "Thank you, Trey. Here, I'd like you to have this. Call it a peace offering."

His eyes held hers as he took it. "Are you sure?"

Beth's cheeks warmed as she released her grip on the paper. Their first argument over. She supposed it was a minor milestone. Trey looked as if he thought so. He probably hadn't expected to get past politeness this soon, either.

"Yes, you're the only person it would mean anything to."

Trey took the drawing back to the house. He returned with a revolver in his hand. Beth's jaw dropped.

"What . . .?"

"I don't suppose you've ever fired one of these."

She stared at him. "No, of course not."

"Well, I'm going to teach you. Starting now."

Goosebumps rose on Beth's arms. Was he testing her, or was he serious? "Do you really think that's necessary?"

"Yes." Trey looked very serious as he took the bullets from the gun and held it out to her. "I keep this in the middle drawer of the dresser, loaded. Being here alone as much as you will be, you should know how to use it. New people are showing up in this country all the time, and they aren't all angels."

Beth swallowed hard. The thought of being alone here hadn't frightened her until now. Her fingers trembled as she took the revolver. "All right, show me."

Trey nodded. "This is a Navy Colt. It doesn't recoil as much as the Army model. A good thing if you're on horseback. You shouldn't find it too hard to handle." He showed her how to load, aim and fire, then watched while she practiced. After she'd emptied the weapon twice he took it from her and put a hand on her shoulder. "That's enough for now. You shoot as well as a lot of the recruits I enlisted with. I'd say you could hit someone coming toward you at close range."

Beth shivered at the thought. "Thanks."

Their eyes met, his challenging, hers refusing to back down. After a moment, he nodded. "I'll teach you to use my Winchester, too. You should carry a rifle when you're riding alone. Your horse could fall and break a leg, anything could happen."

Beth stared at the stump she'd just riddled with bullets. "I don't know if I could ever use it."

Trey handed the gun back to her with one of his appraising looks. "You won't know until you have to. Hopefully you never will, but at least now you know how. I'd better go get some work done."

Beth re-loaded the revolver and put it away. A few minutes later, Trey left to work on a waterhole he was improving. Alone in the house, Beth sat at the table, gazing out the window. The quiet screamed at her.

Did you ever think you'd see the day when you'd learn to fire a gun? Beth, you certainly have some thinking to do.

CHAPTER 5

After supper, which more than lived up to Mrs. Grant's billing, Nathan decided to treat himself to a beer and an informative chat. He headed for Neil's place and settled himself on the same stool he'd used that afternoon.

It wasn't yet dark, but the warped wooden tables in the saloon were filling up with a mixture of sodbusters and ranch hands. The place smelled of liquor, smoke and sweat. The tables didn't go with the rather elegant mirror behind the bar, but good furniture wouldn't have lasted long here.

"Neil, I was wondering. Does this town have a mayor?"

Neil handed Nathan a full mug. "No, just a town council. That'll probably change soon, though, the way the place is growing. If you want my opinion, the longer we can get along as we are, the better."

Nathan hitched his stool forward so he could be heard over the growing racket behind him. "I don't know. I heard today the schoolteacher's leaving, and there isn't a new one ready to step in. There've been a few robberies. New people moving in means more complications. They want a doctor and a teacher and a bank and a sheriff."

Neil stopped wiping glasses and gave him a sharp look in the mirror.

"You a doctor or a banker?"

Nathan took a swallow of his beer. It wasn't bad at all for a place like this. "No, I'm not. I've never taught school, either, but I've been a sheriff."

Neil looked around at his patrons and raised an eyebrow. "Good luck, friend. It wouldn't be an easy job."

"Probably not." As he took another swallow, Nathan caught himself peering into the back hallway, looking for Lorie. He shook his head and grinned when Neil noticed. "Who's on the council?"

"You won't see Lorie this early. She went out a while ago and hasn't come back yet. As for the council, there's the blacksmith, John Reeves, and the storekeeper, Frank Baker. The minister's there too, Paul Baxter. And Dale Turner— he's got the biggest ranch hereabouts, and he represents the folks who live outside of town, but do their business here. Then there's Harriet Grant. They meet once a month, or when something comes up."

"Missus Grant's on the council?"

Neil chuckled. "She sure is. One of the members died a couple of years back and no one else wanted the job. Harriet's got shares in half the businesses in town, and there's nowhere else to go for a decent meal. She's a sharp one, and when she talks around here it's wise to listen."

Nathan had seen enough of his landlady already to believe that. "So the council's responsible for hiring town officials?"

"Yeah, only they haven't hired any yet. They're meeting tomorrow night, I think."

Nathan finished his beer and slipped off the stool. He'd found out what he needed to know. "Thanks, Neil. See you around."

Back in his room Nathan sat by the window, watching the street. There weren't many people around, except for the ones coming and going from the saloon. Lorie was down there, sitting on the bench under Neil's sign. She'd tossed a shawl over her bare shoulders and piled her hair on top of her head in soft loops. It made her look younger and, somehow, more vulnerable. She bantered with a man walking by, her laughter floating up to tease Nathan. He laughed at himself.

Forget it, Nate. You can't afford the money or the distraction. He'd given Harriet a good portion of his cash. If he couldn't convince the town to hire him within a week or two, making room and board could get interesting.

Well, he'd been there before, and the other towns had hired him. He knew the game. Why should things to be any different here?

He sure hoped they'd pay in advance.

* * * *

Beth peered into the small blue crock on the Kinsleys' kitchen table.

"That's the starter," Maddy told her. "I've got a spare jar. I can let you have some to take home. You make it from potatoes. I'll show you how another day. You use warm water, not too hot—feel it—and add a bit of sugar and some starter." Maddy added the ingredients to her bread bowl and mixed them with a careless, practiced hand while Beth tried to store the amounts in her memory. "Then you add salt. Don't forget it, it controls the yeast. Leave it out and the bread will puff up and collapse. Then mix in flour till it forms a dough. After you've done it a few times you get to know what it should feel like." Maddy stirred the mixture, threw in another handful of flour and stirred again. "There. Now you turn it out and knead it for a while."

Feeling thoroughly incompetent, Beth prodded the dough with a finger. "Maddy, how long is a while? The shameful truth is: I've hardly set foot in a kitchen before. You should have tasted the hash I made for lunch today. All Trey would say about it was that he'd eaten worse."

Maddy's eyes crinkled as she let out an infectious laugh. "I'll bet he has. About ten minutes, I guess. Here, you try."

Beth started folding and turning the dough. Her arms were aching by the time Maddy said it looked right. "Now you let it rise until it's twice this size. Cover it with a cloth and put it somewhere warm, but not too warm. At your place I'd say the kitchen dresser would be fine. It'll take a few hours. I usually start last thing at night, then get up early to finish it. You punch it down until it feels like this again, then put it in the pans. Do you have any bread pans?"

"Yes, I saw some in the dresser."

"Well, you only make a loaf about half the size of the pan, because it's going to rise again. When it's doubled again, it's ready to go in the oven. Bake it about forty minutes. When it's done, it'll sound hollow if you tap on it."

"How do you know if the oven's hot enough?"

"You throw some flour in and see how long it takes to burn. Like this." Maddy threw a pinch of flour in her oven and Beth counted the seconds until it browned. "I've got a couple of loaves ready to go in. You might as well stay 'til they're done and have some."

58

Jennie Marsland

Maddy tucked two pans into the oven and pulled the kettle to the middle of the stove. "Trey told us you were living in Denver, but that was all he said. Where are you from?"

Beth gave her a brief history as she washed her hands. Maddy didn't look too surprised.

"You must find it so different out here, Beth."

Beth dried her hands and moved to the table. Maddy had created a cheerful room, with blue gingham curtains at the windows and a braided rug on the sand-scrubbed pine floor. A sideboard painted the same blue as the curtains took the place of a counter, and a matching pantry cupboard filled one corner. Beth had never realized how welcoming a kitchen could be.

"I do. I really haven't got my feet on the ground yet. I could probably count on my two hands the number of times I've been completely alone anywhere. I guess you're used to being alone in several square miles of country, but I'm not—not yet."

Wiping her hands on her apron, Maddy sat down across from Beth. "Does it bother you?"

Beth pictured the tree stump she'd used for target practice then recalled the hour she'd spent outside painting this morning after Trey left. "Sometimes, but there are things I like about it, too."

A reminiscent smile spread across Maddy's face. "I know what you mean. I was married when I was eighteen. Will and I went to live on his farm, fifty miles from town. I'd never been away from home for more than two nights at a time. For the first couple of months I think I cried a bit every day."

"Will?"

"Logan's my second husband, Beth. We've only been married six years. I used to work in the store in my hometown, and Will came in for supplies every couple of months. He started hanging around to chat. Oh, he had a smile, and he could talk the hind leg off a mule." Maddy's eyes shone at the memory. "One day I realized I was in love with him. The next time he came to town I told him so, and he said he loved me, too. The circuit preacher happened to be in town, so we went and told my parents and we were married that night."

From Maddy's expression, she'd never regretted it. Beth thought of all the rules, the proprieties surrounding courtship in the world she knew.

"You just…told him?"

Maddy nodded, eyes twinkling. "Not exactly ladylike, was I? But I knew I wouldn't see him again for two more months, and the preacher wouldn't be back for another six. There wasn't much time to play hard to get. By the time we'd been married three months, I was pregnant."

Beth tried to imagine it and couldn't. Her married friends had all given birth with family members and a doctor in attendance, as well as a nurse to look after them and the child afterwards.

"Oh, Maddy, you must have been frightened."

"That's the truth." Maddy sighed then smiled again. "But I was as happy as I was scared. Will helped me when David was born, and everything was fine. We had just the one, but we had twenty-four good years. David's in California now, married and happy. Sometimes you just know it's right."

"What happened to Will?" Beth asked quietly.

"He had a heart attack. It was sudden and quick." Maddy's voice turned thoughtful. "I believe in fate, Beth. He was given so many days on this earth, no more. I think we all are.

"David had itchy feet. I knew he wasn't really interested in farming, so we sold the place and I went back to town. I got a job in a new restaurant that had opened there, and a year later Logan walked in. He stayed in town that winter. His wife had passed away two years before, and his daughter was married. He'd sold his place and come looking for some new country to explore. In the spring we were married and came out here."

Beth could tell Maddy hadn't regretted that decision either. "It must be comforting to feel so sure."

Maddy moved to the stove and filled the teapot. "Beth, you've got as much nerve as I ever had and then some. I wonder if you know it. It's none of my business I know, but why did you decide to come here?"

On the surface it was an easy enough question to answer. "Well, my aunt and uncle were gone and I didn't want to be dependent on my cousin. I really can't say anything against Graham. He's always been good to me in his way, but he's fifteen years older and he has very definite ideas about a woman's place." So much for the surface.

"It's hard to explain, but I wanted something of my own, something I'd chosen, not something that was chosen for me or given to me. At home there were always expectations—Uncle Robert's, Aunt Abigail's, Graham's. Never mine. If I'd gone anywhere back East it would have been the same. Does that make any sense?"

It appeared to make sense to Maddy. She nodded as she set the teapot on the table. "I've never had a lot of money or things, but I've had freedom and I like it. Do you think you'll stay?"

Beth glanced at Trey's ring on her finger. She hadn't taken it off since he put it there, but she'd been tempted to. It still felt foreign to her, like something of his that she had no right to. As for staying, she still felt too dizzy with change to have any idea. "I wish I knew. Trey's certainly not like anyone I've ever met before."

"No, he wouldn't be. Before the war he might have been more like the men you're used to, but not anymore. People change out here. You'll change if you stay."

"I guess I'll have to." Beth imagined the look on Graham's face if he saw her with a gun in her hand. He couldn't be more surprised than she'd been herself. "On the drive home the other day, Trey made me feel like jumping out of the wagon and running back to town. Yesterday he taught me to shoot. It scared me out of a year's growth. He can be very curt, but when he talks about his family, or when he's handling his horses he's different, though I'm not sure he realizes it. It surprised me to find out he served in the Union army."

Maddy got a pitcher of cream from the pantry cupboard and poured tea for them both. "We didn't find that out until his second summer here. I'm an incurable busybody and our children are grown and gone, so when Trey came here we sort of took him under our wing, or tried to." She shook her head as she stirred cream into her cup. "He hardly had two words to say the first few times he came to the house. He'd filed on his land that summer, and he worked as if a devil was driving him. He looked like it, too. We told him he'd kill himself, but he just said he slept better after a hard day's work. Logan helped him when he could, but he had his own work to do. We'd just finished this house."

Beth forgot her tea. She wasn't likely to hear any of this anywhere else. Maddy brushed some flour from her sleeve and went on.

"Before the snow came, he had the barn up and got his first two mares. He stayed in the barn that winter. We told him he was welcome to stay here, but he wouldn't. He looked like something was eating at him, but he never would say what. The same things that would eat at any of those boys who fought, I suppose. I'm thankful David stayed out of it. The next summer Trey built the cabin and bought the other two mares. He had them all shipped from back East somewhere. Now he's got the makings of a future, and he's earned it."

Beth remembered Trey sitting at the table that first night, watching the fire when he should have been asleep. When she mentioned it in the morning, he shut her out. Was a devil still driving him after all this time?

"I know. I can see that by looking at the farm, though Trey's said next to nothing about his time here. He's told me about his father and sister, but that's all. So far we've done more fighting than talking."

Maddy grinned as she refilled her cup. "Well, that's a good sign."

Beth laughed in spite of herself. "I suppose so."

They made their tea last until the bread came out of the oven. Beth enjoyed two thick, fragrant slices, then reluctantly said goodbye. She wanted to linger and hear more about Trey, but there was too much to do at home. Everything took her longer than it should.

She borrowed Maddy's spare jar of starter and just before bedtime, went to work, trying to remember everything she'd learned. Trey lay on his stomach on the rug, reading by the light from the open stove and glancing at her now and then as she thumped and kneaded her dough on the table.

"Reminds me of when I was small. If I was sick, I'd be put to bed on the kitchen sofa. I'd go to sleep, then wake up later and watch my mother setting her bread."

Beth looked up and wiped a sticky arm across her forehead. "It's harder work than I thought. What are you reading?"

Trey held up the book, *Two Years Before the Mast*. "My mother had a brother who was a ship's captain. He sent me this for Christmas one year. It's about a law student from Boston who took a couple of years off from school and sailed around Cape Horn and back on a merchant ship. As a kid, I thought I'd like to go to sea some day."

Beth imagined Trey as a young boy, lying in front of the fire, lost in the same book. She could never have done it if she hadn't seen his picture. "Aunt Abigail and I spent a winter in Europe once. I enjoyed the trip over. Have you ever been on a ship?"

"Only for a few minutes when Dad and Chelle left. My uncle Michel used to send letters to Mother from all over the world. I remember in one of them, he wrote about a ship leaving harbor under a flying cloud of sails. That's where Cloud got his name. I still think about going to sea sometimes. I get it from my mother's family, the Surettes. There's been a sailor or two in every generation."

It felt surprisingly good and natural to be doing this, making bread and talking to Trey, with supper over and the day's work done. Would this become their routine, their time to get to know each other? Beth wanted him to open up to her, but she also liked hearing Trey talk just because she liked his voice, with its pleasant roughness and teasing hint of an accent. She turned her dough, sprinkled on some flour and folded it again.

"What happened to your home?"

Trey looked down at his book. "I sold it. To a New York Dutchman with a big family, who didn't care whether his neighbors liked him. I couldn't have paid the taxes otherwise."

Beth heard the lingering regret in his voice. That would have been one of the things driving him when he built here. "That must have been hard."

He sat up and faced her. "It was, but the home I knew was already gone. We'd buried Mother, Dad was settled at his brother's smithy, and Chelle had married and started a family of her own." Trey grinned. "There was a time when I didn't think the man lived who could corral her. Chelle had the boys on a string by the time she was fifteen. She had a heart as big as a girl could have, but she also had a shape that turned heads, and she knew it. She never made any promises—there's no dishonesty in Chelle—but she'd caused some talk by the time she and Dad left."

"You miss her."

"Yeah. We were closer than a lot of brothers and sisters."

With a sigh, Beth leaned on the table to rest for a minute. The small, plain room looked welcoming in the flickering firelight, with the smell of the baked beans they'd had for supper lingering in the air. Trey had built a home, where a lot of others would have just thrown together a shack.

"You should be proud of what you've done here, Trey."

He looked flattered, and more than a little surprised. "Thanks. I am."

"You haven't seen your family since they left?"

"No, but of course we write. I'll go over some day. I want to meet Chelle's husband. From what she's said in her letters, she led him quite a chase, but he stuck with her. I admire him for that, and I think she does too. "

Trey spoke with a touch of resignation. It would be difficult for him to go overseas now that he had responsibilities here. Maybe in a few years, if she stayed . . . Beth wondered what Trey would think of London.

When her bread dough looked and felt right, Beth left it to rise and went to bed. She got up in the middle of the night, punched it down and put it in the pans, then got up again just before sunrise. Wonderful, the loaves looked perfect, high and round.

She'd added wood to the stove earlier. When she threw a pinch of flour in the oven it browned right away. Too hot. Half asleep, Beth lifted a grate and poured water from the kettle onto the fire.

The rush of ashes and steam knocked her flat on her back as the grate she'd just replaced flew across the room. It crashed into the wall a couple of feet from Trey's head. Jerked out of a sound sleep, he lunged upright and let out a few well-chosen words as Beth scrambled up from the floor.

"What the hell are you doing, trying to blow the place up?"

Beth dusted herself off and tried to muster some dignity. "I needed to cool off the oven, so I poured a little water on the fire."

He shook his head in disbelief. "You poured—for Chrissake, Beth, you're lucky the stove didn't explode and kill us both. Did you get scalded?"

Beth felt her face. No burns, only a scorching blush.

"No, but you nearly got scalped." She crossed the room and gingerly picked up the stray grate with a potholder. Trey's eyes opened wide.

"Looks like it." He ran a hand through his hair and glanced at her again, a bit shame-faced. "Sorry for the language. I don't worry about it much when no one's around."

"Well, I don't blame you," Beth muttered. She cast a sheepish look at the bread pans on the dresser. "I guess I'll put the bread in now."

Even in the dim light she could see his smirk. "You might want to look in the mirror first."

Beth grimaced at her sooty reflection. Grumbling under her breath, she grabbed a towel and a basin. Still grinning, Trey settled down to go back to sleep. Well, she told herself as she scrubbed, at least they'd have fresh bread for breakfast.

* * * *

The town council met in the church. Generally a handful of townspeople attended, but tonight the crowd was especially sparse. There was nothing in particular on the agenda, just routine business.

They set up a table at the front of the church, beside the pulpit. Tonight it was John Reeves' turn to chair the meeting. It didn't take long. When they were ready to adjourn, he addressed the stranger in the front pew who raised his only hand.

"Yes, what's your name?"

"Nathan Munroe. I'm new in town."

"Planning on staying?"

"Well, Mister...it's Reeves, isn't it?"

"Yes."

"Well, Mister Reeves, I've been here for the last few days looking around, and I've decided I want to settle here. From what I see and hear this town is doing some growing and having some growing pains, too. I think you could use a sheriff and I want the job. I hear there've been a couple of robberies lately."

Frank Baker nodded. "That's true. They're bound to hit the store sooner or later. People around here depend on me for supplies, but I'm past the age where I want to be sitting up all night with a shotgun."

The council members took a minute to look over the out-at-heels stranger. They all knew it was time for some law and it wasn't going to be easy to find someone, but with one arm . . . Harriet Grant spoke up.

"Mister Munroe, no offense meant but what makes you think you're qualified for the job?"

Nathan leaned back and smiled at each council member in turn.

"Well, I took my first job as sheriff in a little hole in the wall in Wyoming almost four years ago. I was broke, I knew I couldn't sit behind a desk and I didn't like my chances at punching cows. Place wasn't much different from this, really. People were moving in with families and they wanted things safe. I dealt with the drunks and convinced a lot of the rougher crowd to move on. Things got boring then, so I moved on, too. Three towns later, here I am." Nathan's smile widened. "I'm still broke. I didn't learn to hang onto money when I had it, and I doubt I will now, though it's never wise to say never."

John looked into Nathan's cool gray eyes. He didn't back down. The man must have sand to even consider the job.

"So how did you *convince* people to move on?"

"I'm still alive, which means I use my head. I don't shoot off my mouth or my gun more often than necessary. I'd say that's my main qualification. Of course you don't know me, but by the time you folks meet again I think you'll find you do." Nathan gripped the back of the pew and pushed himself to his feet. He stepped forward, fished in his pocket and handed a slip of paper to Harriet. "Here's a list of the places I've worked. Go ahead and wire them about me if you like. Good night to you all."

John watched Nathan limp out of the church. John trusted his instincts, and he liked what he'd just seen.

"Well, we can send some wires tomorrow, but before we go home I guess we'd better do something about starting that jail."

Harriet frowned. "I'm not sure he'd be up to the job. I mean, look at him."

"I'd bet he can move when he has to," Frank said. "If he uses his head more than his gun I'll be pleased. I'm with you, John."

CHAPTER 6

"Easy now, Chance, almost done." Beth ran through Trey's instructions in her mind one more time as she finished saddling the mare. As much as she'd ridden, she'd never done that before, and Trey wouldn't be impressed with saddle sores.

Satisfied she'd done everything right, Beth stuffed the package of sandwiches she'd made into a saddlebag, swung up and put Chance into an easy canter. She'd decided on the spur of the moment to take lunch out to Trey. He'd said he would be working at the waterhole, across the river and a mile or so downstream from the cattle, but she didn't find him there.

He'd been shoring up the sides of the small pond with rocks and deepening it to hold more water. It looked like a lot of hard, slow work, but it could make a difference during a drought. Another of the never-ending jobs on a place like this. Beth hoped it wouldn't be long before she could be of some real help to him, but right now, after four days on the homestead, she felt like more of a hindrance.

She'd learned not to pour water in the stove, but she struggled with managing it, especially for baking. Trey had explained that she needed to use hardwood, but when it was split and peeled Beth couldn't tell hardwood from soft. Since her first batch of bread had turned out light and only slightly burned, she'd gotten brave and tried to make biscuits, only to have them collapse into hard, doughy mounds. Grinning, Trey picked one up, tested its weight and pitched it out into the yard, aiming at one of the corral posts. He hit it dead on. The biscuit fell to the ground unbroken.

"I have to hand it to you, Beth, you make fine ammunition."

Beth dumped the rest of the batch in the pig's bucket and dropped the baking sheet on the counter in disgust. "What a waste. I don't know why they didn't turn out. I followed Maddy's recipe."

"The oven wasn't hot enough." And so it went. Beth's johnnycake turned out as soggy as the biscuits were hard. She cooked salt beef without soaking it first and forgot to put salt in the porridge. Her only comfort was that Trey took her mistakes as a joke. At least she hadn't made the same one twice—yet.

Hoping Trey wasn't already on his way home for lunch, Beth turned Chance around and rode back upstream to the cattle. When she reached the herd, she spotted Trey a short distance away, kneeling, busy with something on the ground. Riding closer, she saw that the *something* was a very small calf, which he was deftly skinning. Another lay tied on the ground next to him. A few yards off, two crows waited for their chance at the remains.

Beth's stomach turned over. He couldn't be killing the little things. They looked newborn. With an effort, she kept her face and voice calm when he looked up.

"What are you doing?"

"There were a couple of late calvings overnight. This one was born dead and the other's mother died. If I tie the hide on the orphan calf, the other cow might mother it.

Works sometimes." Trey glanced down at his bloody hands. "I wasn't expecting company."

He turned back to his work, leaving her wondering if he was pleased or annoyed that she'd come out. Fighting her nausea, Beth watched Trey tie the hide onto the living calf, then carry it over to a cow standing not far away. He let the cow sniff the little animal, picking up her own young's scent, before he untied the calf's legs and set it on its feet. When it touched noses with the cow, she didn't chase it away.

"Do you think it'll work?"

"We'll have to wait and see." Trey washed his hands in the river and returned, wiping them on his legs. "What brings you here?"

Beth reached back and slapped the full saddlebag. "Lunch." She relaxed when he smiled. He wasn't annoyed.

"Thanks. I was going to head home as soon as I was through here."

Not sure she could eat after what she'd just seen, Beth dismounted, unsaddled Chance and pulled out the package of sandwiches. She and Trey walked to a shady spot under a clump of aspens while the cow and calf wandered back to the herd. As she sat, Beth scanned the valley for Trey's horse.

"Where's Cloud?"

"There's a patch of grass he likes upstream a ways." Trey pointed toward another stand of aspens. "He's over there."

Watching Trey make short work of a corned beef sandwich changed Beth's mind about eating. She nodded toward the package. "I guess I want one of those. You don't tie him?"

Trey handed her a sandwich and took another for himself, then stretched out his long legs and leaned back on one hand, grinning. "Wouldn't be any use. He can untie knots. Taught himself as a colt."

"He did?"

Trey nodded as he chewed and swallowed a bite of sandwich. "He had it figured out by the time he was six months old. He won't stay tied unless he's where he wants to be. It's a real nuisance sometimes. Anyway, he'll come when I call him."

Glad she came, Beth made herself comfortable beside him. She wanted to know how he spent his days. It was pleasant here, with a snatch of birdsong on occasion and Chance grazing nearby, the muted sound of her tearing grass blending with the music of the water. Minutes passed before Beth felt the need to speak.

"How many cattle do you have?"

"About four hundred between us." Trey sat up and ran his eyes over the herd. "As many as Logan and I can manage. It's a good thing he wanted a partner. I didn't know squat about raising cattle this way when I came here."

Beth took another sandwich and curled her other arm around her knees. "What do you mean?"

"Out in the open this way. I had a lot to learn."

She certainly sympathized with him there. "That sounds familiar. I suppose you felt a lot like I do these days."

"I guess so."

Looking up and down the valley, Beth remembered Trey's description in his letter. *Bleak and of little interest.* She could see now what he meant. Nothing in the landscape commanded attention. A small patch of early wildflowers, the play of light and shadow over the river, the tender blue of the spring sky—all those things were easily missed, but Beth noticed them.

"I agree with what you said in your letter, Trey. It's beautiful out here. Beautiful and peaceful."

Trey smiled. "Just wait. When I first arrived, the thing I liked most about it was the quiet. Then, after a few weeks, I started to hear things I hadn't noticed before. Things I'd forgotten. The same thing will happen to you."

Beth closed her eyes and listened. She heard the sweet notes of the same thrush that had called earlier, but now she also picked up the faint answering song of its mate some distance away. She opened her eyes to find Trey watching her.

"See what I mean?"

"Yes, I do." If she wasn't careful, the place would be working a spell on her the way it had on him. Beth wasn't ready for that to happen. When her gaze met Trey's, she looked away.

"Trey, you've been here four years."

"Yeah, it'll be five later this summer."

"So, why did you decide to write to the agency when you did?"

She saw him pull back into himself, just as she'd expected. "Well, like I told you, the work was getting to be just plain too much."

Beth watched him out of the corner of her eye. "With what you offered me, you could have hired some help."

"Yeah, but hands who can cook are hard to find."

Beth thought of her attempt at pancakes that morning and laughed. "I'd hardly say I could cook yet."

Trey pulled a piece of dried apple from a shirt pocket and bit it in two. "Well, I'm not fussy."

"You're lucky."

"Guess so. Anyway, I offered you a one-time deal. Look." He pointed at the orphan calf and its foster mother, standing at the edge of the herd. "She's letting him feed."

Beth smiled to herself at the diversion. *Nicely done, Mister McShannon.* She hadn't expected him to admit he was lonely.

"So does that mean she'll accept the calf?"

"No, but it's a start. I may have to put that hide on him a few times. We'll see."

"What if she doesn't?"

"Then he won't make it, not if she won't feed and protect him."

Beth watched the calf as it followed its foster mother, sticking close to the cow's side. "I know we can't, but I wish we could take him home and feed him."

"With what?" Trey shrugged philosophically. "Maddy couldn't sell us enough milk, and even if she could it wouldn't pay."

"Of course. It's a business." Beth glanced down at the sandwich in her hand. "I've never stopped to really think about where beef comes from." Or where any food came from, for that matter. She didn't think she'd be able to take it for granted again. "So, you just turn Cloud loose and he'll come to you? That I'd like to see."

He whistled. Cloud appeared from behind the aspens, cantered over to them and reached for the piece of dried apple Trey offered. Beth shook her head at his smug grin.

"Bribery!"

With an eager muzzle nudging him, Trey pulled another piece of apple from his pocket. "He's not stupid. There has to be something in it for him."

Beth got up and took a couple of cautious steps toward Cloud. This close, he seemed enormous. There wasn't any excess poundage on him, but he looked as different from the mares and geldings she'd always ridden as a grown man did from a teenage boy. His thick, heavily crested neck and broad chest rippled with muscle under his shining coat.

"The stallion at Uncle Robert's farm was dangerous. I was never allowed anywhere near him."

When she reached out to touch the horse, he ignored her. His main concern was getting more slices of apple. Trey looked up at Beth as she stroked Cloud's neck. "He's not mean, but he has a temper. If something annoys him he lets you know."

When the apple supply ran out Cloud wandered off to graze. Beth sat beside Trey again. Listening to him talk intrigued her. At times he sounded educated, at times like a farm boy. Expressions he'd grown up with came and went like his accent. If he'd enlisted at eighteen, when had he had time to study?

"So you came here as soon as you got out of the army?"

"As soon as I could, yes."

"I've been wondering where you got your education."

"Education?" Trey gave her that amused sideways glance of his. "All the education I have, I got at home. My mother loved books and she taught us to read. There wasn't a school nearby when I was small, and later there was work to do. Chelle and I both always read whatever we could get our hands on."

So that explained his well-written letters. Sidonie McShannon had been a good teacher. Beth had an idea Trey could have turned himself into a writer if he'd chosen to.

"Have you read your Longfellow and Whitman?"

"Yes, I have, but don't let it get around town. I'd never hear the end of it."

At the touch of irony in his voice, Beth arched an eyebrow and grinned. "How much is it worth to you?"

Trey chuckled. "Lady, I know where you live."

"True. I've read *Evangeline,* but not much Whitman. We didn't have anything of his in the house. Aunt Abigail didn't think his work was fit for a lady to read. Naturally, I read it at friends' houses when I got the chance."

"Naturally. What did you read?"

"Oh, bits and pieces of different poems. I couldn't quote them, but I liked them."

A verse from 'I Sing the Body Electric' came to Beth's mind – the last verse she would have chosen at that moment, with Trey sitting so close beside her.

'The expression of the face balks account,

But the expression of a well-made man appears not only in his face;

It is in his limbs and joints also, it is curiously in the joints of his hips and wrists;

It is in his walk, the carriage of his neck, the flex of his waist and knees—dress does not hide him;

The strong, sweet, supple quality he has, strikes through the cotton and flannel;

To see him pass conveys as much as the best poem, perhaps more;

You linger to see his back, and the back of his neck and shoulder-side.'

She knew what Trey's back looked like, with subtle lamplight glowing on his skin. The memory made Beth's breath catch. Their eyes locked, and a smoldering fire leapt into Trey's. He'd never looked at her that way before, but Daniel had.

Aunt Abigail was right. Whitman wasn't fit for a young lady to read, not when it made her forget herself like this, made her skin prickle and heat with . . . something dangerous. She and Trey were just beginning to get to know each other, and all she could think of right now was how his mouth would feel caressing hers.

She couldn't look away. Without saying anything, he reached out to touch her face. Beth had barely enough will left to catch his hand and lower it to the ground with a gentle squeeze.

"Trey, it's too soon."

He blew out a breath and ran his fingers through a tuft of grass. "Yeah, I suppose so." One corner of his mouth quirked upward in a lopsided smile. "You sure tempt a man, Beth, but I imagine you know that."

Beth remembered Daniel's kisses, the pleasant, tingling sensations they'd given her. Something told her that when . . . *if* Trey kissed her she'd feel more, a lot more.

"It isn't just you, Trey, but I've only been here a few days. I guess we'd better see if I can last a month without burning you out of house and home."

Trey shook his head, heat still lingering in his eyes. "I know this is all new to you, Beth. You don't have to try so hard."

In control of her legs again, Beth jumped up. *Better leave while you can.* "Thanks, but trying hard seems to be part of my nature. Now, I should go and let you get back to work."

She saddled Chance and stuffed the remnants of their lunch in her saddlebags. When she mounted, Trey stood looking up at her. A heavy silence lay between them.

"I'll see you tonight," she said at last.

He fussed with Chance's saddle for a moment, his hand inches from her leg.

"Yeah, see you later."

Beth's nerves got through to the mare. At a nudge, Chance jumped forward and broke into a run. When she got to the road, Beth reined her in and turned in the saddle to look back at Trey. He was still watching her.

CHAPTER 7

"Come here. You know how good this tastes. Come and get it." Beth leaned over the half door, holding out a carrot. The pinto mustang took a tentative step forward, then another. "That's it, Calico, come on."

Trey's body tightened as he watched from Cloud's stall. Beth's soft tone brought all kinds of distracting ideas to mind, like how good it would feel to silence her with his lips. The pants she wore didn't help.

Her voice dropped so he couldn't hear her words, only that entreating murmur. Trey's edginess increased.

Look at yourself, fool. You're jealous of a horse.

Beth had appeared in the barn yesterday morning at chore time, with a stubborn light in her blue-gray eyes and those pants hugging her hips, determined to start getting to know the horses. Trey had never seen a woman in pants before. He couldn't keep his eyes off her.

Knowing he'd have to give in sooner or later, he marshaled his scattered wits and walked her through his morning routine. Now here she was, smoothing down a half-wild colt as if she'd been doing it for years. He couldn't deny she had a touch.

Calico was a boarder, not part of Trey's breeding program. The colt had been captured as a weanling three years ago, gelded and kept in a rancher's rough string until John Reeves bought him last fall. Trey and John had struck up a friendship when Trey first came to Wallace Flats. Trey was training the colt, getting him ready for John's son Ben to ride.

Without the elegance of the mares or anything like the sheer presence of Flying Cloud, Calico had a wild beauty of his own. What he'd been through had left him with a healthy distrust of men, but he responded to Beth's coaxing, moving closer until he could reach the carrot. When Beth offered him some oats, he ate from her hand, something Trey had not yet been able to accomplish.

Don't sweat it, Cal. Man or beast, we're all the same that way.

Cloud pinned his ears back and snorted, a low, vicious sound. As far as he was concerned, the mares belonged to him and he wasn't standing for another male in his territory. Trey dragged his eyes from Beth long enough to finish feeding and watering the stallion, then joined her in front of Calico's stall.

"Not bad. Cal's had plenty of trouble from men, but he knows you're different."

"Of course he does." Beth glanced down the aisle at Cloud as she stroked Calico's muzzle. "He could do without being bullied after losing his freedom like that. It's a shame."

"Yeah, it is, but it isn't all bad. He's got enough to eat, and he's safe here." Trey reached for the mustang's halter. Calico jerked his head back and half-reared before accepting the restraint. Beth offered him another carrot.

"They never forget, do they?"

"Some seem to, if they're treated well, but I don't think they really do." When Trey let go of the halter, Calico

82

retreated to the far end of the stall. In six months, Trey hadn't been able to win more than the horse's tolerance. He was too much like the men who had roped the young colt, taken him from his herd, held him down and gelded him. From the looks of it, Beth might stand a better chance.

"Would you like to feed him?"

"I'd love to." Beth scooped oats from the grain barrel into a bucket and opened the stall door. Calico hung back for a moment, but when she moved closer and set the bucket down, hunger got the better of him. He stuck his nose into the oats and ignored her while he ate.

"Well now. He never touches his food while I'm in with him." Trey took a slow step forward and held the door, ready to swing it open and let Beth out if the horse spooked, but Calico finished his meal quietly. Looking a little smug, Beth bent to pick up the empty bucket.

At the same moment, Cloud let out a piercing shriek. Startled, Calico charged into Beth and knocked her across the stall. In his shock, Trey didn't get the door open fast enough. It crashed into his midsection with all Calico's momentum behind it as he barged through. Trey felt his breath leave him in a rush, saw a blinding flash of light as his head smacked the floor, and that was all.

Beth picked herself up and stepped into the aisle. Through the open barn door she caught a glimpse of Calico galloping past the cabin, but she forgot him when she saw Trey lying in a heap by the grain barrel.

"Oh, Lord." She dropped to her knees beside him, brushed hair and chaff from his face and turned him on his side. "Trey, can you hear me?"

He didn't respond. Beth felt the lump already forming on the back of his head. She unbuttoned his shirt with shaking fingers.

"Trey, wake up."

He labored for breath, his heart racing under her palm. Barely noting the long, puckered scar on his right side, Beth slid her hand down his chest and pressed against his ribs as hard as she dared. Nothing felt broken, but she couldn't be sure. She drew a bucket of cold well water and bathed Trey's face, but she couldn't rouse him.

Frightened tears sprang to her eyes. She didn't dare move him, even if she'd been strong enough to shift his dead weight. She'd heard the thump of the door against his ribcage. A fractured skull, broken ribs, a punctured lung, all sorts of grim possibilities raced through her mind.

After a few seconds' frantic thought, Beth eased a pad of folded feed sacks under Trey's head, did up his shirt and ran to the house for a blanket. By the time she got back, his breathing had settled down. He must have had the wind knocked out of him.

"Trey, look at me. I need you to help me get you inside."

Still no response. She spread the blanket over him and brushed another bit of straw from his cheek. "I'll be back as soon as I can." After one last look at his still face, Beth threw a bridle on Chance, jumped on bareback and headed for the Kinsleys' as fast as the mare could take her.

Beth had never ridden bareback before, but that didn't occur to her. All she could think of as the countryside blurred past was Trey's smile, and the heat she'd seen in his eyes the day of their picnic. The way he teased her instead of criticizing when she made mistakes. The warmth in his voice when he spoke of his family.

You're falling for him, aren't you?

She pushed the unsettling thought aside and focused on clinging to the galloping horse. Maddy hurried from the house as Chance whirled into the Kinsleys' yard. Legs shaking, Beth slid to the ground and blurted out her story.

"I couldn't wake him up. I tried and tried."

The image of Trey's still, pale face filled her mind. She'd never felt so helpless. Maddy threw a reassuring arm around Beth's shoulders.

"All right, it won't help him to panic. Logan's in the barn. He'll go to town for help and we'll go back to Trey."

Beth choked back a sob. "He told me there's no doctor in town. If he's badly hurt he might not make it to Denver—"

"We don't have a doctor, but we've got Neil Garrett."

"Doesn't he run the saloon?"

Maddy took Beth's arm and hurried her toward the barn. "Yes, he does, but Neil was an ambulance attendant during the war. He's as good as most of the doctors I've met. Come on and help me saddle up."

The ride home seemed to take forever, but at last, two distracted women ran into the barn. Trey still lay where Beth had left him. When she knelt and lifted his head to her lap, he stirred and opened glassy eyes.

"Chelle."

It was only natural that his sister's name would come to him first. After all, he'd only known Beth for a few days, but it still gave her a foolish twinge of jealousy. She leaned closer and stroked his cheek to get him to focus on her. "No, Trey, I'm Beth. Do you remember me?"

He squinted, frowned, and then...

"Hey, Philadelphia."

Oh, thank God. In her relief, Beth would have kissed him if Maddy hadn't been watching. Instead, she contented herself with picking bits of grit from the floor out of his hair.

"How do you feel?"

Trey tried to take a deep breath and winced as pain caught him. "Lousy. Hey, Maddy."

His mind seemed to be clearing. Maddy squatted at his side. "Hey, yourself. Logan's gone after Neil. You look like you're going to live, but you'd better stay quiet 'til they get here."

Trey tried to sit, then pressed his fingers to his eyes and sank back onto Beth's lap. "Yeah. I'm not in a hurry to go anywhere."

"Good. Since you're awake and you seem to be in good hands, I'll go cool down the horses." Maddy stood and looked at Beth with a hint of a twinkle in her eyes. "Call me if you need anything."

Was she that obvious? Beth ignored the warmth in her cheeks and did what she could to make Trey more comfortable. It would be at least another hour before Logan could get back with Neil. She took the blanket she'd thrown over Trey and worked it underneath him to ward off the chill of the barn's earthen floor.

"Better?"

"Yeah." With Beth's arms around him and his head pillowed warmly on her thighs, Trey's eyelids started to droop. She ran her fingers lightly down his arm, acutely aware of its hard contours even through her worry.

"I don't think you should go to sleep."

He blinked and gave her a groggy smile. "It's hard not to, with you holding me like this."

"Then maybe I should let you lie on the floor." Beth tucked the blanket more closely around him, wishing she could speed up time or bring Neil and Logan from town by magic. Trey's face was chalky under its tan, and the occasional catch in his careful, shallow breathing told her how much he was hurting. "You gave your head quite a knock."

He found Beth's right hand and linked his fingers with hers. "I'll be all right. I got my bell rung, that's all. It's not the first time."

And it wouldn't be the last. He accepted that as the price of doing what he loved, and Beth would have to do the same if she stayed. Could she?

"I'm sure it's not." Beth squeezed his hand, struggling for words. "Trey, it's been . . . quite a week. Even if I don't end up staying here, I won't forget you." She swallowed and stopped herself before she said too much. "I suppose we've lost Calico. That's a shame."

"He won't go far. Logan and I will find him." Dark eyes looked into hers. "I won't forget you either, Beth."

Of their own will Beth's fingers threaded into Trey's hair. Without thought she leaned down, drawn by his eyes, his mouth. Then something in his expression stopped her, a shade of the caution she should have been feeling herself. It brought her to her senses. If there had ever been a time when she needed to be a lady, it was now, with all these new, compelling emotions threatening to overthrow common sense. Beth straightened and let her hand drop to Trey's shoulder.

"How could you? I nearly decapitated you with a stove grate. Now you rest. I won't let you fall asleep."

The quiet wove a spell around them as the minutes slipped by. Beth kept her arms around Trey, sharing her warmth with him, keeping him from dozing off. It startled them both when Maddy came in, followed by Logan and the red-haired man who had stared – almost leered – at Beth when she got off the stagecoach.

She slid the feed sack pillow under Trey's head and got stiffly to her feet. Surprise, curiosity and yes, a little embarrassment, mingled on Neil Garrett's scarred face as he recognized her. He only spared her a quick glance before he knelt beside Trey.

"Tried to crack your skull, did you?"

Trey managed a lop-sided grin. "Business must be slow today, Neil."

"Not slow enough that I have time to tend hard-headed fools like you."

"So, send me a bill."

Neil peered into Trey's eyes, checked the contusion on his head, then held up his hand. "Maybe I will. How many fingers?"

"Three."

"Right. Is the lady your sister?"

"No, my wife."

Neil sat back on his heels and looked at Beth again, with more sardonic humor than respect. She should have been offended, but somehow she couldn't be. So this was the man who served Wallace Flats as a doctor, when he wasn't serving drinks.

I'd have to be at death's door before I'd go to him.

"You don't say. I've heard a couple of things in town, but I didn't believe them. Pleased to make your acquaintance, Ma'am." Neil turned back to Trey, undid his shirt and pressed on his ribs. Trey clenched his teeth and bit back a groan.

"Jesus!"

Neil nodded. "Yeah. Sorry." He felt over Trey's abdomen, then stood and dusted off his knees. "I don't think anything's broken, but you're badly bruised and there might be a crack or two. You're not showing any signs of internal injuries, at least not yet. Are you dizzy and sick to your stomach?"

"Yeah."

"Well, you've given your head a good bang, but I'd say nothing worse. Logan, let's get him inside."

* * * *

Trey woke to the sound of Cloud's whistle from the corral. Propped on two pillows he shifted in bed, trying to ease his sore ribs. The movement made his head whirl. He closed his eyes and waited until it stopped.

It must be late afternoon. Following Neil's instructions, Beth had wakened Trey every half hour through the night, but at daybreak she'd let him sleep. He must have gotten a good few hours.

Beth had told him how he'd gotten hurt, but all Trey remembered was her holding him, her arms close and warm around him while they waited for Neil. This couldn't have happened at a worse time with most of the spring work still to be done, but at least she'd gotten off lightly, with only a few bruises.

Trey sat up and swung his legs over the edge of his bunk, setting his ribs throbbing and his head spinning again. He'd had his bell rung all right. Gripping the ladder to the loft, he eased himself to his feet. A wave of pain and nausea forced him back to the bunk. He cursed under his breath. Beth wasn't ready to look after the place alone.

He'd just gotten back under the covers when she came in from the yard, wearing his worn gray canvas jacket over her denims and blue blouse. The jacket dwarfed her, but it brought out the color of her eyes. Vibrant strands of auburn hair strayed from under one of Trey's wide-brimmed hats, a fiery contrast to the dusty black felt. When she took the hat off, glowing curls tumbled down Beth's back and around her shoulders, brightening the whole room. It was the first time Trey had seen her with her hair loose.

She dropped the hat on the table and came to sit on the side of his bunk, teasing him with the scent of cool spring air and lavender. "I've got good news. Logan caught Calico this morning and brought him back."

"Good. That's a weight off my mind. I saw mountain lion scat on the ridge behind Logan's place a couple of weeks ago. Where have you been?"

Beth tucked her hair behind her ears and sat up straight, exuding accomplishment. "Well, you had the vegetable garden dug and you said you wanted to plant it this week, so I did it after chores. I found the seeds in the barn. Corn, carrots, peas, turnips, cabbage, and onions."

It was too early for the corn and turnips and there wasn't a chance in hell that she'd planted the rest properly, but it could be done again. Beth looked so pleased with herself Trey didn't have the heart to grumble, even if he'd had the energy.

"Thanks. Did Logan help you with the chores?"

"No. I had them done by the time he showed up with Calico. Since he wasn't around, Cloud behaved himself."

The thought of Beth handling Cloud in his present temper gave Trey chills. Sitting beside him in his coat with the sleeves rolled up, she looked ridiculously small and fragile, her face radiant in spite of the dark circles under her eyes. He wanted to shelter her, to pull her down beside him and gather her in his arms.

"Did you get some sleep this morning?"

"A little." Not much, he'd guess by the look of her. "I went to bed for a while just after you fell asleep. How's your stomach today?"

"Empty."

Beth stoked the stove and made porridge. Trey noticed that she didn't forget the salt. When she handed him his bowl he saw something on her palm, caught her wrist and turned her hand over.

Four good-sized blisters marred her soft skin. His temper rose at the sight, taking him by surprise.

"For Chrissake, Beth, there are gloves in the barn."

She flushed and pulled her hand away. "I know. I tried them on, but of course they're too big. I couldn't work with them. Next time I'm in town I'll get some that fit. It's nothing to worry about. We had this discussion before, remember?"

Trey's head pounded with frustration – at being laid up, at having a woman do his chores for him, at the feelings churning inside him. "I know, but you've only been here a few days. I told you, you don't have to try so hard. You could have left the garden, and you could have waited for Logan to help with the chores. He said he would."

Chin high, cheeks rosy, Beth held his gaze. "I know he did, but finding Calico was more important. And Trey, you don't have to try so hard either."

His hands clenched on the bowl, as much to keep from reaching for her as from anger. God, she was lovely. He'd have to be a poor excuse for a man not to want her, but having Beth creep into his heart so soon was something else entirely. Already the thought of his home without her left him bereft, and he knew that feeling all too well. His mother, Justin. . .

You're setting yourself up for a fall, McShannon, and you know it.

"Beth, whether you like the word or not, you're a lady. You weren't raised a farmer's daughter, and I don't expect you to work like one."

He spoke more sharply than he intended. The glow faded from Beth's face as she stepped away from the bunk.

"Then maybe you should have written to a farmer's daughter."

Her brittle tone made something snap inside Trey. She sounded forlorn. After she'd been up all night watching over him, he couldn't even show her a little tact. With a quick movement that made pain stab him between the eyes, he caught her wrist again.

"But I didn't. I wrote to you, and I'm not sorry I did." He brushed the inside of her wrist with his thumb. Her skin felt like warm satin. "You were right yesterday. It's been quite a week."

With a gentle tug he brought her closer. Beth yielded a bit stiffly and perched on the edge of the bunk. Trey tasted his porridge.

"I couldn't do better myself."

She shook her head and gave him a grudging smile. Apology accepted. "You told me you couldn't make decent porridge."

"So I did." He set the bowl on a rung of the ladder and reached up to trace the curve of Beth's cheek, raising a blush. When her eyes closed and her lips trembled open, Trey made up his mind. When she left, he'd have one taste of her to remember.

He slid his hand under Beth's hair to cup her neck. Soft curls teased the back of his hand as he stroked her there.

She sighed, braced her hands on either side of his head and leaned into him. Trey felt a shiver run through her as her lips brushed his in a tentative caress.

Easy. Don't scare her. In her well-chaperoned life, he doubted if Beth had been kissed often. Trey hadn't touched a woman since last spring's trip to Denver. Now, with Beth's taste, her nearness, her scent entangling his senses, raw need threatened to overwhelm him.

He clamped down on his urge to devour her and savored her instead, nibbling her lips, tasting the corners of her mouth. When he probed with his tongue, asking entrance instead of demanding as his body screamed for him to do, Beth welcomed him with a soft moan. It felt like being seventeen again with a girl in his arms.

Her sweet response fueled Trey's craving for her. With his willpower crumbling, he put his hands on Beth's shoulders and gently urged her to sit up.

The thrumming in his head competed with the desire singing along his nerves. Judging by her flushed face and shining eyes, Beth felt the same way. She ran a finger over her wet lips, then reached for the porridge bowl and handed it to him.

"Glad it meets with your approval."

Her tone made it clear she didn't mean the porridge. Trey smiled to let her know he didn't either. "Never tasted anything like it."

Beth's hand trailed over his bare shoulder, burning him like a brand before she got up. "You'd better eat it while it's warm." She smoothed her hair, crossed the room and started fussing at the dresser, putting away the dishes she'd washed sometime in the night.

Trey recalled each time her light touch and soft voice had wakened him, making sure he was all right. Jesus, he'd miss her when she left. The thought gave him an ache that had nothing to do with his bruised ribs.

He reached under the bunk for his writing case, pulled out two sheets of paper and a pencil. 'Wanted: Temporary help with general farm work. A dollar a day and board. See Trey McShannon, ten miles north of Wallace Flats. Ask at store for directions'.

He wrote the notice out twice. Beth had an artist's hands – in more ways than one – and he wouldn't have her roughening them with her stubbornness.

"Beth, this afternoon I want you to ride into town and post these at the store and the telegraph office. We need some help."

Pain, present and anticipated, gave his voice an edge. Beth turned to face him.

"If you think it's necessary, of course I will." She didn't look hurt this time. She probably read him too well for comfort.

"I do. There's the plowing to do before the oats can be sown, and there's too much other work for you to manage alone, though I know you're stubborn enough to try. Neil said it could be a couple of weeks or longer before I'm myself again. Logan will have to handle all the work with the cattle. I can't expect him to do more. And get yourself a couple of pairs of work gloves."

A wry smile. "I will." Beth went back to her tidying. Trey settled back on his pillows and closed his eyes. In spite of his pain and the emotions pulling at him, the homelike sound of her puttering lulled him to sleep.

* * * *

June Baker's eyes widened as Beth walked into the store. Of course, Neil Garrett would have spread the word about Trey's accident, and his marriage. In heaven knew what kind of language. Beth put on a determined smile and marched to the counter.

"Good afternoon, Missus Baker."

June radiated curiosity, but Beth saw friendliness and concern there too. "Well now. I hear congratulations are in order, Missus McShannon. That man of yours sure keeps his cards close to his chest. He never breathed a word about you."

"Thanks for the good wishes. If you've heard about our marriage, then you've probably heard about Trey's accident, too. He got knocked down in the barn and hit his head. He's going to be fine, but we need a hand for a while." Beth laid one of the notices on the counter. "Will you let me post this here?"

"I'll do it for you right now. And please call me June." June reached under the counter for a hammer and tacks. She pinned the notice up with several others on the wall behind the cash register. "I'm looking forward to seeing you both around town more. Trey has always kept so much to himself out on that place of his. Most men his age would have been in Neil's place every Saturday night, loaded for bear, looking for a fight and a girl."

"I'm Beth. Of course we'll be in to church once Trey's feeling better. And June, I almost forgot—I need a pair of work gloves."

Beth posted her other notice at the telegraph office and hurried home. When she checked on Trey, she found him still asleep. It was getting late, but instead of starting preparations for supper, she sat on the edge of his bunk and watched him.

His obstinate hair stuck out in all directions. Dark lashes brushing his cheeks, lips slightly parted, he looked more his real age, as if some burden he carried when awake had slipped away.

That mouth. When he kissed her she'd felt it to the tips of her toes, and she remembered his taste. Beth knew he'd felt it too, but it took more than desire to make a marriage work. Their backgrounds could hardly be more different. Trey had a Southern man's notion of lady-hood, even more constricting in its way than the old Philadelphia definition she'd been raised with. A lady didn't marry a farmer and spoil her hands with manual labor.

Beth didn't fit in her own class anymore, not with the family money gone. In Trey's stubborn mind she didn't fit in here either, however much he might enjoy kissing her.

He stirred in his sleep and murmured something she didn't catch. His ribs bothered him, probably. Beth bent over him to straighten the covers, her face close to his.

Gray hair. She'd never noticed before, but a few strands of silver mingled with the dark hair at Trey's temple. A rush of tenderness came over Beth at the sight. He wasn't the only man she knew who'd come back from the war older than his years, but this was different.

Why?

Because it's him.

Very lightly, so she wouldn't wake him, Beth ran her fingers along Trey's temple. Touching him warmed her deep inside, emotionally as well as physically. Her aunt's and uncle's final illnesses had been the only times in Beth's life when she felt needed. Now, for a short time at least, Trey needed her. If she could only feel truly wanted, she'd have all anyone could ask for.

CHAPTER 8

Twilight found Nathan on the bench in front of Neil's place. He couldn't afford to go in and drink, but he preferred sitting there in the fine spring evening, watching Neil's crowd come and go, to killing time in his room. If he wanted the sheriff's job, he needed to get familiar with these people. Not that there weren't other, more interesting reasons to sit there.

The saloon's swinging doors creaked and someone came up behind him. Nathan caught a whiff of talcum and rosewater.

"Haven't seen you yet, Mister."

He turned around, smiling. Lorie certainly could make a man wonder where his summer wages had gone. She wore a dark green dress of some glossy fabric that brought out the green flecks in her hazel eyes. The neckline scooped low over her pretty breasts, and Nathan's eyes just naturally followed it down. It really was a shame he wasn't more of a saving man.

"Can't afford you right now, Lorie."

She gave him a slow, provocative stare, along with one of her sultry smiles. "Maybe I'd see you on my own time. What's your name? You aren't from around here."

Nathan let his eyes run leisurely over her in turn. "My name's Nate. Nobody's from around here but the Indians, and they're almost gone. Lorie, I'm going to sit out here for a while. You too busy to join me?"

"Not unless I want to be. Listen, I . . ."

She broke off as two men staggered up the steps. It looked to Nathan like they'd started drinking hours ago, and by the grimace on Lorie's face she'd seen them before. As she moved away from the door, one of them grabbed her arm.

"Come with me."

She pulled away and glared at the man. "Carl, I've told you before, I want no part of you. You're too damned rough. Go in and have a drink, or else get the hell lost before Neil takes his shotgun and ventilates your skull. He's sick of tossing your sorry carcass out of here."

An angry flush spread from Carl's neck upward as he grabbed Lorie's arm again. "You smart-mouthed little—"

He never finished the sentence. Without saying a word, Nathan jumped up, pulled a knife from inside his jacket and threw it to pin Carl's free hand to the saloon wall. Before Carl could react, he found himself looking down the barrel of Nathan's revolver.

"She said to leave her alone. You strike me as a very impatient man, Carl. Life gets complicated when you're that way. I know, because I used to be a bit like that myself."

Keeping his eyes fixed on Carl, Nathan put his gun down on the bench, pulled a pipe from his pocket, put it in his mouth and lit it. Every movement was calculated, the weapon always only a split second away. Carl stood pinned to the wall, not daring to move. Once Nathan had the pipe going, he sat on the bench again, picked up his gun and crossed his legs in front of him.

"When you're always in a rush it seems to me you never get to enjoy things, like this fine evening. Just stop a minute and take it in. There'll be others, but there'll never be this one again. You smoke, Carl?"

Carl swallowed hard and shook his head. People started to gather around the saloon steps. His companion had vanished. So had Lorie. Nathan leaned back and sighed. How much tobacco did he have left? Three, maybe four pipes full at the most. Another shame. What immortal fool had said the best things in life were free?

"Good man, it's a rotten habit. Guess I'll have to break it when this lot of tobacco's gone. Too bad, I enjoy it." He sat there and savored his pipe while blood trickled from Carl's hand and the gun kept him frozen. When he finished smoking, Nathan got up, gun in hand, removed the knife with his teeth and dropped it. He rested his hand on Carl's shoulder as he dropped to his knees. "Patience is a virtue. Possess it if you can, my friend. You have a fine evening."

Carl got up and staggered away, clutching his hand. The crowd drifted into the saloon. Nathan heard the excited buzz and smiled.

Soon, Lorie. Soon.

* * * *

Bucket in hand, Beth stood by the well, watching the rider coming down the lane. In the middle of morning chores Cloud had whistled from the corral, letting her know they had company.

When he reached her, the man pulled his black mare up, dismounted and took off his hat. Silver-blond hair framed his clean-shaven face, a hard face in spite of fair akin and almost boyish features. The hardness came from the palest blue eyes Beth had ever seen. He'd be as tall as Trey, a couple of years younger and probably fifteen or twenty pounds heavier, all of it muscle, covered by black pants and a gray chambray shirt. An intimidating package, though he spoke pleasantly enough.

"Morning, Ma'am. Is this the McShannon place?"

Beth set the bucket down and held out her hand. "Yes, it is. I'm Missus McShannon."

The stranger shook her hand, nodded politely and put his hat back on. "I'm Gabe Tanner. I saw your notice at the store."

"Certainly. There are empty stalls in the barn. Put your horse up and I'll tell my husband you're here."

Beth felt Mr. Tanner's eyes on her back as she walked inside. Of course, she was wearing her denims. She couldn't expect anything else. Sitting up in bed, Trey lifted his eyes from *Great Expectations.*

"Who's that?"

"A man here about the job." She handed Trey a shirt and pants from the basket of clean laundry by the table. "I'll keep him busy for a few minutes."

Back outside, Beth joined Mr. Tanner by the corral, where he stood watching Cloud. The man looked as surprised as she'd been to see a horse of Cloud's quality on a place like this.

"That's quite a piece of horseflesh, Ma'am."

"He certainly is. My husband grew up around Thoroughbreds, Mr. Tanner, and I have some experience with them myself. You can't manhandle them as you might a range-bred horse. They won't stand for it."

Mr. Tanner's smile was more respectful than Neil Garrett's, but somehow it grated on Beth. "I haven't had much to do with fancy-bred horses myself, but I'll take your word for it."

Not the type who wanted advice from a woman. Fine, she could deal with that as long as he'd work for his money. "As you would have seen in the barn, we have four mares, two close to foaling, as well as the heavy team and a colt my husband is training. We advertised because Trey had an accident the other day and hit his head. He has to rest for a few days, perhaps longer, and there's plowing and planting that needs to be done."

Mr. Tanner turned from the corral to the house, barely looking at Beth as he did so. It couldn't be plainer that he didn't intend to take her seriously. "I'm not afraid of work, Ma'am. Is your husband inside?"

"Yes, he is. Come in."

Trey had gotten up to sit at the table. He wasn't supposed to be out of bed. Beth gave him a stern look as she led Mr. Tanner to him.

"Trey, this is Gabe Tanner. Mister Tanner, Trey McShannon."

Beth washed her hands and climbed to the loft, intending to change into a dress. She took her blue print from its hook and sat on the bed, listening to Trey explaining the layout of the place to Mr. Tanner and telling him whoever took the job would be bunking in the barn loft.

Mr. Tanner's voice came up to her, cool and even. "Fine. I'll be more comfortable out there anyway. I have a reference letter from the last place where I worked, up near

Fort Collins." Beth heard the rustle of paper, followed by a moment of silence while Trey read the letter.

"They seem to have thought highly of you. Why did you leave?"

"Well, the owner's son took over as ranch foreman, and we didn't get along. To be frank, we'd had some differences over a girl and he wasn't willing to forget. It was time to move on. I had no problem with the old man, though. Trust a woman to stir up trouble."

"Yeah, it happens."

Beth's cheeks reddened with indignation. Trey didn't have to agree with the man so easily. Mr. Tanner might come highly recommended, but she didn't warm to him at all.

"So, how did you end up in Wallace Flats?" Trey asked.

"Just drifting. From Fort Collins I went to Denver, but it's too damn easy to spend money there. It was getting so I needed to find work and I'd never been down this way, so I decided to have a look. I saw your notice in the store last night."

"Where are you from?"

"Ohio. I came out here after the war, as I expect you did."

"You've got me pegged. I can't tell you how long we'll be needing help, Gabe, but probably not for more than two weeks. If we're suited, though, I'll be glad to help you find something more permanent when I'm on my feet again. If you want the job, it's yours."

So Trey was going to hire this man without even consulting her, and she was going to have to cook for him and work with him. Of all the high-handed, inconsiderate . . . Beth waited until Mr. Tanner had headed back to town for his gear, then grabbed her paint kit and easel and stormed down the ladder. Trey's jaw dropped when he saw her face.

"What's the matter with you?"

"I can't believe you just went and hired the first man to show up here without even talking to me about it first. I have to feed him and work with him—"

Trey glared at her, his face set in hard, angry lines. "You won't have to work with him. He can do the barn work as well as the plowing and planting. If we have to have help, we might as well get our money's worth. We don't know if anyone else *will* show up. And you'd better wait 'til you've been here a while before you start telling me how to run the place."

Beth clenched her fists and infused her voice with as much acid as she could. "Fine. Forgive me, a mere woman, for expecting to be considered. We are just troublemakers, after all. I'll stay out of your way until it's time to get supper for you and your friend. Birds of a feather."

Before Trey could respond, she marched out. Leaving him alone might not be smart, but at the moment Beth didn't care. She saddled Chance, tied her painting gear to the saddle and headed for the river.

* * * *

Trey stared open-mouthed at Beth's retreating back. "Of all the flighty, unpredictable . . ." Of course he hadn't consulted her about hiring Gabe. It never occurred to him.

They needed help *now*, and what would Beth know about hiring a ranch hand? The man looked capable enough, and if he didn't work out they could pay him and send him on his way.

Moving cautiously, Trey got back into bed. Just sitting up for that short time had tired him, or perhaps Beth's tirade had done that. For a sharp tongue, he'd never known her equal.

Then, as he lay there in the stillness, doubts started to creep in. Guilt followed them. Gabe would be in their home every day, eating at their table. Only, Trey had forgotten it was *their* home now. He supposed he should have spoken to Beth first. He'd have to drop his habit of thinking as if he were still alone if he wanted to 'keep from the rough side of her tongue', as his father would say.

Trey remembered times when his mother's temper flashed and she and his father shouted at each other, but they'd always found a way to compromise. Their fights had never damaged their love, never even dented it. They'd had very different opinions on the Confederacy, for one thing, but even that hadn't come between them.

Trey didn't know how to give and take with a wife, and in Beth, he was dealing with a Thoroughbred. He knew as well as anyone that they demanded respect, and you had to take the risk of being kicked. He guessed he'd have to start from there, if he wanted to have any peace while Beth was with him.

Through the open door he'd seen her ride off, her blouse a flash of yellow on Chance's back, her bright braid flying behind her. She hadn't taken his spare rifle, as he'd insisted she do when riding alone. She hadn't even taken a coat, but she had a blanket tied to her saddle and if the mild day turned cold, that would bring her home all the sooner. It was only April, for Chrissake.

Trey picked up his book and tried to push away his worry. He couldn't do anything but wait. He'd apologize to her when she got back, if she'd listen.

* * * *

By the time Beth got to the river, she'd ridden off some of her anger. She took off Chance's tack, put hobbles on her and left the mare to graze. Beth had been intending to paint a river scene since she'd picnicked here with Trey, and today the light was perfect, with just enough cloud to soften it. A fresh warm breeze played over the water, creating ripples to add interest.

Beth set up her easel, arranged her paints and brushes and filled a jar with river water. She was about to put brush to paper when she glanced at the Western horizon. Thunderheads hung there in ominous shades of purple and gray. Uncommon for April, but what a wonderful subject. It looked like she'd have a couple of hours to try to reproduce it before the storm got close, if it didn't miss her completely.

As she worked, half of Beth's mind stayed on her scene with Trey. Now that she'd cooled off, she knew he'd simply acted without thinking. He wasn't the most high-handed, inconsiderate man in the world, except when he forgot she was around. She'd been right to call him on it, but she could have been less of a shrew.

Thinking about it, she realized she'd been more upset at him for putting Mr. Tanner on the barn chores than for anything else. Was there any way to make Trey understand that she didn't want to be sheltered, that she wanted to be a working partner the way Maddy was a partner to Logan?

Beth started her painting with a pale orange wash and dabbed the clouds on top of it, wet on wet, letting the colors flow into each other. The outline of the distant hills and the grassland in the foreground were minor parts of the composition. The sky was the painting.

She lost herself in her work until a gust of raw, damp wind brought her back to earth. Beth looked up and realized she was almost out of time. The dark clouds she'd been painting were almost overhead now. The first clap of thunder rattled down the river valley. Chance whinnied, the sound surprisingly distant. Even hobbled, she'd managed to drift a few hundred yards away.

Idiot, you should have tied her. Too bad the mare wouldn't come at a whistle like Cloud.

'Oh, whistle and I'll come to you, my lad . . .' the words of the song made her think of Trey, not his horse.

The foreground of the painting would have to wait. Scolding herself for not bringing a jacket, Beth packed up her things, slipped the damp painting on its board into a saddlebag and started after Chance. By the time she reached the mare, the first raindrops were falling and the wind had turned bitter. Cursing her own thoughtlessness, Beth took off Chance's hobbles and hurried her back to the saddle.

Growing nervous, the mare gave Beth a difficult time tacking up. The rain came harder. Winded and shivering, Beth crawled into the saddle.

Halfway home, the storm broke in earnest. Blinded by rain, Beth gave up guiding Chance, trusting the mare to find her way home.

* * * *

Trey swore at the first rumble of thunder. He'd stopped reading half an hour ago, when he'd noticed it getting darker. He'd been watching the storm since then. If Beth didn't get back real soon, it would catch her, but she had better sense than that.

Unless Chance had thrown her, or . . . *don't be a fool, she's as good a rider as you are.*

Trey's imagination worked overtime. He worried about Beth riding alone at the best of times. She didn't know the country yet. With a storm coming, she wouldn't risk staying out, so where the hell was she?

When the skies opened, Trey got to his feet. "Bloody stubborn fool women!" He made his way unsteadily across the room and pulled on his jacket. If he took his time, he could . . .

There she was now. He couldn't believe his relief. It completely swamped his anger. Physically and emotionally exhausted, Trey dropped into a chair at the table and waited for Beth to come in from the barn.

What a sight. Her blouse and pants clung to her, soaked and dripping. Rivulets ran down her face from her sopping hair. Teeth chattering, shivering from head to toe, she hugged herself and moved close to the stove.

"Why do you have your coat on?"

If he hadn't known he'd fall over, Trey would have grabbed her and shaken her. "I was about to come looking for you. I figured you would have beaten the storm here if you'd been able to. I was picturing you lying out there somewhere after a fall, or being lost or running up against some stranger—"

Brushing water from her eyes, Beth turned to face him. "Trey, I got caught in the rain, that's all. I was painting, and Chance drifted further away than I thought she would. It took me a few minutes to catch her. Neil said you could do permanent damage if you push yourself."

"I know. That's why I hired Gabe."

"I know." She took a step toward him. "I'm sorry I lost my temper, but I still wish you'd talked to me before offering him the job."

"So do I." Damn, he couldn't talk to her when she looked like this, wet, disheveled and utterly desirable. He could only think of the hole Beth would leave in his life when she went her way, which she would. Trey didn't dare doubt it. "Go get into some dry clothes, Beth. We'll talk when you come down."

Beth came down from the loft wearing her blue print. She'd undone her braid, toweled her hair and left it loose. Her face still pink from being dried, she joined Trey at the table.

He wanted to do the smart thing for both of them and tell her it wasn't working. Trey needed someone he could live with comfortably, not someone who turned him inside out like Beth did, reaching into corners of his heart he'd walled off years ago and wanted to keep that way. A man didn't come out of four years of war without things on his conscience that weren't fit to see the light of day. Especially not a man who'd turned on his home and the friends he'd grown up with.

But the words wouldn't come. He could only feel his way.

"Beth, I haven't lived with a woman in the house since I left home. I don't mean to be thoughtless. I'm just used to deciding things on my own. Do you really object to Gabe?"

"Not really. I think he's a little arrogant, but I was upset because you shut me out, and it hurt."

Trey looked down at the table. "I'm sorry. It's just . . . it's who you are, I guess. I can't get used to the thought of you working in the barn, knowing you could easily marry someone who could give you the life you're used to. Even if I still had the home place, I could never do that. It always provided, but it was just a comfortable small farm. You deserve more."

The color in Beth's cheeks heightened as she looked at him. Her eyes were big and blue and deep enough to drown in. "Trey, you sound exactly like the man I thought I was in love with in Denver. He didn't propose because his parents would have cut him off. With Uncle Robert's money gone, I was no longer a suitable match. Then when Aunt Abigail died one of my cousin's friends told him he'd marry me, since he had no family to object and my looks suited him. He never troubled himself to speak to me first. So, I contacted the agency. I wrote to you because you sounded honest and I thought you'd give me a chance."

So she'd cared for someone, a man with her own background, and the spineless fool had hurt her. Trey couldn't find it in him to do the same, even if it was the best thing for her in the long run. He'd have to wait for her to decide she couldn't live his life.

"I don't have the answers, Beth, but I won't lie to you. That's all I can promise."

Beth laid her hand over his. "That's all I can ask."

* * * *

"Well, I guess you weren't bragging." Gabe stood in the barn aisle, watching Beth as she gave Calico his morning grain and water. "You know your way around a horse."

Trey had agreed that Beth should continue looking after the mustang, since a strange man would be sure to upset him. Though Gabe had said nothing when Trey told him to leave Calico to her, Beth sensed that Mr. Tanner didn't like giving way to a woman. He hadn't said a word amiss since returning to the homestead yesterday after the storm, but she couldn't shake her dislike of the man.

"I've ridden since I was very young." She came out of Calico's stall and glanced in at Cloud and the mares in turn. Gabe had handled them without trouble and done a decent job of cleaning out their stalls. Impatience flashed in his pale eyes as he watched her check his work.

"You needn't worry, Missus McShannon. I do a day's work for a day's pay. You've got a man inside who needs your attention right now. You'd best pay heed to him and leave the chores to me."

Beth looked him in the eye and gave him a smile with a touch of steel in it. "I appreciate your concern, but Trey doesn't like to be hovered over and these horses mean as much to me as they do to him. They're our future. You'll have to humor me."

Gabe grinned, the next best thing to a smirk in Beth's opinion. "How long have you been married?"

No hired help Beth had ever dealt with would have dared to look at her that way, or ask such a personal question. She was tempted to tell Gabe it was none of his business, but things were different out here. Likely he was just making conversation, and for Trey's sake, she didn't want any friction. She settled for a cool answer and hoped Gabe would take the hint.

"We're newlyweds, actually."

"Congratulations." Gabe sauntered down the aisle, lifted Midnight's harness from the wall and walked into the Percheron's stall. "Tell Mister McShannon I'll have the bottom field plowed by the end of the day."

"I'll go tell him now, and make some sandwiches for you to take with you." Beth returned to the house, glad to get out of Gabe's sight. Trey sat at the table, writing a letter. He glanced up and grumbled at her exasperated look.

"I know, I know. Save your breath to cool your coffee. I'll go back to bed as soon as I'm finished with this."

Beth wrinkled her nose at him. "Getting a bit testy, are we? You're as bad a patient as I am."

Trey put his pen down with a sigh and massaged the bridge of his nose. "I hate sitting around like this. I'm used to being out and doing."

His frustration carried across the room and hit Beth in waves. She'd rarely seen Trey still for more than a few minutes at a time, except at meals. This confinement had to be driving him crazy. She moved to stand behind him, looking over his shoulder at the letter.

She remembered her first sight of his bold, slanted script, when she'd opened his first letter in her room at Graham's. She'd been watching the mail, waiting to intercept any letters from the agency before Graham or Julia could see them. It felt like much more than a few short weeks ago.

"I know. If it's any comfort, Gabe seems to know what he's doing. He said to tell you he'd have the bottom field done by tonight."

"Good."

Standing close enough to feel Trey's body heat, Beth felt a sudden urge to bend down and brush her lips along the line of his jaw. Neither of them had spoken of their first kiss since it happened. She knew Trey had enjoyed it as much as she had, but after their talk when she came in out of the storm, Beth intended to let him make the next move. She turned to the counter to make Gabe's lunch.

"Who are you writing to?"

"Dad."

Beth wondered if Trey had told his family he'd written to the agency, or whether he planned to wait and see if the marriage worked out. She couldn't imagine they'd be pleased at him marrying a stranger. From what he'd said, Trey's sister sounded like a woman with a definite mind of her own, and his father sounded like a forthright, no-nonsense type. Would Beth ever get the chance to meet them and win them over?

She gave Gabe his sandwiches and saw him off with the team, then came in and set up her easel by the table. Trey had finished his letter and had gone back to bed with a book. Beth had the day ahead without a lot to do, and she wanted to finish the foreground of her storm cloud painting. If she got at it, she could have it done by lunchtime.

* * * *

"You're it!"

Trey spun around and chased the crowd of puffing, shouting boys across the grassy churchyard. When they reached the two lines of hitched horses waiting patiently by the long, low white church, the group scattered. Trey paused for breath and eased a finger inside his wilting collar, its starch softened by the hot July sun.

"Hey, are you Cathy Sinclair's brother?"

The familiar voice, edged with contempt, came from behind the Sinclairs' buggy. Trey ran around the parked conveyances. Nate Munroe and half of the other boys stood surrounding a kid Trey had never seen before. The stranger was taller than Nate but quite a bit thinner, without the sturdiness of a boy used to running around outdoors. He looked a little older than Trey, about seven.

Everyone knew Cathy had a brother, but none of the boys had seen him. He'd had rheumatic fever as a baby and the Sinclairs had kept him home so he wouldn't catch anything from the other kids. When the family entertained, he stayed in his room. Trey had never been there, but he knew the Sinclairs had the largest plantation in the county.

This boy had the same hazel eyes and sandy blond hair as Cathy's father. He stood facing Nate with his fists clenched, but he didn't speak. Nate stuck his hands in his pockets and laughed.

"What's the matter with you, can't you talk? Maybe we should see if we can make you."

"S-sure I c-can talk."

The other boys tittered. Trey stepped up, got a dirty look from Nate and glared back. They'd never liked each other. Nate would bully anyone who'd let him.

Cathy's brother looked and sounded scared, but he didn't back down. Trey shouldered his way to the front of the group to get a better look at him.

"Hey. Your name's Justin, isn't it?"

"Y-yes, it is."

"I'm Trey McShannon and that's Nate Munroe. He thinks he's tough, but you're bigger than he is."

Justin stood straighter. "Y-you're right." He took a deep breath and faced Nate again. Trey saw Justin fighting his stutter. This time he spoke without a hitch. "You want me to talk? Fine, I'll talk. If you want me to clean your clock for you, just come on."

Nate took a step forward and smiled again, without the contempt. "Hell, I was only foolin'. You can play if you want to, but you'll have to be it."

Justin looked around at the group, then yelled, "I'm it!" and chased the boys back across the churchyard. But it wasn't the churchyard any more, and the boys...men in uniform, ran with Trey across an empty field. Not Justin or John Hughes or Charlie Bascomb or any of the others from home, but he knew them. He remembered them all.

Shouts mingled with screams and the staccato bark of rifles. Trey heard a bullet strike flesh. The man in front of him fell. Orrin Bates, one of his messmates. Trey jumped over the prone form and dodged another, stumbled and swore.

* * * *

When she heard his curse, Beth dropped her paintbrush and hurried to wake him. At her touch, Trey's eyes snapped open, full of his nightmare. He sat up and hid his face in his hands, his shoulders heaving as he took deep breaths. Beth tried to put her arms around him, but he knocked them away.

"Don't."

She refused to let it hurt. Just having her see him like this, shaken by a dream, would be difficult enough for Trey's pride to handle. She couldn't expect him to accept comfort from her so soon. Beth sat on the edge of the bunk and waited while he collected himself.

"That must have been quite a dream."

Trey looked up, his face closed and remote. "Yeah. Thanks for pulling me out of it."

"You're welcome. If you want to talk about it, I'll listen."

"It was just a dream. It's over." Moving stiffly, Trey got up and washed his face. He'd taken off his shirt when he went back to bed after finishing his letter. The scar on his side showed white against the deep purple bruising across his middle. Beth hadn't asked him about it, but she supposed he'd gotten the scar during the war.

She remembered Maddy's description of the silent young man who'd arrived here almost five years ago. Beth had guessed then that Trey had wounds that still hadn't healed. Now she was sure of it.

"Trey, where were you wounded?"

He kept his back to her as he scrubbed his face with a towel. "Antietam. That's when I met Neil. The surgeons were all busy when I was brought in, so he decided to patch me up himself. I'll never forget waking up to that face."

Beth shuddered. "Who would?"

Trey shook his head. "I thought I'd come to in hell, and Neil barked at me. 'You just lie still. I don't know if I've ever seen a dead cavalryman but if you pull those stitches out, you might be the first.' It's the oldest gibe in the service, that about never seeing a dead cavalryman, but he made me mad as hell, which was exactly what he wanted. I told him I'd seen a few and killed a couple myself."

So that explained the connection she'd sensed between Trey and Neil. Beth warmed to the man. There was a heart beneath his repellent face and questionable manners. "It sounds like Mister Garrett knew his job."

"He did. They shipped me out to hospital the next day. I didn't even know his name, but when I walked into the saloon here, he knew me. 'There's some folks you can't kill with a meat axe', he said." Trey threw his towel over the back of a chair, came back to bed and picked up his book. "I could eat lunch any time, Beth." His way of telling her he'd said all he was going to say.

Beth prepared the meal with her mind elsewhere. When she'd first met Trey, he'd looked like so much more man than she'd bargained for – tall, lean and tough, with nothing yielding in those dark eyes of his. Now, only a few days later, Beth knew the gentleness hidden deep inside him. He didn't like showing it, but it came out in the way he handled his livestock. In the way he'd kissed her. In his protectiveness, when he wasn't furious with her. This sodbuster, as Graham had called him, was as much a gentleman at heart as Daniel Hunter or Jason Pembroke with all their breeding. And, underneath his hard shell, he was vulnerable.

It would have been easier for her, Beth thought, if Trey's toughness had gone a little deeper.

* * * *

Gabe got back to the homestead at evening chore time, while Beth was brushing Calico. He put the Percherons away and came to stand outside the mustang's stall.

"Evening, Ma'am."

With her back to him, Beth didn't know he was close until he spoke. She started. Calico snorted and danced away. Beth curbed her annoyance and turned around.

"Hello, Gabe. Next time, please give me some warning. He's skittish, as you can see."

"Sure. Sorry." Gabe came forward to open the door for Beth as she left the stall. He followed her to the back of the barn and hung up the team's harness while she scooped oats into a bucket for Calico. "Last place I worked, the boss's daughter tried to gentle a mustang. It didn't wash. He needed a firm hand. After a while her father came to his senses and gave the horse to the crew to break. We made him useful, and the old man bought a safe horse for the girl. Worked out better all around."

It's only for a few days. We need him. Beth bit back her temper.

"You really don't think I should be out here at all, do you, Gabe?"

He smiled as he settled the harness on its pegs. "It isn't my place to think anything of the sort, Ma'am. I'd just hate to see you get hurt."

Gabe stood too close for comfort. His tone didn't match his words, and his pale eyes stayed on hers a little too long. With a blush rising, Beth walked away. She gave Calico his oats and went back to the house, fuming.

Gabe had never offered her a word or a look she could call positively disrespectful, but Beth had never met a man who made her more uncomfortable. She should tell Trey, but if he took her seriously he'd fire Gabe and they'd be back where they started, with the plowing and planting still unfinished. And if Trey didn't take her seriously, that would only make things worse. Ugh! Well, Gabe had to behave himself at meals, and from now on she'd wait until he wasn't around to look after Calico.

At supper Gabe and Trey discussed range conditions and cattle prices, sounding as much like friends as boss and employee. Beth listened, counting the days until she and Trey would be alone at meals again.

She couldn't shake off the worry that had nagged at her since his accident. Neil had said head injuries were unpredictable things. The effects could linger for months, even permanently. There was a chance, however slight, that Trey wouldn't be able to do hard physical work again.

But that's not going to happen. He'll be himself again soon. All I have to do is put up with Gabe in the meantime.

CHAPTER 9

Feeling restless, Lorie left Neil's place just before it opened for the day. She walked to the top of a hill outside of town, sat on a patch of soft grass and turned her face up to the sun for a moment, then scanned the huddle of buildings below.

Wallace Flats lay spread out in front of her like a collection of cardboard toys, with children walking to school along the main street and Nathan headed toward Neil's for his morning coffee. Even at a distance, his awkward gait gave him away.

Lorie knew about Nathan going to the council, and she'd heard the talk at Neil's place after the incident with Carl Manning. It looked like Nathan intended to stay in town, and chances were he'd get his chance at the sheriff's job. That knowledge had her thinking about moving on.

It happened now and then that Lorie came across a man she couldn't treat as another customer. When that happened, she stopped seeing him. If she let her emotions interfere with her job, she'd be in serious trouble. Nathan was turning out to be one of those men. Lorie had to protect herself.

If she left Wallace Flats, it wouldn't be easy to find another place where she could set her own terms and hours. In most places she'd be the property of the owner, at his whim. She hated that idea but Nathan might not give her a choice.

Looking down at the town, Lorie reminded herself to see beneath the surface. Some of those homes were no different than hers had been, with the fights and constant bickering. She didn't know if her parents had ever been in love, but she'd never seen them show affection to each other or their children. Then, when she'd gone looking for it elsewhere they'd thrown her out. To Lorie, domestic life meant endless mean, nagging, petty quarrels, nothing more. She had no desire to walk into that trap. She liked her life just fine, thank you very much, and any man who wanted to change that could go straight to hell. She wished Nathan would hurry up and finish his coffee so she could go home.

* * * *

Trey stood by the corral, soaking up the sun and breathing as deeply as his battered ribs would allow. Desperate for fresh air, he'd dressed and come out as soon as Beth rode out of sight on her way to Maddy's. His ribs still ached, but he'd decided they must be only bruised, and after five days rest, his head felt better. Another day or two and he'd try getting on a horse again.

Beth had gone for their milk and, truth be told, Trey needed a break from the physical need and emotional turmoil she created in him. Turmoil she couldn't guess at and he could never explain to her, not without telling her things he couldn't tell anyone.

She couldn't know that when she'd asked about his scar, he'd tasted the sickly sweet remnants of chloroform again, heard the nightmarish sounds of the dressing station around him, felt the burn of new stitches in his side. More than that, he remembered faces.

Like the face of a tall, redheaded kid younger than himself, in a gray uniform that was too big for him. Eyes wide with shock, he'd swayed in the saddle for a few seconds before he crumpled and fell, the first of the lives Trey had taken.

They were his to live with, and he'd thought he'd learned to do that until Beth came along. Until the dreams started again. How quickly would she leave if she knew?

His one taste of her had only left him wanting more, but if he kissed her again Trey didn't think he'd be able to stop. Sooner or later he'd end up tying Beth to him for life – and then hurting her more than that man in Denver had. She deserved a man with a whole heart to give her.

He could still see her face, flushed and glowing with pleasure after he kissed her. Beth might start caring for him if he let her. Trey wondered at times if she didn't care already. She'd been unusually quiet around the house for the last few days. At meals she barely spoke while he talked to Gabe. That thought gave him a twinge. He'd noticed Beth avoided the barn when Gabe was around, and she didn't have much to say to him in the house. For some reason she didn't like him much.

Or did she like Gabe too much?

A knot formed in Trey's chest, hard and painful. His marriage to Beth only existed on paper, after all. He supposed a lot of women would find Gabe attractive. Why not her?

McShannon, you're going stir-crazy. She hasn't had time to get her feet under her yet. And you bloody well know she's attracted to you. That's the problem, isn't it?

In the corral, Shiloh lifted her head and whinnied. At a distance another horse answered. Trey looked down the lane and felt his spirits lift at the sight of John Reeves' chestnut mare. He'd been expecting John since the accident, but his timing couldn't have been better.

John swung heavily to the ground, looked Trey over sharply and gave him a cautious slap on the back. "It's good to see you on your feet. Neil told me what happened. I'm sorry it was my horse that did it."

"Cloud's been giving him a hard time. Calico just reacted." Feeling better already, Trey returned the back slap. "Put your horse up and come in. Beth will be home any time, and she'll give me hell if she catches me out here."

Inside, John parked his two hundred and thirty pounds on Trey's bunk. John was Trey's physical opposite, blond, round-faced and massive, but they'd discovered early on that they spoke the same language. Trey had told only John's family and the Kinsleys he'd written to Beth.

"Neil spread the word that you were married." John grinned and shook his head. "I asked him what Beth looked like and he clammed right up. 'A little redhead' was all he said. She must be quite something to leave Neil tongue-tied."

"He'll stay that way if he knows what's good for him." Trey liked Neil, even if he was only as honest as he had to be and drank almost as much as his customers. The man had a surprising amount of compassion for anyone sick or injured, but that wouldn't keep Trey from decking him if he talked about Beth in the saloon.

"You know Neil better than that, Trey. From what I hear, she's a real lady."

"Yes, she is." Trey pulled a chair away from the table and sat on it backward, facing his friend. "I suppose June Baker has pretty much worn her tongue out by now."

"More or less." John's shrewd blue eyes turned thoughtful. "Watch yourself. Beth sounds like the kind of woman who could have you pushing a pen in a city somewhere if you're not careful."

Trey chuckled in response, but the laughter carried a note of uncertainty. Maybe John didn't know him as well as he thought. *Or maybe he knows me better than I know myself.*

"Do you really think any woman could do that to me?"

John wasn't laughing. "You tell me. She's gotten to you already. I can see it. Get in too deep and she won't be easy to forget."

Hell, he'd figured that out before he got her home, but Trey wasn't about to say so. "John, there are six young, single women in town. Two of them are on the point of being engaged. I've got no more interest in any of the other four than I would have in a stranger. I might as well gamble. If it doesn't work, Beth's free to go when and where she chooses. Here she comes now."

* * * *

Beth turned Chance into the corral with the other mares and hurried to the house. She knew Trey was feeling better each day, but she still worried when she left him. Milk bottle in hand, she stopped in the doorway when she saw him talking to a hulking, bearded stranger.

When Trey introduced them, John engulfed Beth's hand in his. "It's a pleasure. Trey, I have to admire your taste, though I'm not sure about Beth's."

Beth warmed to his teasing. She wanted Trey's close friends to like her and from the way he spoke of John, she knew he was one of them.

The three of them chatted for an hour or so. By the time John left, Beth felt that he'd accepted her as a friend, and that his family would do the same. She and Trey stood in the doorway and watched him out of sight.

"I'm looking forward to meeting Hannah and Ben. I didn't expect people to be so welcoming."

Trey put his arm around her. "Not everyone will be, but the people I consider friends will like you unless you give them reason not to. That's how they are."

Beth turned to face him. Trey flushed and removed his arm. Still feeling its warmth, she looked into his eyes. They held the same smoldering want she'd seen when he kissed her.

Beth had done some thinking since then. Every day she felt more at ease with life here. She'd discovered the sense of accomplishment that came from looking after a house, and every time she went walking or riding she found something new. This empty land wasn't empty at all when you took the time to really look and listen. And since his accident, she found herself more and more drawn to Trey.

She'd done a sketch of him the other day, just from memory, and discovered that she knew every line of his strong-boned, tough-looking face. She knew it was the best portrait she'd ever done.

He'd said he didn't have any answers and neither did she, but she knew what she felt. If she left here without expressing it, she'd always wonder if she'd been too much of a lady.

Trembling a little at her audacity, Beth slipped her arms around Trey, stood on tiptoe and brushed her lips over his. She'd never been so bold with a man before. She'd always let Daniel initiate their kisses.

Trey's body tensed and for a horrible moment, Beth thought he was going to push her away, but instead he wrapped his arms around her and covered her mouth with his. He tasted like she remembered, warm, unique, arousing. He kept the kiss gentle like before, but Beth felt the desire behind his restraint. His body hummed with it, and so did hers. When she moved closer, wanting more, Trey drew back and took her chin in his hand.

"Beth, I'm only human. I want to give you time . . ."

His harsh whisper went right through her. Weak-kneed, Beth leaned against the hard wall of Trey's chest. "I know, but this has been building between us since I got here. We have to start somewhere, don't you think?"

Trey dropped his hands to her waist and gave her a ragged smile. "I don't know how much of this I can stand before there'll be no turning back."

Beth ran her fingers along his spine and felt a little surge of feminine triumph when he shivered. "I don't have the answers either, Trey. We're going to have to find them together."

In reply, Trey pressed his lips to hers again. Beth threaded her fingers into his hair and opened to him, letting his lips and teeth and tongue take her on a slow, sensuous journey. She still sensed him holding back, but somehow that only made it sweeter. Beth felt surrounded by his strength, at home in his arms. She couldn't move when the kiss ended.

"Trey, I think . . ." She looked down and shook her head. "I can't think."

Breathing fast, his gaze still heated, Trey brushed his knuckles over her cheek. "Neither can I." A shadow crossed his face, then he grinned. "I guess we've put the cart before the horse, getting married. Maybe we need to forget we've been to church already and start at the beginning. It just might be too much fun to skip."

"I think you just might be right." Beth closed her eyes, savoring his nearness. Her lips tingled and her legs felt rubbery. She didn't know how much more of this she could take either. "I'd better go feed and water Calico."

When she stepped out of his arms, Trey stopped her with a look. "Beth, is there some kind of a problem between you and Gabe?"

So he'd noticed. Beth chose her words carefully. Over the last few days she'd seen very little of Gabe other than at meals, but she still felt his contempt, and instinct told her something uglier than contempt lay beneath it. She knew if she said so to Trey he'd be furious, and a fight was the last thing he needed right now.

"We just rub each other the wrong way. Gabe doesn't seem to think much of women in general."

Trey's hard hand closed around her wrist. "Has he said or done anything to upset you?"

Cold anger glinted in his eyes. She tried to pull out of his grip, but couldn't. "Trey, there's nothing to get upset about. He irritates me, that's all. He as much as said he didn't think I belonged in the barn, and if I tell him anything he brushes it off and waits to hear it from you, but it doesn't matter. In a few days he'll be gone, and in the meantime I'll spend as little time around him as possible."

Trey held her gaze for a long moment, then let her go. "All right. I imagine Gabe isn't much like the help you were used to in Denver. I'll talk to him."

"Trey, there's no need—"

"I said I'll talk to him."

Beth knew nothing she could say would change his mind. She spent the rest of the afternoon in misery, waiting for Gabe to come in from the fields for supper. Her only consolation was that he should have finished the plowing today. If it came to the worst and Trey fired him, she'd plant the blessed oats herself.

Gabe had to notice his boss's coolness over supper, though he didn't let on. When the meal ended Trey gave Beth a pointed look. Knowing she'd only make matters worse by refusing to leave, she picked up her sketchbook and went out.

She retreated to the vegetable garden, close enough to hear if the men raised their voices in the house. She'd made a mistake. If she'd told Trey how much Gabe bothered her at the start, this could have been avoided. Trey was right – some men out here weren't about to respect a woman if she stepped out of her place. She could have handled Gabe differently.

130

Nonsense. He's been rude and you know it.

In about five minutes, with no sounds of an argument, Gabe strode out of the house. Catching sight of Beth, he came to her and held out his hand.

"Missus McShannon, it seems we've been misunderstanding each other. Mister McShannon told me you're new out here. I figured as much myself, but it never occurred to me that you might take offence at anything I said. Please accept my apologies."

He sounded perfectly sincere, and maybe he was. Perhaps they *had* misunderstood each other, though Beth didn't think so. Still, for Trey's sake . . .

"You're right, I am new here, and perhaps I've taken some things the wrong way. Let's just start over again, Gabe."

Those pale eyes looked into Beth's as he smiled. "Yes, let's. Thank you, Ma'am."

Gabe left for the barn, and Beth went back to the house. Trey sat at the table with his account book.

"Did Gabe find you?"

"Yes, he did. He apologized. Did you ask him to?"

"No. He offered to before I could. He seemed honestly surprised when I said he'd upset you. I told him I expected him to treat you with the same respect he would me, in the house and out of it. If he doesn't, I want to know, is that clear?"

Relieved, Beth started getting ready to wash the supper dishes. "Yes, it's clear. Now let's forget the whole thing."

"Yeah." Trey's eyes met hers with a look that made Beth blush. "I guess we have enough to think about."

* * * *

The next afternoon, since Gabe was sowing the oats and didn't need the team, Beth went to town for supplies. Instead of June, a portly, balding man stood behind the counter. Beth handed him her list with a smile.

"Hello. You must be Mister Baker."

"Yes, and you must be Missus McShannon. My wife's mentioned you." To Beth's surprise, he leaned forward and whispered, "Can I speak to you privately, please?"

Beth nodded. Mr. Baker came out from behind the counter and beckoned her into a quiet corner. He ran a hand through his thinning salt-and-pepper hair and fiddled with his watch chain.

"Damn, this is awkward. We've never even met before." He cleared his throat, looking more uncomfortable by the moment. "Well, two nights ago after closing up I went over to Neil's for a beer. I was having my drink and I heard these men at another table talking. Ugly talk, about a woman. Most of it was coming from this blond. I knew Trey had just hired help and this man was a stranger, so after listening for a couple of minutes I put two and two together. I'm sorry, but Trey would want to know what kind of man he's hired."

Elizabeth Underhill of Philadelphia had never been more outraged in her life. Gabe Tanner had wormed his way into her husband's good graces, eaten at her table . . . "Mister Baker, what exactly did he say?"

The storekeeper turned beet red. "It wasn't fit to repeat to a lady."

June came out of the back room in time to hear him. Eyes snapping, she bustled over, nudged her husband aside and spoke in an angry hiss.

"If Frank won't tell you, I will. He said you and Trey weren't sleeping in the same room and it didn't surprise him that you had an eye for the help, that you were the kind of woman who needed a real man. For heaven's sake, Frank, don't look like that. You told me. I'd like to be there to see Trey put his lights out."

Beth felt as if she'd just turned over a rock and found something slimy and loathsome underneath. She'd like to see Trey put Gabe's lights out too, but he couldn't, not now. Gabe wasn't worth jeopardizing Trey's recovery, which meant it was up to her to send him packing. Beth put one hand on June's shoulder and the other on Frank's. "Thank you for telling me. This will be dealt with as soon as I get home."

* * * *

She found Trey sitting on the doorstep, finishing a set of braided reins. He helped Beth carry in the supplies, which made it difficult for her to sneak the revolver from the dresser drawer and into her skirt pocket, but she managed it. On her last trip out to the wagon, while Trey was inside, she ducked into the barn and stuffed the weapon in her saddlebag.

She changed into her denims. "I'm taking Cheyenne for a little run before supper." Trey didn't question her. Beth returned to the barn, climbed to the loft and rolled Gabe's belongings up in his bedroll. Not giving herself time to think twice, she saddled Cheyenne and started for the river.

She pulled up at the edge of the bottom field and took the revolver from the saddlebag. Gabe was sowing oats. His black mare stood tied to a nearby cottonwood.

Beth waited for him to see her. When he did, he sauntered toward her. As soon as he stepped within reach Beth dropped her reins and backhanded him across the face, hard enough to snap his head back.

"You've got a filthy mind and a mouth to go with it."

Red-faced from her slap and his temper, Gabe reached to pull Beth off her horse. She anticipated him, kneed Cheyenne away and brought up the gun in her other hand. Gabe stopped in his tracks.

"You little hell-cat, have you lost your mind?"

"No, I've just heard an earful about you in town." With her free hand, Beth tossed the bedroll at his head, making him duck. "You're fired. Get your horse and get out of here."

Gabe glared up at her, his pale eyes glowing with fury. "Your husband owes me a week's pay—"

"My husband owes you a punch in the face, and he'll pay you if he ever sees you again. You ate at his table, got him to like you . . . get moving. Now."

Smirking, Gabe stood his ground. "Are you going to shoot me if I don't?"

Beth fired a shot into the ground in front of him and grinned when he jumped. "I guess I missed. I'm not much of a shot, but Trey says I could probably hit someone coming at me at close range. Want to try me?"

Swearing, Gabe picked up the bedroll and untied his horse. Beth waited until he rode off, then let Cheyenne run home, wanting to be sure Gabe didn't return and surprise Trey. He came out of the cabin when he heard her in the yard.

"Beth, you look like you ran into a pack of wolves. What's the matter?"

Seeing him – hearing his voice – made reaction set in. She hadn't been here three weeks yet and she'd had to defend herself with a gun. When she got off her horse, Beth's legs would hardly hold her. She walked into Trey's arms and laid her head on his shoulder.

"Not a pack of wolves, only one. Trey, I just fired Gabe."

She'd expected anger right away, but he only held her closer. His warmth and familiar scent worked like magic to calm her. "What happened?"

Beth repeated what the Bakers had told her. Trey flushed, then turned pale with anger. "Beth, what were you thinking?"

"I was afraid if you fired him it would come to a fight, and he isn't worth it. I took your revolver with me—"

Trey's eyes turned black in his pale, angry face. "You *what*?"

Beth shivered at the memory of Gabe's look as he tried to pull her off her horse. "I took the gun and I needed it. I had to fire a shot at his feet to convince him to leave."

Before she could blink, Trey caught her shoulders in a painful grip and gave her a sharp shake. "Jesus, Beth! You need a bloody keeper! If you'd let me handle it, it would be over and done with, but now it's anyone's guess what he'll do."

With her own temper rising, Beth pulled free. "He insulted both of us. I had as much right to do it as you."

He swore, swung his leg over Cheyenne and sent her down the lane at a gallop. Beth watched him out of sight then ran to saddle Chance. Trey would be furious with her, but she'd started this and she wasn't about to wait tamely at home while he finished it.

CHAPTER 10

John looked up from the stove he was repairing as Trey stepped into the forge yard. "Hey. I thought you were staying put for a few more days."

"Yeah, well, I changed my mind."

When Trey told him what Beth had done and why, John let out a low whistle. "That, I would have liked to see. She's got nerve, I'll give her that." He closed the stove door and took off his leather apron. "You aren't ready for this right now, Trey."

"Maybe not, but it looks like I've got it to do."

With a gleam in his eyes, John nodded. "Mind if I come along?"

"That's why I'm here."

John wove his way through the collection of stoves, boilers and scrap metal that filled the yard. Anticipation lightened Trey's anger. Now he'd be able to concentrate on Gabe without worrying about his back.

A man who despised women as much as Gabe did wouldn't let one run him off. If Trey didn't find him in town today, he'd keep looking. He had to make sure Gabe didn't come back to lurk around the homestead, waiting to catch Beth alone. From what she'd said, the man sounded capable of anything. Trey still couldn't believe Beth had faced him herself.

More nerve than common sense. He walked out of the forge yard with John – and stopped dead when he saw

Beth tying Chance in front of the store. Trey swore under his breath and went to meet her.

"What the—? Why couldn't you stay home?"

Beth lifted her chin and looked him in the eye. "Because, I couldn't. Don't bother shouting at me, Trey. I'm already here. Hello, John."

The grin on John's face as he returned Beth's greeting only made Trey angrier. He spun on his heel and walked into the store. Frank came out from behind the counter, his smile tinged with concern.

"Good to see you, Trey."

"You too, Frank." Trey threw an irritated glance over his shoulder at the door. "Beth told me what you heard at Neil's the other night."

"I knew you'd want to know." Frank pressed his thin lips together. "Pretty cheap of him, if you ask me. I guess you've fired him."

"Yeah, he's been fired. I want to know who he was talking to."

"Three of Dale Turner's new hands. You know he hired a few back in March. I don't know their names." Frank shrugged his wide, bony shoulders. "I got the impression that your hand didn't know them very well either. He was a stranger, so he caught my attention."

"Well, I'm going to catch his attention if I see him. If he comes in here, tell him I'm looking for him." Trey stepped back outside, where John waited with Beth. Her eyes dared him to try to send her home, but Trey didn't want to argue with her now, not any more than he wanted to think about how her concern made him feel. He beckoned to John and started down the street toward Neil's.

A few regulars sat in their usual places at the saloon's battered tables. Trey stopped when he saw Gabe standing at the bar with a beer. The polite mask was gone. He looked furious.

Trey knew he'd be in serious trouble if he didn't make this quick. He motioned John to wait by the door, then walked up behind Gabe and tapped him on the shoulder. When he turned around, Trey knocked him down with a right to the jaw. Gabe hit the floor and got up cursing. Before he could get set, Trey hit him in the belly, sending him sprawling again.

"There's your wages, Gabe. If I see you in town again, you'd better be carrying a gun. If I see you within a mile of my place I'll shoot you on sight."

Winded and dazed, Gabe grabbed a toppled bar stool and sat up. Neil reached under the bar and pulled out his shotgun. The other men in the saloon weren't paying much attention. They saw this sort of thing too often.

Trey's head buzzed with the jarring of the punches he'd thrown, but he felt good. He'd been carrying a load of physical frustration since Beth arrived, and releasing some of it this way helped. Neil gave him a sour look.

"You're more of a damned fool than I thought. What was that about?"

"He worked for me, ate in our house, then came in here at night and bad-mouthed Beth. She fired him today, and I wanted to second the motion." Trey watched Gabe struggle to his feet and fought the urge to knock him back down. "Get out."

A bruise already forming on his jaw, Gabe steadied himself against the bar and held Trey's gaze. "That was a cheap trick, McShannon. I'll see you again."

Trey grinned, planted his feet and readied his fists. "There's no time like the present." John crossed the room to stand beside him, his cool blue eyes on Gabe.

"You won't see him again if I see you first. Where's your horse?"

Flashing his crooked grin, Neil gestured toward the door with his shotgun. With a last glare at Trey, Gabe left, John at his heels. Neil watched them go out, then turned back to Trey and raised an eyebrow. "So, how's married life treating you, anyway?"

Trey chuckled and shook his head. He knew Neil's opinion of married life. "Well, it isn't boring."

Before he could say more, another customer walked in. Trey's voice failed him as he took in the man's sandy blond hair, gray eyes, broken nose and missing arm. Through the shock of recognition, he dimly heard Neil's voice.

"Coffee, Nate? It's on the house."

* * * *

Hidden in the alley between the saloon and the barbershop, Beth watched Trey's altercation with Gabe through an open window. Graham would die of embarrassment if he could see her now. She laughed at Trey's comment on married life, imagining what he would have liked to say, angry as he was with her. Then a blond, one-armed man walked into the barroom and all the humor left Trey's face. He spoke in a tone that went through Beth like ice water.

"Small world, Nate. I can't say you haven't changed."

The stranger smiled, a genuine smile. Beth remembered to breathe. Whoever he might be, he didn't seem to be looking for trouble. "That's partly thanks to you, but I'll allow I asked for it. No hard feelings on my side." He glanced at the barstools lying on the floor. "Trouble, Neil?"

"Not for me. Trey—"

But Trey was almost at the door. Beth dashed out of the alley just in time to meet him.

He looked like he'd been sucker-punched. Jaw tight, eyes dark with shock and anger, Trey started down the street. Beth hurried to keep up with his long strides.

"Are you all right?"

"Yes. Let's go home."

He wouldn't look at her. That stranger had upset him to the core, but Beth shelved her questions for later. They separated to get their horses, then rode home together in silence. Trey took Chance and Cheyenne to the barn. A few minutes later, without a word, he left on Cloud.

Beth watched him from the cabin doorway. She didn't want to be alone after all the stress of the day, and Trey could have at least told her where he was going, even if he was still annoyed with her. She blinked away tears as he disappeared around the bend in the lane.

Beth, this isn't about you. He's hurting, and he doesn't want your help.

Turning away from the door, Beth's gaze fell on her trunk. She'd wired Graham to send it, and Trey had picked it up on his last trip to town before his accident. Since then, she'd been too busy to think about it. It stood against the back wall of the cabin, still waiting to be unpacked. Feeling the need to do something, Beth opened it.

She hadn't bothered to ask Graham to pack her mother's china or most of her dresses, but he'd sent her lamp from her room at home, a tablecloth and set of napkins she'd embroidered, a picture of Uncle Robert and Aunt Abigail, some of her books, and a couple of small paintings she'd had framed before coming to Denver. She'd been looking forward to having some of her own things here, but she couldn't enjoy them right now, with this ache of loneliness at her heart.

She took the clothes up to the loft and was about to put everything else back in the trunk when she stopped. She hadn't sent for her things so she could keep them packed away. She'd sent for them because she was thinking of staying. This was her home as well as Trey's, at least for now, and he was going to have to get used to the idea.

She filled the lamp and put it on the kitchen dresser, put the cloth on the table, hung the paintings and stacked her books on the shelf. It was satisfying after all to see something of hers in the place.

What will he think?

She doubted if he'd care, but *she* cared. If Trey needed to get away by himself, he was entitled, but Beth intended to be there for him when he came back. If he didn't want her, he was going to have to tell her so to her face.

142

* * * *

Trey rode into the yard at sunset, still on edge. He felt cheap for leaving Beth alone, but he'd needed to think.

It had to be Nate, here, now – a living reminder of things that weren't fit to see the light of day. Trey would never be able to see the man without recalling the March evening in '61 when they'd met last. He'd just finished plowing for the day, and Nate, Justin and the others were coming home from drill – what they called an hour spent riding, yelling and shooting off their rifles in the name of training. They all knew war was coming, and for most of them, it couldn't come soon enough.

Trey had never joined them, and with Nate adding fuel to the gossip, people were starting to wonder why. He took in Trey and his muddy team with a contemptuous glance.

"Well, looks like you've been busy. Are you going to be too busy to defend your country when the war starts?"

That was Nathan. He had to be pushing someone all the time, and Trey just wasn't in the mood to be pushed. He'd taken on most of the farm work that spring, so his father could spend as much time as possible with his mother in the few weeks she had left to live. Nate's taunt brought all Trey's doubts about the war and about himself boiling to the surface as rage. He left his team at the side of the road, walked over and pulled Nate out of his saddle with one jerk.

"I'm not running now, Nate. Come on!"

Nate got to his feet with a reckless light in his eyes. They circled each other for a moment while the others whistled and cheered, then Trey charged in, took a solid punch to the gut and landed one of his own. Nate was a tough and canny fighter. Trey had fury on his side, but he would have been in trouble if he hadn't managed to flatten his opponent's nose five minutes into the fight. He'd felt the results of their scrap for weeks, but not as badly as Nate. The thought still brought a bitter smile to Trey's face.

But he hadn't spent the last few hours thinking about Nate. For years, Trey had wondered if he wasn't the coward and traitor the man had called him, but he didn't have an eighteen-year-old's definitions of those words anymore. He'd paid a heavy price for the choice he'd made in '61 – no one knew how heavy – but he'd been true to himself.

After leaving Beth, he'd ridden to a favorite spot of his, an abandoned Arapaho camp by the river. Logan had taken him there when Trey first arrived. He'd gone back often that first summer. The quiet of the place, the sense of age, had steadied him when he needed it. He'd needed it again today.

He'd sat there until the tree shadows grew long, thinking about Beth. There were things about him she could never know, parts of himself he could never share with her, but he'd known that when he sent for her.

So why did I send for her?

Because I'd been alone too long. I hoped she'd be someone I could live with, but . . .

Trey wasn't ready to admit he was falling in love. He only knew he came home at night looking forward to seeing her, and that he was very tired of shaking off a web of half-formed longings every time he looked at her.

Those longings had as much to do with feelings as with the attraction between them, strong as that was. He wanted to make love to Beth, and he wanted to fall asleep afterwards with her in his arms. He'd never felt that way about a woman before. No, he wasn't a coward – except when he thought about Beth getting on the stage to Denver and not coming back.

She stood by the front window now in a glow of lamplight, furious with him no doubt. Trey smiled at the thought. Beth in a temper was enough to make him forget his fears. Enough to make him think maybe, if he gave her all of himself that was worth having, it might be enough. What she didn't know wouldn't hurt her.

He put Cloud away, glanced into Shiloh's stall and stopped in his tracks. She lay stretched out on her side, bulging with her foal, her rich chocolate-colored coat dark with sweat. She groaned with the pain of a contraction as Trey hurried to her side. When he checked her, he could tell her water had broken a while ago, but there was no sign of the foal.

Damn. *Damn.* He'd been sure she'd go another few days. Cursing himself, he grabbed a bucket and ran for the house. Beth got up from the table as he slammed the door behind him. She looked like she'd shed some tears. Trey felt like a heel, but explanations would have to wait.

"Beth, Shiloh's foaling and she's in trouble. I'm going to need your help."

She had a right to be angry, but she didn't waste time punishing him. "All right, what do you want me to do?"

He filled the bucket with warm water from the stove's boiler and looked over his shoulder as he hurried out. "Bring some soap. I won't know what we'll have to do until we find out what the problem is."

Beth followed him and watched while he took off his shirt and lathered an arm. His ribs protested as he stretched out on the barn floor and felt inside Shiloh for the foal. The first thing his fingers touched was a small tail. A biggish foal, coming rear-end first, stuck like a cork in a bottle and getting dry. He should have been in here helping her hours ago.

"Damn, it's breech."

Beth knelt down to stroke Shiloh's damp neck, brushing away bits of straw, her blue eyes filled with worry. "So what do we do?"

Trey got up and took a couple of careful breaths. *Good question.* Losing this foal would be a major setback. He didn't want to think about losing the mare. It might already be too late.

"Well, the foal can't be born as it is, so we're going to have to push it back in and turn it around."

"Have you ever done that before?"

Trey ran his clean hand through his hair, wishing with all his heart he could answer differently. "No, but I've seen it done once, the night Cloud was born. We've got to get ropes on the front feet and the muzzle then one of us has to push on the foal's backside while the other pulls on the ropes. I'll do the pushing."

146

"All right." She had the grace to hide her doubts. Beth stayed by Shiloh while Trey took a soft cotton rope from a hook, cut it and tied a slipknot in one end.

"Hold her head and keep her down. I don't want a broken arm."

Beth held the mare's halter with one hand and kept stroking her. "You're going to be fine, Shiloh. In a little while you're going to have a beautiful baby."

Trey rested his hand on Shiloh's sleek flank. She was a fine mare with a sweet temperament, and she deserved better than what he'd given her today. "She will, if I have any say about it. She's too good to lose." He got down on the straw again, reached into Shiloh and started feeling his way along the foal's side. It twitched as his hand moved over its ribs.

"It's still alive." An instant later, the mare squeezed his arm numb with a powerful contraction. As soon as enough feeling returned, he reached further and got his fingers around a front hoof. The loop slid over it, then slipped off again before he could pull it tight. He used a couple of words he hadn't said in years and tried again.

Hallelujah. This time it held. Trey flashed Beth a grin.

"Got it. Now for the other one."

The second leg proved more difficult. Vital minutes ticked away before he managed to snare it. Sitting by the mare's head, Beth kept up a flow of soft, encouraging words. Trey knew Shiloh meant almost as much to her as she did to him. Getting the last rope on the muzzle took more precious time. At last Trey got up, caught his breath and handed the ropes to Beth.

"Right, we're in business. I'll push. You pull when I tell you."

By timing their efforts with the mare's contractions, they gradually turned the foal until it was coming head and front feet first. Two more contractions had the foal on the ground, a little filly with a coat like crumpled black velvet. Her muzzle had been scraped pink in places by the rope, and she wasn't breathing.

"Clear her nostrils." As Beth wiped the remaining membrane away, Trey pushed sharply a few times on the foal's ribs. They both cheered when she sucked in air with a convulsive jerk.

Shiloh got to her feet, shook bits of straw from her coat with a snort, as if to say, 'I'm glad *that's* over,' then nudged Trey out of the way so she could get close to her foal. The little black filly trembled as her mother's rough tongue dragged over her. Trey and Beth stood back and let Shiloh finish cleaning up her baby. Beth's voice hovered on the edge of tears, hushed with amazement.

"I've never seen anything born before."

Trey felt the wonder, too. It never got old, but seeing Beth's reaction made it even better.

"What do you think?"

She shook her head. "It's . . . incredible. I can't describe it, so I won't try."

Blood-smeared, sweating, pumped with success and with the glow in Beth's eyes, Trey stood there watching her. It took a stern effort of will to step away.

"I'd better go clean up."

A pink flush colored the eastern sky. The night had flown while they worked. When Trey returned to the barn after washing, Beth was watching the foal struggle to stand. Trey pulled on his shirt and moistened his dry mouth.

"Beth, I'm sorry for taking off like I did earlier, but I needed to think. I met someone in the saloon, someone from home. He brought back memories I'd rather do without."

She turned to face him. "I know. Trey, I have to confess. I eavesdropped at the saloon window. I couldn't help myself. I saw you punch Gabe, and I saw your face when that other man came in. Is there any way I can help?"

The uncertain look in her eyes made Trey's chest tighten. He reached out then dropped his hand again. "Well, while I was thinking, I was mostly thinking about you."

"What about me?"

He realized his fists were clenched and released them. If he didn't find the words now, he didn't think he ever would. "Well, about us. Beth, I know you deserve better than I've got here. You've got your art and I couldn't blame you—"

Beth cut him off as she stepped forward. "I told you before I can make up my own mind. Trey, things have never been that important to me. I've always had too many of them. And I'm doing better work here than I've done before." Close enough to touch, she held his gaze. "I'm not anxious to be anywhere else."

The emotion Trey saw on her face dried up his voice. Beth's lips parted as she watched him, then she reached for his mouth and he met her half way.

This time Trey couldn't keep his hunger back. He kissed her hard and deep, spurred on by Beth's sigh of pleasure and the boldness of her response. She explored his mouth as eagerly as he did hers, while her hands fisted in the back of his shirt, holding him to her.

The small sounds of pleasure she made shot through Trey like liquid fire. The reality of her was as sweet as his dreams had been . . . no, sweeter.

Make her yours. Lips still clinging to hers, body overriding his mind, Trey backed Beth into an unoccupied stall filled with hay. He lowered her onto the fragrant pile and buried his mouth against her neck, losing himself in the warm, welcoming taste of her, making himself dizzy with her scent. He fumbled with the top buttons of her blouse and reached inside, cupping her breast through the thin fabric underneath. Trey's breath caught at the feel of her, soft but firm and subtly round, her nipple tight and hard. His own hardness pressed against Beth's hip, demanding release.

She breathed a sigh against his hair and slid her hand inside his unbuttoned shirt. Her fingers trailed down his back as she arched against him, giving him more of her breast. Through a haze of need, Trey heard one of the horses blow softly.

The sound brought him back to reality. He was losing control, and Beth deserved a damn sight better than to be deflowered in a barn. He groaned, rolled away from her and sat up.

"I'm sorry, Beth. I didn't mean to go so far."

"I didn't stop you." Her morning-colored eyes wide and dreamy, lips wet and swollen from his kisses, Beth buttoned her blouse. Trey settled her in the crook of his arm, closed his eyes and rested his forehead against her hair. This tender feeling was harder to fight than lust.

"Where did you come from? Where do witches like you come from?"

With a quiet laugh, Beth reached up to stroke his cheek. "You know where I'm from. Trey . . . there are so many things I'd like to know about you."

Icy fingers of fear stole around his heart. *Don't ask questions I can't answer.* "Like what?"

"Oh, silly little things mostly." Beth drew back to see his face. "When's your birthday? I never thought to ask before."

The tension in Trey's gut eased a bit. "September third. When's yours?"

"June twentieth." Beth found Trey's hand and linked her fingers with his. That dangerous tenderness grew. "What's your favorite food?"

"Well, that stew you made the other day was good."

Her voice turned playfully stern. "Tell the truth."

"All right. I'd have to say chicken fricassee and pecan pie." Memories of home rushed in, tangling with Trey's heightened awareness of Beth so close beside him. She rolled her eyes and smiled.

"Aunt Abigail's cook used to say she'd never known a man with a soul above pie." Beth's face turned serious as she lifted their joined hands to his knee. "Trey, who was that old . . . acquaintance of yours?"

Of course she wouldn't leave it alone. Trey couldn't keep the irritation from his voice.

151

"His name's Nathan Munroe. The last time we met I flattened his nose for him."

Beth squeezed his fingers, her eyes soft and calm on his. "Why?"

"Why? He'd been calling me a coward all over the place that spring before the war started, because I wasn't chomping at the bit to fight. When he finally said it to my face, I shut his mouth."

Beth tilted her head to one side, her kiss-swollen lips pressed together in thought, looking utterly tempting. "I don't blame you, but he sounded like he wanted to forget it. People change."

Knowing he'd kiss her again if he didn't, Trey got up. "Nate always was a bully and I'd bet he still is. It was nine years ago, Beth. Forget it." He needed to put some distance between them. His eyes felt gritty from lack of sleep, but he doubted if his body would let him rest. He didn't know where he and Beth were going to end up, but it sure was turning into one hell of a journey.

CHAPTER 11

Nathan walked down the steps of the boarding house smiling. He'd just eaten the best lunch he'd had in months. Mrs. Grant had told the truth – no one would complain about her cooking. Nor was that his only reason to feel pleased with himself.

He'd gotten wind of a poker game happening at Neil's place later on that night. Two men in from the mining country had taken rooms at Mrs. Grant's just before supper yesterday, planning to blow off a little steam before heading for Denver to spend some serious money – serious from their perspective at least. There would be a few hundred dollars up for grabs in the game tonight, and they'd let it be known they were looking for takers.

That kind of news would spread quickly, with predictable results. The players wouldn't be the only people interested in the game's stakes. If trouble came up, Nathan intended to be the one to deal with it.

Those men with the money didn't seem like cautious types. They could well have been followed. It would be smart to have a look around town, but Nathan didn't have a horse. He could gamble and spend some of his remaining cash, but maybe there was a better way.

He headed down the street toward the forge. John came out of the yard to meet him.

"Morning, Nathan. I wanted to let you know we're going to get started on the jail this week. The council hasn't made it official, but you're the only person in the running for the sheriff's job and I don't see much point in waiting any longer."

Don't count your chickens just yet, Nate. "Thanks. I was hoping you'd lend me a horse for the day. Have you heard about the card game happening tonight?"

"No. Big one?"

Nathan shrugged. "Fairly. Big enough to attract some attention. I'd like to look around outside of town, see if anyone's around."

John nodded toward the three stalls at the side of the forge yard. "Sure. Take your pick."

Nathan chose a stocky sorrel gelding and did a slow circle around town. He saw no one until he rode along the wagon track leading north. Not far from the road, a thin belt of woods offered some shelter. Nathan rode closer and spotted a couple of horses almost hidden by the trees.

That didn't make much sense at this time of day, unless the riders didn't want to be seen in town. Fine, he would oblige them for now. He'd know the horses if he saw them again.

Nathan kept riding north, passing the occasional homestead, until he came to the top of a hill and saw a horse coming toward him at a full gallop, with its rider crouched low over its neck. He must be in one hell of a hurry. Nathan pulled off the road and waited.

Not he, she. An auburn-haired young woman, wearing pants and riding astride on a long-legged chestnut mare that looked no more than warmed up by the run.

It didn't take much guesswork to figure out who she was. Not many people out here would own a horse like that.

Nathan took the woman in with a glance as she brought her mare to a neat stop beside him. When she reached up to tuck some loose hair back into her long, thick braid, Nathan recalled Cathy Sinclair. Apparently Trey's taste in women hadn't changed any more than his taste in horses. He'd found himself a very attractive wife.

Her way of holding her head reminded Nathan of his mother, who'd made a religion out of being a lady. This girl had as much breeding as the horse she rode. A big step up for a farmer's son like Trey.

"Hello, Mister Munroe." So Trey had mentioned their meeting. From her expression Nathan guessed Trey had also told her about their long-ago fight, but she seemed to be reserving judgment.

"Hello. It's Missus McShannon, isn't it?"

Her delicate brows lifted. "Yes, it is. How did you know my name?"

"I knew your husband years ago. You and that mare would both have suited him then. I just put two and two together."

Color rose to her cheeks, setting off those blue eyes. When the mare sidestepped and tugged at the bit, Beth controlled her with a deft, unconscious movement. Yes, Trey had done well for himself. Nathan couldn't resist giving her a teasing smile as he tipped his hat. "I see you've got your hands full. It's a fine day for a ride. I won't keep you. I'm sure I'll be seeing you in town."

Trey's wife responded with a polite nod, but didn't return his smile. "I'm sure. Goodbye, Mister Munroe." She nudged her horse forward again and didn't look back.

Nathan watched as the mare's ground-eating strides took her out of sight. Trey had probably spent the war years out here, building a home. Now here he was, healthy and whole, with her to share it.

Charlie Bascomb and John Hughes and Justin, so many of the others killed . . . such a damned waste, and for what? He'd thought about that more since running into Trey than he had in years.

As for himself, he'd always been the type who had to learn the hard way. Nathan turned back toward town, surprised at the dull ache in his gut. He recognized it as loneliness, but he'd thought he'd gotten too used to it to notice it anymore.

Then he thought of Lorie and the ache began to ease. It didn't occur to Nathan to judge her. People did what they had to do to survive, and for a woman alone in a man's world, that wasn't easy.

Before the war, Nathan had been expected to marry a lady like Beth, all cool self-possession. He smiled to himself. He guessed there was plenty of fire underneath the poise, but he'd never found her type particularly appealing. A little hellion like Lorie, now, that was another story. Once he had a job and a place to live, he'd go see her like he'd promised. Maybe, just maybe, it was time to settle down.

* * * *

Maddy looked up from her butter molds at the sound of a horse in the yard. When she saw Chance trot by the window, she set the butter in the pantry cupboard and wiped her hands on a rag. Beth, right on time for a sewing lesson.

156

When she pulled up a chair at the kitchen table, it struck Maddy that Beth looked very different than she had the day of her bread-making lesson almost a month ago. She had a tan now, and her hair had taken on highlights from the sun. She usually wore it in a braid or a loose knot instead of a careful bun. She'd gained a little weight and it suited her, but the biggest difference was in her eyes. The girl had found her feet, and Maddy wondered if Beth hadn't found something else besides.

Beth un-wrapped a parcel, and laid a length of red muslin on the table. "I can't get used to not having curtains at my windows, even though there's no one around for miles. This will brighten the place up, won't it?"

"I think so." Maddy went to the bedroom for her sewing basket and pulled out her scissors. "Let's get them cut out."

After they measured and cut the fabric, Beth practiced pressing the remnants. She scorched one scrap and burned a finger slightly before she got the feel of Maddy's iron, but she got the curtains pressed and ready to sew. They each took a panel and stitched quietly for a few minutes, until Beth noticed Maddy watching her.

"Am I doing something wrong? Aunt Abigail thought needlework was vital to a lady's education, but she never taught me to sew a plain seam. I think this looks fairly even."

Maddy smiled. "No, you aren't doing anything wrong. You look happy."

Beth looked down at her sewing. "Maybe hopeful's a better word. You know, Maddy, when I came here I knew how to set a table for a formal dinner, but I couldn't cook. I could tell you what kind of a dish to serve vegetables in, but I couldn't grow them. I could make a point lace handkerchief, but I couldn't sew. I'd been riding for years, but I'd never saddled a horse. Now I can do all those things." She adjusted the fabric in her lap and ran her needle into it again, pursing her lips in concentration. "Trey would have lost Shiloh's foal last week and probably Shiloh, too, if I hadn't been there to help. If he'd had to go for someone else, it would have been too late. It feels good to do something that matters. At home the only thing I did that actually had a result was my painting."

"I'm glad." Maddy decided to do a little harmless probing. She pulled a box from a cupboard and took out a length of royal blue cotton. "I'm going to make this up for the spring dance next month. What do you think?" Beth had to know about the dance. There were posters all over town.

Beth fingered the material. "It's beautiful, just the color for you. I'm going to wear something I already have . . . no, I'm not." She dropped her sewing in her lap and eyed Maddy with sudden determination. "None of my dresses would be right and most of them are too tight now. I'll make something. There's some lovely organdy at the store. Trey told me about the dance the other day. I'm looking forward to it."

For the past five years Wallace Flats had been holding two dances a year, one in June and one at Christmas. They were the town's only public social events and everyone who could walk attended, but Maddy knew Beth wouldn't be looking this pleased about it unless things were going well at home.

"We'd better get working on these curtains then. Making a dress will take some time. The Bakers have some good patterns to choose from. What do you have in mind, something special?"

Beth blushed, giving Maddy another clue. "Maybe a little. I'll get a pattern the next time I'm in town."

Maddy smiled to herself. She'd liked Trey from the start, and she'd come to like Beth as well. The changes in her, coupled with some comments Logan had made lately about Trey – 'I'll be glad when those two get things settled so he'll be good for something again' was the gist of it – led to some pleasing conclusions.

You're a meddler, Maddy Kinsley, and you always will be. Just keep your nose out of it and see what happens.

* * * *

Beth got home at twilight and found Trey in the corral with Ben and Calico, in the middle of a training session. She dismounted and leaned on the corral fence to watch. Since his meeting with Gabe, Trey had insisted on going back to work, cautiously at first. It hadn't bothered him except for his ribs, which he ignored.

Trey got a firmer grip on Calico's halter while fifteen-year-old Ben, a taller, much lankier version of John, lowered a saddle onto the trembling horse's back. As soon as the mustang felt the weight, he bolted. Trey hung on and did his best to stay with him, following him around the corral until he managed to bring him to a halt. Very slowly, as Trey and Ben both fussed over him, Calico relaxed.

Ben swore under his breath as he lifted off the saddle. "I can't believe he's still this spooky. Are you sure this is going to work?"

Trey took the halter in his other hand and shook out his tired arm. "You've got to remember Calico's a wild animal. When he feels something on his back, his instinct tells him it's a cougar. He'll never be just like a farm-bred horse, but he'll learn to trust you if you give him enough time."

Ben's shoulders slumped. "At this rate I still won't be riding him at Christmas. Sometimes I think I should just turn him loose."

Busy with the horse, Trey looked over his shoulder at the boy. "He wouldn't survive, not now, without his herd. He'll learn, but if you rush things he'll never really accept you and you'll never be able to trust him."

Ben took a deep breath and hoisted the saddle again. "All right, Cal, one more time."

This time Calico stood still, shaking, when the saddle touched him. Ben broke into a wide grin.

"That's better. It's not the end of the world, is it? Especially when it gets you carrots."

While Calico munched his reward, Trey tied a rope to the halter. "Here, Ben, lead him around a bit and let him get used to it."

After a couple of turns around the corral, they decided to end the lesson on a good note and headed for the barn. Beth followed with Chance. Cloud pinned back his ears and kicked the wall as Calico passed his stall. Ben shook his head at the sound.

"I'll bet you had a time with him."

Trey closed Calico's stall door behind him and rolled his eyes. "Oh, yeah. I was just about your age. Dad gave me advice and an extra pair of hands when I needed it, but he left the training to me. Cloud wasn't like Calico, though. He wasn't scared, just stubborn. He wanted things his own way. Then he figured out that being ridden meant he got to go places and run."

Ben lifted the saddle to its peg and looked over his shoulder, grinning. "Come on, Trey. Do you really think he figured that out?"

"Sure he did. A horse like him won't give in. You have to come to an agreement. We did, but that doesn't stop him from trying to rewrite it once in a while, even now." Trey slipped an arm around Beth as she came out of Chance's stall. She hid a smile when Ben joined them. John had passed along his son's first impression of her after church on Sunday.

"He asked me if I thought that agency would still be around in ten years. You hit him between the eyes, Beth."

Ben treated Trey like an older brother, but he was painfully shy with Beth. His face reddened now as he looked down at her. "Miss Beth, I want—I need to ask you a favor."

"Of course, Ben. What is it?"

"Well, I need to learn how to dance. Ma will give me no peace if I ask her, so . . . ."

Ben's voice died away in embarrassment. Trey quirked an eyebrow. "Who is she?"

"Her name's Holly Grier. I asked her to the dance today, and she said she'd go with me if her father would let her. I figure I'd better practice."

"It's not difficult, Ben. Come here, I'll show you." Beth stood beside him and showed him a waltz step. "Watch my feet. One-two-three, one-two-three, like this."

After Ben imitated her steps a few times, Beth placed his hand on her shoulder and took his other hand in hers. "Now you do it and I'll follow you. Ready? One-two-three, one-two-three . . ." Ben took a few tentative steps, then missed a beat and brought his foot down on her toes. Beth caught a glimpse of the grin on Trey's face before he ducked into Cheyenne's stall. Ben's blush deepened.

"Sorry."

Beth put his hand on her shoulder again and vowed to settle Mr. McShannon's hash later. "Never mind, Ben, you'll get it. One-two-three, one-two-three . . ."

After two more tries, Ben managed to circle the aisle with just a bit of stiffness. He looked profoundly relieved when they stopped. "Thanks. Now I just hope Holly's father lets her go. Trey, do you know him?"

Trey came back to the aisle, frowning. "No, but Simon Grier's not well thought of in town, I'm sure you've heard that. I've seen him a couple of times slumped over a table in Neil's place. I'd say he spends most of his time and money there. By the look of his farm, he isn't spending much of either on it."

Ben glanced down at his feet as he shifted from one to the other. "I know. You've probably seen Holly at church. Her mother died a long time ago. I don't think Holly remembers her at all. I just wondered . . . a couple of times last year she came to school with bruises on her face. When I asked her what happened she said something about tripping and falling, but it didn't make much sense. Then one time, she was out for a week. She said she was sick, but I'm pretty sure she was lying. I wanted to tell Dad, but she made me promise not to. If I knew for sure . . ."

Trey's jaw tightened. A dangerous glow built in his dark eyes. Beth felt just the same. She knew as well as he did that legally, the girl would be better protected if she were a horse.

"If it happens again, tell your father anyway," Trey said. "He and I will deal with it."

After Ben left, Beth had to vent her anger. "Trey, I don't care what the law says. That man should be in jail."

Trey sat on the grain barrel and looked up at her in frustration. "I know, but if Simon did go to prison, what would happen to Holly? He keeps a roof over her head, more or less. You should see the place. Poor kid." He got up, walked into Cloud's stall with a pitchfork and stabbed it into the straw. "If I find out he's hit her again, he's going to wish he'd never been born."

CHAPTER 12

After supper, Nathan sat watching the street from the window of his room. When he heard the men who'd talked up the card game going downstairs, he waited a few minutes and followed.

A boisterous mixture of music and voices poured from Neil's place, but the benches out front were empty. Nathan waited in the alley beside the saloon, watching the quiet street. Just after dark the two horses he'd seen outside of town appeared. He kept himself in shadow while he took careful note of the riders.

The chatter inside the saloon died down as the card game got into full swing. When Nathan glanced in there were eight men at the table; the two who'd stayed at the boarding house, and six locals. Nathan recognized Derek Blake, the telegraph operator, and Carl Manning's companion from the other night. The rest he didn't know. The two men who'd ridden in earlier were nowhere to be seen.

Nathan slipped inside, unnoticed, and watched the game from a quiet corner. At the moment, Carl's friend seemed to be having the luck. Nathan heard Derek Blake call him Bruce. There were glasses on the table, but none of the players looked like they'd been drinking much yet.

Derek played smart poker, unobtrusively winning small pots and losing very little. The stakes hadn't started to climb yet. One of the mining men was a risk-taker, betting and bluffing on low odds. Bruce was simply reckless, riding his luck.

After a few minutes, Nathan spotted the two men he was looking for, keeping an eye on the game from the opposite side of the room. Then he noticed a glance pass between one of the strangers at the table and one of the watchers. As the game went on, Nathan realized Bruce's luck seemed to depend on who was dealing. The two strangers were giving him consistently better hands. At other times, he completed hands when the odds were very much against it.

The stakes got higher. Derek bowed out, a little bit ahead of the game. One by one, the others were cleaned out. When the last hand had been played, Bruce was left holding seven hundred dollars. Three hundred came from the strangers, the rest from the local players.

With the post-game celebration in full swing, Nathan slipped out and waited in the shadows of the saloon. Bruce staggered out well after midnight. The two men Nathan had seen ride in weren't far behind.

It always amazed him how predictable these things were. The strangers would follow Bruce a few blocks down the road, then pull him into an alley, knock him unconscious and steal the money they'd helped him win. It was no more difficult and a lot less risky than cheating to win the money themselves. They'd split the profits with their two associates who'd set up the game, and all four of them would walk away a hundred dollars richer. Not bad for a place this size.

Nathan didn't bother to go after them. He'd seen that Bruce wasn't carrying a gun and these were con men, not murderers. He figured a knock on the head might teach Bruce something. Instead, he untied the strangers' horses and hurried them in behind the saloon while the men were out of sight. When they came back, they found Nathan standing where their horses had been. They didn't look impressed.

"Mister, did you see anyone walk off with the horses that were tied here?" one of them demanded. His clean-cut face would look out of place on a wanted poster. He would be the front man, Nathan thought. His partner wasn't quite as straight looking.

Nathan kept his face grave. "No, afraid not. Too many other things on my mind."

The strangers looked suspicious, but they wouldn't want a scene. "Well, come on," the one with the face growled to his partner. "We'd better find them."

Nathan casually lifted his hand to rest it on the hitching rail, holding his revolver. "Before you go, gentlemen, I think there are some folks inside who want to talk to you. Then again, they'd probably be just as glad not to see your faces again as long as they got their money back."

"Who the hell do you think you are?" the tough-looking one snapped.

Nathan grinned. "Does it matter? This gun doesn't care who pulls the trigger. Now I've got an idea. If you give me the money you just took from that fool, and then go in there and get your friends, you can all ride out of here alive. Otherwise, the odds are pretty good that some of you won't. I'll give you five minutes before I go in and tell folks what happened out here. I wouldn't care much for your chances then. And gentlemen, I'll be wiring descriptions of the four of you around the territory tomorrow. This party's over."

He waited, knowing what they were thinking. They were both wearing guns. They knew they could kill him, but not without at least one of them getting hurt and certainly not without drawing a lot of attention. It wasn't worth it. With a glance at his companion, the front man pulled the money from his pocket.

"Just bring it over here and put it in my left jacket pocket," Nate told him. With the gun pointed squarely at his head, the man did. "Right. Your horses are out back. You've got five minutes."

The men ducked into the saloon. Three minutes later, they came out with their two friends. Once they'd ridden off, Nathan stepped inside and climbed up on a chair. The room gradually went silent when he waved the money in the air.

"Folks, I've got some cash here that some of you lost in that game this evening. It was rigged, but the gentlemen who set it up kind of changed their minds. Since we've got no place to lock them up I decided to let them go, but they got something to think about. Your money's here, and I figure the town can use theirs."

By ten o'clock the next morning, everyone in town had heard the story. By noon, Nathan Munroe was sheriff of Wallace Flats.

He got paid in advance.

CHAPTER 13

Beth stood at the dry goods counter, breathing in the scents of molasses and peppermint as she flipped through a catalog of dress patterns. She'd never had trouble deciding on a style for a dressmaker to sew for her, but choosing one she could make herself was another matter. Wavering between two patterns, Beth looked up when the bell above the door jangled. June spoke to the person coming in.

"Hello, Holly, haven't seen you in a while."

"Hello, Missus Baker," a young voice answered.

This must be Ben's friend. Beth stole a look at her out of the corner of her eye.

Holly seemed aptly named. In her red calico dress, with her dark green eyes, pale skin, black hair and delicate features, she would have been a good choice for the role of a winter sprite in a Shakespearean play. No wonder Ben was smitten.

Holly walked over and stood looking at the bolts of fabric on the wall. When she saw the smoky-blue organdy Beth had laid on the counter she reached out to touch it, then drew her hand back. When her eyes met Beth's she blushed.

"It's a beautiful color."

Beth smiled and laid a hand on the fabric. "Isn't it? I'm trying to find a pattern for it – one that isn't too difficult."

Holly looked up and down the shelves. When she spotted a spring green cotton, figured with leaves of darker green that matched her eyes, her face lit up. She had a good sense of color. After a quick mental calculation, Beth made up her mind. Watching the girl, she reached for the green fabric, laid it beside the organdy and unrolled a yard or two.

"Did I hear Missus Baker call you Holly?"

"Yes, Ma'am."

"My name's Beth McShannon. Ben Reeves boards his horse with us. He and his parents are friends of ours. Holly, I've never made a dress before and I don't know how I'm going to get this done in time for the dance. I wonder if you might know someone who could help me with it, for the price of a dress length of this cotton?"

Holly hesitated. She'd have to ask her father, of course. Beth wanted to see him and get an idea whether Ben's suspicions were true.

"Well, I can sew, Ma'am, but I'm usually needed at home when I'm not at school. I could probably work a couple of Saturday afternoons between now and the dance, but I can't promise when. Oh, there's Pa now."

The man who had just entered the store looked surly and mean, but Beth thought that most of all he looked defeated. A fairly big man, he appeared to have shrunk into himself. His hair must have once been black like Holly's, but it was graying now. He kept his gaze fixed on the floor. Beth could easily see him bullying someone smaller and weaker.

"Mister Grier, may I speak with you for a moment?"

He glanced at her out of dull gray eyes before his gaze slid to the floor again. "You're speaking to me now."

He didn't sound as if he cared to listen. With her doubts growing, Beth introduced herself.

"I was just telling your daughter I could use help with some dressmaking. If you could spare Holly for a couple of afternoons I'd be willing to pay her two dollars, along with a piece of fabric."

Simon grunted and gave her a suspicious glare, but as Beth had hoped, he couldn't resist the money. No doubt Holly would have to give that to him, but it was the dress she wanted. He shrugged as he turned away.

"She can suit herself." Simon jerked his head toward the door. "Well, come on girl, let's go."

"Missus Baker's not finished with our order yet, Pa. This lady was first. It'll be another fifteen minutes or so," Holly lied coolly. Beth could see that Mrs. Baker had just finished putting the Griers' small order together. When Simon walked out a faint gleam of mischief came to his daughter's eyes. Life hadn't taken the fight out of her yet. Remembering his tone as he spoke to Holly, Beth repressed an urge to call the man back and give him an unbridled piece of her mind.

With Simon gone, she chose the last pattern she'd looked at. "All right, Holly, I guess it's going to be this pattern for me. Find one for yourself, then help me find whatever else we're going to need. We've got a couple of dresses to make."

* * * *

The morning after the sheriff's office and jail were completed, Nathan walked over to the saloon for coffee. He leaned on the bar and looked around the empty room while Neil filled his cup.

"Lorie around?"

Neil turned in the general direction of Lorie's room and shouted. "Lorie, man here looking for you!"

Nathan grinned. "Thanks, Neil. You're a real helpful man."

When Lorie came out, Nathan realized he'd never seen her so early in the day before. She wasn't wearing any makeup, though she had on one of her usual revealing dresses. It did a better job of opening his eyes than the coffee.

When she recognized him, she stopped halfway across the room. Nathan walked over to join her.

"I told you I'd be coming around, Lorie. Feel like taking a walk?"

She smiled and shook her head. "No thanks, Nate."

He sat at a table beside her and took a sip from his mug. "You said you'd see me on your own time."

Running her fingers through hair that hadn't seen a brush since yesterday, Lorie sat across from him. "I've changed my mind. My choice."

Nathan looked into her eyes and felt their impact like a solid punch. "Why?"

"That's my business, Nate."

He took another sip and let a grin spread slowly across his face. So, she was going to make this interesting.

"Lorie, have you heard the news?"

"Your news, you mean? Yeah, I heard. Congratulations."

"Thanks. Well, the jail was finished yesterday and it's a shame to keep it empty. I guess you're going to have to come along for that walk after all. You're under arrest."

She laughed and Nathan decided he liked to hear it, almost as much as he liked the edge to her voice when she spoke.

"You're joking."

She got up to leave, but Nathan reached for her wrist and held it just hard enough to let her know he wasn't going to let go. "Lorie, I don't have handcuffs and I'd look a sight hauling you down the street in broad daylight. It'd make a lot more sense for you to just come with me."

Lorie sat back and smiled. Nathan kept his eyes on hers, telling her he wasn't giving her a choice. After a few seconds, she sighed and got up.

"All right, have your fun, Nate. It's no skin off my nose."

She walked with him down the street to the new sheriff's office. The small building smelled of sawdust and new lumber. A room off to the side contained a bunk and a washstand. The main room had a desk at one end with a window behind it, and three cells at the other. Lorie's smile disappeared when Nathan walked her into one of them, beat her to the door and locked it.

"Nate, a joke's a joke, but this has gone far enough. I've got things to do today. Let me out of here."

He slipped the cell key into his pocket and grinned at her through the bars. "If I want to, I can keep you here 'til the circuit judge arrives next month. Soliciting's very illegal, you know."

Lorie completely lost her sense of humor. "Next *month!* Listen, you bastard, if you keep me in here my customers will pull this shack down around your ears." She stepped forward and rattled the bars as if she could pull them down herself. *"Now let me out of here!"*

Nathan sat and put his feet up on his new desk. "Well, we can talk about bail, but I want to ask you a few questions first."

Lorie glared at him with pure fury. He figured he knew what she was thinking. 'Keep it professional' had always been her rule. Now, here she was in a mess she wasn't sure she could get out of. Nate intended to keep her off-balance. At the moment, it was worthwhile to see her eyes spitting sparks at him.

"You've got no right to ask me anything."

Nathan shrugged and started unwrapping packages from a small pile on the desk. "Fine. I don't object to company."

Lorie threw herself on the bed against the wall and turned her back on him while he stocked his desk with paper and supplies. When lunchtime came, he went to the boarding house and brought back food for both of them. He half-expected her to throw hers in his face, but she huffed at him and then cleaned her plate. Nathan guessed she'd gone without breakfast. Anyway, she was smart enough to know dousing him with Harriet's beef and barley soup wouldn't get him to turn her loose.

With another mutinous look, Lorie pushed her empty soup plate under the cell door. "All right, ask your damn questions and make it quick."

Nathan picked up the plate and sat again, watching her. "Lorie, how long have you been here?"

"Five years."

"Have you ever looked for any other kind of work?"

Lorie returned to the bunk, pulled her feet up and rolled her eyes. "Spare me the reforming speech, please. I like what I do. I'm my own boss, the money isn't bad and I'm putting some away. I work when I want and come and go as I please." She hugged her knees, then let them go and straightened her shoulders. "If I don't like a man's looks, I tell him to get lost, and if he gives me trouble Neil handles it, or else I just handle it myself." Lorie fingered the gold pendant lying at the top of her cleavage. "A lot of the women who cross the street when they see me can't spend a nickel at the store or walk from one end of town to the other without asking their husbands. I'm a free woman, Nate, and I intend to stay free. If you're going to make that difficult for me, I'll be moving on."

Nathan knew she meant it. He'd better not push her too hard. He took his feet off his desk and looked out the window behind it.

"Tell me something else, Lorie. As a kid, what did you dream of being?"

Lorie snorted. "Well, I sure didn't dream about a husband and brats and a house with a white picket fence. My parents cured me of that."

"So what was it then?"

"Nothing."

Nathan grinned, picked up his keys and dangled them from a finger. "Lorie, do you want out of here today or not?"

She kicked off a dainty sequined shoe and sent it skittering across the cell floor. "Oh, go to hell, Nate. I wanted to be a teacher. I did all right as a student, and I finished school before I left home." She retrieved her shoe and jammed her foot into it. "As if any mother would send her kid to school with me teaching."

"There are other towns, Lorie." Nathan unlocked the cell door and looked her in the eye before he opened it. "I'm going to let you out without bail, but you aren't to leave town. If you do, you'll find yourself back in here waiting for the judge." He took her arm as she brushed by him. "And I'm going to come around once in a while for a walk or a chat. There's no law against you having a friend."

She stopped and glanced up at him. "A friend? I'm not sure I know what the word means."

Nathan smiled. "I'm not sure I do either. See you later, Lorie."

CHAPTER 14

Trey stared over Cloud's back at the street while John pulled the nails from a front shoe. When the horse shifted his weight and leaned on him, John dug him in the ribs and glanced up in exasperation.

"Trey, if you expect me to hold him in my lap as well as shoe him, it's going to cost you double—no—make that triple."

Trey came back to earth and made Cloud straighten up. John pulled off the shoe, put the hoof down and turned to see what had caught Trey's attention.

Nathan was walking toward them. John felt the tension in the air as soon as the man entered the forge yard.

"Morning, John."

"Hey, Nate. Trey, have you met our new sheriff?"

"We've met." John wondered at Trey's curtness, but then again, Trey had shown a surprising lack of interest when John told him about Nathan's appointment.

Nathan addressed himself to John. "I'm looking to buy a horse. Do you know anyone who's got something decent for sale?"

John's pulse quickened a little. He liked nothing better than haggling over a horse, and the ones he rented out were always for sale. "That depends on what you call decent."

Nathan nodded at Cloud. "Well, I'm not expecting to find anything like this one. He looks as good as he did nine years ago."

Trey didn't answer. John looked from him to Nathan, wondering where the animosity was coming from. Nine years ago? They would have been boys. He couldn't see Trey holding a grudge that long unless it went pretty deep.

Nathan went on as if nothing was amiss. "You haven't got anything for sale, have you?"

Trey responded in a flat tone. "No, I've just got my brood mares and a young foal. I'm still getting started. I had to buy young."

They exchanged a less than friendly glance, then Nathan turned to rest a hand on Cloud's back. "So, you're raising horses out here?"

"Raising giraffes, you mean," John scoffed. "He works cattle with this bean-pole. I don't know how. Must be like turning a freight train."

Trey ignored him. "I'm starting to, after feeding them for four years. Just had the first foal."

Nathan glanced at Trey over his shoulder. "I was out north of town the day of the poker game and came across your wife going like a bat out of hell on one of your mares. Figures. Well, where should I look?"

John grinned and nodded toward the stalls across the yard. "I've got three."

"Thanks, but they're too good for what I can pay right now."

"Well then, do you know Dale Turner? He might have something for sale. You might want to go to Denver. You aren't going to find much to choose from out here."

Nathan gave Cloud a final pat and turned to leave. "I've met Dale. I'll talk to him. See you around."

John picked up another hoof as Trey watched Nathan walk out of the yard. "Where did you two meet?"

Trey shrugged and took his place by Cloud's head again. "We were neighbors growing up. We never got along."

John glanced at him and knew that was all the answer he was going to get. "Well, let's get this done. And keep him from leaning, will you?"

* * * *

Nathan had moved into the room attached to his office, but he still ate at the boarding house. After leaving the forge he headed there for lunch. When he'd finished, he took a piece of Harriet's corn bread over to Lorie.

He found her sitting on her usual bench at the saloon. He saw her body tense when he sat beside her.

"You look nervous. I can't believe you're afraid of me, Lorie."

She shifted on the bench and snapped at him. "I'm not nervous. Why would I be?"

Nathan gave her a sharp glance then smiled. "I am. I'm no more used to having friends than you are." He handed her the cornbread in a napkin. "Here, I brought you this from Mrs. Grant's. Eat it while it's still warm."

Lorie put the napkin down beside her on the bench and looked him in the eye. "Why are you doing this?"

Nathan leaned back and made himself comfortable. "Because I like your company better than I like sitting in my office. Is that so surprising?"

A middle-aged woman passing the saloon gave them a scathing look. Nathan beamed at her. "Lovely afternoon, isn't it, Missus Montrose?"

Mrs. Montrose snorted and quickened her pace. Lorie watched her with a sardonic smile. "If she knew how much time and money her son spends here, she'd bust a corset string."

Nathan chuckled. He'd met Jake Montrose in an official capacity a couple of times already. "Probably. If my mother knew how much time I spend here, and with whom, I know she would. I bet she'd be a lot more comfortable afterward, though."

Lorie didn't look as if the thought made her more comfortable. Nathan wouldn't be surprised if she could make some good guesses about his background. He knew there were still traces of it about him, though he rarely thought about it. She proved him right a second later.

"Where are your parents, Nate?"

He pulled out his pipe, clamped it between his teeth and filled it. There had never been any sentiment in his memories of home. "Well, Father's gone. After he lost our place, he had a stroke. Mother lives with her sister in Savannah."

"Do you have brothers or sisters?"

"No." Nathan knew now that once his father had a son he'd lost interest in having more children, and his mother had been quite content with that. They'd had a very civilized marriage.

Lorie took another bite of cornbread as he lit up. "I have a brother, four years older. His name's Caleb. He left home three years before I did. I'm not sure where he is now. What was your home like?"

Two words came instantly to mind. "Big. Empty. But that was just the house. I never spent much time in it." Nathan had much preferred raising hell with the slave children and roughhousing with his peers to anything he could find to do indoors.

Lorie looked down the road at two little boys playing near the well. "Ours was small and loud. I didn't spend much time in it either."

Nathan smoked in silence while she ate her cornbread. Trey rode by on his way out of town. The way Lorie watched him gave Nathan a quick stab of jealousy.

"You know him?"

Her eyes held his for a moment, letting him know she'd read his reaction. "No. He came in to the saloon one night when he'd just arrived here, and we talked, but I've hardly spoken to the man since. He was just out of the army then, I think."

Well, I'll be. I wonder which army. Nathan could picture Trey riding with Jeb Stuart's Black Horse regiment, Virginia gentlemen on their own blooded horses, but no . . . Cloud had the pedigree for it, but Trey didn't. His parents were a blacksmith's son and a storekeeper's daughter. Their farm was comfortable, but small enough that they ran it without slaves, leaving them no claim to any social status worth mentioning. Colin McShannon had earned respect because he was a scrappy little terrier of a man, who backed down from no one, and Sidonie had possessed an easy warmth that endeared her to her neighbors, but they weren't in the same class as the Sinclairs and Munroes. Yet, Justin had drawn Trey and his sister into the big planters' social circle, and they'd held their own there. Nathan had resented them both for it at the time, but that sort of thing didn't matter much to him anymore.

He watched Trey until he disappeared behind the corner of the saloon. The way a man rode was as unique as the way he walked. Trey held his reins in his right hand to keep his left free – Nathan had forgotten he was left-handed – and something about his posture nagged at Nathan's memory. Well, whatever it was would come to him.

Nathan would have been quite content to sit there with Lorie for the rest of the afternoon, but he knew she wouldn't stay and, anyway, he had business to attend to. He got up with a sigh.

"Lorie, I've got to see about getting myself a horse. I'll see you later."

Their eyes met and held again as Lorie looked up. "You know where I'll be."

CHAPTER 15

Beth stared in complete bewilderment at the pile of paper pattern pieces she and Holly had just finished cutting out. They were making Holly's dress first because it was the simpler of the two, but if it was simple Beth didn't want to think about her own, with its puffed sleeves, elbow cuffs, three-tiered skirt and fitted bodice.

Maddy had just arrived at the McShannons'. She smiled at Beth's expression. "I told you this would take time. It's not as difficult as it looks."

With experienced hands, Holly smoothed out the green fabric and began placing the pattern pieces on it. Beth started pinning them in place.

"I think it's a shame there are only two dances a year in town and nothing else, no music or anything. The place could use a little culture."

Maddy hooted. "Culture! What did you have in mind, Beth, a symphony concert?"

Beth's chin tilted. "Maybe a concert wouldn't be a bad thing. The Sunday school had one just before I came here, didn't they?"

"Yes, but . . ."

"But what?"

"Beth, you don't know Wallace Flats very well yet."

"So?"

"Well, let's just say the town's never had much time for that sort of thing."

182

Maddy's tolerant expression only made Beth more stubborn. "No, I suppose not, but maybe it's time that changed."

Maddy stared at her. "You're serious, aren't you?"

Suddenly Beth was. "You know, I did some acting and helped put together some fundraising affairs at home. I think people here might enjoy a concert if they got the chance. We could raise money for the church relief fund, and it would be a good way for me to get to know the town better. There must be some people with talent. Who's doing the music for the dance?"

"Spencer Hall."

"He's a good fiddler," Holly put in. "He always plays for the dances. And Missus Henderson plays the organ in church. Some of the kids at school can recite, too. It might work."

Beth made a decisive stab with a pin. "I think I'll talk to Reverend Baxter about it tomorrow. If he's in favor of it, maybe I'll try to organize something. Holly, if I do, will you try to get your friends interested?"

Holly nodded. "I don't think I'll have to try very hard. We haven't had a school concert since Miss Jakeman came here. She doesn't believe in them. I think it would be fun."

"Good. I suppose it makes sense to have it just before the dance, since people will be coming into town that night anyway."

Maddy shrugged and started basting a sleeve into her dress. "Well, all I can say is good luck. I'm glad we have a sheriff now anyway. There's always a ruckus of some sort at the dance. Logan says he wouldn't bother going otherwise. He hates dancing."

Beth smiled as she reached for more pins. "What do you mean by a ruckus?"

"Well, last year George Chalmers and Calvin Springer got into it over Allie Shaw." Maddy re-threaded her needle and shook her head. "She'd been playing up to both of them, of course. They should have known better. When they started, Allie told them Dan Watson had just proposed to her and she'd said yes, so they could both go to the devil. They got mad and took after Dan and his brother. The four of them ended up fighting on the platform. Spencer told them he'd shoot them all if his fiddle got broken. Nobody complained about being bored, anyway."

Holly grinned. "Remember the time Mister and Missus Thompson got into a shouting match? I wasn't there, but I heard about it."

"Remember?" Maddy's infectious laugh bubbled up again. "I can still hear her. 'Hank Thompson, I know you're a jackass and so does everyone here, but for heaven's sake pretend you're not for ten minutes!'"

Beth giggled. "Sounds like a lovely pair."

"Oh, they are." Maddy reached for her scissors. "They've been fighting for forty years and loving it."

Holly frowned as she righted a pattern piece she'd placed upside down. "Allie was only sixteen this time last year. They won't be able to marry for a couple of years, but still . . ." Her voice changed, sounding very adult. "If anyone proposes to me when I'm sixteen, I'll laugh in his face."

Beth winced as she pricked a finger. "Ouch! I had my first proposal at sixteen. He was fifty."

"Fifty!" Maddy and Holly laughed together, and Beth got the feeling Holly didn't laugh often.

"Well, he was a little drunk at the time. It happened at a large dinner party my uncle and aunt were having. Mister Clark was a widower and I think he had the impression that Uncle Robert and Aunt Abigail were anxious to get me off their hands. He didn't know them all that well. After dinner, he cornered me in the pantry and asked what I would think if he spoke to my aunt and uncle about a wedding on my birthday in the spring. I told him I couldn't have cared less if he asked, but he was wasting his time. I didn't exactly laugh in his face, but Uncle Robert did when Mister Clark actually spoke to him."

Holly grinned. "How many others have you had?"

Beth smiled back. "Well, there were three more before we left Philadelphia. Two from proper young men who were interested in a social contract and a merger of bank accounts, and one from someone who I knew didn't mean it. If I'd thought he did, I might have considered it. He really was very nice. Then we moved to Denver and I met Daniel Hunter. I thought I was in love. I thought we both were, but he never proposed. His parents wouldn't let him."

Beth's dry irony wasn't lost on Maddy. "And that one hurt," she said quietly.

"For a while," Beth acknowledged. She didn't mind Maddy knowing.

Maddy shrugged as she finished basting. "Well, they weren't put here to make our lives easier, they were just put here. Makes life interesting though."

Beth chuckled. "True enough. Holly, are we ready to start cutting?"

"Yes, I guess so."

Holly glowed with repressed excitement for the rest of the afternoon. Beth was glad the concert idea appealed to her. She just hoped they could pull it off.

Maddy lingered for a few minutes after Holly left for home. "I haven't seen Holly up close for over a year. She's certainly growing up. It's hard to believe she's Simon's daughter. How did you meet her?"

Beth gathered up the pieces of the green dress and put them away. "I met her in the store last week, and I could tell she wanted a new dress so badly she could taste it. I just hope her helping me doesn't get her into trouble with her father. Ben Reeves asked her to the dance. I think he's quite taken with her."

"That's a bit of a shame."

Beth looked up in surprise. "Why? Ben's a decent boy."

"Of course he is. I was just thinking that if they met when they were older it might well come to something, but now it likely never will. I'd better be going." Maddy gave her a significant look as she folded up her sewing. "Speaking of coming to something, Trey stopped at our place for a few minutes with Logan the other day. You're good for him, Beth."

Beth blushed and glanced out the window. Trey had come home about twenty minutes ago and gone straight to the barn, avoiding the hen party in the house. She listened for him every evening now and felt a silly little rush of gladness when she heard him. Maddy must have noticed.

"I'm still waiting for him to figure that out."

Maddy put a hand on Beth's shoulder and met her gaze with a bracing hint of a challenge. "He's no fool. He knows, whether he can tell you yet or not. See you soon."

* * * *

Kneeling in an empty stall, Trey spread feed sacks over a small pile of lumber then covered the sacks with straw. Satisfied nothing would attract Beth's attention, he got to his feet. Before he could leave the stall, the barn door opened and Beth stepped in.

Damn. She would have to catch him. Trey came out to meet her, trying to look innocent. She wasn't fooled.

"What are you hiding in there?"

He shut the stall door behind him. "A surprise. For your birthday."

He knew he looked just like a boy caught with his hand in the cookie jar. Beth tried to peek into the stall, but Trey stepped in front of her. She laughed and slipped her arms around him.

"My birthday's not 'til next month. Do you expect me to stand the suspense that long?"

Trey pulled her closer, enjoying the feel of her in his arms as he always did. "It's something that takes time. Don't spoil it."

Time. Ever since they'd delivered Shiloh's foal, he'd been telling himself that seeing as Beth hadn't had a proper wedding, she at least deserved a few weeks of courtship. Keep things easy, keep things gentle. Trey had never dreamed it would be so difficult, nor would he admit to himself that he needed the time more than she did.

The more he realized how much he needed her, the more frightening the thought of losing her became, and he knew he could lose her even if she stayed. Young women lost their lives all the time.

He dealt with death often in a day's work. Calves died of scours, cows and mares died giving birth, predators claimed the weak. That kind of hard truth applied to people out here as well. The only protection was not to care too much, and that was becoming more difficult every day.

As for her not staying – Trey had noticed the changes in Beth. The place suited her, for now. He also knew she cared for him, for now. When the novelty of freedom and independence wore off, would that be enough to keep her from regretting the life she could have had? He didn't know, but he was sure of one thing. He didn't ever want to see resentment in her eyes.

But he couldn't resist her. He kissed her and felt her whole body respond, telling him she was his. He wished he could be sure of that, but he couldn't. Not now, perhaps not ever.

Trey stepped back to look at her. She was so beautiful she made him hurt. He kissed her again and let her go.

Beth watched as he began feeding the horses, starting with Shiloh and her foal. They'd named the little filly Diamond because of the dainty white mark on her forehead. When Trey entered the stall she was nursing, while her mother braced herself patiently against the rhythmic pull. He half-turned his back to them to unfasten the water bucket and didn't pay attention when Diamond finished feeding and stepped toward him. Before he could move, she flashed the whites of her eyes, jumped forward and bit Trey on the backside.

He yelled and dropped the bucket, soaking his legs. The foal scooted behind her mother. Beth doubled over in the aisle, laughing. Trey rubbed a hand over the bruise starting on his behind and growled at her.

"What are you crowing at? That hurt!"

"I'm sorry, I couldn't help it," Beth spluttered. "The little devil!"

"She's Cloud's all right." Trey shook his head at the stubby switching tail just visible behind Shiloh. "She's got to be broken of that real quick. I'm soaked."

When the foal reappeared Beth stepped in, caught hold of her halter and looked her in the eye. "You cut that out. When you're a little bigger it won't be funny."

Diamond stood her ground, ready to assert her independence as soon as Beth let her go. They were certainly in for some interesting times with her. Beth loosened her hold on the halter and looked back at Trey.

"You've got to appreciate a girl with a mind of her own. I think—"

Before she could finish the sentence, Diamond butted her in the shoulder, knocking her off-balance. Beth sprawled on the floor. Trey reached out to help her up, feeling avenged.

"You were saying?"

"Never mind." Beth took his hand and scrambled to her feet, brushing straw from her hair. "Trey, I've been thinking. In her last letter, Isobel said she was quite sure she had a buyer for my other painting, and that it would sell for a better price. I've got two more at Graham's place that I can send. If they sell, we could buy another yearling this fall."

Trey's stomach twisted. He wasn't prepared for the jolt of fear he experienced at hearing her talk long term.

What's wrong with you? You want her to stay, don't you?

But you can't pay her back if she doesn't. He hated the thought of being obliged to her that way. A few seconds ago, he'd been ready to bundle her into his arms again, but now he took a mental step back.

"Maybe. Let's not count our chickens before they're hatched."

Beth dropped his hand. "You don't like that idea?"

Trey's body tensed. Damn it, he hated seeing her withdraw from him. "I didn't say that. I just don't think you should rush into sinking your money into this place."

Beth stood her ground and kept her eyes on his. "Why not? I thought we decided a long time ago that I had a stake here, too."

He knew he was hurting her, but he wouldn't lie. "Of course you do, but when it comes to taking your money I don't feel right, that's all."

The look in Beth's eyes made him hate himself. "If we were really a team it wouldn't be taking my money, but it seems we're not. Sorry for assuming."

She turned to leave, but Trey got hold of her arm. "Beth, that isn't what I meant. Well, maybe it is in a way. Logan's my partner with the cattle, but the horses are my operation. I'm not looking for another business partner."

Beth pulled her arm away. "I'm not looking to take over, I just want to help. I'm sorry you have a problem with that."

He sighed and ran a hand through his hair. Wherever he turned, she had him cornered. Why did she have to read him so well? Against his will, he found himself stepping toward her.

"I just don't want you to do anything you'll end up regretting. Look, let's not argue about something that might not even happen. If it does, we'll talk about it then." Of its own volition, his hand reached out to touch her cheek. "You know, I'm starting to wonder how I managed this place without you."

He couldn't stop himself from reaching for her. With a small sigh, Beth allowed herself to be drawn into his arms. Her head dropped to his shoulder. Holding her close, Trey felt his heartbeat slow and his body relax. His doubts didn't get in the way when he held her. The feel and scent of her made it difficult to think at all.

Beth stepped back, those morning-colored eyes searching his for answers. He didn't have them. After a long moment she turned away.

"All right, we'll talk about it later. Let's get to work."

* * * *

Sleep didn't come easily to Trey that night. When Beth went to the loft he'd listened to the sounds of her getting ready for bed – the floor creaking as she moved to hang up her blouse, the soft thud of her denims hitting the floor as she stepped out of them. He kept his back to the blanket curtain, picturing Beth's slender body silhouetted in the light of her candle, arms stretched over her head, breasts lifted as she slipped into her nightgown, her rich hair loose around her shoulders, flowing down her back. The image stuck in his mind like a burr, goading him with need, making him restless.

When the sound of Beth's slow breathing told him she was asleep, Trey blew out the lamp and went to bed. Thoughts of Beth's body arched in union with his mingled with thoughts of her smiling, holding his baby in her arms. A family to love, a family to lose . . .

* * * *

"Lose? We can't lose. You know what will happen if we do, just as well as the rest of us. We need you. I haven't picked a first lieutenant yet. Just say the word and it'll be you."

"Justin, I'd be proud to if this fight was right, but it isn't."

"Trey, it seems like only yesterday that you and Chelle were babies. It's selfish of me, I know, but dear God, I wish you were five years younger."

"Maman, I told Dad last night I'll be going West when the war starts. I know how you feel about States' rights, but this way . . . it's suicide. I have to go."

"I've never been anything but proud of my children, and I've never been prouder of you than I am right now."

"I don't know if you should be."

"Oh, cher, I do. Don't ever forget it."

"Trey, there are so many things I'd like to know about you..."

* * * *

The memory of Beth's voice, throaty with desire, pushed Justin's and his mother's words from Trey's mind. He saw Beth flushed and sparkling with laughter and exhilaration after their race. Saw her soaked and dripping, with sparks of anger in her blue-gray eyes. Saw the worry on her face the night after his accident, her light touch waking him.

I love her. Whatever might come of it, he was through dodging the fact. For the first time in his life, he was in love. Admitting it brought Trey some relief. He closed his eyes and let the remembered feel of Beth's soft hands ease him into sleep.

CHAPTER 16

Holly arrived home to a dim, empty house. She breathed a sigh of relief and hurried to light the lamp. She hadn't intended to be this late getting home from the sewing session, but now it wouldn't matter.

The place wasn't much smaller than the McShannons', but Holly always turned away from comparisons. They weren't flattering to her home. The windows and pine floor were bare. Simon's bunk was built against one side wall, and the table and chairs with their peeling green paint stood against the other. Boxes under the counter held pots, pans and groceries. The only books and pictures were in Holly's room at the back. Her father resented anything unnecessary in the main space.

Holly got a fire going and put yesterday's leftover soup on to heat, then sat down to do her homework while she had the table and the lamp to herself. She had a history essay to write and, although she liked history, she found it hard to concentrate with her mind so full of the concert idea.

For as long as she could remember, Holly had loved to sing. She thought she had a good voice, but she'd never sung in public other than at Sunday school concerts as a small child. She had dreams, and if the concert came off Mrs. McShannon would hear her. She must have heard plenty of good music before. Then there would be the dance, and Holly's father had said she could go. She'd waited to ask him until he was drunk enough not to care much, but not too drunk to remember saying yes.

"Pa, some of the girls at school are going to the spring dance together. Would it be all right if I went with them?"

Holly held her breath, but Simon only shrugged. "Fourteen's too young to be running around to dances, but you'll probably go whatever I say. Suit yourself, but be back here at a decent hour or you won't be wanting to look in the mirror for a while."

His threats didn't worry Holly much. She'd come to realize her father was a bit afraid of her at times. The last time he'd slapped her she'd told him she'd leave the territory if he did it again, and he hadn't.

"I'll be coming straight home as soon as it's over, Pa." It had always been the same whenever she wanted anything. Choose her moment; size up his mood. She was sick of it. Two more years and *I'm gone.* She wasn't sure how she'd manage, but she didn't intend to stay here a moment longer than she had to.

Holly had started page three of her essay when Simon opened the door. She could read his moods with a glance. By the time he'd hung up his coat, she'd moved her books off the table.

"Hi, Pa. Supper's ready."

"Get it on the table then."

Holly filled two bowls with soup. After a few minutes' silence, Simon glanced up from his dinner with a suspicious frown.

"That woman pay you today?"

"No, she's going to pay me when we're finished." Holly would give him the money, but she wasn't about to let him see the dress. She'd leave it with a girlfriend and go there to change before the dance.

"Well, I want to know when she does. She'd better not try to cheat you or she'll hear from me."

Holly let her eyes flash at him. "Missus McShannon won't cheat me. She isn't like that."

Simon lifted his hand. "You watch your mouth, girl, or I'll—"

Holly kept her gaze on his and didn't budge. "Go ahead. I promise you it'll be the last time."

Simon glared at her, but he dropped his hand. He needed a housekeeper and they both knew it. He looked down and muttered into his soup bowl.

"Who do you think you are?"

"Nobody. Nobody yet. Excuse me, Pa, I've got homework to do."

Simon's hand trembled, making him drop his spoon. That sort of thing had been happening to him more and more often lately. He picked up the spoon, cursed under his breath and shoved his chair back. "Always got your nose in a book. What the hell good is it going to do you? What the hell does a girl need books for?"

Holly got up and marched to her room without looking back. *To get as far away from you as I can.*

* * * *

After service Sunday morning, Beth walked back into the church with Reverend Baxter. In a few short weeks she'd come to like him very much. As Trey had said, all he had to do to win people over was be himself.

He looked at Beth with the same inquiring smile she'd seen that first day. "Something on your mind, Missus McShannon?"

She gathered her ideas as they walked up the aisle. "Yes. I've been hearing a lot of talk about the dance that's coming up next month. I understand there aren't many social opportunities of the kind in town, and I'm thinking it might be worthwhile to organize a concert beforehand since people will be coming in anyway. I wanted to know what you thought of the idea."

Reverend Baxter frowned as he considered it. "What kind of concert were you thinking of?"

Beth took a seat in a front pew. The church still smelled of a mixture of perfume and sweat from the bodies that had been packed into it earlier. "Well, I thought we could get the school children to do a few songs, and some of the older boys and girls could do some skits and recitations. I'm sure we could get a few adult performers, too. We could raise money for the relief fund. Of course, being new here I don't like to attempt it without your help. Do you think it might work?"

Reverend Baxter pursed his lips in one of his characteristic expressions as he sat beside her. "I'm not sure. You've never been to one of our dances. A lot of people consider the whole day a holiday. By the time evening comes things can get rather . . . unpredictable."

Beth grinned. "So I hear. I thought perhaps if there was something organized happening before the dance, it might help keep things a little more orderly."

In the short time she'd known him Beth had learned that Reverend Baxter didn't like disappointing people. He didn't disappoint her.

"Well, I suppose we can try. Spencer would probably help, and I can ask Missus Henderson if she'll accompany the singers. I'd need you to organize the program and run the rehearsals. There isn't a lot of time, but we'll see what we can do."

After posting a notice and agreeing with Reverend Baxter on a tentative rehearsal schedule, Beth started down the street toward the forge. She and Trey were having lunch with the Reeves and Trey had gone directly there after church. Her fears of being looked on as an outsider certainly hadn't materialized among Trey's friends. She already thought of John and Hannah as her own friends as well.

In front of the store, she met Lorie Carter walking toward Neil's. Beth was going to pass without speaking, but something made her stop.

I came out here to marry a man I'd never met for a home and a hundred dollars. How different are we?

"Hello, Lorie."

Astonishment, then suspicion flickered in Lorie's eyes. "Hello."

Beth intended to make some commonplace remark, but she surprised herself. "My name is Beth McShannon. I'm new here, but I've seen you a couple of times. I think you know my husband. He's mentioned you."

"Yeah, I've met him." Lorie hurried away, leaving Beth wondering if she'd made a fool of herself. If she had, she decided she wasn't sorry.

She found Trey and the Reeves in their kitchen. The two men looked as if they'd just enjoyed a good joke. John put on a teasing smile as Beth walked in.

"Trey tells me you're setting up the Wallace Flats Philharmonic Society."

Beth had been expecting something of the sort. Trey's reaction to the concert idea had been exactly like Maddy's.

"Beth, you're asking for trouble. You'd better wait until there are a few more people in town who know what you mean by culture."

"Your faith is touching," she'd answered tartly, and got one of his smug grins in response. He was wearing another one now.

"If you believe what he tells you you're not as smart as I thought you were," Beth told John with a grin of her own. "Are you going to take part in the concert?"

John's face turned grave, but his eyes twinkled. "Well, if you ask me the right way I might sing."

With a pained expression, Trey shook his head. "John, I'd never embarrass a man in front of his family but—"

"Too late, it's already been done," Ben put in.

"More than once," Hannah added. Square-built and calm-eyed, ringlets of dark hair escaping from her heavy bun, she set plates on the table and pinched John's arm. "Now you two stop it. Beth, what did Reverend Baxter say about the concert?"

Beth arched her eyebrows at Trey as she sat down. "He agreed with me that Wallace Flats could use some entertainment outside of the saloon. He's going to help. Ben, I asked Holly yesterday to try to get the school interested. Will you help her?"

Ben shifted in his chair. "I guess so, as long as I don't have to get on stage."

Trey laughed. "Amen to that. Stick to your guns, Ben."

After lunch, Ben left for a friend's house. Trey and John cleared the table while Beth helped Hannah get ready to do the dishes. "Holly's quite a young lady," Beth said as she started scraping plates into the pig's bucket. "She must have gotten her backbone from her mother."

Hannah ladled hot water into the washbasin. "We never knew her, but it certainly didn't come from Simon. Ben says Holly's a good student. I'm amazed that she gets to school at all."

"So am I." Trey turned to John with a smile. "John, maybe I was wrong. I think you should sing at the concert. If word gets around that you're going to, we can be sure there won't be any trouble. The town will be as empty as the church."

* * * *

On Thursday morning, Trey and Logan started branding the spring calves. They set up under the shade of some aspens close to the river, but it was still hot, dirty work. It had turned out warm for May, and by the time they quit for lunch they were both grimy and tired. Logan let the last calf go and straightened up with a groan.

"That's it for me, Trey. I've got work to do at home this afternoon. I swear I'm getting too old for this."

Trey watched the calf run bawling to its mother. "All right, be a slacker. Too old, my arse. You can outwork me any time you want to."

His tone robbed the words of any insult. Logan retrieved his buckskin gelding from the water's edge and mounted up, a grin on his weather-beaten face.

"Why would I want to? Say hello to Beth for me."

After Logan rode off, Trey put out their fire, unsaddled Cloud and turned him loose. The stallion rolled, got up covered in dust and splashed into the river for a drink. Trey shielded his eyes and looked down the wagon track toward home, watching for Chance.

Beth had said she'd be out at lunchtime, a habit Trey appreciated more and more as time went on. On the days when he expected her, he looked forward to it all morning. They talked about his plans for the homestead and the cattle. Trey showed Beth what he'd learned from his mother about healing plants, and pointed out patches of coneflower, yarrow and tansy. Beth told stories about her uncle's breeding farm and questioned Trey about his family. Sometimes they didn't talk much at all, but they didn't have to. Sitting in silence with Beth felt good.

They didn't talk about their marriage. Neither of them knew what to say. Every kiss they shared bound Trey to Beth more deeply, but every time he tried to tell her his conscience stabbed him, whispering that she didn't know him. He pictured the disgust in Beth's lovely eyes if he told her the truth, told her what it really meant to be a turncoat. He thought he could survive her hate, but it would destroy him to have her despise him. And she would. He didn't merit hate, not for being criminally foolish.

Trey's eyes stung with sweat and the back of his neck felt sunburned. The river sounded deliciously cool. There was a deep pool about fifty yards upstream. He might as well clean up before Beth arrived.

He stripped, dove into the achingly cold water, swam a few quick strokes and climbed out. The warm air felt like a lover's touch on his chilled skin. He let the sun dry him then dressed, got the blanket he kept tied to the back of his saddle, stretched out on it and closed his eyes.

How long would it be before he crumbled? If he didn't make Beth his real wife and give her his heart, she'd leave him, and he knew he was in far too deep to let her go. Trey turned the thought over in his mind as he'd been doing since the day Shiloh foaled. Loving Beth would be the biggest risk of his life.

The bright sun beat down on him, soothing tired muscles and clogging his mind. He laid a forearm over his eyes and took in a breath laden with the scent of warm earth. Another . . . three . . . four . . .

He knew this scent, too. Lavender. He felt the warm, soft weight of Beth's body draped over his and reached for her, molding her to him. He heard her sigh as her lips met his and parted to let him in. He reached under her loose hair to cup the back of her neck as he tasted her, then her flavor and fragrance vanished, along with the sun's warmth.

The acrid reek of burning brush, combined with the odors of sweaty horse and his own unwashed body, stung his throat. The last two days fighting had taken place over a burning landscape, set ablaze by artillery fire. A pale, smoke-hazed moon hung above him in the night sky.

Cloud stumbled and nearly fell to his knees. Dizzy with fatigue, Trey pulled him up. Sheer instinct kept him in the saddle. He no longer cared if he fell. He only knew they couldn't stop, not with troops from both sides moving through the darkness.

The screams of the wounded they hadn't been able to save from the flames that day still rang in Trey's mind, drowning out the subtle night sounds around him. Sounds he shouldn't have ignored.

Why weren't you listening?

He looked back to check on the rest of his patrol, but they blended into the darkness. Trey nudged his spent horse forward, living only for the moment when he would be able to rest.

Turn around. Just get out of there.

He shouted the words, but they made no sound. In another minute, he'd be turning the corner he could barely see up ahead. His pulse hammered in his ears as he shouted again. He couldn't make himself heard, couldn't make himself stop.

He rounded the bend in the road, heard a shout from the darkness of a stand of trees. Metal flashed in the moonlight. Trey pulled his rifle from its scabbard and fired in one smooth motion. A cry of pain mingled with the sounds of horses and riders moving. The rest of his patrol came up behind him. The group under the trees disappeared, except for a lone horse and a dark shape on the ground. Trey dismounted and walked toward the still figure, knowing what he'd see. He turned the body over and looked into the face of the man he'd shot, a face he knew as well as his own.

"Sweet Christ . . . Justin. Justin, hold on, I'm going to get you out of here . . ."

The darkness broke up and gave way to sunlight again, the cool, smoky night to the warmth of Beth's arms.

"Trey, it's all right. It's over." Her voice barely reached him through the remains of the nightmare. Stomach heaving, muscles frozen, he clung to Beth while she stroked his hair and murmured soothing nonsense. Long, humiliating seconds passed before he regained enough control to pull away. Beth clasped her hands around her knees and waited while he gathered what was left of his dignity.

"Maddy told me she and Logan asked you to stay with them your first winter here. I think I know now why you didn't."

Still sick and shaky, Trey wiped his face with his sleeve and looked out over the river. "Yeah, I guess so." Back then, the dreams had come almost nightly. He couldn't have spent a week under the Kinsleys' roof without them knowing.

"How often does this happen?"

"Not often now. Not for a year, until . . ."

"Until I came." Beth reached for his hand. "Trey, talk to me."

Trey pulled his hand back. He'd rather have Beth's contempt than her pity, but then he glanced at her and realized she wasn't offering him pity. What he saw in her tear-filled eyes was love, plain and simple. He couldn't destroy it with the truth.

"There's no point, Beth. Some memories aren't worth sharing. It wouldn't do anyone any good."

Beth sat up straight, her voice brisk and matter-of-fact. "No? I've always found that putting things into words cuts them down to size. Besides, I think I can piece things together fairly well from what you were saying when I woke you."

A fresh wave of horror rolled over Trey. "I was talking?" *How much did you tell her?*

"Yes. Correct me if I'm wrong. You had a friend, Justin, who was killed. You saw it happen."

Trey picked up a rock and tossed it in the river. The ripples it made spread and vanished with the current. How many times had he relived that night? Yeah, I saw it happen. *I knelt there in the road and held him while he died, after I'd* . . . "No, you aren't wrong."

He wanted to get up and leave, find somewhere to hide, but Beth's calm, even voice held him there. "I'm sorry. Tell me about him."

Perhaps if he gave her that much, she'd let it rest. "Justin and I were friends from the time we were six or seven. The first real friend for both of us. We played together, chased girls together, got drunk for the first time together. As close as a lot of brothers are, I guess."

Trey hadn't spoken Justin's name to anyone since his death. It was harder than he could have imagined. Beth moved a little closer. Her scent got through to Trey, lavender and woman, warming the chill from his tense body. "So you enlisted together? Justin felt the same way you did about the war?"

205

"No, he was ready to fight his way to hell and back for the Confederacy. The local troop elected him captain." *I haven't picked a first lieutenant yet. Just say the word and it'll be you.* "He tried so hard to get me to go with him and the others, but I told him I was going West. He didn't understand, but he never blamed me."

"But you didn't go west, and you ended up on opposite sides."

"Yeah." Trey didn't want to feel this need, this emptiness, not now. He had to fight it, brace himself for what he knew was coming. He'd already told Beth too much. He stole a glance at her, saw her piecing the story together.

"You both had your reasons. You can't blame yourself. But if you weren't fighting together, then how . . ." Her hand went to her mouth as she arrived at the answer. "Oh, Trey, of all fiendish things. I'm so sorry. How did it happen?"

No disgust. No recriminations. She simply assumed he'd had no choice. Floored by Beth's acceptance, Trey found himself telling her.

"I was with a small patrol on the way from the Wilderness battle toward Spotsylvania. It was late, and we were all exhausted. We'd been through two days of pure hell. I was taking a turn riding ahead. I rounded a corner and there they were. If I'd heard them ahead of time – but I didn't."

Beth put her arm around his shoulders. Trey left it there. His need for her touch overcame his pride. Just that simple contact grounded him. "What happened then?"

"Well, for a split second I didn't know if they were our troops or enemy. They had a clump of trees behind them and I couldn't see them clearly. They could see me better. One of them yelled and went for his rifle. I got to mine first. I don't know why he was so slow. I don't know why he didn't know me."

"Trey, it was night. He probably couldn't see you as well as you thought. Neither of you had time to think."

"No, we didn't. I fired, and someone shot at me and missed. Then the rest of my patrol came up behind me. The others ran. There were twice as many of us. I got down to see if the man I'd shot was alive, and he was." Beth's arm tightened around him when Trey stopped to get control of his voice. "He knew me then. He didn't say anything, but he knew me. In a few minutes, it was over. We couldn't stay, not even long enough to bury him. We left him there like trash at the side of the road."

His voice broke. Beth drew his head down to her shoulder, cradled him against her and laid one soft cheek against his hair. Her slender arms folded around him, powerful in a way he could never have imagined. "You were fighting a war, Trey. You defended yourself. You would have expected Justin to do exactly the same thing in your place."

Unable to fight his need, Trey relaxed against her. The sense of freedom that came with accepting her comfort amazed him. He'd never expected to feel like this again. Hurting, but whole; completely alive. "I guess I would have, but I've never been able to think of it that way."

"I know." Beth's hand moved in a gentle circle over his back. "You've never told anyone about this, have you? Not even your family."

"No. It would only have hurt them." Trey looked up, saw his grief reflected in her eyes and shook his head. "It hurt you."

"Of course it did." Beth cupped his cheek in her palm. "Anything that hurts you will hurt me, because I love you."

She meant it. Trey saw it written on her face and stared at her in wonder. In so many ways, he was the last man she should have chosen.

"Beth, why?"

She'd never looked more beautiful than she did at that moment, flushed with emotion, a smile playing across her pretty mouth. "Why? Because I've seen you be patient with a frightened horse. I've seen you take the time to try to save a calf, though you knew its chances were slim. What happened to that calf, Trey?"

"He disappeared. Coyotes, probably."

"That's a shame, but you tried. And I've seen you with your friends. I've seen how hard you've worked to build a life here. All those things tell me who you are. Knowing you had the courage to fight for what you believed only makes me love you more. Trey, why didn't you go west like you'd planned?"

With years of tension dissolving, Trey lay back and rested his head in Beth's lap. Here in the circle of her warmth, the memory of that last difficult year at home lost much of its sting. "Mother died in March of sixty-one. Heart failure. Dad was lost. We all were. He decided he wanted to go home, but I couldn't see much of a future for me in England, so I stayed.

After Dad and Chelle sailed from New York, I went back to Washington. I'd left Cloud in a stable there. Two days later Fort Sumter was shelled. All the rhetoric and recruiting . . .it was going to come down to numbers, I really believed that. I got the idea that the best thing I could do was to join up and help end the war as soon as possible, before it reached home. An eighteen year old's impulse."

Beth's fingers interlaced with his. "An impulse? Maybe. Who knows? Maddy told me once that she believes in fate. Perhaps she was right."

Trey closed his eyes, inhaled a breath perfumed with Beth's scent. "Maybe, but I'd been feeling like I was the only person walking away. I suppose Nate had a lot to do with it. I thought I had something to prove." He brought her hand to his lips, kissed her palm. "Mother believed in the Confederacy with all her heart. She hoped it wouldn't come to war, but she thought the break had to come, and she thought it should. Still, when I told her I planned to go West she said she was proud of me. If she knew what I decided to do—"

"She'd still be proud."

Yes. Lying there with the sound of the river in the background, Trey felt certain his mother and Justin were both near, listening, understanding.

Cher, you survived. You did what you had to do. What your father's son had to do.

Trey, you'll have to live for both of us. No regrets. Not between you and me.

"She probably would." Trey got up and helped Beth to her feet. All around them, the spring afternoon shouted its message of new life, and he intended to take that message to heart. It was high time he claimed his bride.

"Beth, let's get the horses. There's a place I want to show you."

* * * *

They rode into the woods, following a narrow trail beside the river. When they reached a clearing, Trey stopped and waited for Beth to come up beside him.

She reined Chance in and looked around her, wondering why Trey had brought her here. It was the only open space nearby; everywhere else the forest came to the water's edge. The grass smelled warm and sweet and a breeze rustled the young aspen leaves. A pleasant spot, that was all. Then, looking at the old fire-pit, the bare, compacted earth around it that was slowly being reclaimed by grass, she began to understand. This must be the Indian camp he'd mentioned to her. She dismounted for a closer look at the blackened stones.

"I wonder how long this has been here."

Trey led Cloud and Chance a few paces upstream and came back carrying his blanket. He spread it on the grass, sat cross-legged and drew Beth down beside him.

"The Arapaho used this campsite for generations. Births and deaths and weddings happened here. I can't think of a better place to say what I want to say to you." Emotion

210

flared in his eyes as they locked on hers. "Beth, I didn't think I had it in me to feel this way."

Like the world was about to be handed to you with all its colors brightened? Beth nodded as a wave of warmth washed over her, leaving a glow deep inside. "I didn't think I did, either."

He gave her one of his heart-twisting smiles as he took her hand. "It feels good, doesn't it?"

Beth's cheeks colored as his fingers curled around hers. "Yes, it does."

Trey slipped Sidonie's ring off her finger and put it in his shirt pocket. The quick, sharp sense of loss Beth felt made her want to laugh at herself, but the impulse died when he spoke.

"Reverend Baxter and territorial law say we're married but I don't, not yet. I want to marry you here."

He must be able to hear her heart pounding. Beth found it as difficult to speak as she had the moment they met.

"What do you mean?"

Trey reached out to run a finger down the length of her braid. She'd never seen him smile quite like that before. With no reserve, nothing held back.

"Logan traveled quite a bit when he was young. He told me once about an Indian wedding he saw, with a ceremony called the Seven Steps. It's pretty simple. We build a sacred fire, and I take one step clockwise around it and make a promise to you. Then you take a step to join me and make a promise to me. Seven steps, seven promises."

"And then what?"

"Then we're married."

Married. Beth looked into Trey's smiling dark eyes and lost her breath. When she'd heard him scream, seen the sheer horror on his face as he relived the night he killed his friend, she'd felt his pain as if it were her own. Now, she felt his relief just as keenly. The woman who'd come to Wallace Flats no longer existed. What had happened to her?

She'd learned to keep a farmhouse, worked in a barn and gained the trust of a half-wild mustang. She'd used a gun in self-defense, been kissed like never before. She'd touched her husband's scarred heart and lost her own in the process. Beth knew she couldn't go back. She was ready to promise heart, soul and body to Trey if he wanted her, and thank God, he wanted her.

"Build a fire."

Trey kindled a small fire in the old stone circle and Beth got up to stand with him beside it. He took a step and turned to face her.

"Beth, I love you and I want to spend my life with you. I can't give you a lot of things, but I promise to do my best to make it a good life."

Near tears, she took a step to stand close to him. *Beth, don't you dare start crying now.* She fought off the urge before looking up.

"And I love you. I want us to be together, to raise children together. I promise to do my best for you and for them."

Facing her, Trey took another step back. "My mother always said I had her father's temper. I like to blame it on him, anyway. We'll fight, but it won't change how I feel about you."

Beth stepped forward again. Now he had her smiling. She'd never enjoyed fighting with anyone as much as she did with Trey.

"I blame my temper on my mother. I promise to be honest with you, even if it hurts." Her smile widened to a grin as her gaze settled on his mouth. "And making up has its good points."

Trey took his third step then reached for Beth's hand. For a moment he was quiet, examining her slender, tapered fingers.

"I promise I'll always be proud of you and your talent. It's one of the things I love about you."

Beth knew he meant that, but she also knew he still had moments of doubt when he was afraid she'd regret what she'd left behind. She stepped forward and traced the line of his jaw with her finger.

"I drew a sketch of you my first week here. I think I was already in love, though I didn't know it. I promise nothing will ever be more important to me than our life together."

They were halfway around the circle now. Her breath caught in her throat at the fierce joy in Trey's eyes as he stepped back again.

"I'll be with you through good times and bad, I promise you that."

"We'll get each other through the bad times. I promise you that."

Trey took his fifth step. The joy turned to resolve. "I'm going to trust you, Beth."

He couldn't have paid her a higher compliment. On the verge of tears again, Beth held his gaze. "I promise you won't be sorry for trusting me."

Two more steps. "We've got a lot of years ahead. I want us to be like my parents were. Like Maddy and Logan and John and Hannah. I promise to do what I can to see that we grow together, not apart."

Beth put her hands in Trey's as she stepped forward. "So do I."

He took his last step away from her, back to the beginning of their circle. "I promise to laugh with you every day."

Beth let a giggle escape as she joined him. "I promise that when I'm eighty, I'll still want to laugh with you."

They were standing where they'd started. Trey took Sidonie's ring from his pocket and put it back on Beth's finger. She walked into his arms.

"You may kiss the bride."

Trey kissed her breathless, this time showing her all the passion he'd been keeping in check over the past weeks. They made their way back to the blanket, and a blush – half shyness, half eagerness – warmed Beth's cheeks as he worked the buttons on her blouse. At last he pushed the material back, brushed aside ribbon straps and trailed soft kisses across her shoulder.

"There's a lot to be said for you wearing men's clothes, Beth," he murmured against her throat. "A dress can be a nuisance."

Scorching heat flooded through her as his lips grazed her skin, tracing the line of her collarbone. Beth glanced down at the lace and cotton she wore. "What about this?"

Trey slid a hand underneath the thin muslin to cup her breast, his palm lightly rubbing her nipple. Pleasure rocketed through her to pool in her lower belly. He grinned when she trembled.

"It's interesting."

Beth's chuckle ended in a moan. She didn't care much what she was wearing at the moment either. Trey lifted the camisole off over her head and pulled her close. His mouth came down on hers in a deep kiss while he caressed her, then he broke the kiss and let his lips stray again, finding the sensitive spots on her neck while he toyed with her breasts, tracing her curves, teasing her aching nipples. She let her head fall back to give him better access, relishing the sweet torture.

Beth had felt her body respond to a man before, but not like this. No one had ever had this kind of power over her, power to turn her bones to liquid. She wanted to melt into Trey so completely she didn't know where she ended and he began, and she wanted him to feel the same way.

She slid her hands up between them, unbuttoned his shirt and began exploring him with her hands and lips. She loved everything about the way he felt to her touch – the mat of crisp dark hair on his chest, the fine texture of his skin, the muscles that contracted and gave under her fingers as she ran them up his back. She felt his pulse with her lips and sent it racing faster to match her own. Trey took her chin in his hand, lifted Beth's face to his and whispered to her, his voice husky with need.

"Lie down with me."

They hurried out of the rest of their clothes like a pair of eager children. Trey eased Beth down to the blanket with him. Leaning over her, he ran a finger from the hollow of her throat down between her breasts to her stomach, then let his palm rest warmly there.

"Are you nervous?"

Beth reached up to touch his face, aching with the vulnerability she heard behind the need in his voice. He'd had women before, but had there been one he loved? It seemed this was a first time for him too.

"A little. I don't want to disappoint you."

Trey's eyes darkened to black as they roamed from her face down her body and back again. "Good Lord, Beth. You're the loveliest thing I've ever seen. I've been thinking about you, dreaming about you for weeks. You couldn't disappoint me. I just don't want to hurt you."

Beth drew him down to her and kissed him softly.

"Hurt me? Trey, I love this. I love you."

There wasn't anything else to say. Trey began caressing her with a gentleness that amounted to reverence, molding her with his hands, skimming over her with his mouth, suckling and tasting her until her whole body burned for him. Beth couldn't get enough, but she was just as greedy for his response, needing to feel his pleasure as much as her own.

Watching Trey's face, she slid her hand down his chest, following the trail of dark hair past ridges of muscle, until she came to his hard arousal. She felt his belly contract as her fingers curled lightly around him. His eyes drifted closed.

"Don't be shy, sweetheart. I'm yours."

For a moment Beth kept her hand still, absorbing his heat, his thickness. Then she began stroking him, running her fingers along his taut, silky skin, watching him respond to her touch.

"Jesus, Beth, you really are a witch!" Jaw rigid, eyes closed in rapt concentration, Trey moaned deep in his chest. The sound went straight to Beth's core, spurring her desire to a throbbing ache only he could ease. With a throaty little laugh, she wrapped her arms around him and reached for his mouth. He plunged into the kiss, gentleness forgotten in passion as he covered her body with his.

Beth had always thought that when this moment came she'd be a little bit afraid, but the flood of delicious new sensations left no room for fear. The rasp of Trey's chest hair against her sensitized nipples, the burn of his lips on her mouth and throat, drove everything from her mind but him. When she felt his hard length nudge her opening she instinctively wrapped her legs around him, inviting him inside her, where he belonged.

The flash of pain when he entered her dissolved as Beth's body relaxed, flowing around him. Resting on his elbows, his dark eyes on fire for her, Trey bent his head for a kiss.

"All right, love?"

He spoke in a harsh whisper against her mouth. Beth gasped as her inner muscles pulsed around him in welcome. "Oh, so much more than all right. Trey, please . . ."

Her voice died away on a sigh as Trey began moving, stroking her inside. The friction felt like nothing she could have imagined. With a will of their own her hips rocked to meet him, again and again, building exquisite tension until Beth thought she would shatter. When release came, it felt like flying.

She arched her back, taking Trey deeper as her climax rippled around him. When his body shuddered with his peak and he called her name, Beth knew he'd given her his heart as she'd given him hers. It gave her the sweetest, strongest sense of triumph she'd ever known. She cradled Trey against her with his head on her breast, loving the weight of him lying quiet in her arms, the feel of his ebbing flesh still filling her. While his breathing slowed she ran her fingers over his shoulders and down his back, tender touches that said what her full heart couldn't put into words.

We can trade old nightmares for new dreams, love. One day at a time. Together.

After a few minutes Trey rolled her onto his chest and folded the blanket over them. Beth lay with her head tucked against his shoulder, his body warm and solid under hers, his strong arms holding her close.

"My beautiful Beth. My wife." She heard the whispered words and murmured a response with her lips against his throat. She tasted his sweat there, smelled her scent on him as well as his own.

He was beautiful, too. All warm shades of brown, hair and eyes and skin. All long lines and lean muscle. She'd love to paint his portrait, just like this, but of course she'd have to knock him unconscious to do it.

His wife.

Possession. The word had never occurred to her in connection with Daniel. She would have found it repugnant if it had, but she didn't now. There was such a thing as belonging *with*, not belonging *to*.

Elizabeth Marie Underhill. In the middle of the woods, in broad daylight.

No, not Elizabeth Marie Underhill. Elizabeth Marie McShannon.

A few minutes later Trey's lips grazed her ear.

"What are you thinking?"

Beth glanced up. That sultry, sated look on his face was for her and her alone.

"I was just remembering sitting in the stage on the way here, wondering what on earth I'd gotten myself into. Now here we are. It's . . . strange."

Her hair had worked loose in their passion. Trey ruffled it gently and let it tumble in bright disarray over both of them. "I know. I feel the same way. I thought I was being pretty smart. Write to the agency, take a chance. It might even work. I deserved to get knocked flat, and I did."

Beth nestled closer, listening to his heartbeat. "I'm thinking of something I found in your Whitman a while ago. A magazine clipping. 'Singing all time, minding no time, while we two keep together.' That's how I feel right now, like I could lie here all day."

"I know what you mean." Trey pressed a kiss to the top of her head. "'Winds blow south or winds blow north, day come white or night come black, home, or rivers and mountains from home, while we two keep together.'"

Beth looked up with a grin. "So, you memorized it. Where did you get it? You never cut that out yourself."

"Well, a friend of mine gave me the book when I left home. The clipping was in it."

"Really." Beth raised an eyebrow at the hint of smugness in his voice. "Who was she?"

Trey's eyes went wicked. "She was the prettiest girl in the county, and she was crazy about me." He only winced a bit when Beth pinched him. "Well, she was, for a few weeks when I was sixteen. And I was crazy about her, along with half the boys in the county, but not enough to hurt. She told me she'd cut the poem out then, but didn't have the nerve to give it to me."

A wayward breeze lifted the edge of the blanket. Beth shivered and pulled it down. "A while ago, I would have sworn cold didn't exist. So she didn't break your heart?"

"No." Trey tightened his arms around her. "We stayed friends. She was Justin's sister, so it would have been awkward if we hadn't, but we wanted to. She was engaged when I left."

"What did she look like?"

"She had amber eyes, and skin like new cream, something like yours." His fingers moved down her back, making her tingle again. "And her hair was a few shades lighter than yours, but pretty much the same color. I guess it's a weakness of mine."

Beth brushed a few stray strands of sweat-darkened hair from Trey's forehead. "I'll keep that in mind the next time I see a pretty redhead. Now I'm thinking we should have lunch. I'm hungry, and you must be starving."

Trey stretched lazily and nodded. "Guess we'd better." But he wrapped his arms around her again, clearly in no hurry to go anywhere. "I'll get no more work done this afternoon with you here like this. Lady, you're a bad influence."

"Really? That's too bad." Beth trailed her fingers down his side to trace his scar, white and puckered against his brown skin.

Bless you, Neil Garrett, satanic as you look. I owe you, too.

"Trey, I just thought of something. We don't have a bed."

"What?"

Beth propped herself on an elbow and rolled her eyes at him. "A bed. You have one, I have one. *We* don't."

Trey chuckled and kissed her smiling mouth. "I'll fix us a bed. It won't be difficult." He shook his head. "Women. Always coming up with work to do."

Beth grinned and kissed him back. "I'm so sorry for you. Now, what about lunch?"

Trey's fingertips brushed lazily across the top of her breast, leaving a trail of heat on her skin. His eyes glowed with desire and she felt him hardening once more against her thigh.

"Lunch can wait."

Beth's breath caught in her throat, then released on a sigh as she lowered her mouth to his. "I guess it can."

CHAPTER 17

"All right, Ben, I'm going to let him go. You ready?"

Ben got a firm grip on the saddle horn with one hand and shortened his reins. "Go ahead." Trey let go of the bridle and stepped back.

Calico took a couple of tentative steps forward, then stopped. He'd learned to accept Ben on his back while being led, but he didn't seem sure what to do now.

Ben got a little over-eager and squeezed with his legs a bit too hard. Calico jumped forward, then knocked the bit against his teeth and stopped abruptly, nearly unseating his rider. The same thing happened two more times, while Beth and Holly watched from the fence. Beth giggled and Holly called out, "What're you riding, a grasshopper?"

Ben rolled his eyes at Trey across the corral and mouthed, 'I should have left her home.' Trey grinned and mouthed back, 'Smart man.'

"Go real easy," he said aloud. "Keep his head up, but be soft on his mouth."

Ben loosened the reins and urged Calico forward as gently as he could. This time he started at a walk, wary of bumping his teeth again. As they circled the corral, he gradually began to get the idea of stopping in response to the reins and starting in response to leg pressure. Ben looked triumphant as they passed Trey.

"He's getting it!"

Turning in the saddle to speak made him nudge Calico with his heel. The words were just out of Ben's mouth when the horse bolted, dumping him on the ground. Beth and Holly had another laugh at his expense before they went back inside to their sewing.

* * * *

Holly's green dress was finished except for the hem, and Beth was glad of it. She didn't know how she was going to get her own dress finished in time for the dance, even with Holly's help. The concert was turning out to be more of an undertaking than she'd expected.

Beth had gotten up amateur entertainments before, but not with such a cast on her hands. She wasn't sure which was the bigger problem – the lack of performers with talent, or the attitudes of the ones she had. Two or three boys had put their names on Reverend Baxter's list for no other reason than to hang around the rehearsals and tease the older schoolgirls, who were trying to practice the witches' dialogue at the beginning of scene four in *Macbeth*. None of them could remember their lines, and the first witch kept looking over the edge of her script to make eyes at one of the boys while saying, 'Round about the cauldron go; in the poison'd entrails throw', which did nothing to enhance the desired eerie effect. The second witch kept giggling in the middle of her lines, which didn't help either. Beth knew she could make the boys toe the line or leave by threatening to tell the girls' parents what was going on, but she didn't want to start alienating people.

No more than half of the younger children ever showed up at the rehearsals, and Beth had gotten on the bad side of Miss Jakeman, the teacher, who didn't believe in concerts and was annoyed because her students were being distracted from their schoolwork. When Beth came home after the second rehearsal she sounded off to Trey in the barn.

"Whose idea was this anyway?"

Trey hung up the bridle he'd been cleaning and shrugged. "Tell the boys to get lost. If they don't, tell Nate. That's what he's there for."

"But then the girls would quit too."

"So what?" Trey reached for another bridle and turned to face her. "I couldn't care less about the concert, but I do care that you're upsetting yourself over it. If they quit, call the damn thing off and forget it. It's not worth worrying over."

Beth rolled her eyes. "Thanks for the sympathy. I would call it off if it weren't for Holly. Have you ever heard her sing, Trey?"

"No. Like I said before, I didn't even know she existed until Ben mentioned her."

"Well, she has talent. Real talent, I think. I'd like to tell her so, but . . ."

"But what?"

"Well, I just don't know if it would be fair of me to encourage her. I'm no expert, and it would be such a struggle for her to do anything about it."

Beth sat on the grain barrel with her shoulders slumped and her back against the wall of the barn. Trey dropped the bridle, took her hands and lifted her to her feet.

"How old were you when someone told you that you had talent, Beth?"

It was hard to remember. As a child she'd loved to draw, without worrying about what anyone thought of the result. "About Holly's age I guess, when I started taking lessons."

Trey took Beth's chin in his hand and touched his lips to hers. "Do you think you'd have worked as hard if no one had told you?"

"How do you expect me to think when you're doing that? No, I suppose not, but that was different. I could afford lessons and . . ."

"And Holly will find a way to get training if she really wants it. I think she's as stubborn as you are." Trey kissed the tip of her nose and let her go. "Tell her. And don't worry so much over the concert. You don't have to. You're not the minister's wife."

Beth understood now why that position was still vacant, even though Reverend Baxter was an attractive man. Still, it went against her nature to give up. So, she wouldn't. If this was going to be her home, she wanted to be a part of it. The place and the people. If the concert failed and she and the cast ended up looking foolish, who would care?

She reminded herself of that at least three times a day as the concert date got closer. Now it was only a few weeks away.

She knew one person would care. Beth looked at Holly, intent on her hemming. Trey was right. She should tell her.

"Holly, what do you think you'd like to be when you're older?"

Holly hesitated for a moment. Beth doubted if anyone had ever asked her that before. "Well, when I was small I used to think I wanted to be a singer."

Beth unfolded her pattern pieces and started laying them out on the blue fabric. "But not anymore?"

Holly kept her eyes on her sewing. "I don't know. It would be a lot of work, and . . ."

"And you're not sure you have the talent," Beth finished for her. "Well, I'm no expert but I've heard professionals, and you've got quite a voice for someone your age. You'll never know unless you try."

"I've thought about it," Holly admitted. "About finding a job and getting some training. Maybe someday."

"I might be able to help." Beth formed a plan as she spoke. "I've got a few friends in Philadelphia with young families. In a couple of years, if you were willing to work as a nanny, I could put you in touch with some of them." As Holly's eyes lit up Beth hoped again that she wasn't setting the girl up for disappointment, but she was glad she'd spoken. "Keep it in mind. Now where is this sleeve supposed to go?"

* * * *

The fourth concert rehearsal took place the next evening. After supper, Beth took a wistful look around the cabin before following Trey outside. She'd much rather spend the evening curled up with him on the bunk that now served as a couch, talking or reading to each other, until sooner or later they decided to go up to the loft. Probably sooner, she thought with a smile.

Among the books that Graham had sent in Beth's trunk was a copy of *Pickwick Papers*. Dickens' first book had always been Beth's favorite. She and Trey had been reading it to each other and laughing over it for a while every evening lately. It lay on the bunk now, and it gave Beth an idea. She grabbed the book and hurried out to the wagon.

Trey was going in to town with her to get their supplies and spend the evening with John and Hannah. With an appreciative smile, he helped Beth up beside him.

"You're looking pleased with yourself."

Beth held up her *Pickwick*. "I am pleased with myself. I think I've come up with a way to deal with those boys, and I think the girls will help me."

"Good. What is it?"

"The skating scene from *Pickwick*."

"What about it? Don't think you can drag me into this scheme of yours, just because I can imitate Dad as Sam Weller."

Beth flashed him a teasing grin. "You'll see on the night of the concert."

When they arrived Reverend Baxter met them at the church, gave Beth a smile that said 'good luck' and left her to it. He'd made it clear that the rehearsals were her job. To do him justice, he really was busy.

For once, most of the younger performers showed up and Beth got their pieces out of the way first. Spencer and the organist didn't need to practice. She'd asked the older performers to come later.

By the time the children had left and the older girls began practicing their dialogue as the witches, the usual three boys were lounging in a front pew. The flirting and giggling began. Beth laid her *Macbeth* on the front pew, picked up her *Pickwick* and gathered the girls by the pulpit.

"You know, ladies, since you seem to have a problem being serious I think maybe we should see how you do with a comic scene. Have any of you read *Pickwick Papers*?"

One of the girls nodded. "Good." Beth opened her book to the skating scene. "Tell me what you think of this."

Beth had done her share of reciting, and by the time she finished reading through the scene the girls were laughing. One of them took the book to look over the lines.

"But how could we do it? It wouldn't work with us playing the men's parts."

That wasn't Beth's intention, but she played along. "If you did it properly it would just make it funnier. Let's try it. Jen, you read Mister Winkle. Carrie, you try Mister Weller. Becky can be Bob Sawyer and Martha, you take Mister Pickwick. I'll read everyone else for now."

The girls were in the mood to show off for the boys, so they agreed. The scene was pure physical comedy, centered on a very awkward first-time skater creating havoc at a skating party. As Beth had expected, they weren't sure what to do with it. The boys laughed and made comments until Carrie got annoyed.

"It's too bad you three don't have the nerve to get up here and do this."

That caused a brief whispered conference. When it ended, Jack Barron, the boy Carrie had been making eyes at, stood up.

"Who says we don't?"

His friends were right behind him. They came up front and passed the book around to read the main parts, with the girls filling in as needed.

"We can do this as well as you four can do your witch scene," Jack declared when they were finished.

That wouldn't be difficult, Beth thought. She had to hide her triumph when Carrie retorted, "Well, we'll see about that. You'd better find people for the other parts before you start bragging. You're going to need them."

Beth handed the book to Jack. "I'll write out the parts for the next practice. You're going to have to get moving, we've only got three weeks."

To her carefully concealed delight, the girls went to the other end of the church and began practicing their Macbeth scene seriously for a change, while the boys stayed up front and worked at their parts with equal determination. When Trey came by to pick Beth up, he found her tired but exultant. He reached for her hand as she climbed into the wagon.

"Well, how did it go tonight?"

Beth held up her *Pickwick* with a smug flourish. "My idea worked. We're going to have a concert, O ye of little faith."

Trey shook his head with a long-suffering smile. "Stubborn women. They're my fate I guess."

Beth sidled over and slipped her arm around him as they left town. The night had grown chilly enough for her to relish his warmth.

"Trey, you're good at mimicking your father. Maybe you could help the boys with their scene." She ran her hand up his back to gently tease the hair at the nape of his neck. "Feel like going over the lines when we get home?"

He gave her a wickedly suggestive grin and spoke volumes in one word. "No."

A full moon was rising over Beth's right shoulder, turning the road and the open land around it into an enchantment of silver and shadow. As they drove through it she wondered if it was possible to be any happier than she was at that moment.

"Trey, I'm very glad I'm not the minister's wife."

CHAPTER 18

With some careful nudging on his part, Nathan and Lorie had fallen into the habit of having breakfast at the boarding house most mornings. He hadn't given her much choice. After he let the usual sobered-up, hung-over drunks out of jail, he'd walk over to Neil's. She'd be waiting for him in a dress like most of the women in town wore, with her hair tied back. He suspected she'd dressed that way the first time to get a reaction from him. He hadn't obliged her.

Nathan knew Mrs. Grant wasn't exactly comfortable with Lorie coming to the boarding house, and he imagined Lorie wasn't exactly comfortable there herself, but then she never really was comfortable around him. Still, she hadn't pushed him away, and he'd decided she was going to have to push hard if she wanted him gone.

Nathan had settled into a routine with his job. He knew the local troublemakers now, and they knew him. As for trouble from outside, there hadn't been any since the rigged card game. He would have been starting to find Wallace Flats a little dull if it hadn't been for Lorie.

This morning as he walked to meet her, Nathan passed a poster advertising the dance and started remembering the dances and parties at home. He'd never been much of a dancer, and he'd been even less of one since the battle for Richmond when a shell had exploded next to him, shooting fragments into his left side. He'd been lucky not to lose his leg as well as his arm, damned lucky to survive at all. Lorie would have been sixteen then. Nathan found it hard to realize she was only twenty-one now. He'd found out her age from Neil. She would never have told him.

When he got to Neil's place, Nathan found Lorie waiting outside on the bench, wearing a blue dress he hadn't seen before. It looked like something Beth McShannon would wear. On her, it would have looked cool and graceful, but on Lorie it was bright and vivid. She'd pinned her hair up, but it didn't make her look prim. Nathan didn't think anything she could do would make her look that way.

"Morning, Lorie. Where did you get that dress?"

"Made it a couple of years ago. I was going into Denver for a few days."

She came down the steps and took his arm. No one paid them any attention as they walked down the street. People were getting used to seeing them almost every morning. Maybe too used to seeing them. A couple of Lorie's regular clients seemed to think so. Nathan had found out that they weren't clients anymore.

Her hazel eyes had their usual effect on his pulse as she looked up at him. "Quiet night?"

"Average. Bruce Allen, Drew Holland and Mark James." Bruce hadn't learned much from the poker game. He was still a magnet for bad company. On the other hand, Carl Manning had caused no more trouble since that night at Neil's. Maybe he'd changed, or maybe it was just that his hand was still sore.

They passed the same poster Nathan had walked by before. He glanced at it again, then at Lorie.

"You got anything planned for that night?"

Lorie put a little more distance between them. Nathan knew she wouldn't be working. Under pressure from the town council, Neil's place always closed early the night of the dance. Lorie seemed to be having a hard time coming up with an excuse on the spur of the moment. That surprised him. Nathan considered her good at thinking on her feet. After an awkward few seconds she looked at him out of the corner of her eye.

"No, I haven't got plans."

Nathan smiled to himself and said nothing more about it until they were sitting at their table at Mrs. Grant's, starting on more of her cornbread. Along with the table she kept for her boarders, Harriet had three smaller tables in another room for drop-ins. This morning Nathan and Lorie were the only customers in the 'restaurant.'

"I won't be going to the dance either. Don't see much point in both of us sitting around alone that night. Maybe we could help look after the babies or something."

Lorie stared, then laughed. "No thanks, Nate."

"Well, maybe not." Nathan poured coffee for them both and sat back, enjoying the uncertain look in Lorie's eyes. As long as she looked like that, he figured he was on the right track with her. "I'll have to be around town, but there's no reason you can't come over to the office for the evening. I'll be in and out."

Lorie stirred some sugar into her coffee, taking her time before she answered.

"I don't think so."

Nathan put on a teasing smile. He'd never seen her back down from a challenge.

"How's that different than having breakfast here?"

Holding her cup in both hands, Lorie leaned on her elbows and looked him in the eye. "It's different. We're friends, Nate. Let's keep it that way. You're going to ruin my business at this rate, which is probably just what you have in mind. Let's just eat."

Nathan said nothing more. He didn't have to. Lorie refused to show it but he knew he got to her, whether she liked it or not.

"Did you see Jake Montrose when he left Neil's last night?" she asked a bit too carelessly as they finished their breakfast. "You should have locked him up, too. He probably would have appreciated it. He wouldn't have dared go home to Mama in that condition."

Nathan downed the last of his coffee. "No, I didn't see him. He must have found a place to go. He can usually get one of his friends to put him up. I've told the Montroses what he's up to, but they're deaf and blind where Jake's concerned. Anyway, I've got a stack of paperwork waiting. See you later."

He paid his bill and left. Lorie would never let him pay hers. She'd made that clear the first time he tried. He knew she'd linger over her coffee until she was sure he was back in his office before returning to Neil's.

No, he wasn't bored with the town. Not by any means. Not yet.

* * * *

The last two weeks before the concert went by in a blur for Beth, what with getting her dress finished, drilling the performers and painting backdrops – the only painting she was getting done. Of course, regular daily chores went on as well.

"You're going to run yourself into the ground," Trey told her one evening when they were sitting out on the doorstep after supper. As the evenings grew gentler and longer, it had become their favorite place to relax at the end of the day.

Beth made a sound between a laugh and a sigh. "I'm fine. I'll slow down once it's over. I'm enjoying it, but it'll be nice to get back to my own work for a change."

The extra activity certainly wasn't hurting her. She guessed she'd gained ten pounds since coming to Wallace Flats – gained them in delightfully appropriate places, Trey seemed to think. He reached for her now and gathered her close.

"Is everyone behaving themselves?"

Beth smiled and leaned back against him. "Yes, they are. The girls actually know their lines, and the boys are getting close. You should see Jack Barron as Mister Winkle. He must be black and blue from the rehearsals. Holly's got her two songs down cold. She hasn't been to the rehearsals, but she goes over them when she's here. We finished my dress yesterday."

Trey pressed a kiss to the top of her head. "Beth, when we get around to having an election I think you should run for mayor of Wallace Flats. You'd have things running like clockwork."

"No, thank you. I've done my bit for the community for a while. Why don't you run?"

"Me? No. I figure you're a better general than I am."

Beth looked up with narrowed eyes. "I'm going to take that as a compliment. Otherwise I'd have to assume you're saying I'm bossy."

Trey bent his head to nuzzle the sensitive skin behind her ear. "It's better to remain silent and be thought a fool, than to speak up and remove all doubt. One of these days, I'll remember that before I open my mouth instead of after."

Beth tried for crispness and failed. "You'd better." She tilted her head to give him better access as he kissed a tingling trail down the side of her neck. "Mmm. Maybe it's getting too dark to sit out here any longer..."

After a few more hectic days, the only thing left to be done for the concert was fastening the backdrops to wooden frames, which had to wait until the platform was complete. That didn't happen until the morning of the concert itself. Beth rode into town after breakfast to see it done and have a last rehearsal. Trey would come in later if he could. After the scare they'd had with Shiloh, he was concerned about leaving Eve alone so close to foaling.

Jack and his friends had managed to come up with performers for the other roles in their dialogue, by methods Beth had decided not to probe. She'd painted a winter scene for them, on the paper the Bakers had donated, and a dark cavern backdrop for the girls. As the boys nailed the backdrops to their frames she prayed that the evening wouldn't be windy. At least there was no threat of rain.

As the afternoon went on, the party atmosphere in town became noticeable. Neil's place started humming as people from the outlying homesteads made their way in, businesses closed and the townspeople joined the celebration. Beth spent the afternoon at John and Hannah's, getting increasingly jittery. She knew a lot of the performers were more nervous than she was, which didn't help at all.

Early in the day, she'd seen Simon Grier slouch into the saloon. She hoped he'd be too far gone to move by the time the concert started. She hadn't asked, but she didn't think Holly had told him she was taking part. He didn't appear when people started to bring out chairs and assemble in the twilight in front of the platform.

Behind the blankets they'd strung up as a curtain, Beth marshaled the Sunday school children into rows and checked her watch. Ten past seven. They should be starting, but the Masons' three children hadn't appeared and she knew Mrs. Mason wouldn't be thrilled if they began without them. Thank goodness, there they were now. Beth hurried them into their places and nodded at Reverend Baxter, the master of ceremonies.

When Jack Barron and one of the other boys pulled open the curtains, one of the nails holding the cord they were strung on promptly fell out. The boys scrambled to mend matters while the little ones sang, or attempted to between giggles. At least the audience was laughing, too.

Neil had flatly refused to close so early, and a shouted obscenity carried clearly from his porch to the stage during the children's final song. Beth's face burned behind the curtain. *Keep your sense of humor.*

Spencer Hall got up next and played through a set of fiddle tunes that ranged from haunting slow airs to jigs and reels. Beth forgot her nerves as she listened. Spencer had a real gift.

Holly was next on the program. As she stepped to the front of the platform in her green dress, Beth crossed her fingers. She knew the girl was nervous, and she wanted this to be a success for her. If it went badly it might be enough to keep her from trying again. After a tense pause, Holly began her first piece.

'By the lake where droops the willow
Long time ago,
Where the rock threw back the billow,
Whiter than snow . . .'

Her nervousness disappeared as she settled into the ballad. Scanning the crowd, Beth realized that the faces out there were appreciative and maybe a bit astonished. Holly was singing well.

Her second song was a lively one she'd found in a book of Mrs. Henderson's.

'My love has gone to France
To seek his fortune in advance,
If he comes home there's but a chance . . .
I'll sell my rod, I'll sell my reel,
I'll sell my only spinning wheel,
To buy my love a sword of steel.'

Holly had everyone clapping to the lilting beat. Spencer picked up his fiddle, she nodded to him and he joined her. When they finished, the audience whistled and cheered. Holly bowed quickly and fled. Backstage, Beth met her with a hug.

"You're going to have to learn to make an exit, Holly. You couldn't have done better. Congratulations."

A crimson blush spread over Holly's face. "Thanks. They did like it, didn't they?"

Beth laughed. "They certainly did."

There was a brief pause while the boys lifted the backdrop for the witch scene into place. With a moment to think, Beth remembered two things. The first was that it was her birthday. She was twenty-four. It had slipped her mind in all the hurry and excitement of the day. The second was that Trey seemed to have forgotten it as well.

* * * *

As soon as Beth left for town, Trey started carrying the pieces of her birthday present one by one up to the loft. They'd had some fine birch at the sawmill and he'd made a bed frame and headboard, simply carved but carefully cut with a graceful curve and lightly stained to bring out the grain of the wood. A better job than he'd done on the rest of the furniture. He'd borrowed tools from Logan and spent his first winter at the homestead taking apart some old junked pieces he'd picked up, then copying them as best he could. The results couldn't be called beautiful, but he'd learned as he went along and this time he was pleased with what he'd done.

As he put the bed together, he grinned at the memory of the day he'd brought Beth home. It didn't make him smile, though, to remember how close he'd come to sending her back to Denver.

She couldn't banish his memories. He'd dreamed of Justin since that day by the river, but each time, before the dream became a nightmare, Trey woke with Beth in his arms. Life was richer and fuller than he'd ever dreamed it could be, even before the war. He knew now what plentiful lovemaking and a woman's good sense and tenderness could do for a man.

He guessed he'd always be a little afraid of losing Beth, but the fear only made him appreciate every moment. Trey supposed he was like every other newlywed on earth and it would have been sad if he hadn't been, but deep down he'd always known he wanted the kind of strong, deep love his parents had shared. What he and Beth had was still growing and strengthening, that was the miracle of it.

When he'd finished with the bed, he worked his way through some other chores then went out to take care of the barn before heading into town. He looked in on Eve first. She seemed uncomfortable, as Beth had noticed that morning. "You've had enough of feeling big and clumsy, haven't you?" she'd said as she ran a hand over the mare's bulging side. "Well, it'll be all over soon."

The muscles around Eve's tail had relaxed, telling Trey her time was near. He went on with the chores, keeping an eye on her as he worked. By the time he'd finished, she'd started pacing her stall. He put a hand on her side and felt a contraction ripple through her.

"You sure know how to pick your time, don't you?" So much for the concert. Resigned, he settled down to watch the birth.

* * * *

By the time everything was ready onstage it was deep twilight, perfect for the candlelit witch scene. Neil's place had closed and the rowdies had dispersed until the dance, so things were quiet.

Beth had been afraid the girls would get nervous and make the dialogue gruesome rather than eerie, but they didn't. When Martha finished with, 'By the pricking of my thumbs, something wicked this way comes', they got an honest round of applause. Then the set had to be changed for the boys' dialogue, which finished the show.

Trey still hadn't appeared. He must have needed to stay with Eve. Beth wished she were there, too. If it were another difficult foaling, he wouldn't find anyone to help him. Maddy and Logan were in town. Helpless from where she stood, Beth pushed her concern aside and forced her mind back to her performers. In a few minutes, the backdrop was up and lanterns hung around the platform. The curtains opened to reveal the skating pond with Mr. Pickwick's party gathering.

With perfect timing, Jack flailed around in character as Mr. Winkle. His friend, Hugh Johnson did Sam Weller almost as well as Trey did. Then, as Mr. Winkle collided with Bob Sawyer, Jack tripped and staggered into the corner of the backdrop. The frame collapsed and the whole contraption fell on top of the boys, while the female characters at the side of the stage shrieked, then burst into gales of laughter. As a finale, Jack's head pushed through the paper. The audience cheered and whistled. They sat through Reverend Baxter's closing remarks more or less politely and then dispersed, laughing, to come back in half an hour for the dance.

Beth, Reverend Baxter and the boys cleared away the mess on the platform. Jack couldn't have been happier. His performance would be remembered now for years instead of days. Beth didn't know whether to laugh or cry, but eventually her sense of humor asserted itself. In spite of it all, she savored a sense of accomplishment. They'd made a decent amount of money for the church fund, and she knew almost every face in town. Now if only Trey would show up.

Beth went back to the Reeves' house to change into her blue dress and wait for him. Through an open window, she heard Spencer tuning his fiddle as people started to gather again. Her concern had shifted to worry by the time she finally saw Cloud cantering up the street.

Trey's eyes widened as he stopped in the doorway and looked Beth over. The organdy dress clung to her body down to the waist, then flared over her hips and fell in three graceful tiers to the floor. Beth had been devoutly thankful when hoops went out. This softer look became her much better. The scooped neckline showed a hint of cleavage, bringing a slow smile to Trey's face.

"So, this is it. Are you looking to cause a brawl?"

Beth blushed. "Is it too revealing?"

His smile widened to a grin as he drew her into his arms. "Is there such a thing?"

"Trey!"

He chuckled and kissed her. "You're beautiful. Sorry I'm late, but Eve decided it was time for her own party."

243

He wouldn't be here if it hadn't gone well. Beth laughed with relief. "I thought that might have happened. Colt or filly?"

"A bay colt with legs a mile long. He's a dead ringer for his daddy. Everything went like clockwork. How was the concert?"

"Memorable." Beth told him the tale as they walked over to the square ahead of John and Hannah. Trey found it as amusing as everyone else had.

"I'll bet Jack did that on purpose to make an impression."

Beth recalled Reverend Baxter's face as the set collapsed. "He made an impression, all right."

They took their place among the dancers as Spencer played the opening bars of 'The Ash Grove'. As they eased into the waltz, Beth looked up in surprise. Trey was guiding her as smoothly as if he'd been doing it all his life.

"You're good at this."

That sly look again. "Thought I'd surprise you. There were plenty of dances and parties at home. Happy birthday, Beth."

Beth moved closer and smiled up at him. "It's the happiest one I've ever had." Then she gave herself up to enjoyment of the night. The concert was over, Eve had given birth safely, and Trey looked delightfully out of character in his charcoal broadcloth suit and cream brocade vest. She'd never felt more like dancing.

* * * *

Standing on the sidelines with Ben, Holly still glowed with excitement over the concert. Her energy made

244

him feel shy. Holly had a toughness about her that scared Ben a little at times. After a few minutes, he worked up the courage to reach for her hand.

"Your songs sounded great. Were you nervous?"

"A little at the beginning, but not for long. I was just happy the audience was enjoying it."

Her eyes strayed to the stage, watching Spencer. Ben felt like she was a million miles away, but then she turned and smiled at him. It gave him some nerve.

"Would you like to dance?"

Holly looked shy too, and that put him a little more at ease.

"Sure."

As they joined the others John caught his son's eye and winked. Hannah rolled her eyes. "For heaven's sake, John, you'd think you were fifteen yourself."

John twirled her around and kissed her. "You can't help getting older, but you don't have to grow up."

* * * *

To Lorie, sitting in her room, the music sounded muted and dreamy, like a hazy memory of something that had happened a long time ago. She closed her window to shut it out.

She supposed Nathan would have given up expecting her by now. He'd never said anything more about them spending the evening together, but the unspoken challenge had still been there. If she'd thought he'd read her absence as indifference that would have been fine, but Lorie knew he wouldn't. Maybe she should have gone to meet him after all.

He'd be out there unobtrusively watching the dance, keeping an eye open for trouble. He might be outside Neil's place right now. At the thought, she closed her curtains and pulled her blue dress from the closet. The hem needed fixing in a couple of places.

It's no good, Lorie. You don't know how to be the kind of woman he's looking for. You don't want to be that kind of woman. You can't keep working here, not with him in town. Time to move on.

That was the truth, plain and simple. Too bad the truth made her feel so rotten.

The tricky part would be getting out of town without Nate catching her. Lorie believed what he'd said about throwing her in jail again if she left, and who knew what kind of a choice he'd give her if he did. She had enough cash to live on for two or three months, so the sensible thing would be to get to Denver, but she didn't like the thought of working in any of the places she knew there.

But, as Nate had said, there were other towns. For the first time Lorie considered finding another line of work. She could clerk in a store or wait tables. There had to be something.

Damn you to hell, Nathan Munroe.

Lorie threw the dress on the bed and started stuffing clothes into a suitcase. She knew Nate usually kept an eye on the stage when it arrived, but that was mostly to be aware of strangers coming into town. He wasn't as concerned about passengers getting on. If she wore something he hadn't seen and fixed her hair differently she might have a chance.

No. He was too observant and he'd watched her too closely. She'd need a diversion. Lorie planned it as she packed. She'd have breakfast with Nathan in the morning so he'd have no reason to suspect anything. When the stage arrived, he'd be busy, and when it left she'd be on it.

* * * *

The dance turned out to be a quiet affair, relatively speaking, with only three actual fights. Everybody managed to find their own horse and conveyance without too much trouble afterwards.

After she changed back into her old dress, Ben drove Holly home in his father's wagon. When they came within sight of the house, she put a hand on his arm.

"Better let me off here. Pa's still up. The lamp's burning." She jumped from the wagon and flashed him a quick smile. "Thanks, Ben, I had fun tonight. See you Monday. 'Bye."

When Holly went in, she found her father sitting at the table, rubbing his temples. One glance told her he was sober and furious.

"Where the hell have you been 'til this hour?"

"The dance just ended, Pa. I had to wait to get a drive home."

Her father was an apathetic drunk, but the apathy turned to belligerence when the hangover set in. He jabbed a finger at the chair across from him. Holding her breath, Holly sat. She knew from long experience not to speak at a time like this. Her father sat back and smacked his hand on the table.

"It's past midnight. A fine time for you to be getting in. That was a boy who drove you home. Who was it?"

"Ben Reeves. He was nice enough to offer me a drive." In spite of her fear, a note of defiance crept into Holly's voice. *I had such a good time today. Why should I have to come home to this?*

Her tone pushed her father over the edge. He leaned across the table and grabbed her arm. "You listen to me, girl. I'm not going to have you running the roads with boys at your age."

Holly jerked away. "We weren't running the roads. He was being a gentleman. Would you be happier if I'd walked two miles home at this hour? I'm going to bed."

Her father gave her a look that kept her in her chair. "You're not going anywhere 'til I'm through with you. I don't know what kind of ideas that woman you've been working for has been filling you with, but I've had enough. Did she pay you like she promised?"

"Of course she did. Here." Holly fished the money out of her pocket and threw it on the table.

"You're lucky. I don't want you going out there again, you hear?"

Holly met his gaze with her eyes flashing. She'd proven something to herself that day, and at the moment she just didn't care what her father thought. "You know something, Pa? In another two years I'll be through school and I'm going to get out of here. I'm going to forget this place ever existed. And there won't be one thing you can do to stop me."

For a moment Simon sat motionless, looking at her. She knew what was coming as soon as he got up.

CHAPTER 19

In spite of bleary eyes and dragging feet, Beth had to take a peek at the new foal when she got home. Trey lit a lantern and they both leaned on the half-door, watching the little replica of Cloud weaving around on spindly legs.

"He's perfect, Trey. I'll have to make his acquaintance properly in the morning, but right now I can't keep my eyes open."

Trey looked tired himself. They'd both been on the go since daybreak, and now it was past one. He stepped into Eve's stall for a final inspection of her and the new arrival.

"You go on up to bed, Beth. I'll be there in a minute. Your birthday gift's up there waiting for you."

Beth went in, lit the lamp and a candle and climbed the ladder. When she saw the bed, she let out a yelp of surprise.

"Trey, you dear, how did you find time for this?" She got into her nightgown, dropped onto the mattress and reached up to trace the design on the headboard. The day she'd found him looking like a guilty schoolboy in the barn, Trey must have been hiding the wood when she walked in. Had he known she was for him, even while he was still afraid he couldn't have her? The thought made Beth smile as she got under the covers. She'd tell him how pleased she was as soon as he came up to bed. She blew out her candle, snuggled under the quilt and settled herself to wait.

She opened her eyes to a stream of morning light pouring in the window. Trey slept beside her, lying on his side with his face toward the wall, the quilt down around his waist, his back a tempting expanse of smooth tanned skin. Beth watched him for a few minutes, thinking she should let him rest after their late night, but the urge to wake him grew too strong. She nestled close and placed a soft kiss between his shoulder blades, then another.

"You keep that up and there's gonna be trouble."

His lazy growl brought a wicked smile to Beth's face. "Is that so?" She brushed her lips and tongue along his shoulder. "Well, I think you're all talk."

"Oh, yeah?"

"Yeah."

In one quick move Trey rolled, caught her wrists and held her hands above her head, pinning her with his weight. Beth struggled until she was breathless, just to enjoy his strength, then she let herself go limp. Her sudden surrender brought a hot light to Trey's eyes.

"Is this your way of saying thank you?"

Beth lifted her hips to rub against him, sighing when she found him already aroused. "You might say so."

Trey released her hands, pressed her into the mattress and covered her mouth with his. She wasn't looking for a slow, tender taking this time, and he knew it. She matched the fierceness of his kiss with her own passion, threading her fingers into his hair to hold him to her. Beth's nightgown rode up as she wrapped her legs around him in invitation. Trey moaned into her mouth as he slid inside her.

"You sure know how to wake a man up, Beth."

With a little gasp Beth slid her hands down his back, pressing him closer. "Thanks, McShannon. Now do you know when to stop talking?"

He didn't say another word. They lost track of time as they lost themselves in each other. Familiarity had only made this better. Beth knew Trey's body well now, knew just how and where to touch him to give him the most pleasure, and he'd learned to do the same to her. Trey would never be a man who talked easily about his feelings, but it didn't matter, not when he showed them by taking her to places she hadn't known existed.

By the time they came back to reality, the morning had nearly flown. After a belated rush through chores, Beth got her first good look at the new foal. He was smaller than Diamond had been at birth, a lighter bay than Cloud, already bold and curious. He walked right up to Beth when she entered the stall.

"I think we should call him Viking. He's an explorer all right."

"Sounds good to me." Trey came up beside her and slipped an arm around her waist. "Looks like all of Cloud's get are going to be little spitfires. Sorry I didn't make it to the concert."

"Well, you were needed here." Beth reached out to stroke the inquisitive little muzzle Viking poked toward her. "I'm just glad it all went well this time."

Trey went out to toss a couple of armfuls of hay into Calico's stall. "Ben asked me last night if he could take this one home today. I think they're both ready."

Beth joined him, looking in at the mustang with regret. Calico had come a long way with them, and she hated to see him go now that they'd earned his trust. "I'll miss him."

Trey shook his head when Cloud loudly demanded his late breakfast. "So will I, but Cloud sure won't. He'll be easier to deal with, at least."

Ben had said he'd be coming for his horse before lunch, but he didn't show up until afternoon. It wasn't like him to be late. When he rode into the yard, one glance at his tense, white face told Trey and Beth something was wrong. Trey asked him what it was as soon as he was off his horse. Ben spat out his words as if they tasted bad.

"I saw Simon Grier in town, so on my way out I stopped by to see Holly. She wouldn't come to the door, but I figured she was there so I looked in the window. I saw her. Her face . . ." Ben clenched his fists and took a deep breath. "For two bits I'd take my rifle and give him what he deserves."

Beth made an indignant sound. A dangerous spark flared in Trey's eyes, but he kept his cool. "You could do that, Ben, and chances are people would look the other way. He's not exactly popular. He'd probably do something so you could call it self-defense. But to Holly you'd always be the one who killed her father. Is that how you want her to think of you?"

Ben had to think about it before he could answer. "No, but I'm not going to let him treat her that way."

Trey put a hand on the boy's shoulder and looked him in the eye. Ben almost matched his height, and the look that passed between them was very much man-to-man. "Neither am I. You get Calico ready and I'll ride back in with you."

"Trey, I'm so glad you took him seriously about shooting Simon," Beth said when Ben was safely in the barn. "He would have been even more upset if you hadn't."

Trey's grip on his temper slipped a little. "I took him seriously because he meant it. At fifteen, I was as good a shot as I'm ever going to be, and so is Ben. If his father and I don't handle this, he'll figure he's got no choice. This isn't Philadelphia, Beth."

Beth's tone sharpened with her own anger. "No, but there are ways and there are ways. Don't you think this is a job for Nathan? What else did they hire him for?"

She didn't like what she saw in Trey's eyes at that moment. "Nate can have what's left of Simon when John and I get through with him. This has been going on for years and no one's done anything about it. We're going to."

"But you can't blame Nathan for this," Beth protested. "It hasn't happened since he's been here."

Trey shot her a smoldering look. "I'm not blaming him. He can't do anything, anyway. Simon hasn't broken the law." His tone softened at the worry Beth couldn't help showing. "We won't lose our heads. I'd better get Cloud saddled. Damn it, I've got work to do today."

* * * *

Simon was spending the afternoon at his usual table in the saloon. Nathan leaned on the bar, talking to Neil over a beer. They both looked up when Trey and John walked in, grabbed Simon's arms and hauled him out of his chair.

"Come on, Simon, we're taking you home."

The shock on his face turned to fury as he looked from Trey to John and back again. "The hell you are!"

Trey bent Simon's arm behind his back until he flinched. "What's it going to be, Simon, the easy way or the hard way? I don't give a damn myself. It's up to you."

Nathan crossed the room, studied the situation for a moment and then spoke to John. "Problem?"

"Yeah, there's a problem. Simon here has been slapping his daughter around. She's a friend of my son's, and we don't appreciate it."

Nathan glanced at Simon, then turned to Trey. "You?"

"I just don't like his face." Trey spared Nathan a quick glare, then got a tighter grip on Simon's arm and turned toward the door. "See you around, Nate. Let's go."

Before they could take a step, Nathan held up his hand. "Hold on. Neil, come over here a minute."

Neil came out from behind the bar and joined them. "Yeah, what?"

"It seems like our friend here has a problem holding his liquor. I don't think you should sell to him anymore."

Neil's voice took on an edge. "Seems to me it's my choice who I sell to."

"Not when your customers go home and beat their kids it isn't," Nathan said in that soft, dangerous tone of his. "Keep him out of here."

"Well, if you put it that way, fine." Neil shrugged. "Tough luck, Simon. Serves you right."

Neil headed back to the bar. Nathan nodded to John and Trey. "Fine. Now you two can walk him over to the jail for me."

"You can all go to hell!" Simon wrenched his arms free and glared at Nathan. "A man's got a right to deal with his kids. She needed a lesson. What about these two? This is assault!"

Nathan chuckled and shook his head. Trey remembered that don't-give-a-damn smile very well. "Well, if you want to press charges, Simon, I guess I'll have to lock all three of you up. You for disturbing the peace . . ."

"What peace?"

"Mine. I was having a peaceful drink before this happened. You for disturbing the peace, and them for assault. I guess one cell will do for all of you. Come on, let's go."

Trey might not appreciate Nate interfering, but he had to appreciate the man's sense of humor. Simon didn't seem to relish it, though. Seeing the look on his face was almost as satisfying as landing a few punches. Trey decided it was payment enough for cooperating with Nate. He and John frog-marched Simon over to the jail, with stares from several curious onlookers as they went. Nathan walked in ahead of them and opened a cell.

"How long are you going to keep him?" John asked.

"'Til tomorrow." Nathan gave his prisoner an offhand glance. "He isn't worth feeding more than once."

Trey let go of Simon's arm. "Keep him a couple of days. We should be able to find a place for his daughter to stay by then." He gave the man a cold stare. "This isn't going to happen again."

Simon planted his feet and jabbed a finger into Trey's chest. "She'll stay home where she belongs. You've got no right—"

Before he could finish the sentence, John buried his right fist in Simon's midsection, knocking him into the cell. "Think about this, Simon. You make a fuss about it and I won't be shoeing your horses. The Bakers won't be selling you supplies. Neil's already not selling you liquor. And Nathan will have you in here if you put your little toe out of line."

Simon lay doubled up on the cell floor, gasping. Trey walked in, picked him up by his shirt collar and gave him another punch in the belly, knocking him backward onto the bunk. "And you'll have me to deal with. You'd better do some thinking. The next time you get a hate on, why not work it off putting a roof on that house of yours? John, let's get out of here before I do something I wouldn't regret at all."

The next thing to do was to check on Holly. When Trey and John arrived at the Grier place they found Beth and Maddy already there. Beth had ridden over to the Kinsleys' as soon as Trey and Ben left for town.

Holly had some nasty bruises. Trey doubted if Simon had ever been that violent with her before. All in all, she seemed to be doing as well as could be expected. She was sitting on her father's bed between Maddy and Beth when the men came in.

"What happened to Pa?" Holly spoke with real regret. Trey couldn't believe anyone could be as blind as Simon Grier.

"He'll be in jail for a couple of days, and then he'll be free to come back here, but you won't be here. We're going to find a place for you to live. John and Hannah would be happy to have you and so would Beth and I, but neither of us have a spare room."

"We can take her," Maddy said, "and we'd be pleased to. Beth and I talked it over with Logan before we left." She put an arm around Holly. "What do you think? It's a ways from town, but we've got a horse you can use to get back and forth to school and your friends will be welcome. There are times when I miss having someone young around."

Beth smiled. "And we're not far away. You'd be welcome any time. I still have plenty to learn about sewing. Will you give it a try?"

Holly hesitated, eyes on the floor, but after a moment she glanced at Maddy. "All right, I'll give it a try."

Maddy gave her a light squeeze. "Good. We brought our wagon, so let's just pack whatever you want to bring with you and we'll be going."

* * * *

Rather than listen to Simon, Nathan took his paperwork to his room. He didn't come out until Jack Barron and three of his friends knocked on the office door.

"Mister Munroe, we think there was someone picking pockets at the dance last night. We're all missing money."

Nathan gave Jack a cynical look. "Why do you think a pickpocket would target you boys? He couldn't expect you to be carrying much."

"No, sir, but maybe he was just hitting as many folks as he could."

Nathan smelled a rat, but the boys looked serious and he supposed it was possible. He waved them inside. "All right, I'd better write this down. Come in."

They trooped into the office and stood around Nathan's desk. He turned to Jack first. "Well, how much money are you missing and when did you notice it was gone?"

"A couple of dollars. Hugh and I were heading home after the dance, and some change fell out of his pocket when he got on his horse. I checked my own pocket and found out my money was gone."

Preserve me from idiots. "So, you had holes in your pockets. Haven't you heard of needles and thread? I should talk to your mothers about you boys."

Luke Connor spoke up. "This morning I found I was missing five dollars. It doesn't make sense that we'd all have holes in our pockets, does it? I'll bet if you ask around, you'll find we aren't the only ones."

Between the four of them, they occupied Nathan for half an hour, giving a confused account of where they'd been, whom they'd talked to and how much money each of them was missing. When Nathan had gotten all the details and promised to ask around to see if anyone else had been hit, the boys thanked him and left. It wasn't until the next morning that he found out Lorie was gone.

CHAPTER 20

When she and Trey got home from the Grier place, Beth remembered she still hadn't opened the mail she'd picked up the previous morning. There was a letter for her from her friend Isobel James in New York. Beth read it while Trey put the horses away and was still sitting at the table, stunned, when he came in ten minutes later. He took one look at her and crossed the room in two long strides.

"Beth, what's the matter?"

She handed him the letter. "Read it."

Dear Beth,

I suppose it will be close to your birthday when you get this. I'm enclosing a little gift for you, a check for the sale of Meadow at Sunset.

The buyer was Vance Hickstead, the man I mentioned in my last letter. You really should meet him, Beth. He's very impressed with your work and he has a lot of the right connections here in the city. If you're serious about selling your work, he is a very valuable man to know.

A close friend of Mr. Hickstead's has a private gallery, small but highly rated. They're starting to spring up in the city now. I'm sure we could arrange a showing if you have enough work ready and could be here to attend. In fact, Mr. Hickstead suggested it. I read in the Times that the rail line to Denver has just been completed, so you've really no excuse. You aren't going to get any further without meeting people like him, Beth, and he'll lose interest if he doesn't think your work will appreciate in value.

Besides, I'm selfish. I like to bask in reflected glory without having to work for it myself. Get on the train and bring that husband of yours with you. I want to meet the man who could convince you to bury yourself in Colorado Territory. Wire me and let me know your plans as soon as you can. It's important. Walter sends his regards.

As ever,

Isobel

P.S. I haven't told anyone E.M. Underhill is a woman. They haven't asked.

Trey dropped the letter and picked up the check. "Congratulations," he said, sounding as shocked as Beth felt.

Beth scanned the letter again, folded it neatly and laid it back on the table. "Two hundred dollars. I don't know what to think. When Aunt Abigail and I would go to New York I used to dream that something like this might happen someday, and now it has. It'll be good to see Isobel again."

Trey froze in place and looked at her with all his old wariness in his eyes. "You're going?"

That quickly, a wall sprung up between them. Beth's excitement drained away. The biggest opportunity of her life, and he looked like she'd just slapped his face.

"Don't you think I should? This could mean a lot to us. I hoped you'd be happy if something like this happened."

Trey still had the check in one hand. He took a step forward and rested the other on the back of a chair. The distance between them grew as he spoke. "I'm proud of you and pleased for you, Beth. You know that."

The words sounded so forced Beth wished he hadn't said them. She reached out and took the check from him, very tempted to tear it up. He'd spoiled the joy of it for her.

"Well, you don't look it."

With what looked like a conscious effort, Trey unclamped his hand from the chair back, but he didn't sit down. He looked poised to walk out the door. "Beth, I know you've been happy here, but how can you live at both ends of the country? You have talent. I don't want to feel like I'm holding you back."

Beth's temper got the better of her. She snatched the letter off the table, crumpled it and threw it across the room as hard as she could. It quite simply broke her heart to think he could doubt her now.

"You just don't get it, do you? After that day by the river, after the way things have been between us since then. What do I have to do to convince you? I belong here, too!"

Trey's voice rose to match hers. "Then why do you have to go to New York? If your work's good it's good, and people will buy it whether or not you're there. You just found that out."

In spite of her anger, Beth had to hide a smile. After all, city life as she'd known it was as foreign to Trey as his life had once been to her. "It isn't quite that simple. A lot depends on reputation, and a lot of that is very political. You have to make yourself known to the right people. I need to make connections so I can ship my paintings and get good prices for them. I'll probably have to make a couple of short trips over the next couple of years, and fewer after that if things go well. If that isn't enough, then it isn't enough. I know I'm needed here, too."

Trey rested his hands on the chair again, obviously struggling with his own temper. After a few seconds he spoke quietly. "And what if it isn't enough? I know how important your work is to you, Beth. Once you're back in that world . . ."

Beth got up, moved toward him and stood close, looking into his eyes. "Trey, do you seriously think I could walk away from you now?"

He put his hands on her shoulders, but he wouldn't bring her closer.

"I still wouldn't blame you if you did."

The contact didn't bridge the distance between them. Beth fisted her hands in frustration.

"Trey, you know I'm satisfied with what we have here. We settled that when Diamond was born. And you also know this place is what my work is about. I can't do it anywhere else." Something flickered in his eyes, behind the remoteness. Beth's instinct told her it was fear. She decided to pursue it. "But this isn't really about me, is it? You know what I think? You're afraid, plain and simple."

That earned her a smoldering look. "What's that supposed to mean?"

Good. She could deal with his anger, and she knew it meant she'd read him right. Beth stood her ground and returned his glare. "You were eighteen when you lost your mother and your father left. Three years later it was Justin, and I have no idea how many other friends before him. Now you think it's going to be me. Well, if you keep thinking that way it will be. If we don't have more trust than that between us, there'll be no reason for me to come back here. I can't give up my work for you or anyone else."

Trey took his hands off her and stepped back, his face closed and angry. "I don't want you to give it up. Go to New York. That's where your future is."

God, ten minutes ago she could never have imagined this. "You're telling me to leave, just like that?"

Trey's voice cracked with hurt and frustration. "I'm not telling you to leave. I want you to do what's best for you. I love you too, Beth, but sometimes that isn't enough."

He turned and walked out. A few minutes later, sitting at the table with her head in her hands, Beth heard Cloud leave the yard. She got up, washed her face and went out to saddle Chance. She needed to talk to Maddy.

Beth found her sitting on her front step, peeling carrots. Maddy's welcoming smile faded when she got a look at her visitor's face.

"Well, it's plain you haven't got good news."

Beth plopped down beside her, picked up a carrot and snapped it in two. She wasn't going to cry. . . but a tear ran down the bridge of her nose. Then another. She threw the carrot in Maddy's pot and wiped them away.

"To put it in a nutshell, I'm going to New York for a while. Maybe a long while. Maybe for good, I don't know."

Maddy put an arm around her and sighed. "I thought the sailing was just a little too smooth to last for you two. Tell me what happened."

Beth told her about Isobel's letter. "This could be important for us, Maddy. I could really help Trey build the horse business. We could put something away for our children. I've dreamed about something like this happening, and Trey's acting like I'm abandoning him. If I thought he was just being selfish I'd tell him so, but the truth is he still doesn't trust me."

Maddy smiled, but her blue eyes were full of sympathy. "Trust takes time, and that's something you and Trey haven't given yourselves much of. He doesn't know the world you came from, and now you're going back there. He's afraid of losing you."

Beth wiped her eyes and clasped her arms around her knees, picturing the look on Trey's face before he walked out. "I know. I told him that, but it just made him angrier."

"Well, that's not surprising." Maddy shrugged. "It isn't something he'd want to admit. When do you have to go?"

"As soon as I can, to be back in time for haying. If I come back."

The thought of not coming back, of never waking up next to Trey again or listening for him to come home at night, brought the fiercest heartache Beth had ever known. Her smile gone, Maddy picked up her paring knife and shook her head. "Whatever happens, come back. You love him, Beth, and he loves you. He also needs you. Trey's not a fool. He'll come around."

"I know you're right, but I can't *feel* it right now. I do love him, the infernal idiot. Things have been so good between us." Beth gave Maddy a fierce hug. She didn't feel quite as hurt and hopeless as she had when she'd arrived. "I'd better ride into town and wire Isobel. Maddy, I'm going to miss you."

Maddy pulled back to look her in the eye. "I'll miss you too. And Beth, when he wakes up, don't hold out on him. It isn't worth it."

"I know." Beth took a deep breath and got up. "Wish me luck, Maddy."

After another hug, she mounted and started Chance at a slow jog toward town. Beth wanted to think, to look past her hurt and disappointment and see what she'd find.

She recalled Trey's face as she'd seen it in his picture. A boy's face. His world had come crashing down around him before he'd had time to grow up, and she knew now that the war had nearly shattered him. She sensed it in the slow, cautious way Trey had come out of himself over the last few weeks with her, as if a long, hard winter had finally given way to spring.

When he'd arrived in Wallace Flats, instead of gravitating toward the other young homesteaders and cowhands he'd chosen John and Hannah and Logan and Maddy for friends. Trey had pushed himself to the breaking point trying to replace the home he'd lost, and he'd sought out people who had the stability he missed. Now he thought he'd found that stability with her, only to have it taken away again. How could she do it?

If you don't, you'll drift apart. If she didn't go to New York now, Trey would never find what he was looking for, because he had to find it in himself. Beth couldn't give it to him, but it would take every ounce of will she possessed not to stay with him and try.

* * * *

Trey arrived home just before midnight. He put Cloud away, stepped quietly into the lightless cabin and stood there in the dark, listening to the soft sound of Beth's breathing coming from the loft.

It didn't sound as if she was asleep. He wanted to climb up there, gather her in his arms and hold on for dear life, but he couldn't. If he had to let her go, why make it more difficult for both of them?

She had him pegged. He was afraid. He wasn't sure he could go back to living the way he had when he'd arrived here, with nothing but work to keep him sane. But he'd promised himself that if Beth left she wasn't going to take his heart with her, and he intended to keep that promise. He owed it to himself, and he knew it was the only way Beth would go forward and take what the future offered her.

That meant he had to start the painful process of pushing her away.

Trey pulled off his boots, stretched out on his old bunk and closed his eyes. He'd exhausted himself before heading for home, but sleep evaded him. Pictures kept revolving in his mind. He saw himself sitting beside his mother's bed, holding her hand while she whispered goodbye. Standing on a pier in New York, watching a ship disappear over the horizon. Kneeling in the road that night with Justin, seeing the light of recognition in his eyes before they went sightless. This was different, but it didn't feel like it.

His feelings weren't the issue, though. Beth couldn't build her career if the people who mattered had never seen her face, and he had no right to ruin that for her.

When the first light showed through the east-facing front window, Trey got up and made a pot of coffee. Beth heard him and climbed down from the loft, still in her nightgown. The heartbroken look on her face nearly cracked Trey's resolve. He busied himself at the stove until the coffee was ready, then poured two cups and sat across from her at the table.

"Beth, I think it'll be easier for us both if you go as soon as you can."

She nodded. "If that's what you want. I wired Isobel that I'd start next week, but I can wire her again."

She sounded as if she'd cut him loose already. Trey tried his coffee while he got a fresh grip on himself. It couldn't hurt this much for long.

"Beth, you're not to blame for this any more than I am. We both should have done some more thinking. I guess it's going to take a while for us to work this out, but you have to go."

He hated himself for the bruised look in those blue eyes. "Yes, I have to go. I'd never forgive myself if I didn't, but it doesn't have to be all or nothing. I wish you could see that."

If she started arguing, Trey didn't think he'd be able to keep from reaching for her. He clenched his hands on his coffee cup and took a deep breath. "Beth, let's not fight. Not now."

"No, let's not." Beth sighed and took a moment to steady her voice. "It won't take me long to get ready. I'll pick up most of my clothes at Graham and Julia's in Denver. I can make this afternoon's stage." Without tasting her coffee, she got up. "I'll start packing now."

* * * *

They got to town with half an hour to spare and waited in silence on the sun-baked street for the stage. To Beth, the whole scene seemed as unreal as their wedding had.

She'd sent another wire to Isobel and one to Graham, asking him to pick her up in Denver. She would be spending two weeks in New York, and more than that traveling, if she came back. Neither she nor Trey could speak. When the driver loaded Beth's suitcase she turned into Trey's arms, but he put his hands on her shoulders and held her off.

"Wire me when you arrive, Beth. Knock them dead. Write and let me know how things go."

He sounded like he was talking to an acquaintance. Beth searched his eyes for some sort of feeling, but he'd closed himself off.

"I will. Trey—"

"You're going to need some time, Beth. We both are. Go on, he's going to leave without you. I love you." He gave her a quick kiss on the cheek and a gentle push towards the coach, then walked away.

Once Beth was in, the driver started the horses. Beth watched the town roll past the window. There were other passengers this time, so she couldn't indulge in a cry. She hurt too much to cry, anyway. It wouldn't do to think of

Trey arriving back at the homestead alone, so she tried to fix her mind on New York.

Late in May, she'd sent two paintings for Isobel to have framed, and Graham had sent three that were stored at his house. She hoped they'd be done by now. Beth also hoped she'd be able to squeeze into some of the dresses she'd left in Denver. If not, she'd have nothing to wear on her trip.

She spent the night with Graham and Julia before catching the eastbound train. Though Graham had been lured west by opportunity years before his parents joined him, he and his family had never left Philadelphia in any way that mattered. Neither he nor Julia would unbend enough to ask her about Trey. Beth thanked heaven for that. She had no intention of telling them how he felt about her trip.

The next morning, she was on her way over the new railroad line to Kansas City. From there the trip mirrored the one the family had made when they moved to Denver. Finally, Beth found herself searching the crowd in the hubbub of the brand new Grand Central Terminal for Isobel's face.

It didn't take long to find her. Isobel hadn't changed as much physically in the last three years as Beth had in the few weeks she'd been in Wallace Flats. Isobel was still the same tall, willowy blonde, perhaps a little thinner than she'd been at her wedding, but with the same elegance. Isobel Stanton and Beth had known each other all their lives, and had seen each other regularly until Isobel married the son of an affluent New York family. Beth had seen her last on the day she had become Isobel James. She had a two year old son now.

Beth walked up behind her and tapped her shoulder. Isobel turned around with the smile Beth remembered.

"You're really here! I've been having visions of having to explain to Vance Hickstead and everyone else I've told about you that you'd been waylaid by thieves or Indians." She gave Beth a quick hug. "Oh, it's good to see you."

Beth returned the hug. "It's good to see you too, Isobel. Now for heaven's sake, take me somewhere where I can hear myself think. I'm not used to this racket anymore."

"I'll take you right home. Where are your baggage checks?"

Outside, Isobel handed the slips to her driver. He retrieved the luggage while she and Beth settled themselves in the carriage. As they pulled away from the station, Beth watched the traffic a little nervously. She'd forgotten what it was like to drive on busy city streets.

"I still can't believe you married out West, you know," Isobel said when they'd exhausted their do-you-remembers. "Why didn't your husband come with you?"

Beth sat back and steeled herself for the inevitable questions. "He couldn't. He has nine horses and a herd of cattle to look after."

"Yes, you mentioned the farm. I'm not surprised that you enjoy it." With an unconscious, characteristic gesture, Isobel smoothed her skirts. "You always did like riding, but surely the help could handle things for a short time."

"I'm the only help Trey's got," Beth told her with a wry smile. "Except for his partner with the cattle. Try and picture me as a farmer's wife, Isobel."

Beth almost giggled at Isobel's astonishment. She'd always prided herself on being unflappable, but it took her a few seconds to find her voice.

"You're serious. You actually work on the place."

"Yes, I do. And, as strange as it might seem, I've come to enjoy it."

"Why?"

Beth didn't mind her friend's blank stare. She'd expected Isobel to ask her outright if she'd lost her reason. "Because it's real. Everything I do matters."

A tolerant smile spread across Isobel's face. She hadn't lost her cynicism. "And it didn't before?"

"Not in the same way." Beth searched for the right words to explain. "You know, a few weeks ago I helped Trey deliver a foal he was counting on for a good part of next year's income. If he'd been alone, he probably would have lost the foal and the mare, too. It would have set him back two years at least."

"I see." Isobel's smile widened. "Beth, I believe you're in love."

Beth decided the painful truth might as well be told now. "I am, but things aren't going any too well, Isobel. Trey was very upset about my coming here. He doesn't want me to give up my painting, and I can't convince him that I can stay with him and not give it up. He put me on the stage the day after I got your letter. I don't know right now if I'll even be going back. I'm afraid I've made a fool of myself, just as Graham predicted."

Isobel put an arm around her. "You aren't a fool. Whatever happens, you're going to be all right, I'll see to that. In the meantime, you have a responsibility to yourself. I think it would be a shame to bury your talent out there."

Beth shook her head. "It looks like it's my feelings I'm going to have to bury."

"I can tell you're hurting, Beth." Isobel gave her another squeeze. "Try to put your worries aside for now. I'm going to convince you to go to the Adirondacks with me. I'll be leaving with the baby in three weeks. Walter's family has a place up there." She paused to close the carriage window against the dust. "He doesn't care for it himself. He prefers the city even in the heat, but I like to spend as much of the summer there as I can. You'd love the place."

Isobel's words gave Beth a sinking feeling, not so much because of what she'd said but how she said it. And what she hadn't said. This was her first mention of her husband and son.

"I'm sure I would, but—"

"Now, don't say no right away." Isobel grinned as they turned off Fifth Avenue. "You know I've always been a bad influence on you, Beth. We're almost home. Walter's parents bought the house for us as a wedding present when we came back from our honeymoon. It took us a year to get it done up to our taste, but I'll admit I'm proud of it."

Isobel's home was a four-storey brownstone three blocks away from the busy avenue, far enough to dim the noise but not far enough to muffle it completely. Similar houses lined the street. The neighborhood exhaled an atmosphere of money and culture. It felt more foreign than Beth had expected. As she climbed the front steps, she tried to pull her thoughts back into the patterns she remembered.

Isobel had become interested in art through her mother, an amateur sculptor and collector as well as a financial supporter of several galleries in Philadelphia. Walter James indulged his wife's interest and many of their friends were like-minded. Isobel had arranged a dinner party for the following evening to introduce E.M. Underhill to the circle, including Vance Hickstead.

Thinking of the dinner, Beth's spirits sank. Since moving to Denver, she'd fallen out of touch with this world. She didn't know whose work was fashionable and current anymore. She'd have to watch her step tomorrow night.

Upstairs, she changed into one of the dresses she'd picked up in Denver. It was a year behind the style, but that couldn't be helped. She comforted herself with the thought that it would look a lot more out of place in Wallace Flats than it did here. She found she was out of practice in doing her hair the way she wanted it, but with some fussing she got it done and went down to dinner.

Beth had always enjoyed a late dinner. The dining room was in perfect taste, with wallpaper in a muted stripe and a Sheraton table and sideboard gleaming in the light from a beautiful chandelier. There were only Beth, Isobel and Walter at the table.

Beth had only met Isobel's husband twice before, but he greeted her with easy charm. Superficially he reminded her of Trey, with dark hair and eyes and a similar build, but he didn't have the dark complexion Trey had inherited from Sidonie and his relaxed grace contrasted with Trey's restless energy.

"I haven't forgotten the prettiest bridesmaid in our wedding party. Welcome."

Beth shook Walter's hand, wondering why his cordiality left her cold. "Thank you. It doesn't seem possible that it can be three years. I can't wait to meet your little boy. If he's anything like you, Isobel, I'm sure he's a handful."

Isobel smiled. "You'll meet him tomorrow. He is a handful, but we flatter ourselves that we aren't among those parents who bore others with their children. As charming as we think him, the nurse takes care to remind us that Michael is a perfectly ordinary toddler and I'm sure she's right." She sipped her wine and adjusted her napkin in her lap. "The woman's a treasure. We were so lucky to find her. You wouldn't know there was a baby in the house most of the time."

Disappointment prodded Beth again at the detachment in her friend's voice. Walter topped up her glass. "We want to hear more about you. How did you meet your husband? Through your cousin?"

If I told them the whole truth, they'd never believe me. "No, we met by accident."

"How long has he been in Colorado?"

"He settled there right after the war."

"Well, there's more than a few here in the city that should have done the same thing in my opinion. Immigrants who signed up to fight for a few dollars and came back to roam the streets. We certainly don't need them here."

275

Walter spoke with casual contempt. It was on the tip of Beth's tongue to say, 'Did one of them take your place?' She knew he hadn't served during the war, and it hadn't been unusual for affluent young men to pay substitutes to serve for them if they were called up.

Be fair, Beth, you don't know he was one of them. She remembered her first opinion of Lorie Carter and got a grip on her temper before she replied.

"Trey was very lucky. He came out of the war healthy and with enough money to give him a start, and he knows farming."

Isobel had on her tolerant smile again. "He sounds nothing like the kind of man you used to prefer."

Beth remembered saying much the same thing to Maddy the day she learned to make bread. Beth and Isobel had critiqued each other's suitors in a teasing way since men first started to pay attention to them, but Beth didn't intend to spend the whole evening explaining herself. She also didn't think she could bear any more questions about Trey at the moment.

"That's because he isn't. Trey is very direct. When he says something, I don't have to wonder if he really means it. He has backbone. Now tell me about this dinner tomorrow night, and about Mister Hickstead. Do you know when my paintings will be ready?"

Beth's crisp tone wasn't lost on Isobel. Still smiling, she went along with the change of subject. "Late next week, I hope. The people I've invited to the dinner are all people we've met since we married. We attend openings and fundraising events together. Mister Hickstead is a male version of Mother, really. He collects art, and he makes a hobby out of sponsoring young and little-known artists. He's one of the people critics here talk to." Isobel flashed a sly grin. "It will be interesting to see what happens when everyone finds out you're a woman. I didn't intend to keep it from them at first, but when it didn't come up right away the temptation grew overwhelming."

That was so like Isobel. Beth had to smile herself. After all, it wasn't fair to blame Isobel and Walter for holding the attitudes they'd been raised with, even if her own had changed.

"You don't think Mister Hickstead has much of an opinion of female artists?"

Isobel frowned and toyed with her fork. "I've never heard him say so, but I've heard him say he thinks the field has become overcrowded since the war, and of course women have been flooding the art schools since then. There's even some woman here in town, Candace Wheeler, promoting classes in design for working class women as a way for them to make a living."

"And you think that's a bad thing?"

"No, not if they have some talent. As far as Mister Hickstead goes, it would be rather embarrassing for him to change tacks when he finds out you're a woman, now that he owns one of your paintings. I wouldn't worry about it."

Beth couldn't help worrying. She hadn't been to art school and most of her teachers had been women, so she hadn't had to deal with much prejudice, though she knew it existed. Then, she'd never tried to get her work into the exhibitions that were the usual route to sales and a reputation. She was asking a lot to expect to be taken at all seriously here, and if this didn't work out, she had no idea what her next step would be. She swallowed a mouthful of poached salmon and sighed.

"Well, tomorrow night should be interesting. I hope I don't make a mess of it."

"You won't," Isobel assured her. "You've been to Mother's dinners, Beth."

As soon as she decently could, Beth pleaded fatigue and went up to her room. She hadn't taken the time to really look at it earlier. Isobel certainly had reason to be proud of her home. It wasn't as ornate as the Underhill home in Philadelphia had been, which suited Beth's taste. Her room had red toile-patterned wallpaper, a fine oriental rug on polished hardwood, a dark-stained cherry bed and dresser, and a full-length mirror in a matching cherry frame. She wouldn't have chosen much differently herself.

Isobel's maid had already put Beth's things away. Yawning, she got into her nightgown, hung her dress in the wardrobe with the others and sank into the feather bed. When she closed her eyes, she could almost feel Trey's wiry, solid warmth beside her. Thinking that way would only make her more miserable, so she turned her mind to Isobel.

In some ways, she was the same friend Beth remembered, but in others she seemed very different. There'd been a lot of water under the bridge since then, of course. Isobel had married into a class a sizable step above the one in which she and Beth had grown up. Beth wasn't sure what she thought of Walter or their marriage. She hadn't sensed any of the unspoken communication that existed between Maddy and Logan or John and Hannah. She wondered how much of the change she felt was in Isobel, and how much was in herself.

* * * *

Trey rode into the yard just at moonrise. He dismounted and stood still beside Cloud for a moment, listening. Except for the faint yipping of a coyote somewhere near the river, everything was quiet.

He unsaddled Cloud and put him in the corral, then walked quickly into the house and lit the lamp, eager to banish the emptiness he'd felt at the sight of the dark windows reflecting the moonlight. It hadn't taken Trey long to get used to coming home to light and warmth. To Beth.

He'd gone into town to see if her wire had come in yet, telling him she'd arrived in New York. It had. She was back in her old world.

Trey put the chimney on the lamp, turned down the wick and went out to sit on the doorstep in the sweet-scented night air. The moon was high enough now to shine into the yard. The barn and corral cast crisp shadows across the cool glow.

For all he knew, Beth was thanking her lucky stars right now. Trey told himself again that her going was for the best. He knew he'd go crazy living in a big city. He'd put five years of his life into this place, and he belonged here. Just like she belonged there. She'd realize that after a while, once the hurt faded.

He wasn't selling her short. She might come back, but if she did, could things be the same between them? Trey didn't think so, and he didn't think he could bear it if he was right.

It had all happened so fast, it still felt like a bad dream. Trey couldn't get used to not having Beth there beside him at night, not having her there to look forward to all day. Time wasn't making it any easier, but he knew it would only have made things worse if they'd waited. Chances were they'd both have ended up saying things they'd never forget. Quick and clean was best.

He got up and walked over to the corral. Cloud came to the fence and sniffed Trey's shirt pocket, looking for a handout. Trey obliged him with a piece of dried apple.

"We'll get along, Cloud. She's where she needs to be, and so are we."

Cloud nudged him again, then wandered off when no more treats appeared. Trey leaned on the fence, waiting for the tightness in his chest to subside before he went back to the house. It didn't. He gave up, rode out to the river and managed to fall asleep there just as the moon was setting.

* * * *

Morning came soon enough. Beth allowed herself the luxury of a lazy hour in bed before going downstairs. At home, she and Trey would have finished breakfast and done the chores by now.

As she passed the nursery, a small boy darted out to collide with her knees. The nurse was right behind him.

"I'm sorry, Ma'am, he's just learned to open the door this minute."

Beth laughed and got down on one knee. "And you're going to have your hands full because of it. Hello, Michael."

The little boy reminded Beth strongly of Isobel's father. He looked at her with dark blue eyes full to the brim with mischief.

"Run!" he crowed, then turned and scooted away. The nurse darted after him.

"Not so fast, young man." She caught Michael and brought him back. Beth reached out to him. He seemed quite content to have her pick him up.

"What a charmer you are." Beth felt a pang of longing as she smoothed his dark blond curls. "He's just turned two, hasn't he?"

The nurse smiled as she took Michael from Beth and set him on the floor inside the nursery. "Yes, he has. He knows how to twist you around his finger already." She nodded politely before she closed the door. "Have a pleasant day, Ma'am."

The woman looked to be about Beth's age. She went down to breakfast thinking of Holly working in a house like this in a few years, spending most of her time confined to one room, looking after small children. If Holly wanted vocal training badly enough it might be worth it to her, but it certainly wouldn't be easy.

Walter was spending the day with his parents. Beth found Isobel waiting for her in the breakfast room, with a table nicely spread for two. Beth sat down and reached for a muffin, then chose an orange instead.

"I just met Michael upstairs. Isobel, he's adorable."

"Isn't he?" Isobel poured coffee for them both and handed Beth her cup. "I hope you slept well. We have plenty to do today, or at least I have. You're under no obligation to help, of course. You're the guest of honor."

Beth started peeling her orange to cover her sudden sadness. Isobel spoke of her son in the same tone she might have used in commenting on an attractive piece of furniture or an efficient servant. She had never been sentimental, but . . . *Doesn't she know what she has?*

"Of course I want to help if I can. If I sit around all day, I'll be a nervous wreck by evening. What can I do?"

Isobel's long fingers drummed the table as she ticked off items on a mental list. "Will you check the silver for me? Anna polished it yesterday, but she isn't always as careful as she should be."

They spent the rest of the morning making sure the house would be ready and then paid a call on the framers. Two of the paintings were finished. After getting them home, Beth snatched an hour to play with Michael while Isobel held a council of war with the cook and saw to the flowers. Before Beth knew it, it was time to dress for dinner.

Standing in front of the mirror in her room, she thanked heaven again that she'd learned to sew. She'd let out the seams in her dress during her days on the train, but she couldn't call it comfortable. She wasn't used to lacing into a corset anymore.

At last she decided she was ready. Beth gave her reflection a last critical glance. She'd piled her hair on top of her head in graceful coils and her watered silk gown was her favorite shade of blue, but she thought she liked the dress she'd made for the Wallace Flats dance better. She'd certainly enjoyed wearing it more, dancing with Trey under paper lanterns and a clear June sky.

Beth gave her skirt a final twist and headed downstairs, lecturing herself. She couldn't think that way. Tonight would have a bearing on her future, and she didn't want to be distracted.

As the guests arrived, Isobel introduced them to Beth while Walter mingled. One after another their faces registered surprise, quickly covered by politeness - in some cases, icy politeness. It puzzled Beth to see that from the women as often as from the men. Fortunately a few of them showed genuine interest under the politeness, or she thought she would have crept upstairs and locked herself in her room. She felt as if she would have gladly given her paintings away if this collection of smartly dressed, well-informed people could have been replaced with the down-to-earth faces of John and Hannah or the Kinsleys.

Isobel had previously shown Beth's work to many of the guests and she got a few guarded compliments, but to her relief, they seemed more interested in hearing about life in Colorado than in talking about current trends in art. She was telling the story of the Wallace Flats concert to a small group and didn't see Vance Hickstead when he arrived, but when she found herself alone for a moment and he approached her, she recognized him from Isobel's description. He was of medium height with a stocky build, a long, clever face and wide amber eyes that went well with his russet hair. He carried himself as if he had a comfortable conviction of his own importance, but he did have a certain charm.

"Missus James appears to be occupied, so we'll have to introduce ourselves." He smiled and extended a hand to Beth. "Vance Hickstead here."

His slightly patronizing manner prodded Beth to mischief. She hadn't intended for Isobel to hide the fact that E.M. Underhill was female, but since she had . . . Beth met Mr. Hickstead's hand and answered as guilelessly as she could.

"Pleased to meet you. I'm Beth McShannon, an old friend of Missus James' from Philadelphia. I'm staying with her at present."

"Oh, so you will have met Mister Underhill." Mr. Hickstead glanced around the room. "Where is he? I know everyone else here."

Beth had to drop her lids to hide her eyes. "I haven't seen him."

"Well, that's odd. I'm really rather curious to meet him. If you're staying here you've seen his work, of course."

Beth met his gaze with a straight face. "Actually, I haven't."

Mr. Hickstead glanced down at Sidonie's ring on her finger. His tone became a bit more patronizing. "Perhaps you haven't much interest in art, Missus McShannon, but I purchased one of his paintings recently through Missus James. It's a hobby of mine. Very interesting use of color and a gift for interpreting a subject, I think. He has real potential."

Beth decided she didn't dare take the game any further. She gave him a frank smile. "I'm glad you think so. You'll have to forgive me a joke, Mister Hickstead. I'm

E.M. Underhill. I became Missus McShannon two months ago."

Mr. Hickstead's jaw dropped for an instant, but he recovered his poise as quickly as he'd lost it. "I don't understand. You just said—"

"I told you the truth. I am from Philadelphia and Missus James and I are old friends, but I've been in Colorado for a little over two years now."

"I see."

He didn't have a chance to say any more before Isobel joined them, looking apologetic. "I see you and Mister Hickstead have made each other's acquaintance, Beth."

"Yes, and I've also introduced him to E.M. Underhill."

"Oh." Isobel put on her most charming smile. "Well, I'll have to ask your forgiveness, Vance, but I just couldn't help myself. I hope you're pleasantly surprised."

Beth laughed. "I hope so, too, Mister Hickstead. You'll have to pardon us both."

"Of course." Underneath his smoothness, he didn't look at all amused.

The parlor maid appeared and informed Isobel that dinner was served. She laid her hand on Mr. Hickstead's arm. "Vance, you must take Beth in."

Beth took his arm with a sinking feeling. It would be her luck that the man didn't seem to have a sense of humor. At the table, she took a deep breath and started trying to repair the damage.

"I only arrived yesterday. I haven't had a chance yet to look around the city. I'm looking forward to it. It's been several years since I've been to New York."

Mr. Hickstead responded politely, but with an undercurrent of annoyance. "You must have been very young then. There have been a lot of changes since the war. Did you study here?"

"No, I took private lessons in Philadelphia."

He smiled. "It seems you've taken things a step further than the typical young lady amateur. What made you decide to send your work to New York?"

His tone made Beth feel she'd done a very presumptuous thing. She met his gaze and held it. "Because I thought it might do well here. I understand that in France there are some younger painters doing landscapes in an informal style similar to mine."

"Yes, in oils. A more robust medium, you might say. I was in France this winter. They call themselves impressionists. Your work has less weight."

Beth read him easily. *Of course, with a woman's hand on the brush.* "But you thought it significant enough to buy, until now."

Mr. Hickstead's eyes turned cool. "Of course. And I'm sure if you were to stay here in the city and promote it for a few years you could carve out a niche in the market, but it is becoming very competitive. As a married woman you will want to consider that carefully."

You narrow-minded, prejudiced creature. Beth smiled sweetly. "Of course I will. When Missus James wrote that you'd purchased 'Meadow at Sunset' she said you suggested a gallery that might be interested in a small showing while I'm here."

"Oh, yes. I can't make any promises of course, but Missus James has the name and address. You can only try."

The snub couldn't have been more obvious. Beth gave him another sweet smile. *If I kicked you under the table, would you be too polite to yell?*

"I intend to. I wouldn't have made the trip otherwise."

The annoyance in Mr. Hickstead's voice became more than an undercurrent. It seemed he didn't take kindly to being challenged. "To be frank, I'm surprised your husband allowed it. If one can believe the newspapers, Colorado Territory is no place for a lady to travel alone – or for a gentleman, for that matter."

Wouldn't it be worthwhile to see what would happen if you said that to Trey? Or John. Or Logan or Nathan. Beth answered with a strong touch of venom. "I'm curious, Mister Hickstead. Exactly what is your definition of a gentleman? Mine includes keeping your word."

She had the satisfaction of seeing his face redden before he turned to speak to the woman seated at his other side. Beth's other neighbor had apparently overheard enough of their conversation to make him uncomfortable. He studiously avoided speaking to her for the rest of the dinner. As for Mr. Hickstead, he looked furious. Beth was miserable, but not ashamed. She had a good idea of what Vance Hickstead would amount to in Wallace Flats.

When the ladies left the table, Beth chatted with a woman a few years older than herself who had paid her a compliment earlier. The woman repeated it, and it heartened Beth up enough to get her through the rest of the evening, but she couldn't have been more grateful when it ended. She slipped off to bed and left Isobel and Walter to hear her story in the morning.

Is this what I came here for? She shook the thought off with a sigh. She'd been working toward this, dreaming of it for years. Even if the dream looked a little tarnished at the moment, she wasn't going to give up now. She couldn't afford to.

CHAPTER 21

"Oh, Beth," was all Isobel could say at breakfast when she heard the tale of Beth's evening.

"That just about sums it up." Beth put her elbows on the table and rested her chin in her hands. "I just lost my temper. It wasn't so much what I said as how I said it. Well, there's no point in crying over spilt milk."

Isobel rolled her eyes and sighed. "I had no idea Vance felt that way about female artists."

"Oh, I don't think he minds female artists as long as they know their place and don't take their work seriously." Beth grinned mischievously at Isobel over the rim of her teacup. "Is he married?"

Walter shook his head. "No, but it isn't for lack of opportunity. He comes from an old New York family and he's very comfortably off. He's considered quite a catch."

"By whom, I wonder?" Beth sat back as the maid placed a bowl of porridge in front of her. Her stomach clenched in protest. It seemed Mr. Hickstead had upset her digestion as well as her temper. "Anyway, I suppose we can forget about the Caldwell gallery without his backing."

"If so, I've got some other possibilities in mind," Isobel said. She studied Beth's face for a moment. "In the meantime eat some breakfast, Beth. You look like last night did you in."

"I'm not very hungry." Beth grimaced at the fresh hot rolls and bowl of fruit on the table. "I think something I ate last night upset me, or maybe it was just the company." She

289

forced down a roll anyway, then set her lips. "I'm going to call on that gallery this afternoon, and I'm going to use Vance Hickstead's name. If they turn me down, they're going to know I know why. Why don't we take Michael and go to the park this morning? I could use some fresh air."

Walter checked his watch and got up. "You might as well, Isobel. Frank Graves asked me to go with him to call on Hugh Putnam this morning."

Isobel lifted a brow. "I see."

Walter returned her significant look with one of his own. "I don't know what Frank thinks we can accomplish. Of course, his wife is putting him up to it. Anyway, I probably won't be back 'til dinner time."

"Fine, I'll see you then, dear. Bring in the mail on your way out please. It just arrived."

Beth turned to Isobel after Walter left. "Ignorance is bliss?"

Isobel glanced down the hall at the retreating maid before speaking. "Exactly. It's become far too fashionable for young wives to court attention, and for single young men to pay it. Oh, it's usually harmless, but not always."

Beth couldn't think of anything to say that wouldn't sound as naïve as she felt. Isobel shrugged. "You won't be meeting any of the involved parties anyway. They're all part of Walter's old set. The park it is, then. Let's get Michael and go."

They spent the morning in Central Park, letting Michael run wild along the tree-shaded paths and dabble in the pond. Beth got the exercise she'd wanted chasing him. Isobel laughed at her.

"He'll run you off your feet."

Beth caught her breath after another dash. "He's certainly a whirlwind. Well, my stomach has settled anyhow. Here, Michael, you hold on to Aunt Beth's hand for a while." With the toddler clinging rather unwillingly to her hand, they started back the way they'd come.

When Michael got tired, they found a bench to rest on. Isobel took her son on her lap and Beth wriggled her hot, aching feet. Her shoes weren't made for chasing children. She wished she could take them off and soothe her toes in the cool grass.

"You said you had some other ideas about my paintings. I'd like to hear them."

"Yes. I've been wondering if it might not have been smarter to send them to Mother in the first place. She knows you well and she'd know who to show them to." Isobel shifted Michael to the bench between them and gave Beth a rueful smile. "I shouldn't have taken Mister Hickstead at face value like I did, but he did seem genuinely interested. I really am sorry, Beth."

Beth reached over Michael to put her hand on Isobel's knee. Sitting here under the trees, she could put Vance Hickstead's pettiness into perspective. "Don't worry about it. New York's a pretty big pond to start in. Maybe you're right about your mother, but I'm not giving up yet, not when I just got here."

"Of course not." Isobel put her hand over Beth's. "We'll call on Mister Caldwell this afternoon, but he's not your only hope. Private galleries are new here, but there are a few and I know the owners of a couple of smaller ones.

They aren't as well known, but they may be more accessible for that. Some of the people who were at dinner last night have connections as well. We'll keep trying."

Beth thought of all the times she and Isobel had gotten each other out of scrapes as girls. It warmed her to know the old loyalty hadn't faded.

"Isobel, you're the same old scout."

"That's what friends are for. Beth . . . last night I told Walter you were having problems. He said you're welcome to stay with us for as long as you need to."

Beth winced. She had a feeling she'd quickly find a limit to Walter's generosity if she tested it. If she stayed in New York, she would become a huge social liability when the truth about her marriage became known. A divorce, if that were even possible, would put her outside the pale completely.

"Thanks, but if I don't go home I guess the best thing you'll be able to do for me is help me find a place to live and keep promoting my work. Let's just take it one day at a time."

Once Michael was rested they hurried back to the carriage. In spite of her nerves about meeting Mr. Caldwell, Beth found her appetite when they sat down to lunch at home. Whatever happened, at least she wouldn't have to deal with the man on an empty stomach.

After lunch, the carriage took them to a quiet side street in Greenwich Village. Beth looked around appreciatively when the Caldwell Gallery door closed behind them, shutting out the traffic sounds and leaving them to enjoy the artwork in near silence. At the moment there was no one else in the gallery except the owner, a tall, thin gentleman with salt and pepper hair and the unmistakable air of old New York money. After giving Beth and Isobel a few minutes to themselves, he joined them with a pleasant smile.

"Good afternoon, Missus James. Please introduce me to your friend."

"Of course. This is an old friend of mine, Elizabeth McShannon, until recently Elizabeth Underhill. You've heard her name I believe, and seen her work. Beth, this is John Caldwell."

Mr. Caldwell acknowledged Beth with a slight bow. He showed the same surprised politeness as the guests at Isobel's dinner. Beth's hopes sank.

"E.M. Underhill? Yes, I've seen one of your paintings; the one Vance Hickstead bought recently. Interesting work, I must say."

"Thank you." Beth's hopes dwindled a little more. 'Interesting' was as noncommittal as one could get. "I have several more pieces here in New York. I'm only visiting for a short time, and Mr. Hickstead suggested that you might have space for me to show them while I'm here."

Mr. Caldwell looked embarrassed. Beth surmised he'd had a visit from Vance Hickstead that morning. Just how vindictive had he been?

"Well, I'm sure you'll understand it's very short notice, Missus McShannon."

Just what she'd expected. Beth straightened her shoulders and looked him in the eye. "Of course. Mister Caldwell, I'm going to be frank with you. I've traveled here from Colorado Territory with my work on the strength of

Mr. Hickstead's suggestion. I met him for the first time last night, and he seemed rather nonplussed to find out I was a woman. If you've talked to him since, you probably don't feel quite comfortable about showing my work. If you've only seen one piece I don't blame you. I'd like to show you some others."

Beth watched Mr. Caldwell weighing his words. She could imagine what he was thinking. He might be a good friend of Mr. Hickstead's, but Isobel was someone a man in his business wouldn't want to alienate. After a tense few seconds for Beth, he nodded crisply.

"Well, I think it would be churlish of me not to do that much after you've come all this way."

Don't get excited, Beth, it's probably just a gesture. "Thank you. I should have the last pieces back from the framers by Thursday. Would Friday be convenient?"

"Friday morning would be fine."

Beth restrained an urge to hug the man. "Thank you. We'll be here."

Mr. Caldwell bowed again. "I look forward to it. Now if you'll forgive me, I'm expecting a client in fifteen minutes. We'll discuss your work thoroughly on Friday. Until then, goodbye."

He retreated to his office. Beth and Isobel spent a few more minutes looking at the paintings on display before leaving. Beth couldn't see that any of them had much more merit than her own. She took a deep breath as they stepped into the summer afternoon again.

"That was quick, but I don't think I'm sunk yet."

Isobel frowned as she glanced over the gallery pamphlet she'd picked up. "We might have been lucky he was busy. At least he doesn't seem to have already made up his mind, or had it made up for him. We'll see."

Reaction set in as Beth settled herself in the carriage. Her head swam and her heart raced. *Don't be silly, Beth, it's a chance. Nothing more.* If she couldn't do better than this at controlling her nerves, she might as well get on the train back to Colorado tomorrow. She leaned her head against the seat back, closed her eyes and imagined herself alone at the homestead, surrounded by stillness as she went about her day, knowing Trey would be home at the end of it. She held on to the vision until it calmed her.

Visiting the other galleries Isobel had mentioned took up the rest of the afternoon. One of the owners was unreceptive, but the other agreed to see Beth's work on Friday afternoon. By the time they got home, Beth was so tired she didn't even want to think about what Friday would be like. She definitely didn't feel like herself.

After dinner at nine she went up to her room, lit the lamp and threw herself on the bed. Whatever happened with Mr. Caldwell, she'd learned one thing already. She didn't belong here anymore.

She pictured Trey sitting alone at their table. It would be suppertime there. Homesickness swamped her. She couldn't help hoping he was miserable, too.

She'd thought she'd gotten behind Trey's defenses, that they'd found something solid to build their lives on, but perhaps he wasn't capable of that kind of trust. If so Beth couldn't find it in her to blame him, knowing what he'd been through, but that didn't make her feel any better.

He'd asked her to write. She could hold on to her hurt feelings, or put them aside and reach out to him. She moved to the desk and rummaged for paper, ink and a pen.

Dear Trey,

By now, you should have my wire saying I arrived safely. I've been here forty-eight hours, and half of me is still at home with you. Right now, I think I agree with you that I'd be happy never to see New York again.

That sounds dismal. I'm sorry. I've had a tiring day and so far, things haven't gone any too well. I've managed to lose my temper and offend the man Isobel wanted me to meet, so I don't know if I'm going to get to show my work or not. Right now, I'd have to say I feel old.

It's been good to see Isobel, but nothing seems the same. I used to love New York. A trip here with Aunt Abigail was always a treat. Now I find that since moving to Denver, and especially since moving to Wallace Flats, I've grown in a different direction. I think Isobel has, too. As for Walter, I find I can't like or dislike him. He's attractive – I think he looks something like you – and he's been as nice to me as he could be, but he doesn't leave an impression on me. Sometimes I don't think he's left much of an impression on Isobel either.

The baby, Michael, is adorable. I think it would be wonderful if an artist could see with a small child's eyes. My best times here so far have been with him.

I have a couple of meetings with gallery owners coming up, but it all seems rather unimportant to me right now. I'm starting to think you were right. If my work's good, it's good and people will buy it eventually, Vance Hickstead be . . . canonized.

I want to make this work in spite of him, but Trey, I miss you so much. I want to come home. Please write and let me know what you're thinking. I can't believe that what we had between us wasn't as real for you as it was for me.

Love,

Beth.

It would take Trey two weeks to get the letter. Would he wire or write back? It could be a month or more before she heard from him. She didn't know how she was going to wait that long, but she couldn't go back until they understood each other.

Beth went to bed as soon as she'd finished her letter, and woke feeling worse than she had the previous morning. She forced down some breakfast and then had to run from the table to be sick. When she returned Isobel sat her down and put her hands on Beth's shoulders.

"Beth, how long have you been having morning sickness?"

Beth's stomach clenched again as the words sank in. "Morning sickness? Only yesterday and today."

"Are you late?"

"Yes, but only by a couple of days. I thought it was just the traveling." Dazed, Beth gripped the arms of her chair. "Isobel . . . you're right, I know you are. I don't know why I didn't realize it myself."

"Well, it is your first and you've been a bit preoccupied." Isobel turned to the pitcher and glasses on the dresser behind her and poured Beth a glass of water. "We'll get you to my doctor to make sure, but I don't think there's much doubt. Oh, Beth, I'm sorry."

Beth looked down in disbelief at her flat belly. She was carrying a child in there. Hers and Trey's. If only things were right between them it would be wonderful for him to have a son to raise, to teach the way his father had taught him. Or a daughter. She could picture Trey spoiling a little girl rotten. Perhaps the baby would look like Beth's mother or father, whose faces she couldn't remember. A dozen conflicting emotions surged through her, but regret wasn't one of them.

"Sorry? I'm not. We both wanted this."

"When are you going to tell Trey?"

"Not 'til I've heard from him. I wrote to him last night to tell him I want to go home."

Isobel gave her a little shake. "Beth, you're in shock. You'd better go back to bed."

Still dizzy, Beth got up. "Yes, I think I will."

The next day she went to see Isobel's doctor. An image of Neil Garrett flashed into her mind as she sat in the imposing waiting room. When she walked into the oak-paneled consulting room after her examination, Dr. Graves looked up from his desk with a smile.

"Missus McShannon, it seems you're going to be a mother sometime late in March. Is your home anywhere near a doctor?"

Weak-kneed, Beth dropped into the chair across from him. "No. The nearest doctor is a ten-hour stage ride away, in Denver."

Dr. Graves shrugged. "Well, I wouldn't worry. You're young and healthy. The sickness should pass, though it doesn't always. Unless it gets really bad or something happens in the meantime, I'd say go to the doctor in six months for a check-up. Congratulations."

Congratulations. She'd never been more frightened in her life, and she had two days to pull herself together before visiting Mr. Caldwell.

In a way, the news helped. The gallery showing didn't seem as important anymore. Sooner or later, her work would find its place. She had more pressing things to worry about.

When Friday morning came, Beth skipped breakfast and supervised as the coachman loaded the paintings into the carriage. When she and Isobel arrived at the gallery, John Caldwell came out to meet them and help bring everything inside. As he looked the paintings over so did Beth, remembering when she'd done each one. The approaching thunderstorm sweeping toward the river valley – she'd never forget getting caught in the rain that day, or the look on Trey's face when she stepped into the cabin. Each canvas carried a memory.

Mr. Caldwell took his time. Beth felt like screaming with the suspense before he finished.

"Missus McShannon, how long can you leave these with me?"

Beth forgot completely about her stomach. "For as long as you like. I wasn't planning on taking them back home."

"I'm glad. It would be a waste. I'd like to have a few days to spread the word, but I think we can be ready for an opening next Thursday night."

Beth couldn't keep a slight tremor out of her voice. "Thank you. Thursday would be perfect. Mister Caldwell, I really appreciate this."

He gave her a dry smile. "Don't thank me, young woman. I expect to make a healthy profit here."

She'd discussed commission and prices with Isobel beforehand, but Beth still felt very inexperienced as she negotiated with Mr. Caldwell. They agreed on asking prices that totaled eight hundred dollars for the five paintings. The gallery would keep them for a year, then return any that hadn't sold to Isobel.

"Tell me I didn't sound as green as I felt," Beth said as soon as they were back in the carriage. "Was he being reasonable?"

Isobel sat back with a satisfied nod. "Not exactly generous, but reasonable. Now let's concentrate on the opening."

"Do you think Mister Hickstead will be there?"

"I'd expect him to be. There might be a critic or two as well. That's why you're here. Now we're going to call on most of the people who were at dinner the other night and invite them. We've got a busy week ahead of us, Beth."

* * * *

Trey looked up from his supper at the sound of a horse in the yard. Logan's buckskin. He stifled his irritation and called out through the open door. The last thing he wanted right now was company, but that wasn't Logan's fault.

"Get down and come in, coffee's on."

Logan stepped in, joined Trey at the table and pulled two envelopes from his shirt pocket. "I'm on my way back from town. Here's your mail."

He handed over a letter from an old army friend for Trey and one from someone in Philadelphia for Beth. Seeing 'Beth McShannon' scrawled across the envelope felt like biting down on a sore tooth. Trey got up, moved the frying pan he'd used to the edge of the stove and reached for the coffee pot.

"Thanks. Want a cup?"

"Sure." Logan leaned his elbows on the table and watched Trey pour coffee. When the silence became awkward he started to speak, then appeared to change his mind. Trey let out a sigh as he sat down.

"You might as well say your piece." He knew Beth had been to see Maddy before she left, and no doubt Logan had been filled in on what had happened, though he and Trey hadn't discussed it.

Logan took a sudden interest in a crack in the table. "Trey, I've always made a point of staying out of other folks' business."

Trey turned and slammed the stove door shut. "Smart thing to do."

"Yeah." Logan took a sip of his coffee, tipped back in his chair and then rocked it forward again. "Maddy, now, she hasn't got the gift."

Trey shot him a sardonic grin. "No, I guess not. Did she send you here to pester me?"

"No, I told her to leave you alone, though I wouldn't be surprised if your milk's been a little sour lately. Maddy likes Beth."

"Yeah, I know." Trey picked up his fork and pushed the beans on his plate into a neat pile. "So you just stopped by with the mail."

Logan nodded. "Yeah, but while I'm here I'm going to have my say. Trey, Beth is without a doubt the best thing that ever happened to you."

Trey dropped his fork and scraped back his chair. "I know. What kind of a fool do you take me for? But I just might be the worst thing that ever happened to her." He picked up his dishes and shoved them onto the kitchen dresser with a clatter. "She's talented, Logan, even I can see that. She deserves her chance. She can't make a name for herself from here."

"Don't you think she's the best judge of that? And isn't it up to her how much of a name she wants?" Logan held Trey's gaze when he glared at him. "If you think you're doing this for her own good, you are a fool. A miserable one. That's been plain enough since she left." He took a swig of coffee and got up. "Well, I'm done. Maddy'll have supper waiting. Get some sleep. You look like hell. I'll see you tomorrow."

Logan stepped out before Trey could think of the scathing words he wanted. He sat at the table until dark, fighting a losing battle with his feelings.

Deep down, he'd known from the start that what he'd done to Beth was abandonment. He'd made coming back to him an almost untenable option for her. What had taken him days to understand, what he still didn't want to admit, was that Logan was right. He hadn't done it for her own good; he'd done it for himself, because it scared him so much to think of losing her.

A wave of self-disgust hit him so strongly he couldn't sit still. Trey climbed to the loft and sat on the bed. The sheets still held Beth's scent.

His gift. They'd spent one night there, the night of the dance. And in the morning . . . when he closed his eyes he could feel Beth's lips against his skin, the memory of their lovemaking was so vivid.

Her sketchbook lay on the edge of the nightstand. Trey picked it up and leafed through it until he came to the sketch she'd done of him during her first week at the homestead. He hadn't seen it before. For some reason she wouldn't explain, she'd refused to show it to him.

Good Lord. That trick with his eyes. He'd had no idea he did that, but he'd seen Chelle do it every day at home. Beth hadn't just copied his face, she'd managed to put a bit of his soul on paper, just as she'd done with Cloud.

I think I was already in love, though I didn't know it. She'd said that to him, and what had he done? He'd broken her heart and sent her off to make it on her own in New York if she could.

Trey lay back on the bed and, for the first time since reading Isobel's letter, he started thinking about a compromise. Racing had always held a thrill for him. Working for a good stable, training young horses and seeing them succeed, seeing Cloud's get become winners, could be a very satisfying life – and it could be lived a lot closer to where Beth needed to be. He'd considered himself settled here, but the truth was that without her, it wasn't home. Not any longer.

He could only hope it wasn't too late. He climbed back down to the main room, found his writing case and filled two pages with apologies and explanations, then crumpled them up and threw them in the stove. A letter would take too long to reach her. He'd caused her too much pain already. He'd go back into town and wire her tomorrow. It would only take a few words to tell her what she needed to hear.

For the first time since Beth had left, Trey slept in their bed; slept soundly, without waking once.

* * * *

Isobel wasn't lying. She dragged Beth around relentlessly in the afternoons until she no longer cared if anyone came to the opening or not, but Thursday arrived at last.

When Beth and the Jameses got to the gallery there was a nervous half-hour of waiting, then people began to arrive. Isobel's friends, and the people Mr. Caldwell had spoken to, made a respectable crowd. Beth found herself in the middle of a scene from the life she'd always thought she wanted. One man came up to her after looking at her painting of the thunderstorm and said, "I stayed in the army and went West for a couple of years after the war. I remember those storms."

Beth smiled. "I certainly won't forget that one." She sensed the general mood of appreciation in the room. It was all she had hoped for and more, and the icing was put on the cake when Vance Hickstead arrived.

"Congratulations, Missus McShannon," he said as smoothly as if their conversation at Isobel's dinner had never occurred. "You're a very enterprising young woman."

Beth let her amusement show. "Not really, Mister Hickstead, just a stubborn one."

"Yes, I suppose so."

Before he could say more, the woman who had complimented Beth at the dinner appeared at Beth's shoulder. "Missus McShannon, I was just telling my husband that we should have had our wits about us like Vance did. He got himself a bargain, I believe."

Mr. Hickstead put on his most winning smile. "Of course I did, Missus Jeffries. That's how the game is played. Now, if you ladies will excuse me, I see Larry Andrews over there and there's something I have to tell him."

He moved across the room, and through the rest of the evening Beth heard him gracefully accepting compliments on being the first to appreciate her work. Each time she caught his eye she let her eyes twinkle with amusement. Then it was over, and she was blessedly alone in her room back at Isobel's.

Exhausted, she crawled into bed and turned down the lamp. That was when she noticed the piece of paper lying on the nightstand.

A telegram. Nobody would be wiring her except Trey. Her hand shook as she picked it up.

I'm sorry, Beth. Come home when you're ready. I love you so much. Trey.

He wouldn't have her letter yet. He hadn't waited to hear from her. He'd finally decided she really was his. The relief was so sharp it hurt, but she'd never known a sweeter pain. Beth lay back and rested the hand holding the telegram on her belly.

"Well, little one, we're going to have a story to tell your father when we get home."

* * * *

The next morning Beth was still in bed when Isobel came in with the *Times*, wearing a broad grin.

"This should settle your stomach, but it probably won't do much for Vance Hickstead's. Here, read."

She'd circled two very small columns about the opening. Two very small, positive columns.

'. . . highly original use of color . . . sensitive interpretation of ordinary subjects . . . a young artist of significant promise.'

Beth put the newspaper down. Her grin matched Isobel's.

"I don't believe it. Who are they talking about?"

"Enjoy it, you've earned it." Isobel flipped up the window blinds, flooding the room with bright sunlight. "Now get up. We're going to spend the day celebrating."

306

Beth sat up cautiously, then swung her feet to the floor. "All right, but let's keep it low-key for another hour or so. My stomach and I need to get used to the idea. I've got something else to celebrate, too." She handed Trey's telegram to Isobel. "This came last night while we were out. His timing couldn't have been better."

Isobel laid the paper back on the nightstand and hugged her. "I'm glad, Beth. You've hidden it well, but I know how unhappy you've been. You really do love him, don't you?"

The words held a bare hint of wistfulness. Beth stifled another pang of regret for her friend. "More than I can say, Isobel. Now, let's get the party started."

She had more to celebrate two days later, when Mr. Caldwell sent to tell her that her thunderstorm painting had sold to the man who'd admired it at the opening. She wired Trey the next morning.

Starting tomorrow. 'Til we two keep together. Beth.

* * * *

On Beth's last evening in New York she sat up in her room with Isobel, side by side on the bed as they'd done so many times in Philadelphia. Isobel put on the coaxing smile Beth remembered so well.

"Are you sure I can't convince you to come to the country with me for a week or so? You deserve a real holiday after what you've been through."

Beth couldn't quite hide her sadness. It might be a fact of life that friendships had to change, but it wasn't a pleasant one.

307

"Isobel, you've been a brick. I really can't thank you enough, but I have to get home. It'll be time for our second cut of hay when I arrive and Trey needs me to be there."

"Of course." Isobel leaned forward and put a hand on her knee. "You know, Beth, when you wrote that you'd married I thought you'd taken leave of your senses, but I can't think so now. I expected to dislike your Trey, but I can't do that either. I don't understand how you can be, but I'm glad you're happy."

"I am happy." Beth looked into Isobel's eyes. "Are you?"

The hand on her knee gave a little squeeze. "Of course I am. I'll be frank, dear. I've never been in love with Walter the way you seem to be with your husband. I prefer it that way. I couldn't afford to let my heart rule my head in the matter of marriage. The stakes were too high. Walter and I like and understand each other."

Beth didn't know what to say. She could so easily have fallen into the same trap of disillusionment, especially after her breakup with Daniel. She felt sorry for Isobel, but worse for the child asleep in the nursery.

"And Michael . . .?"

"I'm fond of my son, Beth. You know I've never had it in me to coo over babies. All is as it should be for both of us, it seems. And it's been *good* to see you again. You will take care of yourself when you get back, won't you?"

"Of course I will. I don't think Trey will give me any choice." Beth got up and gave Isobel a fierce hug. "Isn't it a shame people have to grow up?"

CHAPTER 22

Beth's morning sickness stayed with her as she traveled home, but the closer she got, the less it mattered. All she could think about was how Trey's eyes would look when she told him he was going to be a father.

She reached Denver longing for a night's rest in a stationary bed, but when she got off the train Graham didn't appear. Perhaps he hadn't gotten her wire. She was about to hire a carriage when someone cleared his throat behind her. She turned around to find herself in Trey's arms.

She noticed briefly that he wore his good suit, but all that mattered to Beth at that moment was the dear, familiar feel and smell of him, a light mixture of hay and animals and soap. Then she reached for his lips and his taste was there too, and they could have been alone on the street. He took her breath away with his eagerness to close the rift between them. When the kiss ended, Trey settled her head on his shoulder and buried his face in her hair.

"You're back. Beth, I'm so sorry."

"I'm sorry too, but you didn't give me time to understand. Oh, it's good to be home." Beth held him to her for a long moment, then stepped away to look at him. "What are you doing here dressed up like this? Who's looking after things at our place?"

Trey warmed her from the inside out with the light in his dark eyes. "Ben. I decided I couldn't wait another day to see you, so I came up yesterday and knocked on your cousin's door."

Beth grinned and ran her hands down the lapels of his jacket. How could she ever have thought Walter James looked like him? "So, that explains this. I wish I could have seen Graham and Julia's faces."

"So do I. They were worth the price of admission. For a minute I thought they were going to shut the door in my face, but we've been getting along fine since they got over the shock." Trey let out a long sigh as he drew Beth back into his arms. "I got your letter two days ago. If I hadn't known you were almost home I would have jumped on the train and come after you. God, I've missed you. What happened with the show?"

Beth stood on her tiptoes and kissed him again. "Oh, I've got plenty of news. I'll tell you when we get to Graham's. I'm glad you did this. I didn't want to wait another day either."

When they sat down to dinner in Graham and Julia's elegant dining room, Beth had to hide her amusement at the change in their attitude. Trey put on the polish so well they didn't notice his occasional sly glances at his wife between forkfuls of roast chicken and buttery mashed potatoes. He seemed perfectly at home with the silver and crystal on the polished mahogany table. Beth knew she shouldn't be surprised, but at home it was easy to forget he'd had friends who lived like this.

Graham looked a little perturbed when he heard about Vance Hickstead. "It sounds as if that man deserved to be shown up, but I can't imagine Isobel Stanton allowing such a thing to happen in the first place. Your trip could have been wasted."

Beth shrugged. "You know Isobel never could resist a joke. She thought she knew him better than she really did, that's all."

Trey smiled at her the way he never did at anyone else. "The main thing is, you had your show. Trust you for that, Beth. He should have known better than to get in your way."

Graham put down his fork with a restrained chuckle. "It sounds like you've gotten to know her quite well already."

"Of course I have. I grew up with two stubborn women in the house, so it came naturally."

Beth gave Trey an overdone sweet smile and batted her eyelashes at him. "How very lucky for you. Graham, you're going to have to visit, and bring the children. They'd love the place."

"That'll give me a reason to get the house set up for company," Trey added. "I never thought much about that until Beth came along. We'd be glad to have you."

Graham and Julia exchanged a glance Beth read perfectly. She could almost hear the heavy clink of their opinions of her marriage turning over.

"We'll do that," Graham promised.

The promise healed a small ache in Beth's heart. She'd told herself when she answered Trey's letter that she didn't care what they thought, but Graham and Julia were her only relatives and she would rather not be at odds with them. Underneath their stuffiness, they meant well.

The maid came in with the coffee pot and Julia began filling cups. "So, Isobel is keeping well? It sounds as if she hasn't changed much."

"Yes, she's well." Beth handed a cup to Trey, then took her own. "She's got a lovely home and a beautiful little son. She has everything she wants."

Julia spoke with a hint of indulgence. "You make that sound like a tragedy."

Beth looked across the table at Trey again, anticipating telling him the rest of her news in private. Had Isobel ever felt this way? "Maybe it is, Julia. I think she married for money. What I find sad is I think that's what she wanted, too."

Beth barely managed to contain her impatience through coffee and dessert, but at last she and Trey found themselves alone in their room for the night. As she finished braiding her hair, Trey came up behind her and ran his hands down her sides, watching her in the mirror as he molded her cotton nightgown to her skin.

"You've lost weight, Beth, and you look pale. Are you all right?"

Beth glanced down, not wanting him to see her eyes just yet. "Well, I started feeling nauseous in New York so I went to Isobel's doctor. He said I'd get over it." She braced herself for his reaction, laid her hairbrush on the dresser and turned around. "In about two months probably. I don't think I'm going to have to worry about gaining the weight back either. I'm due in March."

After a moment of stunned silence Trey whooped, lifted Beth off the floor and swung her around in a circle.

Dizzy and breathless, she clung to him when he put her down.

"You'll wake the whole house!"

"Good, let's wake the whole street." He turned toward the open window and shouted. "We're gonna have a baby!"

"Congratulations," Graham muttered sleepily from down the hall.

Weak with relief, Beth blushed and dissolved into laughter, then sobered and took Trey's hands in hers. "It's pretty early for this, I know. We've hardly had time to get to know each other. Trey, we need to talk."

His eyes locked on hers as their fingers interlaced. "I know. Love, I know now how selfish I acted over you going to New York. You were right. I didn't think I could stand to lose you, so I pushed you away. I'm not making excuses. I can only promise to make it up to you."

Beth searched his face for doubt and found nothing but joy. The last of her own fears melted away. "You just did. But Trey, you have to believe that being with you and our children is more important to me than anything else. You promised to trust me."

"I know, and I do. I did a lot of thinking while you were away." Trey's hands moved up her arms, raising goosebumps. "I could be happy working on a breeding farm somewhere back East, as long as you were with me. If it'd help your career…"

Beth couldn't believe her ears. Trey was willing to give up a part of himself for her. With tears in her eyes, she put a finger over his lips. "No. I could never let you do that, not when you've worked so hard to have a place of your own. Anyway, I work better without the distractions we'd have back East. But I love you so much for offering."

Trey brought her other hand up to his mouth and kissed it. "Fine, we'll stay where we are and fill the place with sons and daughters."

"Sounds good to me." Beth moved closer. "If the baby's a boy I'd like to call him Matthew. That was my father's name."

"And I'd like Rochelle if it's a girl, since Chelle beat me to the punch and used Sidonie." Trey took her chin in his hand. "Are you happy, Beth?"

"Happy and scared, but mostly happy. Very happy." Watching Trey's face, Beth started slowly undoing the buttons on his vest. "You know, I've always thought this suit looks good on you."

The spark she loved to see kindled in his eyes as he smiled. "Is that so?"

"Yes, it is." His shirt buttons came next, then her hands made contact with his warm skin and the spark in his eyes became a glow. "But I think it looks even better off you."

"I agree, Missus McShannon." Trey closed his eyes while Beth indulged herself with the feel of him. When she pushed his shirt back and pressed her lips to his chest, he captured her hands in his.

"Beth, you must be tired."

His body was tense, almost trembling with want for her, and he was talking nonsense about her being tired. If she wasn't careful, she'd find herself wrapped in cotton wool until the baby came. Beth gave him her most seductive laugh.

"We've got ten hours on the stage tomorrow to sleep."

"Now there's an idea." Trey took her hand and led her to the bed. Beth linked her fingers behind his neck and brought him down to her for a slow, lazy kiss, teasing him with gentle strokes of her tongue. Then she let her lips stray to the hollow of his throat, caressing him lightly.

"I've missed the taste of you so much."

With a deep sigh, Trey lifted her nightgown off over her head and pulled her close, pressing against her where she ached for him the most. He trapped her roaming hands between them and looked down at her, a look that left her boneless with anticipation.

"You're mine, Beth, wherever you go. I'm going to make sure you never forget it."

He shed his clothes as quickly as he'd dealt with Beth's nightgown, sat on the bed and lifted her over him. In one shattering, blissful instant he claimed her, making good on his promise. Beth gasped into his mouth as it covered hers again, then she was his completely, moving to his rhythm, welcoming his hungry kisses. She could feel his control crumbling as quickly as her own.

"We belong to each other," she whispered, looking into his eyes. "You believe that now, don't you?"

"Yes. Oh, yes." Trey held her gaze as he arched into her again, pushing her closer to the edge of the world. Beth anchored her hands on his shoulders, ready to fall.

"Come to me, Trey. Now."

He did. Beth followed almost instantly. They collapsed backwards on the bed, damp skin fused to damp skin. Beth lay limp on Trey's chest, relishing each aftershock that rippled through her. When he'd caught his breath, he wrapped his arms around her and settled her against him, his front to her back. His hand came to rest on her belly as he nuzzled her ear.

"Welcome home, both of you."

Beth snuggled closer and rested her hands on his. "Maddy said something to me just before I left . . . she was right, we haven't given each other much time, but it feels like we've been together forever, doesn't it?"

She felt Trey's smile against the nape of her neck. "To me each time's like the first, but I know what you mean." He reached down, untangled the bedcovers from their legs and pulled them up. "Now go to sleep, Beth. Tomorrow will be a long day."

"I know. Maybe we should spend a hundred years or so right here first." With all the tension drained from her tired body, Beth closed her eyes and let herself drift, giving in to her fatigue one sense at a time. Wrapped in Trey's arms, lulled by his heartbeat, she fell asleep and dreamed of home.

* * * *

In the morning, Beth settled into the same seat on the stage she'd had when she'd traveled to Wallace Flats. That had been a bright spring day and today the sky threatened a downpour, but this time she wasn't alone and frightened. She was only a little queasy, for the best of all possible reasons. As soon as they were moving, she asked about Holly.

Trey took off his tie, undid the top button of his shirt and tried, without much success, to arrange his long frame comfortably in the cramped coach. "Maddy says she's doing well. She didn't have much to say for the first couple of weeks, but she's starting to come around. The hell of it is she misses her father. She told Maddy that when she was little he wasn't like he is now. I'll never understand him."

Beth looked out the window, feasting her eyes on the landscape of home. "Neither will I. Has Simon been leaving her alone?"

"Yes. As far as I know, the only time he leaves his place these days is to go to the store for supplies. John says he hasn't seen him since the day we threw him in jail."

"What else is new in town?"

"Well, I guess the most surprising thing is that Lorie Carter left just after the spring dance, and hasn't come back."

Beth felt a mixture of surprise and regret. At least Lorie had been relatively safe where she was. There were many worse places.

"Really? I thought she was more or less a fixture at Neil's."

"So did I, but she had breakfast with Nathan one morning and then got on the afternoon stage without a word to anyone."

Like everyone else, Beth had heard the talk about how much time Nathan and Lorie spent together. Her leaving seemed a shame for both of them. "I wonder what Nathan thought of that?"

Trey shrugged. "Not much, probably. I think he liked her. The girls he liked didn't run from him at home."

It would be a waste of breath to say anything, but Beth wished Trey could ease up on Nathan. Maybe they were too different to ever be friends, but it would mean he'd eased up on himself.

When they reached Wallace Flats the air was hot and still, waiting for the storm to break. Trey had left his wagon and team with the Reeves and John and Hannah pressed them to stay until the weather passed, but Beth wanted to be done with traveling. In the end, they decided to race the rain. Once they were out in the open country they could see it coming from the west, a gray curtain blotting out the landscape.

It caught them a mile from the homestead. When they reached home they ran into the cabin breathless and dripping. Ben grinned at the sight of them.

"Welcome home. I guess you brought it with you. I'll help you with the team."

Beth went up to the loft, got out of her wet clothes and pulled on her denims, thinking a little wistfully that they weren't going to fit her for long. Everything had its price, she reminded herself. It was worth it. At any rate, she hoped it would be quite a while before she'd have to lace into an evening dress again.

CHAPTER 23

On her third day back at the homestead, Beth took lunch out to Trey and found the chicken coop open when she returned. She spent a frustrating hour rounding up the hens. Trey shrugged when she told him.

"You must have forgotten to latch the door this morning." Beth supposed he was right, but the next morning she came back from a walk to find the corral gate open and Eve, Shiloh and the foals wandering free. Beth had put them in the corral herself, and she distinctly remembered fastening the gate.

Trey was more than a little annoyed when she told him that evening at chore time. "The gate didn't open itself. Make sure you really check next time."

Beth glared at him from Chance's stall. "I *did* check!" He didn't answer, but she knew he didn't believe her.

Two days later, they went to town for supplies and to visit with John and Hannah. They started home well after dark. When they came to the top of the last hill before the homestead, they saw a glow coming from the yard and picked up the tang of wood smoke on the air. Beth's voice almost failed her as she grabbed Trey's arm.

"The barn . . ."

Trey froze beside her. "Sweet Christ, they're all inside."

He yelled to the team. Numb with horror, Beth clung to the wagon seat while they careened down the hill.

The smell of smoke grew heavier as they went. Beth closed her eyes, desperately trying not to be sick. All of Trey's hard work would be the smallest part of the loss. After all he and Cloud had been through together . . . that bond could never be replaced, and the other horses meant almost as much to Trey. And to her. The worst two minutes of Beth's life passed before Trey spoke.

"It isn't the barn. It's in the corral. What the hell . . ." Beth opened her eyes. They were close enough now to see that someone had piled a large mound of brush in the middle of the corral and set it alight.

Trey stopped the team halfway down the lane, looped the reins around a young pine and sprinted to the well. Beth ran to the house for an extra bucket. Eyes burning, choking on ashes and smoke, she cranked the windlass on the well until her hands blistered while Trey threw water on the fire. When only glowing coals remained, they drenched the cabin for safety and took a moment to catch their breath. Trey wiped his hands on his legs, threw an arm around Beth and rubbed a finger across her smudged cheek.

"Good work for a city girl."

"Thanks, I think." Coughing, Beth looked down at her ruined dress. "If only that crowd at Isobel's could see me now. Well, I wouldn't have been able to wear this much longer anyway." She stood back and looked Trey over. A greasy black film covered him from head to foot. "You look worse than I do. Any damage?"

Beth saw only a couple of small, superficial burns as he gave his hands a quick glance front and back. "Nothing serious. Come on, we'd better check on the horses."

Trey lit a lantern and hung it in the barn doorway. A thin haze of smoke lingered in the air, enough to frighten the horses. The mares paced their stalls while Cloud almost galloped around his. Sweat lathered his coat. He'd kicked the stall door until it cracked. Trey eased himself in and started talking the stallion down.

"Easy now, slow down. It's all over, just slow down." He kept talking until he managed to get hold of Cloud's halter. As he brought the horse under control, he looked over his shoulder at Beth.

"He's terrified of fire. Has been ever since the war." Trey started walking Cloud in slow circles, cooling the horse down as if he'd run a race. He spoke with suppressed fury. "He must have been even more scared then, but he never bolted. At the Wilderness, when the battlefield went up in flames, he was one of the only horses controllable enough to help bring the wounded in. I could have put a baby on him." As they came to a stop, Cloud dropped his muzzle into Trey's hand. He took the halter off and stroked the horse's face. "I'd sure like ten minutes alone with whoever did this. Hand me a feed sack, will you, Beth?"

He began rubbing Cloud down, fussing over him until he relaxed. Beth watched from the aisle until the horse settled, then went in, rested a hand on his neck and spoke to him softly. It seemed he had his own dark memories.

"Poor brave old fellow. Trey, who would do something like this to us?"

Trey's eyes smoldered as he looked at her over Cloud's back. "Can't you think of anyone? If there'd been any wind at all, it would have been a whole different story."

"Gabe?" The thought made Beth's stomach roll.

"No. Gabe would have done it right. Anyway, no one's seen him since that day at Neil's. If he'd been to the store or the saloon, we'd know it. I was thinking of Simon."

"Simon?" Beth couldn't picture him expending that much energy. "You think he'd ride all the way out here and do this? How would he know we weren't home?"

Trey moved to check Cloud's hind legs for injuries. "We're lucky. Looks like the door got the worst of it. He could have broken a leg." He dropped Cloud's hoof and straightened up. "The wagon was parked in front of John's place. If Simon saw it, he'd figure we'd stay a while. I think you did latch the corral gate, Beth, and the chicken coop too. Those things were petty, but this isn't. He's probably just trying to shake us up, but it could easily have gotten out of control and he wouldn't have cared if it did. We can't stand guard day and night."

"So, what are we going to do?"

He ran a hand through his hair in a quick gesture of frustration. "Tomorrow I'll take a look for tracks and go into town, find out if anyone saw him around."

Coming out of the stall, Trey slammed the cracked door behind him. Beth was still trying to banish the image of the burning barn that had formed in her mind at the top of the hill. Trey put an arm around her waist as they left the barn. "Come on inside, there's nothing else we can do 'til the morning."

* * * *

Just after dawn, Trey started following in their visitor's footsteps. He pieced things together easily enough.

322

The man had taken what he needed from a pile of small stuff Trey had saved for kindling when he trimmed the branches from his firewood the previous fall. It was good and dry. The culprit also used his horse and a rope to knock down the woodpile and scatter the wood around. It would be a couple of days' work to stack it again. Trey could picture Simon doing something like that. There were tracks from one shod horse in the yard, but no strange boot tracks. He'd worn moccasins.

Trey bridled Cloud, jumped on bareback and followed the hoof prints across the wagon road. The tracks were plain enough for anyone to follow. They led into a small belt of woods about a mile from the cabin and stopped near the remains of a small fire. Someone had spent two or three nights there by the look of it. He'd built his fire in a bit of a hollow where it wouldn't be easily visible, but he'd made no other effort to conceal himself. That certainly sounded more like Simon than Gabe, though he couldn't be ruled out. Cursing under his breath, Trey turned Cloud back toward the homestead.

Beth joined him in the barn. He heard the anxiety in her voice. "What did you find?"

"Nothing very useful." Trey rammed Cloud's bridle onto its peg. "He wore moccasins. He camped about a mile from here. It looks like he spent a couple of nights there recently. I'd say he's been back and forth over a few days, watching the place." The idea chilled him as much as it infuriated him. Trey knew because he'd asked that no one in Wallace Flats had seen or heard from Gabe since he left. If the man wanted revenge badly enough to come back now, he'd be a dangerous enemy. As for Simon, he could be trouble enough in his own vindictive way. "I'll go into town after breakfast. We'll leave the cleanup for now. Do you want to come along?"

Biting her lip, Beth glanced out the door at the mess in the corral. "No, I'd rather not leave the place alone. I'll be fine."

Trey wanted to insist that Beth come with him, but she was right. It would be best to have someone watching here, and she'd be armed. "All right. I'll make it a quick trip. I don't think he'll come around while you're here, but keep your eyes open and don't leave the house without the gun."

* * * *

After Trey left, Beth made a quick mental list. She hadn't had chance to catch up with things since coming home. The garden needed attention, she'd gotten some pickle recipes from Maddy that she wanted to read through, she needed to think about cooking for the haying crew, and she wanted to paint. It felt like a year since she'd picked up a brush.

The garden first. Beth got to the door before she remembered the gun. She went back, lifted it from the dresser drawer and stood for a moment, holding it.

Could I? She spun the chamber, emptied it and loaded it again. The movements came naturally to her now.

Yes. Gabe had taught Beth that. To protect her home or her loved ones, she could pull the trigger. Beth settled the weapon in the pocket of her apron, picked up a basket and went out.

Before she started weeding, she scanned the horizon in all directions. There were too many places where a person could hide. Beth felt completely exposed, but she forced herself to get to work. She didn't think Simon had the stomach for outright murder, and she refused to live in fear because of him. As for Gabe, he'd want more satisfaction than to shoot her from a distance.

Trey hadn't had much time to spend on the garden while Beth was away, so cleaning it up took her a good hour. As she worked, she began to relax in spite of herself. She heard nothing except the movements of the horses in the barn and an occasional bird's call. The peace and quiet felt wonderful.

Before going back in, Beth pulled some carrots for dinner. She stopped at the well to wash them and was halfway to the cabin when she heard the bark of a rifle, followed by a soft thud. She spun around and saw a splintered hole in the roof over the well.

Out in the open with nowhere to hide, Beth didn't stop to think. She made a lunge for the door and dropped on Trey's bunk just as her legs gave out.

Calm down. He wasn't that close, and he wasn't shooting at you. He could have killed you if he wanted to. That sounded like Simon. He'd get his revenge by terrorizing them.

Anger took the edge off Beth's fear. When her hands stopped trembling, she took the gun from her pocket and moved to the rocker near the stove. Through the front window, she could see anyone approaching the cabin door. If she saw Simon Grier or Gabe Tanner she'd fire, and she wouldn't be shooting to frighten.

* * * *

When he got to town Trey pulled Cloud to a stop in front of John's place, then changed his mind. John would be willing to help, of course, but what could he do? It wasn't his job to follow Simon Grier around. As much as Trey disliked the idea, he had to take this to Nate.

When Trey opened the door to Nathan's office, he looked up from his desk. Trey fought down the usual surge of dislike when their eyes met. Nate just looked a bit surprised.

"Morning. What brings you here?"

"We've got a problem out at our place." Trey pulled a chair up to the desk and told him the story. "There's always the chance that the man we fired is around again, looking for trouble, but I don't think so. If he was, I think he'd be shooting off his mouth here in town. I want to know what Simon Grier's been up to."

"Uh-huh." Nathan tapped the desk with his pen. "Mean and spiteful, that would be his style. I saw him at the store last night around six o'clock."

"Which was right around when we arrived at John and Hannah's." Trey's hands slapped the desk as he got up. His chair tipped and fell. He'd never felt this kind of cold, satisfying rage before. "I'm going to go over there and tear him apart."

Before he got to the door, he heard Nathan open his desk drawer. The sound of a revolver being cocked came next. "You do and I'll lock you up."

Trey turned around. Nathan set his gun on the desk. Those cool gray eyes held a faint gleam of amusement, but more understanding.

"Put your Surette temper on the back burner for a minute and think. Unless you kill him, you'd never be able to sleep easy at night again. Someday, somehow he'd pay you back. Being Simon, I'd expect him to try to do that through your wife."

The hell he will. Trey's anger turned to joy at the thought of getting his hands around Simon's neck. "Then I'll kill him. Nate, Beth's expecting and she needs her rest. I've got work to do. We could have lost everything last night, the house, the barn, the horses. A month before the place is due to be mine, free and clear. I'm not in the mood to play games."

"Then what we need to do is put him away for a good, long time, and for that we need to catch him in the act." Nathan put his gun back in the desk drawer and got up. "I'm going to call in a few favors and get some people to keep an eye on him for me."

Trey took a deep breath and decided to listen. "Who?"

"I've found out that Jack Barron and his friends played a little trick on me a few weeks ago. They owe me."

"A bunch of kids?" Trey snorted in disgust. "Come on, Nate."

Nathan looked him calmly in the eye. "They've got the time and it's not what he'd expect. I'm going to get them to help me watch Simon. When they know what's happened, they'll take it seriously. They got to know your wife when they were practicing for the concert, and they like her. What Simon did last night could earn him a few years."

Trey hesitated, weighing the satisfaction of dealing with Simon himself against the risk. If any harm came to Beth, killing the man afterwards wouldn't ease his conscience. "All right, Nate, we'll try it your way first. I'll talk to John and the Bakers, too. The more eyes, the better."

Nate followed him to the door. "Trey, I've been doing this job here and there for the last four years. If Simon sneezes I'm going to know. Trust me, this is the right way to handle it. You don't want to do anything to risk what you've got. You're a very lucky man."

Their eyes met again for a moment. "Yeah, I am."

* * * *

Trey had another argument with himself as he passed the lane to the Grier place on his way home. He lost to the extent that he rode far enough in to see the house.

He found himself thinking Simon's life was revenge enough. The barn and house were tottering. Garbage littered the yard. There Simon was, with no one who cared if he lived or died except Holly, and he'd alienated her. When Trey saw the man come out of the barn, he rode off before he could be seen himself.

When he got home, he found a basket of carrots emptied on the floor of the cabin and Beth sitting in the rocker, with frightened, dilated eyes and his revolver in her hand.

"Beth, what . . .?"

He'd never heard her use such an odd, restrained voice. "Someone took a pot-shot into the yard while I was

out there. I don't think they were trying to hit me, but . . ."
Beth looked down at the gun. "I would have used it. I really
would have."

"When did it happen?"

"When?" It seemed to take a moment for her to
understand the question. "About twenty minutes ago, I
guess."

Anger battled with bewilderment in Trey's mind.
"Then it wasn't Simon. I saw him in his yard forty-five
minutes ago." He swore hard. If Gabe had come back, there
would be hell to pay before this was over. "Are you sure
about the time? Come show me where the shot came from."

Beth followed him out to the yard. "Yes, I'm sure. It
couldn't have been any more than twenty minutes ago,
maybe less. I was walking from the well to the house. I was
just about here." She stopped halfway to the well. "You can
see where it hit the well cover."

She still looked frightened. Trey hated to leave her,
but every second was putting the shooter further away. He
gave her a reassuring hug and got back in the saddle. "I'm
going to see what I can find. You stay inside and keep that
gun handy."

After an hour's tracking, Trey knew where the shot
had been fired from and that the shooter rode the same horse
as the person who had set the fire, but he hadn't caught sight
of the man. He did find two or three light red tail hairs
snagged in a bush where the horse had been tethered. He
checked the campsite he'd discovered before, but found no
sign that anyone had been there since. Knowing Beth would
be worried, he headed home. He couldn't shake the feeling

that he was a moving target for this man, and he knew she felt the same way.

He saw the relief on Beth's face when he walked into the house, but no more fear. She looked as angry as he felt as she came to meet him.

"Any leads?"

She'd made coffee. Trey poured himself a cup and gratefully took a soothing swallow. "Well, I know he rode a sorrel horse, about as heavy as Cheyenne, with a shorter stride and small hooves. Simon doesn't have a horse like that. Neither did Gabe."

"John would know who does."

It drove Trey crazy to feel this helpless. "Yeah, probably. There might be twenty sorrel horses in town – if this idiot is even from town. I don't know what to think anymore."

Beth put her hands on his shoulders and trailed them down his arms. "It's something. Sooner or later we'll get him."

"Well, it had better be sooner." Trey set his coffee on the counter and took her in his arms. The idea of danger, any danger, coming near her was unthinkable. "Maybe you should go in and stay with John and Hannah 'til I do."

Lips pressed together, eyes glinting, Beth looked up at him. "No. I'd worry too much about you, and I wouldn't want any tricks played on them. I have an idea."

"What's that?"

"Maybe we should try and trap him. I could be the bait. Tomorrow morning you ride off as if you're going to town, then circle around. I'll go out and start puttering around the yard. If he's still out there, hopefully that will lure him and—"

Trey cut her off with a little shake. "Absolutely not. Whoever this person is, he's sick and unpredictable. You're going to stay in the house until he's caught, is that clear?"

Beth stepped back, looking mutinous. "It isn't nearly as risky as it sounds. He's not trying to kill me, he's just trying to scare us. Anyway, I don't see why I should let you take all the risks. How do you think I feel sitting here waiting while you're out looking for him? If he's cornered, we don't know what he'll do."

Trey drew Beth close again and looked into her eyes, floored by the toughness he saw there. At that moment she reminded him strongly of his father. More nerve per pound than anyone had a right to possess.

"And what if he's a really bad shot? I know waiting is the hardest part, Beth, but it won't be long, I promise. I'm going to go back out and start going over the country within rifle range of here with a fine-toothed comb. I'll go tell Logan what's happened and ask him to go to town to talk to Nate and get some people to help me look. I need you to keep an eye on things here at home and take care of Chelle or Matthew." He ran a hand gently over her belly. "I'm not going to let our lives be turned upside down like this, not now. I've never had this much to lose before."

He was betting that the thought of the baby would be enough to dissuade her. He was right. Beth gave in with a sigh.

"All right, I suppose you're making sense. I'll keep watch here."

Cloud had already put in thirty miles that morning, so Trey saddled Cheyenne and rode back to the spot where the shot had been fired. Standing there looking down at the homestead, he racked his brain trying to think of someone, anyone other than Simon or Gabe, that he might have seriously offended in the last four years, but he drew a blank.

The shooter had approached this place at different times from different directions. If Trey followed each trail, he might find some kind of a pattern to the man's movements. He was just about to start tracing the first one when he saw Beth come out into the yard.

"Damn it, Beth." She'd promised to stay inside. Trey watched as she walked directly to the well, filled a bucket and turned back to the house. She was almost there when a rifle sounded off to his right. Beth dashed inside and Trey sent Cheyenne at a dead run in the direction of the shot.

When he found the sorrel horse half-concealed in a small stand of scrub pine, he backed off, hid Cheyenne and found a spot out of sight to wait.

Less than ten minutes later, he heard someone coming. When Trey saw who it was, he couldn't believe it. He stepped out into the trail with his rifle ready.

"Terry, what are you doing out here?"

Terry Pike was a smallish, blond, round-faced, round-eyed young man who lived in a shanty on the southern edge of Wallace Flats. He was nineteen or twenty, with a mental age of eleven or twelve on a good day, but people considered him harmless. Terry had no known family. He'd somehow managed to earn enough money to buy an old horse, and he kept body and soul together by doing odd jobs around town, usually for food. Reverend Baxter made sure he and his horse didn't starve. Trey only knew Terry by sight. He could think of no earthly reason why the boy would want to harass him.

Terry stopped in his tracks, instantly defensive. "I was hunting."

Trey slowly came forward. When he reached for Terry's rifle, he met no resistance. The rifle had been fired very recently.

"Terry, someone fired a shot into our yard this morning, and again just a few minutes ago. I have the bullet from the shot this morning. It's the same caliber as this rifle." Trey had no doubt that when he dug the bullet from the well roof, he'd find that was true.

Terry's face turned red like a child's would when caught in a lie. "So, maybe it was me. Thought I'd teach you a lesson, you and that snooty wife of yours. I know what you say about me in town. You've got no right. I'm not dirt under your feet."

Completely at sea, Trey stared at the young man. He couldn't remember ever mentioning Terry's name and he knew Beth had never even heard of him, but this would have to be sorted out in town. He nodded in the direction of Terry's horse.

"I don't know what you're talking about, but I'm going to find out. We're going to have a talk with the sheriff. Let's go."

CHAPTER 24

As twilight faded to dark Beth lit the lamp and picked up a book, but she couldn't keep her eyes on the page. Trey had only stopped in for a few seconds on his way to town with Terry Pike, and her mind was spinning with questions. She was on the verge of starting for town herself out of sheer frustration when Trey rode into the yard.

He came in, dropped on the bunk and ran his fingers through his hair. Beth's heart squeezed at the sight of the dark circles under his eyes and the rigid line of his mouth. She knew he'd been awake most of the night, and he'd been riding all day, driven by worry for her. This was supposed to be a happy time for them, and it was being ruined. She sat beside him and put her hand on his shoulder.

"Talk to me. I've been going crazy."

Trey glanced at her and shrugged. "Well, Terry admitted to doing everything. He was so scared at finding himself in jail that it took a while to get anything out of him, but he said he did it because people told him we'd been badmouthing him. When Nate pressed him, he admitted Simon Grier was one of them."

Beth's face heated. To take advantage of someone like Terry...there just weren't words to describe someone like that. "What a despicable thing to do."

Trey clenched his fists, clearly dying to hit someone. "Yeah, he's a piece of work all right. Nate and I rode out to see him after we talked to Terry. He said Terry had been out there doing some chores, and when he asked where Holly was, Simon told him. He admitted he'd had some things to say about us, but he swore he never told Terry we'd bad-mouthed him."

Beth snorted. "I'll just bet he didn't."

Trey flashed her a grim smile. "Yeah, me too, but it's possible he told us the truth. Terry's memory is spotty, and he seems to have quite an imagination. Anyway, Nate's going to keep him in jail for a few days to see if he can get anything else out of him. If nothing else, the poor devil will get a few decent meals. And I told Simon if we so much as lose a chicken without knowing why, I'd kill him."

Beth ran her hand across Trey's shoulders, gently massaging until his knotted muscles relaxed. "So, we shouldn't have any more trouble. I don't think Simon has the guts to do his own dirty work. Put your feet up, love. You've had a long day."

Trey kicked off his boots and settled back on the bunk while Beth set about making supper. "While I was in town I hired Ben and a couple of his friends to help with haying. We'll start tomorrow. It's about time things got back to normal around here."

Beth grinned at him over her shoulder. "I'll go in to the store in the morning for supplies to feed them. As for getting back to normal, just wait 'til March. Normal, my dear, is in for a big change."

* * * *

Simon Grier leaned on his elbows at the store counter, eyeing the tobacco on the shelf behind it. He couldn't afford to buy any. The thought sent a stab of irritation through him. Then, life in general irritated him these days, since the ban from Neil's place had forced him to stop drinking. Sobriety had sharpened his mind and his temper.

Wallace Flats had more or less forgotten his existence. He supposed Holly had too: his girl, who looked so much like her mother. She'd had no right to leave him.

She'd had no right, and those interfering sons of bitches had no right to take her.

Simon had been doing a slow burn ever since, but his hands were tied. If he tried to get Holly back, the town would shut him out completely and force him to move on. His own daughter, and he had to stand by and let her defy him like that.

Of course, that high-nosed little tramp she'd been working for was behind it. Holly was just a kid who believed what she was told. That McShannon woman could dress and she could talk, but no real lady would leave a fancy home like he'd heard she had, to come out here and shack up with a sodbuster. Oh, they'd made it legal, but there was only one name for a female who would do such a thing.

He should have known better than to let Holly near her in the first place. Before that, he'd had no problems with his girl running around at night with boys and giving him lip. Now she'd left him, and Simon knew where to lay the blame.

As June finished up his order, the bell above the door jangled. Simon didn't look, but when the new customer called out to June, he knew her.

Simon picked up his parcels and turned around. Beth McShannon stood beside him at the counter, completely ignoring him. She had to be furious over what she'd found out yesterday, but she'd be too proud to act angry.

Simon hadn't told Terry to do anything. He'd only said the McShannons thought they were better than others, the kind of people who liked to look down their noses at someone like Terry, and that they deserved shaking up. Then the idiot had started playing 'pranks' and gotten himself caught. Well, he'd cool his heels in jail for a few days and that would be the end of it. Simon's hands were clean.

He brushed by Beth and walked out front to his wagon. When he dropped his supplies in the back, he took a long look at the rifle lying there. No one was close by at the moment.

Simon's anger gave birth to an impulse. He didn't have to take their crap, and he wasn't going to. Trey McShannon could have his wife, but he was going to have to pay for her and bring Holly back to him. With some cash behind them, they could start over somewhere else. Simon picked up the rifle and waited for Beth to come out.

He didn't have to wait long. She stopped dead with her arms full of packages when he leveled the rifle at her.

"Get in the wagon, you're coming with me."

* * * *

For a moment, astonishment crowded out fear in Beth's mind. She stiffened her back and gave Simon a cool stare.

"Are you crazy? Put that thing down. I'm not going anywhere with you."

Simon took a step forward, poked the rifle barrel into her side and tightened his finger on the trigger.

"You just think again. You do what I say and you won't get hurt, as long as your husband does what I tell him. Make a fuss and you'll die right here."

Still in shock, Beth stood her ground. "You are crazy. You know what will happen if you—"

"Maybe, but you wouldn't be around to see it, would you?" He jerked his head toward the wagon. "I'm not going to tell you again. Get up there."

Simon's hands trembled on the rifle. Beth's mouth went dry as she took in the desperation in his eyes. This couldn't be happening. She didn't think she could move, but somehow she put down her packages and climbed onto the wagon seat. With the rifle still pointed at her, Simon followed. "You drive. We're going to my place."

As Beth picked up the reins, June came to the door of the store. She froze when she saw the rifle and Beth's face. Simon's voice shook as he spoke to her.

"You get word to her husband that he can have her back if I get my daughter and five hundred dollars by tomorrow noon. Come on, girl, let's go."

He kept the rifle on Beth as they drove away. No one they passed dared to stop them. Someone yelled. Nathan came to the door of his office, swore and ran for his horse.

As they left town, Beth's mind started functioning again. Simon couldn't be crazy enough not to see where this had to lead.

"We don't have five hundred dollars here. And do you expect Trey to kidnap Holly for you? This isn't going to work, Simon."

Simon glanced at her, then looked away. Even now, he couldn't look her in the eye.

"You'd better hope it does. I don't care if your husband borrows or steals the money. If he wants you back badly enough he'll get it, and he'll convince Holly. A man's got a right to his own children. Maybe you'll both think twice before you meddle in things that are none of your business again."

Beth decided it would be safer not to talk to him. One thing was certain; by doing this, Simon had set Holly free. He was going to be put away for a long time when this was over. *Keep your wits about you, Beth, and wait.*

Beth had only seen the inside of the Grier place once, the day she and Maddy had come for Holly. It was dirtier and more unkempt now. Grime clouded the windows, and the floor felt gritty underfoot. A basin of rancid-smelling dishwater sat on one end of the counter, adding to the sense of degradation that permeated the place. How could anyone live like this?

Simon seemed sharper and meaner than he had when she'd seen him before. Beth hoped he was sharp enough to think of consequences as she sat on the bed in the small, dingy back room that had been Holly's.

She tried to imagine what was happening in town. Nathan would probably have gone for Trey himself. He'd be smart enough to take John with him. Hopefully, Holly wouldn't have to be dragged into this. She'd been through enough already.

Simon sat on his bunk in the main room, with his rifle beside him. He didn't seem to want anything to do with

Beth other than to keep her from leaving. She stayed where she was, waiting for Trey.

Three hours passed before they heard a horse in the lane. Simon picked up his rifle.

"Get out here."

When Beth obeyed, he took her arm and marched her outside. Trey was there, his face pale and set. Simon peered past him, looking for others coming. Trey kept his hands on his saddle horn and spoke quietly.

"Beth, are you all right?"

She gave him what she hoped was a reassuring smile. "Yes, don't worry about me."

Simon pointed the rifle at her. "You stay where you are." Then he turned to glare at Trey. "You're here, so you've heard what I want."

Trey nodded. "I think I can get five hundred dollars by tomorrow. Take it easy, Simon, it's your game."

Even from that distance, Beth could see the cold rage in Trey's eyes. Simon must have seen it too. The defiance on his face was mixed with more than a little panic.

"That's not all I want. You took my daughter from me. I want her back. You tell her that if she isn't here with you by noon tomorrow, your wife will be dead."

"And after you get Holly and the money, what happens?"

Simon smiled. "We ride out of here with your wife. I'll leave her at a place I know a few miles out. I'll tell you more tomorrow. You'll find her, but it'll take you a while. Long enough for me and Holly to put some distance behind us, and for your wife to find out what thirst is. It's been a hot summer."

Trey spread his hands in surrender. "Like I said, it's your game." He swung Cloud around and looked over his shoulder. "I'll be here. Take care of yourself, Beth." He turned a lethal look on Simon. "If you hurt her, if you touch one hair on her head, you're a dead man."

* * * *

Forcing himself not to look back, Trey rode down Simon's lane. John, Nathan and Logan were waiting for him on the road. John and Nathan had found Logan and Trey haying. He'd been too shocked to say much on the way to town, but the shock was wearing off now. He lit into Nathan with a vengeance.

"You useless son of a bitch, I thought that idiot was being watched!"

"He was," Nathan shot back. "He went to the store. Was I supposed to arrest him for that?"

Trey rode closer, putting himself in Nathan's face. "I swear, if anything happens to Beth I'll kill you and Simon both. He's just about scared enough to snap. I should have taken care of him last week like I wanted to. She'd be safer with a real criminal than with a gutless coward like him. He's going to leave her in some hole, miles outside of town, if he gets what he wants."

John urged his horse forward, but Nathan held up a hand. "He's not going to get that chance, Trey. Look, there's no way on earth we could have predicted this. We're going to get her out of there safely tonight." He met Trey's eyes, making it a promise. "Lorie told me once that you ended up in the army after all. Ever do any night work?"

Trey knew he'd have to cooperate with Nathan or shoot him. It wasn't an easy choice, but they didn't have time to waste. He backed Cloud off a step. "Yeah, some."

"Good. It'll be the two of us then, and John and Logan can back us up. We'll go as soon as it's dark. We'll get Neil to come along too, just in case. Beth will be all right in the meantime. Simon knows he's dead if he hurts her, and she'll give him something to think about."

Trey gave in. If Beth didn't come out of this, he'd deal with Simon and Nate both, and then . . . nothing would matter then, but he wasn't going to let that happen. He didn't care if he had to work with the devil himself to free her.

"Yeah, I'm sure she will."

"Yeah. Blood will tell," Nathan said softly.

They got back to town to find a crowd in front of the Bakers' store, armed and angry. They surrounded Nathan as soon as he was off his horse.

"What kind of town have we got when decent women aren't safe on the street in broad daylight?" Ed Barron demanded.

Jack stood right beside his father with his rifle. "We aren't going to put up with this, Mister Munroe."

Nathan pushed through the crowd, climbed the store steps and turned to face them. "I'm only going to say this once. I'll shoot the first one of you who leaves town. All you'll do is get that woman killed. Her husband and I will take care of it. You folks can plan the ceremonies for afterwards."

Frank Baker glanced toward the tall pine that shaded the town well and smiled; a cold smile with no pity in it. "With pleasure."

* * * *

Beth decided to take Trey's advice and look after herself. She expected a rescue attempt overnight, but she didn't plan to go hungry or thirsty in the meantime. Simon watched her as she started rummaging through the boxes on his counter.

"I don't know about you, but I'm going to eat," she told him coolly when he grumbled. "You don't know Trey very well, but I'll tell you this. If he gets me back in good shape, he'll probably be thankful enough to leave it at that and let you find your own way to the devil. If he doesn't you'll be looking over your shoulder for the rest of your life, which probably won't be very long. So, do you want supper or not?"

"You watch your mouth," Simon muttered. "You're in no position to talk smart. There's some beans I put in to soak this morning. Cook those and shut up."

Beth kindled a fire in the stove and got the beans in the oven. It seemed silly, but she felt a bit better with something to do. Simon kept glancing out the windows, looking more and more frightened. When she'd finished with the beans, Beth retreated to Holly's room and quietly looked for something, anything she could use to defend herself if necessary. All she could find was a brick that served as a doorstop.

There was a small window in the room, not too small for Beth to get through. She kept that in mind as a last resort in case Simon really panicked, but Trey and Nathan would be making plans based on her being in the house and it would be smarter not to upset them. A part of her wished she could see them having to work together.

Simon left her alone. Late in the afternoon when the beans were ready, she put coffee on. When it started to perk, Simon came to the table. He didn't speak or look at her as she dished up the food. Beth knew he was listening for anything unusual outside.

By the time they finished eating it was getting dark. When Beth got up to go back to Holly's room, Simon reached for his rifle.

"You stay where you are. I want you right here in case someone out there tries something stupid."

Beth sat back down and tried to hold his gaze, without success. "It seems to me that you're the one who's being stupid. You know, Simon, we did take Holly from you. If this ended right now, I'll bet a judge would take that into account in giving you a sentence."

Simon swore under his breath. His head jerked as his eyes kept darting to the windows. "I'm not going to prison on account of your interference. You're going to be my ticket out of here with Holly."

"And how long do you think you'll keep her? Holly still cares about you. If you hadn't done this, you might have had a chance to win her back. As it is, there's only one end to it, unless you ride out of here right now and give yourself a few hours' head start. If you did, I don't know if anyone would even bother to follow."

She was trying to offer escape, but he wasn't listening. Simon swung the rifle up and held it to Beth's temple. "That's right," he said when the color drained from her face and she closed her eyes. "You think about it. If you want to see tomorrow, you do what you're told and shut up."

CHAPTER 25

Trey clenched his fists on his knees and stared out the window of John's front room at the darkening street. He'd given up trying to fight his impatience, but the waiting was almost over. The moon would be up soon and they'd be smart to get themselves in place before then.

John and Logan sat at the corner table under the lamp, playing cards to pass the time. Nathan leaned back on the sofa under the window, smoking his pipe, looking as relaxed as if they were planning to spend the evening here socializing. Trey wanted to plant his fist in the man's face. Of course, it wasn't Nate's whole life sitting out there at the whim of a frightened, angry weakling.

Nathan looked up, sensed Trey's mood and nodded. "All right, I guess it's time."

The horses were waiting in the forge yard. Neil would join the group at the saloon. As they mounted, Nathan gave Trey a sudden, sharp glance. He ignored it. Then they were finally moving. Trey forced himself to relax. As long as they were doing something, he could stay in control.

As they left town, Nathan urged his horse into line with Cloud. When Trey glanced his way, he smiled.

"Strange to think about it. You gave me the worst beating I ever got in my life because you didn't believe in the war, and then you ended up fighting after all."

Trey held down his irritation. Why couldn't the man leave him alone? "Yeah, on the other side."

346

"Well, is that a fact? I've been wondering about that ever since Lorie told me she'd talked to you." Nathan chuckled softly. "Wouldn't it have been something if we'd ended up shooting each other?"

"Yeah, it would have." Trey nudged Cloud into a trot, hoping to end the conversation, but Nathan kept pace with him.

"Were you at the Wilderness? That was a piece of hell, I'll tell you."

"Yeah, I was there." Alarm bells started going off in Trey's mind. He'd always assumed that some of his old neighbors were with Justin on the road to Spotsylvania the night he was killed, but if Justin hadn't known him Trey had doubted if any of the others would. If he was wrong . . . there had never been any love lost between Justin and Nate, but they'd served together. If Nathan knew what had happened, there was no telling how he felt about it.

"You ever go home, Trey?" Nate sounded casual, but Trey knew better. Fine, he'd play along.

"No. Do you know what became of Cathy?"

"She married Tony and they're living on his place. It's a lot smaller than it used to be, but it's still going. So is Foxglove. Her folks are still there."

He'll think it's strange if I don't ask. "What about Justin?"

"You already know the answer to that, don't you?" Nathan moved his horse closer and kept his voice low. "I just realized that when I saw you mount up tonight with your rifle in your left hand. I was there. If I'd been a better shot

347

that night, you wouldn't be here now. I didn't know you, but I think Justin did. Trey, you did him a favor."

Trey's temper snapped. "What the hell is that supposed to mean? He was twenty-two years old..."

"And he was dying." Nathan was whispering now. "You remember he was sick as a baby. I don't know if that made any difference, but he got lung trouble. He wouldn't give in. Said nobody could do anything for him anyway and he'd rather die fighting."

Trey froze in the saddle with his face turned away.

He did know me. He wouldn't shoot. He let me set him free.

They rode in silence for several seconds before he trusted himself to look at Nathan.

"That would be Justin."

"Yeah."

Neither of them spoke again until they got to Simon's lane. Trey wanted to curse Nathan for his timing, but knew he'd spoken in case he didn't get another chance.

It wasn't something an enemy would do.

By the time they reached the lane, they were fully focused on the present. They left the horses with Neil and continued on foot, keeping to the shadow of the trees on either side. Trey crept to the house, hunkered down by the window and saw Beth sitting at the table across from Simon. His blood boiled at the sight of her pale, strained face.

"Not much longer, love." He turned and hurried back to the others. "They're sitting at the table. Beth looks tired, but I'm a lot more worried about Simon. He looks scared to death."

Nathan nodded. "All right. You go back to the right window and I'll take the left. If you can manage it, let her see you. She'll keep cool. We'll wait for our chance. It's bound to come sooner or later."

* * * *

Simon heard a slight sound outside the cabin, grabbed his rifle and rushed to check the windows, then slumped in his chair across from Beth again.

It's just some animal.

He'd never wanted a drink more in his life. He got a glass of water and told himself again to calm down. When a branch scraped the roof, a branch that had been scraping it for years, his heart jumped to his throat again.

Suppose they didn't come tonight. Suppose McShannon did what he'd asked. It would take them a few hours to find Beth tomorrow, and then they'd be after him. Simon remembered the way Trey had looked at him the day Terry had been caught. The man would never let this go unanswered, whatever that little tramp said. Simon was going to have to take her and run while he still could. And Holly . . . they'd pick her up on the way. She'd go with him to save Beth, and the Kinsleys wouldn't dare try to stop him. They could dump Beth once they were far enough away. Simon pushed his chair back and reached for his rifle.

"Get up, girl. We're getting out of here now."

* * * *

Crouching in the dark by the cabin window, Trey watched the pair inside with growing frustration. He didn't dare move as long as Simon was that close to his rifle and Beth.

It didn't look as if Simon had touched her. He was probably half afraid of her, too. Then the man turned toward the other window for a moment, long enough for Trey to show his face.

Beth blinked to let him know she'd seen him, but otherwise she didn't react. *Good girl.* Trey pulled further back. His biggest fear was that Simon would hear him or Nathan and panic.

A branch scraped the roof and the man jumped. Trey's hands tightened on his rifle, but Simon settled uneasily into his chair again. He couldn't stay still. A few seconds later he picked up his rifle and motioned for Beth to get up.

In the next instant, Beth reached for the coffee pot sitting on the stove and flung it in Simon's face. He screamed and dropped his rifle as Beth dashed for the back room. Shards of glass crashed onto the cabin floor as Trey and Nathan broke the windows at the same time.

When Simon got his hands on the rifle, Nathan yelled. Half-blinded by the coffee, Simon turned and fired wildly at the sound, then again in the direction of Holly's room. A muffled cry froze Trey's blood. Without a second thought he swung his rifle up, pulled the trigger and watched Simon crumple and fall.

That cry had to have come from Beth. Choking with the thought of what he'd find, Trey swiped away glass with his rifle barrel, scrambled through the window and jumped over Simon's motionless body on his way to the back room.

There she was, pressed flat against the wall beside the door, holding a brick. Trey got one quick glimpse of her frightened eyes before she stumbled into his arms.

Trey had thought he knew what fear was, but as Beth's arms wrapped around him he realized he'd never had a clue, not until the moment he thought he'd lost his family. He let out the breath he'd been holding and turned Beth away as John stepped into the main room and knelt by Simon.

"Poor Holly." Beth started to shake and Trey rocked her gently, stroking her back as he held her tight. John looked up and shook his head.

"Shh." Trey closed his eyes and swallowed the bile that rose in his throat. "Holly lost her father a long time ago . . ."

Beth clung to him for a long, steadying moment, then stepped back. Trey's stomach churned again at the sight of blood on her dress.

"Beth, you're hurt. Let's get you to Neil. You're going to be all right—"

"I'm fine." Beth's face grew even paler as she looked him over. "You're the one who's hurt. Your arm . . . I heard you yell."

Trey looked down in surprise. For the first time he noticed the stinging in his right arm and the blood soaking his sleeve. "I must have cut it on some glass on the way in. I didn't yell. It must have been Nate. I heard it too."

John had taken Simon's body outside. Trey and Beth hurried out and found the others gathered around Nathan, who lay unconscious on the ground with Neil on his knees beside him. Trey joined them.

"What happened to him? He never got inside."

"Bullet must have bounced off the window casing." Neil gave the group an irritated glance. "Somebody go get the wagon and a lantern."

When John brought the light, Neil took a closer look at Nathan's wound and pursed his lips. "I think it's lodged in his breastbone, but I can't be sure. This isn't one for me. I can slow the bleeding, but he needs a surgeon." He looked up at Trey's bloody arm. "What about you?"

"I went in through the window."

Beth glanced at Simon's body lying nearby on the grass, shuddered and turned back to the others. "I'll wire Doctor Ross. He's retired now, but he was an Army surgeon and also our family doctor in Denver. He'll come."

Neil nodded as he applied pressure to Nathan's wound. "Fine. John, can we take him to your place?"

"Sure, he can have Ben's room."

Still pale with shock, Beth looked down at Nathan, at the blood staining his shirt.

"A chest wound . . ."

Trey put his good arm around her. "Don't count him out, Beth. You can't kill Morgan County stock that easy. Let's get him back to town."

She moved closer and looked up at him. "You would know."

"Yes, I would. What's so funny?"

Jennie Marsland

Some of the strain faded from Beth's eyes, replaced by a teasing glint. Her mouth curved in the mocking grin Trey loved to distraction.

"Seems like some things have changed. Now let me have a look at that arm."

She pushed up his sleeve and winced at the deep gash just above his elbow. "You're in for a few stitches, I think."

Neil had his hands full doing what he could for Nathan. Trey looked down at his arm and decided he'd rather get it over with. "You might as well do it, Beth. Neil's got what you need in his kit."

Beth eyes widened, but she straightened her shoulders and set her lips. "All right. I guess we don't have time to waste."

Trey had to smile. He could imagine Maddy saying the same thing.

"You've come a long way from Philadelphia, Beth."

Beth found a needle, thread and a bottle of antiseptic in Neil's bag. As she set to work, Trey shut his eyes and thought about Justin. He'd been as good a friend as anyone could have, and now Trey could remember him properly. All the good times. Hell, no one knew half the scrapes they'd gotten themselves into . . . no one who was here now.

Except Nathan. It would be good to have someone to talk to about those times again.

By the time Beth finished stitching Trey's eyes were watering. The fierce bite of the alcohol solution she poured on the cut made him grit his teeth, but she looked as if the job had hurt her more than it had him. She cleaned up his arm, wrapped a bandage around it and then slipped her arm around his waist. Trey let out a long breath and pulled her closer.

"Thank you, love."

"You're welcome." Beth's voice trembled again. "Trey, I'm ashamed of myself. I feel like crying good and hard right now. All I could think about in there was the baby and you. When I heard Nathan yell, I was so afraid it was you . . . and now I'm so relieved that it wasn't. How selfish and horrible is that?"

"It's normal." Trey bent to kiss her upturned mouth. The sweet, welcoming taste of her pushed the throbbing in his arm and the fears of the day to the back of his mind. "I think I would have killed Nathan if anything had happened to you. I just wouldn't have given a damn. It looks like Neil's got him ready. Let's go."

When they laid him down in the wagon, Nathan opened his eyes. Hazed with pain, they widened in surprise when Trey leaned over him.

"Hang on, Nate. We're taking you to John's. Neil can finish patching you up there, and we'll have a doctor here tomorrow. You've made it through worse than this." He'd never stopped to really think about that before. Nathan had paid a heavy price for his beliefs, too. Their eyes met, and an unspoken message passed between them before Nate found his voice.

"Yeah, I have . . . is Beth all right?"

Beth smiled at him from his other side. "I'm fine, Nathan. You two do all right as a team."

With a hint of his usual grin, Nate glanced at Trey's bloody sleeve. "Yeah, right. Look at us."

There were a lot of things Trey wanted to say, but he would have to keep it short for now. Nathan was fading out again.

"Thanks, Nate. For this, and for what you told me earlier. I think Justin would have wanted me to know."

Nate's grin widened. "So, you aren't going to kill me?"

"Not this time." Trey grinned back. "You're right. I'm a very lucky man."

* * * *

As usual, the dry goods store was empty when Lorie got to work. The owner put down the newspaper she was reading and stepped out from behind the counter.

"I guess I'll go get a coffee, Lorie. See you in a few minutes."

"Take your time, Missus Harper."

Alone in the store, Lorie picked up the paper Mrs. Harper had left on the counter. Nicknamed the Rocky Mountain Liar, the Denver paper always made for interesting, if unreliable, reading.

Her eyes flickered to the window as a man with a passing resemblance to Nathan walked by. Lorie's life was so different now that most of the time it was easy not to think of him, but that didn't mean she'd forgotten.

I did us both a favor. Getting out before they got in any deeper had been the smart thing to do, whether it felt like it or not.

She rattled the paper impatiently. "Lorie, you've got a decent job, a decent boss and a decent place to live, with no mean customers to handle. What's past is past."

She turned the page and read a headline, then pulled her handkerchief from her pocket, wiped her eyes and read it again.

It can't be . . .

KIDNAPPING IN WALLACE FLATS. SHERIFF GRAVELY INJURED DURING RESCUE.

The paper was a week old. Lorie put it down in a daze. She'd missed the southbound stage by several hours. She'd have to hire a horse. She scrawled a hasty note to Mrs. Harper, locked the store, slipped the key through the mail slot and ran.

Please God, I know I don't deserve anything from you, but he does. He's the only man who ever treated me like a friend. Please.

She alternately prayed and cursed through her long ride to Wallace Flats. When she dashed into Neil's place it was night, a warm one, and the saloon was busy. Every head turned. Neil looked as shocked as everyone else until he recognized her.

"Lorie? What the—?"

"Nathan. Is he still alive?"

"Yes, he's over at the Reeves' place. He's—" Before Neil could say any more she was gone.

Lorie stood in the street in front of the Reeves' house, trying to scrape up the nerve to knock on the door. *She'll probably slam it in my face, a woman with a young son. And Nate . . . why would he want to see me? I ran off without a word.*

She couldn't do it. Nothing had changed. She still couldn't be the woman Nathan needed, the woman he

356

deserved. She should have stayed in Denver. She was about to run when the door opened and Beth McShannon came out.

"Lorie, is that you? Where have you been?"

The words tumbled out in a rush. "I've been working in Denver. I read in the paper that Nathan was hurt. How is he?"

She thought her knees would buckle when Beth smiled. "He had a close call and he's still pretty weak, but the doctor says he should be fine in time. Trey and I came in tonight to see him. We're just about to head home. I'm glad you came, Lorie."

Surfacing from the warm wave of relief that washed over her, Lorie remembered she hadn't bothered to read the newspaper article. "The paper said something about a kidnapping. What happened?"

"Well, Simon Grier got this crazy idea of using me to get his daughter back. Trey and Nathan had to come and get me away from him. Nathan did a brave thing. He made sure Simon shot at him first. I'm sure you'd like to see him. Come in."

Lorie's heart started pounding. She didn't have any right. "I don't know . . . it's late. I just wanted to find out if he was all right. I don't want to disturb him."

She turned away, but Beth took her arm. "I think you'll be just what the doctor ordered. As for the time, day and night are pretty much the same to him right now. Come with me."

Lorie had no choice but to follow Beth inside. The men were out harnessing Trey's team, but Hannah was in the kitchen. Lorie saw a knowing look pass between the other two women before Beth spoke.

"Hannah, you remember Lorie Carter. She's here to see Nathan."

To Lorie's surprise, Hannah smiled. "He's upstairs, first door on your left. I don't know if he's awake, but go on up and see."

Lorie stepped into the bedroom and shut the door behind her. Nathan's eyes were closed. The dim lamplight accentuated the hollows in his cheeks and gave his skin a gray hue. He looked as if he'd lost a significant amount of weight in a hurry. A lump rose in Lorie's throat as she realized just how close a call he'd had.

He's going to be all right. He has to be. The doctor said so. She sat in the chair beside the bed and spoke to him quietly.

"Nate, are you awake?"

He didn't respond. It would be so easy to reach out, touch his face – Lorie had never felt the urge to touch anyone that way. No one had ever offered her comfort, and she'd never considered offering it to anyone else. The idea scared her more than anything else ever had.

She imagined what Nathan's hair would feel like; thick and soft and slightly coarse. Would she wake him if she touched him? Would he give her one of his ironic smiles, or would he ask her to leave? Or would he not care enough to do either?

"I've missed you, Nate. I'm working in a store in Denver now. The money's not as good as I used to get here, but it's all right. I like the place . . . I thought leaving the way I did would be easier, but it wasn't." Lorie reached out in spite of herself, stopped short of touching him and straightened his blankets instead. "If I'd told you, would you have let me go?"

What else was there to say? Lorie curled up in her chair, her eyes following the rise and fall of Nathan's chest as she struggled against tears. Beth and Hannah meant well, but they really didn't have a clue about her. How could they? As for Nate, he probably knew her better than anyone. He knew her well enough to know that she couldn't settle down here, even if she wanted to, but he was too damned stubborn to admit it. If she stayed, how many times would he have to fight because of her? How many years would have to pass before she'd be able to walk along the street with her head high?

Lorie took a deep breath, reached out, then pulled her hand back again. She hadn't expected it to hurt this much. "You were decent to me, and I won't forget it. Goodbye, Nate, and good luck."

She got up, returned to the kitchen and faced Beth and Hannah with a smile. "He's asleep. Thanks for letting me see him."

She stiffened a bit at the sympathy she saw in Beth's eyes. Hannah nodded. "You're welcome, Lorie. We'll tell him you dropped by."

"I'd like that. Missus McShannon, take care of yourself and that man of yours. He's a good one. Goodbye."

She hurried out before Beth could reply. The warm night air dried Lorie's tears on the ride back to Denver, but it took a lot longer for her to stop crying inside.

EPILOGUE

Beth tightened her grip on Trey's hand and clenched her teeth to keep from crying out as another contraction wracked her exhausted body. When the pain passed, she sank back against his shoulder. After twenty hours, she wasn't sure how much more she could take.

"Almost there, love." Trey wiped the sweat and tears from Beth's face with a cool cloth and stroked her forehead. "Yell if you need to. I know it hurts."

Maddy moved up from the end of the bed to take Beth's other hand. "You're doing fine, Beth. Catch your breath and get ready for the next one." It hit as she spoke. "Push now, as hard as you can. That's it, there's the head. Keep pushing, just a little longer."

Beth screamed as she pushed, feeling like she was being split in two. Then the searing pain miraculously lessened. As if from a distance, she heard a thin, indignant wail, followed by Maddy's laugh. "Beth, you've got a daughter."

A little girl. Utterly spent, Beth collapsed on her pillows, still clutching Trey's hand. He wiped her face again as Maddy pressed Beth's belly to help drive out the afterbirth. A couple of minutes later, Maddy laid a squalling, blanket-wrapped bundle in Beth's arms.

"She's got your eyes and Trey's hair. She's beautiful."

Together, Beth and Trey gazed at their daughter. Trey's eyes filled with raw emotion as he stroked the baby's cheek.

"She's Mother all over again."

Seeing his broad finger brush over the baby's delicate skin made Beth feel like laughing and crying at the same time. Lost in wonder, she looked at what her hours of pain had bought. A miracle.

"Rochelle Elizabeth McShannon. Look at her, Trey. Just look at her." Tiny lips open, a fine down of black hair on her head, her blue eyes fringed with sooty lashes, little Chelle fisted her hands and screeched as loud as she could. Trey's eyes widened.

"She sounds healthy enough. Nothing wrong with those lungs."

Beth laughed. "Nothing at all. Come here, sweetheart." She put the baby to her breast. Chelle's cries turned to small sounds of contentment as she discovered what a nipple was for. A slow smile of amazement spread across Trey's face.

"Beth . . . thank you."

Beth cradled her daughter in her arms and looked up at the man she loved more than she'd once thought possible. A very different man from the one who'd met her in Wallace Flats on a bright April afternoon. Trey laughed easily now and smiled a lot more often, a smile that reminded her of the boy in his old picture. It was worth any amount of pain to give him a family again.

"Trey, life doesn't get any better than this, does it?"

He leaned in to give Beth a slow, sweet kiss. "No, it doesn't."

* * * *

Later, Trey stood at the cabin door and watched a fine drift of snowflakes float through the gray March twilight. Behind him, the main room of the cabin glowed with lamplight. Beth and the baby lay asleep in the new bedroom where she'd given birth, one of two rooms Trey had built onto the cabin last fall. The other was a spare room for now. He'd also covered the earthen floors with pine throughout. To see how proud Beth was of the result, no one would know she'd grown up in a home where spare rooms and wood floors were a given.

A cold gust of wind brought Trey back to reality. He closed the door, added wood to the stove and sat cross-legged on the rug in front of it. A good night to be inside, counting his blessings.

He found himself humming a tune he'd learned from his mother when he was small. In a moment, the words came back to him.

'Mon père, aussi ma mère, n'avait que moi d'enfants . . .'

The rest escaped him. He'd have to remember so he could teach it to little Chelle someday.

As a kid Trey had always been the dreamer, looking for pictures in the fire. It was something he still loved to do, and now the visions he saw in the flames had shapes that were solid and real. He sat there for a long time, watching them come and go, until the fire died down and he was ready to sleep.

ABOUT THE AUTHOR

Jennie Marsland is a teacher, an amateur musician and watercolor artist and, for over thirty years, a writer. She fell in love with words at a very early age and the affair has been life-long. She enjoys writing children's fiction, poetry and lyrics as well as romance.

With a background in Animal Science and molecular biology, Jennie has been a lab technician and a science teacher at different times in her life. She is now pursuing her love of language as an ESL teacher, meeting people from all over the world and helping them learn to communicate in English. She finds it as rewarding in its own way as penning novels.

Jennie has always loved books that take her back to an earlier time. Glimpses of the past spark her imagination. Perhaps there's an archaeologist buried in her somewhere. Everyone has a story, and it's the stories of ordinary people that affect her the most.

Jennie developed a soft spot for Westerns by reading her father's collection of Louis L'Amour and Zane Grey novels as she grew up. She thinks they contain everything a girl – or a woman –could want…handsome, rugged heroes, spirited heroines and horses, but she's planning on trying her hand at other genres as well. So many stories, so little time.

She finds her inspiration in family stories passed down from her parents and grandparents, and in the beauty of Nova Scotia's landscape. When she's not writing or working she gardens, plays guitar and spends time with her husband, two cantankerous elderly cats and the most spoiled dog on earth.

CPSIA information can be obtained at www.ICGtesting.com
231055LV00001B/6/P